"You know I can't love you," he said as he lowered his head and tasted first her temple, then her cheek.

"I know," she said, tipping her head back farther so that her mouth brushed against his as she waited for him to take possession of those lips.

"And I won't ever love you," he murmured against the softness he could taste.

"Of course not," she agreed, leaving her lips parted slightly so that he had no choice but to kiss her fully, soundly, to take her head in one hand and her back in the other and pull her against him until he could feel her heart beating against his chest, feel the crazy throbbing of her pulse as it matched his own.

"Just so there isn't any misunderstanding later, Abidance, I am leaving Eden's Grove," he warned her, his fingers lost in the waves of hair piled on her head. This was madness. Insanity. If he weren't a man of medicine, he'd think he'd been bewitched by some magician with a very strange sense of humor. And with every ounce of strength he had, he fought against the urge to just give in to it all—that it was all too big to fight, too strong.

He could think of nothing else to say, no good reason not to go on kissing her all night and all the next day. . . .

A KISS TO DREAM ON

"*A Kiss to Dream On* is a historical romance that has the typical Mittman Midas magic: a fun-to-read story line filled with two heart-wrenching, wonderful lead characters. Fans of the genre will immensely enjoy this novel even as they dreamily await more magic from the magnificent Ms. Mittman."—*Affaire de Coeur*

"Mittman joins the ranks of the greats in this poignant historical western romance."
—*Oakland Press* (Pontiac, Mich.)

"A VERY POWERFUL BOOK . . . Ms. Mittman deserves heaps of awards for writing some of the best Americana romance around. Ms. Mittman brings daily life into focus so well that you feel like you are stepping into these people's lives. The depth of understanding is unbelievable."—*The Belles and Beaux of Romance*

THE COURTSHIP

"INSPIRING . . . WELL-WRITTEN . . . Stephanie Mittman brilliantly infuses vitality and freshness into the . . . love triangle between a woman and two brothers.*The Courtship* is a splendid piece of Americana that entertains while teaching a lesson on the pioneering days of women's rights."—*Affaire de Coeur*

"PASSIONATE, HUMOROUS . . . this story of star-crossed lovers is bittersweet and poignant."—*Rendezvous*

"Mittman, who does sweet historical romance to perfection, delivers her finest in this gentle tale. [Her] characters are, as always, endearing and well-developed, but here she enriches her story by giving them seemingly insurmountable obstacles."—*Publishers Weekly*

A Heart Full
of Miracles

Stephanie Mittman

A Dell Book

Published by
Dell Publishing
a division of
Random House, Inc.
1540 Broadway
New York, New York 10036

ISBN: 0-440-22556-6

Manufactured in the United States of America

Published simultaneously in Canada

September 2000

10 9 8 7 6 5 4 3 2 1

OPM

This book is dedicated to the following people, who made it possible:

Jennifer Po, dear friend and wonderful nurse, who brought me dusty, antiquated texts on brain surgery from the late 1800s.

John Mangiardi, M.D., neurosurgeon, who spent hours on the phone with me and helped "diagnose" Abidance.

Robert Whitfield, pastor of the Centerport Methodist Church, who spoke with me, lent me his own books, and even invited me to Easter services.

Shelle McKenzie, my sister, who read the manuscript and told me where it needed tweaking.

Alan Mittman, husband, confidant, friend, who listened to every word, rubbed my back, and offered encouragement, advice, and unqualified love.

My friends at LIRW—Roberta Gellis, Pam Burford, Myra Platt, Julie Righter, Happeth Jones, and especially Bernardine Fagan, to name a few, who stroked me and coddled me and forgave me when I was late with articles for the newsletter!

And especially to readers everywhere who wrote or E-mailed and told me to stay at my desk and keep working even though the sun was shining and the trees were calling.

Thank you all.

Chapter One

I KNOW, I KNOW," ABBY MERGANSER SAID, SHAKING her head as she stood in the doorway of Seth's office with yet another steaming pot of soup for his dead sister. "I keep telling myself she's gone yet I still keep making all her favorites." She shrugged, or maybe she was just raising her shoulders against the cold. Seth wasn't sure.

"What is it this time?" If it was anything but her potato-leek soup, he was turning her away, sending her home, or back to the newspaper office where she no doubt caused more trouble than she was worth to her brother, Ansel.

"Potato-leek," she said, stepping around him. He hated that uncanny ability she had to know what he wanted before he did. Confidently—because Abidance Merganser was always confident—she added, "but if you don't invite me in out of the cold, it'll be as freezing as I am."

He watched her as she took over his office, just the way she'd taken over his sister's sickroom, just the way she took over *The Weekly Herald*, heck, the way the girl took over everything. "I have patients to see," he told her, following on her heels, his mouth watering as the smell of her soup filled the air.

"They must be very small," she said, looking around his waiting room as she removed her hat and shook her head, letting loose those chestnut curls of hers. "I hope I didn't step on any of them."

He wanted to shout at her, *No, don't take off your hat, don't stay*, but settled for asking her if that was any way to talk to her elders.

"No. I usually ask them if I can get their canes for them," she answered, pulling off her fine kid gloves. "Or their teeth."

A cane. He felt almost old enough for one, surely old enough for a rocker, especially around Abidance Merganser, who never walked but danced her way around the edges of his life.

"You want some butter on your bread, Seth?" she asked him, reaching into her bottomless basket and pulling out a spread they'd be proud to serve at the Eden's Grove Grand Hotel.

"*Dr. Hendon*," he corrected. With Sarrie gone it was only right to return to proprieties. After all, Abby was barely half his age.

She looked at him in utter disbelief, as if he had suddenly grown a second head and had shaved it bald.

"*Dr. Hendon*, is it?" she asked, not even having the decency to hide her smirk. "Sarah always said you weren't half as smart as you looked." And this from the looniest member of the looniest family in Eden's Grove. Well, not counting her father, the reverend. Years ago Seth had looked in his sister's bird book and found that mergansers were the closest relative of loons. The book had understated the case—obviously the author had never met the Mergansers of Eden's Grove. After an embarrassed glance at him, Abby stumbled on as she held her gloves. "That didn't come out right. Sarah thought you were the smartest man alive. She just always said that men in general—like it always says in the '*Dear Miss Winnie*' column in the *Herald*, when it comes to matters of the heart—"

"Speaking of the *Herald*, don't you have to get back there?" he asked, wondering if the soup was worth having to listen to Abby quote that awful Winifred Dunbury on the superiority of women, the way she and Sarrie used to do. That was, when Sarrie was well enough to tease him. In the end, it was Abby—and that damned Winifred Dunbury—not he, who could still make his sister smile.

"I've hurt your feelings," Abby said, contritely, her wide eyes suddenly awash with tears. Amazing how she could be so lighthearted one minute and so crushed the next. Just watching her exhausted him. "Worse, I've made you think that Sarah—"

"I don't have any feelings to hurt," he told her, enjoying her wide-eyed shock. "And you haven't betrayed Sarah. But you do have work to do, and so do I, young lady."

"Seth Hendon! I am not a *young lady*. You act like I'm ten years old instead of nearly an old maid." Lord help him, now she was unbuttoning her coat and settling in for the duration.

"You can just leave the soup, Miss Merganser, and I'll eat it at lunchtime. Just leave a cover on it, all right?" He opened his supply cabinet, pretending to check it, praying she'd just leave him alone, let him be miserable, let him grieve for what he had been unable to prevent.

"At lunchtime," she agreed, cheerful once again as she carefully folded a napkin next to his bowl and—he should have expected it—one beside hers. "That'd be about half an hour ago, Seth."

"*Dr. Hendon*," he corrected yet again, as if there were any hope of getting through to the girl.

Huge hazel eyes searched his face. "I miss her. I miss telling her how I feel and having her laugh at me. I miss planning and plotting with her. I think a hundred times a day that I should tell her this, or tell her that. I worry about her and then realize there's nothing to worry about anymore." She sat down in the chair beside his desk and played with the soup she'd ladled into her bowl. "I miss her so much that it hurts, and I don't know what to do with the pain."

You swallow it, he thought. *You bury it under a hundred layers of dispassion.* But this was Abby, incapable of either, and so he merely nodded, afraid that if he spoke there was a chance she'd hear the tears that were lodged in his own throat.

"Please let me hold on just a little longer. Let me come for lunch and we can talk about her until I'm ready to let her go. Please, Seth. I'll never call you Seth in front of anyone else, I promise. But here, please, let it be like it was when Sarrie was still with us."

He'd learned a lot in all those years of medical college—to set broken bones, to suture torn skin, to let a fever run its course. But they never taught him a thing about grieving, about losing a patient, about moving on.

He didn't know if her way was the right one—maybe a clean break was what was called for. Maybe they were both supposed to close the door on their memories of his sister and lock it forever.

"Of course, my father says that praying will see me through this," she said, twisting the napkin in her lap. "But then he says that about everything. And Ansel refuses to let me talk about her. But I'm terrified that if I don't, I'll forget her, forget the way her eyes saw right to my soul, forget the way her smile held the darkness at bay."

"You know, you and she were quite a pair of hellions once upon a time," he said, remembering the time they'd been left in his care when he was seventeen and both his parents and Abby's had gone to see a traveling troupe performing Shakespeare. He settled into his desk chair and spread a napkin across his lap. "Not that you've changed much. But once, when you were maybe three and Sarrie was close to six, I got stuck watching you two, and you convinced me that it was a good idea to play hide-and-seek. Do you remember that?"

Abby shook her head. A tear slipped from the corner of her eye and he caught it with his thumb, studying it for a moment.

"You two hid and I couldn't find you anywhere. I called and called and told you that the game was over, but neither of you answered. I was afraid you were dead."

It was a word he almost never said. He had a thousand others in his bag of tricks, all meant to soothe the people left behind. Funny that a doctor, a man of medicine, who was supposedly an expert in matters of life and death, should have such an aversion to a word composed of four little letters. Dead. Sarrie, his beloved little sister, was dead. Despite the years of schooling he had gone through to change the outcome of her illness, despite the trips to hot springs and the steady diet of liver, despite his fervent prayers, Sarrie was dead.

"Eat your soup," Abby told him. "It's getting cold."

"So tell me," he said, fighting the surge of misery that threatened to pull him under. "Which instrument do you see Sarrie playing?"

"What?"

"Which instrument?" He sipped his soup as he watched her mind working—saw it on her face when the pieces fell into place.

"Not in Sarah's obituary!" she begged him, holding the palm of her hand against her forehead. "Tell me I didn't print an error in Sarah's story."

"You commended her into God's 'bands.' I just wondered if she was playing the oboe or—"

"Hands! Hands. It was God's *hands*. Ansel promised me he corrected all the mistakes this time. I wanted Sarrie's story to be as perfect as she was."

He lifted her chin with the same fingers that had dug out bullets from a couple of shoulders, sewn together a good score of wounds, and laid cool cloths upon a thousand brows. "It was perfect," he said softly. "Sarrie would have gotten a good laugh out of it. Like it was a private gift from you to her."

"Thank you, Seth," she said softly. "I'll try to think of it that way."

"And will you try, too, to wear your glasses?" he chided. "You're less likely to make so many embarrassing mistakes that way."

"I *was* wearing my glasses when I set Sarah's type. I do admit that when I wrote that Mrs. Binder's new hut was the latest style, I had pulled off the glasses because, well . . ."

Abidance Merganser felt herself blush. She could hardly tell him it was because he'd come into the shop and she'd wanted to look her best. Not while he was chastising her to grow up. "There was something in my eye."

"I'll miss those mistakes of yours," he said, looking at her with those soft, sky blue eyes, all rimmed with dark lashes that she herself would die for.

"Don't worry, I'll never stop making them, I'm afraid," she said, willing that to be what he meant, knowing in her heart of hearts that it wasn't.

"Just like you'll never grow up?"

"Just like you'll never notice that I already have," she shot back. She stood, ignoring the pain in her head that seemed to never go away, and began collecting the dishes and plates from their lunch, "I'm not ten anymore, Seth. I'm a grown woman. And it's time you noticed."

"Don't be so quick to wish away your youth, little one. What I wouldn't give to be your age again. To feel that life still held promise, the way it does for you. To see the future ahead of me instead of lying crippled in my wake."

"Sarah would be rolling her eyes at you right about now, you know."

"I suppose," Seth agreed. "But it wouldn't change the way things are."

Beside the basket, into which she was depositing the remnants of their lunch, was a pile of letters. She was always impressed by the number of doctors Seth corresponded with, asking for advice and giving it. He was keeping up to date on the latest surgical techniques and medical discoveries, he always said.

She, by comparison, wrote only to her cousin Anna Lisa in St. Louis, who she visited every summer for a month, and sometimes to their mutual friend Armand, whom Anna Lisa was sweet on.

The top letter on Seth's pile was to the Medical College at Philadelphia. The words *to replace me in my practice here* leaped out at her, and, not caring whether she was prying, not caring if Seth saw her reading it, she squinted at the words on the page until he pulled the letter out from under her nose.

"You're not serious," she said. "You wouldn't really leave Eden's Grove, would you?"

He leaned back in his chair until his long legs were stretched out straight in front of him. "The minute I can find someone to replace me."

"Because of Sarrie?" she asked.

"Because I'm done," he said, softly. "Because I don't want to be the one to tell another mother that the child inside her is dead. Because I don't want to have to tell another husband that there isn't anything more that can be done for his wife."

"Because despite all you did, Sarrie died."

Her bluntness shook him. She could see it, but all he said, as softly as he said everything else was, "Because I'm tired of fighting God and losing."

"And all the times you've won? Do they count for nothing?"

He shrugged, as if he couldn't remember a single victory over death, when there had been so many.

"So you've decided to run away? To leave your practice, leave Eden's Grove, leave me?"

"You'll be over Sarrie's death by then, I promise," he said, coming to his feet and poking about in his cabinet once again.

"Perhaps," she agreed. "Given long enough. But will I be over you?"

Abby took off her coat and quietly put it on the peg beside the *Herald*'s door. Seth hadn't said a word in response to her admission. He'd looked at her as if she were some pathetic little creature—which she supposed she was—and had held her coat up for her to put on. "Button up there, Miss Merganser," he'd said as she'd stood in his doorway waiting for any sign that he returned just a modicum of the feelings she had for him.

"How's the doc doing?" Ansel looked up from the freshly printed proof of the week's *Herald*. "I bet he's missing Sarah something awful."

"*Doctor* Hendon," she said, "is the same as always."

"Miserable as ever, then," Ansel said, circling some error. "Mrs. Wilkins is having a public *pee* to raise money for the new church? I wonder how that'll work. And Abby, despite what our father might think, the Lord is not going to fix those eyes of yours. You've got to wear those glasses—"

"Seth is not miserable," she said, placing her spectacles on her nose and hooking the wire arms around her ears. "He's merely serious. And it's *a tea* Mrs. Wilkins is giving."

"While you were out spitting in the wind, Frank Walker stopped by to place an advertisement for a sale at the mercantile," Ansel said. "'Course he said he'd come back when you were here."

Abby nodded. Frank Walker was always dropping by the *Herald* with one excuse or another when it was as plain as the missing tooth in his smile that he was trying to work up the nerve to court her. She did everything she could to discourage him, but still he came by, week after week, always telling her that her dress was pretty or that he admired her penmanship.

"Nice man, Frank," her brother said. "Uncomplicated. Kind. The kind of man that could make a woman happy."

"How would you know what kind of man would make a woman happy? How would you know what tugs at a woman's heart or warms her soul? What would you know about feeling like a piece of yourself is missing and that only one man can fill that place in your heart, whether or not he's willing?"

"More than you might think, Abby. But what if he's just not willing? What if it means being alone forever rather than settling for someone else?" Ansel stood at the press, holding out his hand for Abby to pass him the *t* and the *a* so that he could correct her mistake, and waiting for her to admit that Seth might never love her.

Well, maybe he wouldn't ever love her, but it couldn't change her loving him, wanting to be near him—heaven help her, wanting to touch him and have him touch her. Intimately. The way a man touched a woman. The way she thought a husband touched a wife.

She struggled to find the *t*, squinting behind her glasses. There was no question that her eyesight was getting worse all the time. Despite her father's immutable faith that the Lord would mend her vision, it seemed more likely that she would have to make a trip to Sioux City and have her eyes examined and new spectacles made. For so long she hadn't wanted to leave Sarah, but now she supposed she should make arrangements to go. Maybe Seth wouldn't mind taking her. . . .

"You could learn to love someone else," Ansel was saying. "Okay, maybe not Frank Walker. But what about Emmet Sommers? Emily says that Emmet—"

The thought of Emmet Sommers touching her, even to brush a fly off her arm, turned her stomach. "You know I love your wife like a sister—better than that, actually, but she does have a habit of saying pretty dumb things." From what Abby could see, Ansel loved Emily the same way she did—like a sister. So if anyone was an expert on settling for someone he didn't love passionately, it was surely her brother. But at least he'd gotten Morton Cotter's newspaper, *The Weekly Herald*, along with Morton Cotter's daughter, and he did dearly love the newspaper.

"She just wants to see you happy," Ansel said. "We all want to see you happy."

She found the *t* and thrust it at him. "I am happy. I love my life and my family and my job, just the way they are. I'm delirious with joy. Or at least, I will be."

"When, Abby? You sound just like Pa. Like wanting will make it so. It doesn't work that way, believe me."

"I'm not just sitting around praying for Seth to love me—I've got a plan."

Ansel looked worried. So maybe a plan or two of hers had gone awry in the past.

But this plan had to work. It had to. Losing Sarrie was painful enough. Losing Seth, too, would be unbearable.

Ansel pulled a hankie from his back pocket and wiped her cheek with it. "Tears of happiness?" he asked, brushing back her hair and trying to get her to look at him.

"I've lost my very best friend," she answered, meeting his gaze and feeling grateful that he cared so much about her and was so tender with her. But she was embarrassed that he could pull the thoughts from her head and the feelings from her heart.

"Both of them," he said gently, touching the tip of her nose. "But the doc isn't the man for you, Abby, and now that Sarah is gone, you've got to move on."

"I don't think I can. I think I'm in love with him," she whispered.

"Oh, I am so sorry, honey," Ansel said just as softly,

pulling her against him and letting her find shelter in
his arms. Despite the fact that she had two sisters and
another brother much closer to her in age, it was always Ansel, the oldest, who took the time to talk with
her, who loved her unconditionally. "So sorry."

"Maybe Seth could be the one who learns to love,"
she suggested, her voice muffled against Ansel's apron.

"Honey, he's too old for you."

"Maybe when I first had these feelings it would have
made a difference, but I'm grown now, and fourteen
years doesn't seem like so much. Ma's almost ten years
younger than Papa, so I hardly see—"

"Grown, huh?" her brother said. "Honey, it's not
just the years. Doc's plum old. He's been old ever since
we were children. Ever since he and Sarrie came down
with scarlet fever and she never quite recovered."

"Seth had scarlet fever, too?" And she thought she
knew everything there was to know about Seth.

"We were around fifteen, Seth and me. Another year
and we might not even have gotten sick, since we'd
have been done with school. But we did. Nearly everybody did. At least all the school-age children. Back
then the schoolhouse was up on Healy Hill, and the
wind ran through it like they'd never put up walls.
Becky Chaplain had it first, and then we all came down
with it."

"But Sarah was just a baby then. She wasn't . . ."
Like lightning, it struck her. And suddenly, finally, so
much made sense. "Sarah caught it from Seth."

Ansel nodded. "That's why he became a doctor, I
always figured."

"Poor Seth."

"Losing Sarah had to be hard for him. He really thought, when he came back from Philadelphia, that he could cure her."

"He gave her much more time than Doc Spinner thought she'd have."

"I suppose you pointed that out to him," Ansel said, just as the little bell rang above the shop door.

Abby turned around, ready to see to a customer, but found her father in the doorway instead. His small shoulders were hunched, and his cherubic face was almost hidden by a black muffler that Abby's mother had made. Only his eyes, wet from the cold air and bright with excitement, were clearly visible.

"God bless the Holy Trinity!" he said, then blushed slightly and waved away the words as ridiculous while he unwrapped his muffler to reveal his clerical collar. "Praise heaven for the bright blue air and the clean, crisp sky." And then he sneezed, dug for a hankie in his inner pocket, and blew his nose thoroughly before looking heavenward. "Testing my strength, are You? A cold shall not lay me low, nor all the plagues deter me. I am a man with a mission."

Abby could not remember a time when her father hadn't been a man with a mission. The mission might be to feed the town's hungry, to shelter its poor, or it might be to have the shiniest shoes on Sunday so that they would reflect the Lord's light right back up into the heavens.

Ever since the church had burned down at Christmastime her father had only one mission in mind—to replace the little white church in the woods with a grand affair in the center of town. Late one night he'd admitted to her that he was afraid that since he was only a lay pastor, if he didn't have a church, the bishop in Iowa City would turn his parish back over to a circuit preacher—a fate Abby knew he considered worse than death.

"What is it this time?" Ansel asked, as irreverent as always. From the time Ansel could talk, no one had ever thought that he would follow in his father's religious footsteps. Of course, back then her father hadn't been a minister. He'd been a drunk, and Ansel had never forgiven or forgotten his behavior. "Has God told you how to pay for a new church?"

"Indeed he has," their father said cheerfully. "The Lord taketh away and the Lord provideth."

Under his breath, Ansel muttered a quick "Say hallelujah!" while Ezra Merganser took off his heavy overcoat and hung it beside Abby's.

He put up his hands as if he were at the pulpit and announced, "Joseph Panner has seen the light and shut his eyes in prayer. He has become a citizen of the Kingdom and has decided to make the church the beneficiary of his God-given largess—"

Ansel cranked the press, which moaned loudly. "It sounds like when the Lord *taketh* Joseph, *Joseph* will *provideth* the new church," he said.

"And where do you think Mr. Panner's ill-gotten was gained?" their father asked, flapping his arms to warm up and looking rather like a goose trying to take to the air but failing. "Did it fall from the sky, or did God place it at his feet for some greater purpose than to abuse his mind and amuse his body?"

Abby inked the brayer as she spoke. "Papa, stand by

the fire and warm up. I can't believe you're this excited about Joseph Panner. I thought that you had no use for him and his evil ways."

"A pastor looks after his whole flock," her father said. "Even the stray pig must be found."

"That's the stray *lamb*," Ansel corrected.

"Not in Joseph Panner's case," Abby said. "The man has every dirty habit under the sun, living up there in sin in that big house which, if I'm not mistaken, he won along with that gold mine of his in some bawdy-house poker game when he was no doubt well into his cups, I might add!"

"Exactly!" her father said. "The Lord redeemed me when I lost my faith in the bottom of a bottle, and now the Lord has given Joseph Panner a chance to repent. And to save our church along with his own soul! What a wonder God is! Imagine! The Lord sent me to Ridder's Pond to seek the answer and there it was, drowning!"

"The answer was drowning?" Abby asked.

"That's right! That's right! I got to the pond just in time to witness the miracle."

"How did we get from Ridder's Pond to Panner's mine?" Ansel asked. "Did the Lord write some message in the ice?"

"You can doubt all you want, son, but yes, he did. In a way. He carved a circle, and Joseph Panner fell right through it. If I hadn't come along, he'd have died the sinner that he was, unrepentant, unwelcome in Heaven. But just as I was pulling him out of that frozen hole straight to you-know-where, the Lord spoke to me again and told me that it was a good time to explain to Joseph how leaving his ill-gotten gains to the church would save his soul—just in case he didn't make it, that is." He looked as if his own soul had just been saved. Again. " 'Who desireth not the death of a sinner, but rather that he may turn from his wickedness and live.' Clearly, God gave that mine to Joseph Panner so that he could give the profits he made to me."

"Why didn't God just give them directly to you and leave out the middleman?" Ansel asked. "And the ice?"

"Because I don't gamble," her father said simply. "So how could I have won that mine? And besides, the Lord didn't need to save me again, Ansel. I've already seen the light. I've had the gifts and the graces. It was Joseph Panner's soul that needed saving, and my church that needs building, and with one hole in the ice the good Lord killed two birds."

"So Panner's just planning on giving you all his money?" Ansel asked. "Not that I believe he's got that much left. That mine was played out years ago."

"The man's got more gold than Judas. I'm going for Mr. Youtt now so he can draw up the papers for Joseph to sign, as soon as the feeling comes back to his fingers, that is."

"Did you tell Seth? I mean Dr. Hendon? Has someone gone for him?" Abby asked, pulling off her spectacles and heading for her coat.

"The doctor? My heavens! You don't think the good Lord saved him from drowning just to—"

"You didn't tell Seth?" Abby asked, hitting something with her foot and tipping her head to see that it was one of the cats that roamed the *Herald*'s office because she refused to heed Ansel's warnings not to feed them. She apologized to the kitten and slipped her coat over her shoulders.

"A doctor? After such a miracle?" Her father appeared confused. " *'Blessed is he that hears the word of God'*—and I shouted it in his ear till the poor man couldn't hear anything but the Lord. I'm telling you it was nothing short of a miracle. I summoned the Lord and laid my hands upon Panner's body. And I could feel his soul rise up in worship!"

"I'm very happy for his soul, Pa. But what about his fingers and toes? Who's seeing to those?"

For a moment her father looked confused. "I told you. The Lord is—"

"I'm getting Seth," she said, sidestepping her father but feeling his hand on her shoulder.

"*Seth*, is it? Oh, Abidance. Don't you go losing your heart, now. Remember, this is the same *Seth* who doesn't come to church, who refused the sacraments at his sister's burial. You were surely doing the Lord's work when you saw to Sarah Hendon when she was alive, God rest her soul. But I see that while I've been watching over my flock, your mama and your brother have allowed my littlest, dearest lamb to stray from—"

"All you see is a young lady fetching the doctor for a sick man, the way you should have," Ansel said, coming toward the door himself. "Don't go imagining things. Abidance is no more interested in the good doctor than I was in his sister."

Abby supposed she would have stood there all day, her breath caught in her throat, her jaw dropped, her brother's words ringing in her ears, had Ansel not all but pushed her out the door.

Chapter Two

SETH HAD GRABBED HIS MEDICAL BAG AND HURried to Joseph Panner's home, Abby on his heels, despite his telling her to go back to the newspaper office. He was glad now that she'd come along, since he needed help with the cold dressings he was applying to Mr. Panner's fingers and toes in hopes of saving the frostbitten digits.

"I'm telling you," Joseph Panner said, his teeth chattering so that it was hard to make out his words. "This was the biggest walleye you ever saw. That fish was big last fall, but he's ready for me now."

"Can you feel anything when I touch here?" Seth asked Panner, running his fingernails against the end of Panner's toes and ignoring the man's fish story.

"He can feel the Lord in every breath," Abby's father, who had been hanging back in the doorway until now, hollered.

"Great, but it'd be a shame to save his soul and lose his toes, don't you think?" Seth responded, gently rubbing the unnaturally white skin and directing Abby to do the same to the toes on the man's other foot. She was good in an emergency—better than he expected from a girl her age, not to mention the upbringing she'd had.

"Oh, just so, just so. But it was the Lord saved this man," Reverend Merganser said to Seth as he watched him work. "Dr. Hendon, that was the Lord's hand."

"It was your hands," Panner said, his voice quivering with chills. "You pulled me out of that ice, Reverend, and I owe you my life."

The reverend's face colored, and he waved away the gratitude with his hand. Then his eyes got big and round, and he said, almost as if he were surprised at the revelation, "The Lord brought me to that spot, that very spot, at that very moment, just to do His will. Why, I never go past that old pond. And yet today I was drawn to it. Oh, ye of little faith! Oh, *me* of little faith! I woke up thinking that perhaps my church would never be—that I would remain forever a believer without a home, a servant without quarters in which to do my work for the Lord."

Her father looked out the window and shook his head in amazement. "Just when I was sure that the bishop would decide to take back my appointment, seeing as how I barely passed my course of study and it was only because the town built a church and there wasn't another minister around that he let me be the pastor in the first place. . . ." He mumbled this last, then, in a stronger voice, added, "And now, when I was at the end of my rope, He made a loop for me to hold on to—the means to build my church!"

Panner smiled weakly. "I still can't feel my toes, Doc," he said, raising his head to see over his belly and down to where Seth and Abby were gently rubbing his stiff toes.

"That's not surprising," Seth said. "You were in the pond a while. It'll take some time for the flesh to thaw."

"Can't I just stick 'em in a tub of hot water?" Panner asked, his voice still quivering. "I'm not going to lose my toes, am I?"

"Well," Seth began, not one to lie to a patient, but not anxious to have the man panic, either. "I don't—" he began, only to have Abby interrupt him.

"So, Mr. Panner," she said, her voice light, as if the man weren't in the least bit of danger of losing his toes. "I've never played poker. What do you have to do to win?"

"Abidance!" her father gasped, but Seth knew that Abby was just trying to distract Panner. And it was working. Panner's voice came out stronger and clearer as he answered her.

"You gotta be braver and smarter than the next fellow," he said, and Seth thought that maybe, just maybe, there was a little bit of pink now to Panner's big toe. "You gotta have a good bluffing face, Miss Abby. Like you believe you've got a winning hand despite the cards you mighta gotten dealt."

"That sounds remarkably like my father's philosophy," Abby said, pointing out to Seth that there definitely was a pinkness to Panner's big toe. "Only he calls it blind faith."

Panner laughed, his laughter even louder than the reverend's. "Maybe there is some similarity there. But I've always thought your father really did believe he was holding the winning hand, and I was just pretending. Till now, that is."

"Did you practice that bluffing face in the mirror?" Abby asked him. "Can anybody develop one? Do you think I could?" She made one of the million faces that used to amuse Sarrie so, and aimed it right at Seth.

"Abidance Merganser," he said, adding a bit of warmer water to the wrappings around Panner's feet. "You couldn't lie if your life depended on it. Everything you think is on that face of yours like you inked it and printed it at the *Herald*."

Abby batted her eyelids at him as if she were capable of keeping even the smallest of secrets, which he knew darned well she wasn't, and smiled what he supposed she imagined to be a mysterious smile.

"Looks to me like you'll be all right, Mr. Panner," Seth said, gently bending and flexing each toe. "It'll take a while, and I ought to see you in my office in a day or two to make sure that the damage isn't permanent. Sometimes things look just fine and then gangrene sets in 'cause the tissue's dead."

"I could lose my toes?" Panner asked, looking from Seth to the reverend as if somehow Merganser could stop that from happening.

"Would the Lord stand you on your feet without your toes?" Merganser asked, laying a hand on Panner's arm.

"Well," Abby said, adjusting the covers like a little Florence Nightingale. "If you don't lose your toes, sir, it'll be Dr. Hendon who saved them, and if you don't see him in his office in a couple of days, it'll be your fault if you do."

Seth heard the words and tried to make sense of them. How could it be that he could take the credit and not the blame? If Panner lost his toes, it would be because Seth hadn't done exactly the right things—hadn't used cold enough water, or hadn't rubbed gently enough, or hadn't tried some new remedy that had just been discovered.

"I'll be back to check on you tomorrow," he said with a sigh, knowing that once Joseph Panner was feeling better he wouldn't bother to have the toes checked until it was too late.

Abby simply didn't understand the burden of being a doctor, especially here in Eden's Grove, where a second opinion was a two-day ride away, where an emergency on this end of town meant he couldn't check on Mrs. Denton's baby at the other. Where a small room on the bottom floor of his home was his office, and he'd had to go without new shoes for a whole winter just to get a used autoclave so that his instruments would be sterile.

Well, of course Abby didn't understand. She was a child—a sprite—in a family that danced in the rain and made angels in the snow and relied on the Lord to provide whatever they needed. Her brother, Ansel, hadn't been able to wait to get away from them, to find order in his life.

Seth had liked Ansel, once upon a time. The man should have been his brother-in-law. He'd seen it all spelled out in Sarrie's eyes and he'd seen it in Ansel's. But it had all come to nothing when Sarrie pushed Ansel away, out of her life and right into Emily Cotter's arms, just weeks before she'd become bedridden.

She'd wanted to see Ansel have children, and she had. The closest thing to nieces she would ever see.

"Mr. Youtt is coming with the papers," the reverend told Panner.

"Well, just be sure to leave Mr. Panner enough so he can pay Dr. Hendon," Abby said. "I'll have his bill brought by with your newspaper in the morning."

Seth didn't know what to say. What a patient paid his doctor was a matter of conscience, not a number on a bill most folks couldn't afford to pay anyway. They did the best they could, the richer folks giving what was fair, the poorer bringing him chickens and eggs and slabs of bacon when there was no money in their till. Abby was all business, still rubbing Panner's foot as if she were Seth's assistant, talking about his bills as though she were his bookkeeper.

The sooner he could find a doctor to take over his practice, the sooner he could get out of Eden's Grove, the better for all of them.

"Don't you worry about that," Panner said. "I ought to be able to make a nice donation to the reverend's new church and still sit pretty comfortable. I ain't gonna lose those toes, Doc, am I?"

"Not if you do as the doc says," Abby said before Seth could properly answer the man.

"Abidance Merganser, will you be so kind as to not take over my practice until you've gotten a medical degree? I'll gladly hand you the keys to my office when you show me your diploma. Until then, I'll answer for myself." Rather than looking the least bit chastised, Abby shrugged and indicated that by all means, he should certainly answer Panner's question. Like a fool, he parroted her words. "Not if you do as I say," he added, and Abby smiled brightly at him as if he'd learned a lesson.

Well, he had: never bring Abidance Merganser on another house call.

And then he remembered. He hadn't brought her. Like a stray puppy, she'd followed him.

But he had no intention of keeping her.

None.

Her papa was pouting, sulking like a little boy who couldn't understand why Christmas couldn't be every day.

"How could he not 'be sure'?" he asked, shaking his head, while Abby's mother wrapped a colorful afghan she'd crocheted around his shoulders, and Patience, one of Abby's sisters, poured more hot water into the basin in which he was soaking his feet. "Imagine that! God all but spoke directly to him, and he says he's just not sure. Why, if I had felt that way, I wouldn't be where I am today." He looked around him and sneezed.

"Well, I think you've just done the bravest thing I've ever heard of," Patience said. "I can't wait to put it in my journal so that my great-great-grandchildren will know how brave their great-great . . . wait, I lost count. My great-great—"

"You had two greats and a grand," Jedediah the sibling closest in age to Abby said. Poor Jed, he was fine with numbers and tools, but the train of life didn't seem to stop at his station. Sense just seemed to pass him by. "Was he dead when you saved him, Papa?"

"Well, almost," her father said. "If he'd been dead, then I couldn't have—oh, Jedediah! Make yourself useful, son, and find me my slippers like a good boy."

"I'd have been useful," Jed said. "I'd have saved him myself if I'd been there."

"Oh, sure you would have! You'd have invented some way of getting him out of the pond without getting yourself wet, using winches and ropes, and by the time you got it all together, the man would have been dead a week!" Prudence, the older of Abby's sisters corrected, scooping up one of her children who was trying to sail a toy boat in the basin their father was soaking his feet in. "So, Jed, are you having any luck with that silly flying machine?" she teased.

Nobody waited for Jed's answer. It was always the same anyway—*You'll see. You'll all see.*

"The fact remains that he promised the Lord that money, and now, thanks to Abidance, he's reconsidering his promise." Her father glared at her.

"I never told him not to give his money to you for the church," she defended, feeling disloyal despite herself. "I just said that he should pay Seth—I mean Dr. Hendon."

"And you made the poor man think God would take his toes if he didn't," her father said.

"Now, Papa, I hardly think that paying Dr. Hendon a dollar or two will prevent your church from being built, do you?" she asked, handing him a clean hankie and lifting Disciple, the little furball of a kitten, into her arms before he began drinking the water in her father's footbath. "That poor man is overworked and underappreciated as it is. I'm worried about him," she admitted.

"I like Seth Hendon," her mother said. She took the kitten from Abby and appeared to be thinking deep thoughts before she handed Disciple over to Prudence, and announced, "I think we ought to have him for Sunday dinner."

"The cat?" Prudence asked, and immediately little Gwendolyn began to cry, grabbing the cat and throwing herself over the furry body.

"Oh, no, dear!" Mother said, shaking her head at Gwendolyn, and Prudence, and for that matter at Jedediah and Patience, too. "Dr. Hendon. Why, I would think he must be the loneliest man on earth, now that Sarah's gone. He needs a family."

"Oh, but not ours," Patience said. "I mean, lately he's so surly. I think a smile would break his face."

"The man has a right to grieve, don't you think? And actually his smile is quite dazzling," Abby said, a smile of her own turning her lips. When Patience just shook her head, she added, "And it's all the more precious because it isn't bestowed on just anyone."

"So you've seen it, then?" her mother asked, and Abby watched her exchange a glance with her father that all but shouted *Didn't I tell you so?*

"Everyone's seen Seth smile," she said, trying to pretend it was nothing so that her mother wouldn't start taking measurements for her wedding gown.

"I suppose I'd better ask *Seth* his intentions," her father said with a resigned sigh, making sure his lap was well covered with the blanket her mother had given him when she'd unceremoniously demanded that he remove his pants. "Since Abby's so sweet on him."

"Whose intentions?" Jedediah asked, looking up from the clock he was fiddling with. "Dr. Hendon's? Oh, wait. I see. Abby and . . . No. I don't see. Isn't Dr. Hendon nearly old enough to be—"

"I am not a child!" Abby cried, stomping her foot so that even she could see that she was belying her words. She calmed herself, improved her posture, and said as demurely as she could, considering that Michael, Prudence's little boy, was crawling under her skirts as she spoke. "There is nothing to see, Jed. He has no intentions, Father. He is not surly, Patience. And Mother, I do not think he would like to join us for Sunday dinner."

Everyone just stared at her for a moment.

"And Michael, you come out from there," she added, lifting her skirts to gently boot out her nephew.

"I'll make ham," her mother said. "Or turkey. I bet he's a whiz at carving a turkey, wouldn't you think?"

"No," Abby said, but no one seemed to be listening to her.

"I suppose I could make my quince tarts. Boone always loved my quince tarts," Prudence said.

"No," Abby said again.

"Couldn't I pick up three cigars, Papa, and we could all discuss the world situation?" Jedediah asked.

"Make that four," her father said, shrugging her mother's afghan off his shoulders. "I'd like Ansel here too. He's friends with the doctor and it'll help put him at ease when I ask him when he'd like to—"

"*No!*" Abby said, this time stamping for emphasis.

"He has no intentions. Not yet. At least none toward me. In fact, he's thinking of leaving Eden's Grove altogether."

"Oh, but that's awful," her mother said, sitting down at the table with a pencil and paper. "How I would miss you! Just like when you go to Anna Lisa's in St. Louis—only longer."

"Michael and Gwendolyn would hardly know their cousins," Prudence complained.

"Please," Abby begged them all. "Listen to me. Dr. Hendon has just lost his sister. He's hurting and he's confused. A dinner here with all of you would push him out of Eden's Grove so fast that we'd choke on his buggy dust."

"It's so sweet that she's worried about him, don't you think?" her mother asked her father, as she got up from the table and placed the iron on the stove and her father's pants on the pad on the kitchen table.

"Wouldn't it just beat the Dutch to have that new church built before they took their vows?" her father said.

Abby looked around the kitchen of the home she'd grown up in. It had fallen into terrible disrepair during her father's drinking days and never quite recovered. Now it bore the scars of Jed's inventions, the latest being an attempt to make a clock that would somehow turn on the kettle so that they could wake up to the smell of fresh coffee. He had promised to repaint the kitchen wall as soon as he perfected the clock.

He had promised to replace the window he'd broken when demonstrating how his boomerang would turn before it reached the glass. He had made lots of promises, but in the Merganser house it was the promising and not the doing, the intent and not the execution, that mattered, and so the wall remained unpainted, the window broken, and the table wobbly. She didn't even want to remember that particular invention.

Despite the chaos around him, her father, his legs sticking out from under the blanket, was contemplatively drawing crosses on the wooden floor with his wet toes. Her mother was furiously writing and crossing things off what Abby hoped was a grocery list, not a wedding list. Jedediah was turning last week's *Weekly Herald* into an airship with Michael sitting on his shoulders, covering first one of Jed's eyes and then the other. Prudence, for reasons beyond Abby's understanding, had decided it was the perfect time to sing one of her favorite arias (no doubt what had driven her husband, Boone, to go hunting for gold almost a year ago, with only one letter home in all that time, asking if Pru might send him a few extra dollars for a new pan and boots). Patience, an apron tied around her head, was dancing with Gwendolyn in her arms, humming a waltz that sounded suspiciously like the wedding march.

A big dose of this family all at once would probably kill Seth, she thought. He was, after all, used to a quiet life with Sarah.

But surely Seth would warm to them eventually.

If he encountered them in small enough doses.

He had a broken spirit. Just as if he had a broken leg, he needed to rest it a bit. And then, just as he'd do with a broken leg, he needed to exercise it, strengthen it.

And she could help him.

If he let her.

She took a deep breath. If she waited for him to let her, it could be too late.

"It's hot," Patience told her mother, taking the heavy iron from the stove.

A plan taking shape in her head, Abby came up behind her mother and gave the woman a big hug. "Then it's time to strike," she said, kissing her mother's hair.

Seth had seen six patients since running out to Joseph Panner's house. Three were simple accidents that required little more than a bandage and the assurance that all would be well. Two were coughs and colds that he felt pretty sure would not develop into the influenza or pneumonia. The last, Mrs. Denton's little boy, was the one that was troubling him now, as he read through his latest journal and sipped a cup of the morning's now-cold tea.

He recognized the sound of Abidance Merganser's feet as they climbed the steps and crossed his porch, and what was left of his heart fell into his stomach. What had he ever done to deserve his own little Miss Sunshine? Whatever it was, he was sorry he'd done it. Why she still had faith in him after he'd let Sarrie die, he didn't know.

But she did, still looking at him with that cheerful, hopeful face, those big bright eyes that shouted she was his for the taking. It was as if she were taunting him, holding out a life to him that he could never embrace, a hand he had no right to claim.

First off, she was too young, too innocent, too untouched by the awful things that life could hand a person, to be soiled by the life he led. He imagined trudging home from Mrs. Denton's and having Abby waiting there, glowing, only to have him tell her that the boy had taken a turn for the worse, that all the tricks he had in that medical bag of his wouldn't be enough. And where would her smile go then?

Second, his was an orderly life that ran according to the demands of his practice. He needed the calm, the quiet, the serenity of living alone, having to meet no one else's needs when the day was done. She'd want to see him smile, laugh, engage him in ridiculous conversations. There was no place for that in his life.

Most importantly, he was leaving. As soon as one of the medical colleges or hospitals he had written to could offer him a suitable replacement, he was leaving Eden's Grove—and medicine—behind him.

"Seth?"

The girl didn't speak. She sang.

"Yes?" he said, exasperated.

"Something wrong?" she asked, pushing back her bonnet and freeing a riot of curls.

"This is a doctor's office. Shouldn't I be asking you that?"

"Wrong with me? Don't be silly. I'm healthy as a horse."

"Then why are you here?" he asked.

"Well, I had this wonderful idea for the newspaper.

You know how you tease us about 'Dear Miss Winnie'?"

"You're dropping that ridiculous column?"

"It's not ridiculous. 'Dear Miss Winnie' appears in hundreds of papers. The lady knows a great deal about . . . well, feminine things. Anyway, I was thinking about a column you could write—"

"To warn men about women who take Miss Winnie's advice?" he asked, one eyebrow raised.

"No. You could write a column about health! You could teach people how to take better care of themselves, warn them about what might be going around. . . ."

"That's ridiculous," he said, despite the fact that it didn't seem ridiculous to him at all.

"Now, Seth . . . I mean, Dr. Hendon. People are not as stupid as you think. And what they don't know, they are capable of learning. They just haven't had the schooling you've had. Take, for example, this morning's emergency. Why, nearly everyone would have put Joseph Panner's feet into hot water to warm them up. I mean, it makes sense, doesn't it? Unless, of course, you know better."

She was neatening the papers on his desk as she spoke, and she stopped to look up at him with those innocent eyes of hers that refused to see the problems that were at the end of her nose.

"Where are your glasses?" he asked.

"Oh! Did you want to dictate a column?"

He hadn't thought her eyes could get brighter.

"It's not that your idea doesn't have some merit," he

admitted, thinking that, indeed, there were lots of simple things people could do without medical training. And he could save himself an awful lot of time if patients could at the very least differentiate between what really required his services and what didn't.

"We could run it weekly, in every issue. We could key it to the seasons—frostbite in the winter, sunburn in the summer. We could tie it in with holidays—stomachaches from too much holiday celebrating, that sort of thing. And what to do in case of an accident. And how to stop bleeding. How to—"

"I spent years in medical college learning the answers to those questions," he began.

"Well, would it hurt you to share what you learned?" she asked, finding a pad and a pencil and tidying up the piles they were hidden under. She sat poised, ready to take down his words for all of Eden's Grove to read.

"It's not that simple," he started.

"Well, start with what *is* simple," she said. "Like using cold water to prevent frostbite. That's vital information that people here need, don't you think?"

He did think so. He just didn't think that he wanted to sit in his office with Abidance Merganser's dazzling smile just across the desk from him.

"Your father get himself dry and warm?" he asked, spreading his papers back out across his desk the way he liked them.

"You could add that in about how if there is no frostbite then the patient can be—"

"I'll drop a column by the office later in the week," he said, not admitting that it was a darn good idea. "It certainly couldn't hurt," he said grudgingly.

She put the pad and paper down on the desk and leaned forward toward him. "Why do I make you nervous?" she asked.

He humphed, sounding like the old man he thought he was. "It'll be a fine day in Hades when a girl like you—"

"If I'm just some girl, Seth, then why can't you seem to breathe when—"

"*Doctor* Hendon! And you're imagining things because you've, well, to be frank, Abidance, you've got a schoolgirl crush on me. And while I do admit that it's flattering, it is wholly inappropriate and—"

"I suppose you're right," she said as dreamily as she could. "After all, I am nearly promised to another and you'd probably want someone . . ."

She tried to look as casual as she could, blinking at him innocently, as she continued. "You'd no doubt want someone with less experience than I."

She really did think he'd have the common decency not to laugh out loud.

"Abby, any less experience and you'd still be sucking your thumb and playing with dolls."

Well, that wasn't the kind of remark she could just let pass, was it? She smiled at him as mysteriously as she could, her mind racing wildly for proof of what wasn't.

"I'll give Ansel an article before you go to press on Friday," he said, rising as if the conversation between them was over, and adding, quite patronizingly, "How's that?"

"It's a start," she said.

"Now go on home, Abidance, where you'll be safe under your mother's wing and your father's eye. Be a good girl, huh?"

"Seth Hendon, I am not a good girl," she said, feeling herself blush at the implication and backtracking rapidly. "I mean, I'm not the innocent you suppose."

She'd have stopped there, but he raised his eyebrows with such amusement, such condescending doubt that she couldn't stop herself.

"I have been kissed, you know."

A smirk! "So little Frankie Walker finally worked up the nerve to peck you on your cheek, huh?"

"Frank Walker! A peck on the cheek! I'm talking about thoroughly kissed. Not like a brother or uncle." She knew nothing about kissing, except the innuendos of some of the girls she'd gone to school with, but they'd always hushed at the sight of the Reverend Merganser's daughter. One, though . . . She ran her tongue very slowly over her bottom lip. "*Well* kissed," she said, mimicking Callie Jean Evans, and watching Seth's eyes widen. Maybe Callie Jean, who already had two little babies and another on the way, wasn't all talk, after all.

"I don't believe it," Seth said, his smirk returning to his face, though at his side, where he thought she couldn't see, his thumb rubbed fast and hard against his fingers. "Who?"

Abby ran her tongue over her lip again. Seth opened and closed his fist several times. "You don't know him," she said, rising and reaching for her bonnet.

Seth took her coat from the peg, but held it to his

chest, rather than helping her into it. She wasn't even sure he was aware of what he was doing. "I know everyone you know," he said gruffly. "I probably delivered half of them."

"Not this one," she said coyly. "He's not from around here." She could just hear her mother warning of tangled webs, but words of love and wedding bells rang a good deal louder in her head, drowning out any warnings.

"Abidance," he warned, as if now was the time for her to come clean and admit that she was . . . well . . . *fabricating*. After all, a reverend's daughter never lied.

"St. Louis," she said, the words coming out in a rush of relief. She went to St. Louis every summer. Surely she could have met someone there—a handsome, charming, insistent gentleman who was so taken with her that—

Seth seemed to be considering whether or not this was a real possibility. Abby sensed the vital importance of this moment to the rest of her life.

Well, her mother always did say she had a flare for the dramatic.

"What's his name?" Seth demanded, that darned eyebrow of his raised in his usual disbelief.

She said the first name that came to mind. "Armand," and then added, "I've probably mentioned him before."

"It sounds familiar," Seth admitted. Fortunately he'd apparently paid little attention to her prattling all these years.

"Yes, well," she said, taking her coat from his hands

and putting one arm through the sleeve. "Oh, and maybe you could do an article on the dangers of social diseases."

Turning to smile at him, she caught sight of the blood draining from Seth's face. "I mean, women might need to know—"

"Not here in Eden's Grove, they don't," Seth said as if his words could make it so. He was no doubt right, but she'd surely captured his attention, and she wasn't about to let go.

"As I pointed out, women do travel, Seth. Why, I wouldn't miss my yearly trip to St. Louis"—she paused to concentrate on buttoning her coat—"for anything."

"And are you trying to tell me that you do wild and woolly things there?" he asked her, pushing her hands away as she fumbled with her top button and fastening it himself.

Clearly she had aged years in his eyes. She ran her tongue over her top lip this time and watched Seth's eyes follow the movement intently.

"Better put some pomade on those lips," he said.

"They're plenty soft," she said, offering them up to him.

"Then why is it you need to keep licking them?" he asked, the smirk back in place.

"You are just so full of yourself, Dr. Hendon," she said, opening the door to the early March winds and not bothering to close it behind her before she started storming down the sidewalk.

"And you, Miss Merganser, are full of hogwash!" he shouted after her.

She'd have been sure the whole episode was a total failure if she hadn't stolen a glimpse back as she turned the corner.

Seth Hendon was standing outside his office door in the dead of winter in his shirtsleeves, watching her go.

Chapter Three

S ETH COULDN'T IMAGINE WHAT POSSESSED HIM TO
accept Clarice Merganser's invitation to have
dinner with the "loons" after church, except that
to say no would have been rude, and he was not a rude
man. Except maybe around Abby, who seemed to
bring out his sarcastic, impatient side.

Ansel, taking pity on him, had offered to stop by on
his way so that Seth could at least arrive in the company of sanity, even if it was a soon-to-be-vanquished
illusion. Ansel's wife, Emily, walked ahead with their
daughter, Suellen, shepherding her along on the sidewalk, while Ansel and Seth dragged behind because
each of them was more reluctant than the other to get
to their destination.

"Abby seems to be taking Sarah's death pretty hard,"
Ansel said as he put up the collar to his coat against the
same damn wind that had been at Seth's back for
months, urging him forward, urging him to move on
already before it was too late.

"Really? I thought she was bouncing back rather
well," Seth said truthfully. It seemed to him that she

was as cheerful as ever, as full of life and plans as she had always been.

"That smile of hers could fool the devil himself," Ansel said. "But it's phonier than invisible ink, and fades as fast when no one is looking."

Seth felt Ansel's gaze, but didn't meet it. It wasn't his job to make Abidance Merganser happy, was it? Just because she imagined herself fond of him didn't make it incumbent upon him to be the willing object of her affections, did it? Why, if everyone was obliged to return all feelings, what would women like Lily Langtree do? Split themselves in a million pieces for everyone who thought they were in love—that was the key word—they *thought* they were in love.

After all, what could Abby know of love? She was just a baby, an innocent. *Social diseases!* She probably thought shyness was a social disease. Ineptitude. Gracelessness. Surely she had no more idea what a social disease was than she had of what she was implying with that tongue of hers tracing that soft, luscious lip. At least he didn't think so.

"You ever go with her to St. Louis?" he asked casually, "To see that cousin of hers?"

"Not since we were kids," Ansel said.

"You mean since *you* were a kid. As far as I can see, Abby still is."

Ansel stopped walking and waited for Seth to look at him.

"What?" Seth asked him.

"I don't know where you're looking, but Abby's no kid. She's a lovely young woman, and if you aren't careful, someone else will come along and snatch her out from under your nose."

"From your mouth to God's ear," he said irreverently.

"Far be it from me to tell anyone what to do about their love life, but I'll tell you this, Seth Hendon, and I hope you'll give me more than the half an ear you usually do. True love doesn't—"

"Save it, Ansel," Seth said. "When I want your advice on love, I'll—"

"—disappear. That's all I want to warn you about, Dr. Hendon. True love doesn't disappear. No matter how hard you try, no matter how you go on with your life. No matter even if she dies. The love goes on."

Seth was quiet out of respect. Ansel had never admitted aloud that he loved Sarrie. At least not to him. Not ten feet ahead of them, Ansel's wife and child waddled up the street like a mother hen and her chick. From the looks of it, Seth supposed that Emily might be carrying once again.

"You look to me to be a well-fulfilled man," Seth said softly. There was a piece of him that resented the path that Ansel had taken, the easy path that gave him a wife and a family and washed his hands of Sarah's problems.

"I am," he said, so vehemently that Seth had to wonder who he thought needed convincing.

Suellen dropped back to wind herself around Ansel's legs. "Papa, can you carry me?" she begged with the same big eyes that belonged to Ansel and Abby and most of the Mergansers. She had that little bow mouth that Abby had, but had Emily's sharp nose and pale brown hair.

He imagined the children that Abby would have someday and the breath caught in his throat.

"Does she tell you much about her trips to St. Louis?" Seth asked. "I mean, she always seems to come back so full of excitement. She has a good time?"

"I suppose," Ansel said, busy with trying to keep Suellen on his shoulders and still see while her hands covered his eyes and pushed down on his hat. She was laughing in his ear when Seth asked Ansel whether Abby ever mentioned anyone in particular, and when Ansel asked him what he'd said, Seth thought it best to just drop the subject.

What difference did it make if Abby Merganser had ever been kissed well? What earthly difference could it make to him if there was a man who had pressed his lips to hers and felt that little pink tongue tentatively—

"Watch it there! Careful!" Ansel warned as Seth tripped off the end of the wooden sidewalk.

He'd nearly twisted his ankle.

And he had the bad, bad feeling that Ansel's warning had come too late.

She'd warned her whole family to behave themselves, with threats of dire consequences. Not that she expected it to do a lick of good, but she was just one of those people who couldn't help but hope for the best. Ansel teased her unmercifully, asking if she so often neglected to wear her spectacles because she already had on rose-colored ones that made her see things as better than they were, better than they would ever be.

"They're here," Prudence sang, making an opera out

of the announcement. "Now I can ask him about my throat. It's been sore as long as I can remember," she screeched at the top of her lungs, leaving no doubt in anyone's mind about the cause of her pain. Abby figured that next Jed would complain about the ringing in his ears whenever Patience was singing.

Abby splayed herself against the door, ready to do battle with anyone who tried to open it. If it wasn't Seth on the other side of the door, the throbbing in her head would have made her go running for her bed. But it was Seth, and no headache was going to stop her from keeping her family in check and making sure that this night went perfectly. Well, if not perfectly, then nicely. Or merely adequately. Oh, all right! She was positively determined that it would at least not be a disaster.

"We will not ask the doctor about our ailments," she ordered. "We will not sing, dance, stand on our heads"—she looked pointedly at Jed—"or do anything else that every other family in Eden's Grove doesn't do."

"Will we eat?" Michael asked, eyes big and round and fearful.

"Of course we will eat," Abby assured him. "That's why the doctor's coming."

"Oh, is *that* why?" Patience asked, nudging Jed with her elbow. "So the doctor can eat."

Abby ignored her.

"May we talk?" Gwendolyn asked.

Abby raised an eyebrow at Prudence, as if to ask whether she could be trusted, and then nodded, albeit reluctantly.

And then Seth knocked on the door, and with a million misgivings, she opened it.

Naturally, all hell broke lose.

Did her father say *Please come in. How nice to see you?* No. Instead he asked, "You think you ought to check my toes?" at the same time her mother was reaching for Seth's coat and saying that she hoped that Seth liked stew, which was interrupted by Prudence, asking, "Has anyone seen the cat today?" which sounded like she suspected that her mother had used Disciple for the stew, which made Seth blanch, but not for long, because Prudence, never liking to be told what to do, or maybe never remembering what she was told, was busy angling her head near Seth's chest and opening her mouth wide and pointing at her throat while she made whimpering noises.

"Prudence?" Seth managed to choke out.

"I'm not supposed to tell you that my throat hurts." She glared at Abby while Michael tugged on Seth's sleeve.

"Wanna see what's in my potty?"

Abby rubbed at her temple. The headache was getting hard to ignore.

"I cut my finger with the butter knife this morning," Jedediah said, thrusting it in Seth's face. "You wouldn't think that was possible, would you? I needed something to help me stretch an old rubber gasket around this wire wheel—for the model for my sky cycle," he added as Ansel and Emily wedged their way in, Suellen in Ansel's arms.

"It must be so wonderful to be a doctor," Abby's mother said. "And be able to help everyone."

Seth looked at Abby as if he were going under for the third time and she were holding the life preserver out of his reach.

"Say hello to Dr. Hendon," Prudence directed Gwendolyn. "He's the man who helped bring you into this world, sweetie."

"It has its moments," Seth admitted to Abby's mother, ruffling Gwendolyn's blond curls and letting his hand linger on her head.

"Heard you won't be delivering any more kids to Frannie Wallis unless Bill—" Jed started, then stopped himself when he realized that Bill Wallis's problem wasn't a fit topic of conversation in front of his mama, though he'd told Abby that all Bill's drinking had taken the "manliness" out of him. "Heard he came to see you, Doc, and—"

"Well, he came to see *me*, poor man," Abby's father said as he sat down and began removing his shoes. "All a mess like what was happening wasn't his own fault. And I told him I'd been to the bottom of *that* well myself, and—"

"I'm sure whatever you told him was in confidence," Seth said, looking around the room with what Abby supposed was escape in mind. "It's the same with doctors as it is with men of God, and lawyers too, I've heard. What patients tell us is in confidence. It's meant for no one else's ears."

"You mean that if I went to you and I told you something, you'd have to keep it a secret?" Emily asked. Ansel looked shocked at the question and more than a little annoyed when Seth agreed that he would keep her confidence.

"But surely not from a woman's own husband, or a child's mother, or . . ." Ansel pressed as Seth bent over and took her father's foot into his hand.

"Not a young child," Seth agreed, turning the foot this way and that and spreading her father's toes, "but the doctor-patient relationship is a sacred one. A patient has to feel safe that he can tell the doctor the truth so that the doctor can best treat him. If he—or she—was afraid that a secret might come out, he—or she—might hold something back that could jeopardize her life."

"Oh, that must be the best part of being a doctor," Abby's mother said.

Seth just rolled his eyes and then released her father's foot. "They seem just fine, sir. No damage at all."

Abby's father wiggled his toes and smiled as if they'd done something extraordinary, while her mother continued her discussion with Seth.

"Of course, not being able to tell anyone . . . that would be hard," she admitted. "But being privy to everyone's secrets!"

"Would you like to know a man is going to die and be forbidden to tell his wife? Would you like to know—" He stood and shook his head. "Most secrets aren't happy ones."

"Oh, how solemn we've gotten," Clarice said, "and just when I was going to show you the new crosses that the girls and I are fashioning for Jed to throw out from his skycycle on Easter morning!"

Abby offered to show Seth where he could wash his hands now that he was done examining her father's toes. She stood close enough to him to smell his Eau de Pinaud.

"If you want to pretend you have an emergency," Abby whispered, "I'll understand."

"And no doubt follow me," he said, drying his hands and avoiding her gaze.

"Wherever you lead," she said cheerily before reminding herself that she was supposed to be interested in someone else, someone in St. Louis. "Or perhaps just as far as the train station."

Seth frowned, and Abby bit on the inside of her lip to keep from smiling so widely the grin would have split her face. Maybe she did have a crazy family. Maybe she was much younger than he was.

And maybe men had better ways of showing their interest than a scowl, but it would do, and do very nicely, for the time being.

When he was done washing up, Seth followed Miss Abidance-*the loon*-Merganser to the table, feeling like a lamb being led to slaughter. There was a scurrying around, as if any seat were available to anyone, and he watched as Abby put her hands on the backs of two chairs while she stared at everyone else until they quieted.

Well, some of them quieted. Prudence was still humming loudly, he supposed because he'd told her not to sing so that she might rest her throat. And Patience was being fought over by Suellen and Gwendolyn, while Michael was loudly demanding that Jedediah sit next to him.

When they were all seated, they clasped hands and bowed their heads. Abby's hand was warm in his and sure within his grip. It had been a long time since he'd said grace, since before Sarrie had been called to His side.

"Michael, I believe it's your turn," the reverend said, and Seth was grateful that Merganser hadn't called on him to say the prayer.

"We thank thee, Lord, for sunshine sweet, For a roof above us and food to eat. We thank thee, Lord, for faith and health, And care we not for untold wealth. For in the end our soul is dear, If you, our Savior, hover near."

After the amens and the moment of silence, before everyone started reaching for platters and plates and Prudence started to hum again and somebody's child started crying, the reverend addressed him.

"You weren't at services again, son," Merganser said, looking at him as though he were a chick fallen from the nest.

"No," Seth agreed, offering no excuse.

"God only knows what you're doing to your soul," the reverend said with a sad shake of his head.

"Truer words were never spoken," Abby said, reaching across the table for some green beans and holding them in front of her father as a diversionary tactic. "How's Mr. Panner doing?"

"Or is that one of those secrets you can't tell?" the reverend asked, teasing Seth.

"He's doing well," Seth said. "I don't think there'll be any permanent damage from his dip in the pond."

"Thank the Lord!" Clarice Merganser said, looked at her husband, and added quickly, "and you, too, dear."

"I didn't do anything anyone else wouldn't have

done," he said, waving away the adoration as if he truly meant it. "You know the bishop didn't appoint me pastor of Eden's Grove just because I have a good heart. It was a calling, and he knew it, heard it—or he heard me hear it, anyways.

"Can you just imagine that new church in the square? Of course, we'll have to build a square, too, I suppose. But that'll be easy. You know I read in the *Christian Spectator* that there's a man who makes church bells that can be heard for over a mile."

He watched Abby squeeze her eyes shut at the thought of the noise.

"Headache again, dear?" her mother asked. "She does suffer from dreadful headaches," she told Seth, offhandedly, as if Abby's problems would be of no more concern to him than anyone else. Which they wouldn't. Doctors didn't play favorites. "We tried tying her head with a rope."

"I put scissors under her pillow," Patience offered. "After I clipped some of her hair and put it under a rock."

"And that didn't do it?" Seth asked, feigning surprise that an old wives' tale or two couldn't compete with modern medicine.

"If she'd left that frog on her head until it died, she'd never have a headache again," Jed said with all the finality that ignorance can impart.

"Is it any wonder I get headaches now and then?" Abby asked, gesturing around the table.

It would have been amusing, had the patient not been Abby, and had the headaches not been bothering her long enough to be subjected to all those remedies.

"Just how long have you been suffering from these headaches?" he asked, watching her until she squirmed under his scrutiny.

"Oh, heavens, they're nothing," she said, waving away his concern and reaching for the string beans, which she piled onto her plate and then passed to him.

"Oh, that's not true, dear. Why, sometimes they're positively blinding," Clarice declared. "Once I caught her taking to her bed and she had her head between—"

"Mother! I am fine. Let the poor man eat. If anyone has a medical complaint they should see him at his office. That's what I would do, *if* I had a complaint, which I don't. I would not interrupt the man's dinner with all this shoptalk. Let the man eat in peace!"

But somehow, he couldn't now. The thought of Abby sick took away his appetite. The thought of her head hurting, or her taking to her bed . . . He just sat there with the vegetable dish in his hand trying to swallow.

"I know, I know," Abby said, her smile just as dazzling as ever.. "The doctor in Sioux City said that if I'd wear my glasses more often, I'd suffer less. And my toes wouldn't hurt, either!"

"Your toes?" Seth asked.

She sighed a big exaggerated sigh, raising her shoulders up to her ears and lowering them in a huff. "Well, doubtlessly I'd walk into fewer walls and stub my toes less often!"

"Can not wearing those spectacles that big-city doc gave her really give her a headache?" her father asked.

"Yes," Seth answered, relief washing through him.

"It most certainly can. Which is just one more reason, young lady, that I don't want to see you again without those glasses planted firmly on that cute little nose of yours."

"Oh! He thinks your nose is cute!" Patience drawled out.

He made a fist in his lap rather than bang it against his head. Had he really said she had a cute nose?

"And so it is," Clarice said, exchanging a telling glance with the reverend that made Seth think he was in for it now.

But mostly the table quieted—for a meal with the Mergansers—with compliments on the food and admonishments about table manners to the younger folk becoming the order of the day. And there were so many things to keep a body busy—pulling at ribbons tied to the salt shakers so that no one had to ask or reach, the platters on some sort of wheels so that they didn't have to be lifted to be passed, a stacking device to slide each plate into so that there would be only one trip to the sink. Obviously Jed had been busy.

"Well, I do admit that Abby's idea about the health column could be a wonderful one," Ansel finally said.

"Of course it is," Emily seconded, smiling brightly at Abby and obviously enjoying the Merganser family dinner much more than her husband was. "Did you expect anything less than brilliance from Abby? I even mentioned it to my father and he thought it made good business sense. He was sure that it would increase circulation tremendously because people would be getting a medical digest along with their paper. Of course, I didn't tell him it was a woman's idea until after he'd admitted how good it was! But he thought women were surely likely to clip and save the column, the way they do with the sewing tips and the gardening ideas, and then they could make themselves a little health book."

"I don't think there will be all that many of them," Seth said, figuring that he'd be leaving Eden's Grove before too long and he didn't want Emily getting the wrong idea about this little health column he'd agreed to do for Abby.

"No? But there must be so very many topics," Emily said, and before he could explain that he wasn't afraid of running out of topics but of time, he felt Abidance's hand squeezing his thigh, just above his knee.

He caught his jaw just as it began to drop, and turned his gaze from Emily to Abby. Her head gave the tiniest of shakes, and her eyes sparkled a warning about something, but he wasn't sure just what. Not that he really cared. With Abby's hand squeezing his thigh under the table, heading who knew where, it was hard to think about anything else.

"Dr. Hendon?" Clearly someone had asked him a question, but he hadn't heard it. Naturally not, the drumming of his blood was drowning out even the Merganser family's noise.

"Why, that's a wonderful idea, Emily," Abby said, removing her hand. Seth felt his back straighten and tried to shake off the confusion he was feeling.

Hell, it wasn't *confusion* he was feeling. It was arousal, plain and simple. Excitement. Abidance's touch had awakened something better left dormant. At least where she was concerned.

In the last few years he might have had a few good

evenings with a charming widow in Sioux City who was a friend of a friend. But they had been couplings, physical needs being met within the confines of polite society.

" 'Ask the Doctor.' At first it would be just a short question at the end of the column, but they could lead to whole columns of their own. . . ."

"Oh, it could be just like 'Dear Miss Winnie'!" Emily said.

"Oh, yes!" Prudence seconded. "Did you read her advice in this week's paper? I had never thought of family allegiances quite like that."

"Well, I know when I get married I intend to follow her advice to the letter," Patience said. "I will think of my husband as my family and shift my allegiance from my parents to him on the day we are wed."

"You'll do no such thing," the reverend said. "Unless I tell you to stop listening to me."

"Have some bread," Clarice Merganser said, apparently hoping to fill the reverend's mouth, though it hadn't seemed to Seth that eating had put so much as a crimp in Ezra's talking.

"I think Miss Winnie was absolutely right, don't you, Emily?" Abby asked. "I mean, once you marry, your husband is your family. And everyone knows that saying about a man not being able to serve two masters . . . not that I think that a man is the master of a woman. I just mean that—"

"I read her column this morning before church," Emily said. "And I have to admit that it was on my mind during the sermon."

"But my sermon was about God's miracles and how

he manifests them," the reverend said. "Not that Miss Winnie."

Emily blushed slightly, and if Seth had harbored any doubt that she was carrying again, the furtive movement of her hand to her belly ended it. "Well, I think that one of God's miracles is family," she said.

"Oh, Emily!" Abby gushed, her hands on her face, which was a good thing or her smile might have broken her cheeks. "You're letting out your waistbands again, aren't you?"

"You are?" Ansel asked, clearly taken aback by the news. "Emily, are you?"

"It seems so," she said, almost apologetically, but the moment that should have been a private one between husband and wife was overtaken by the Merganser family's excitement at its impending expansion.

Everyone spoke at once, all the children shouting questions, the adults hushing them as if they shouldn't know what was going on or how it had come to be.

And while Abby and the others shrieked and sighed and asked when and what Emily hoped for, Seth watched as if he were stranded on some island, just out of the reach of all of them. Abby was smiling and waving her arms and touching Emily's belly, completely unaware of how hard he was fighting to put out the tiny spark in his heart which was threatening to ignite.

Which was as it should be. After all, he could not be in love with Abidance Merganser. He didn't think of her in that way at all. She was, he reminded himself—as if he needed reminding—a child. And nothing could happen between them, so that was that.

But something below his gut wasn't listening. Not

with Abby next to him, her eyes sparkling so. He watched her shift around so that she was sitting on one leg, leaning over the table, talking with her hands, smiling that smile.

And he tried to hear the conversation going on around him, but the voices in his head drowned them out.

"Oh, he's doing a column on that," he finally heard Abby say, and he nodded when she asked him if it wasn't so. He could only hope he hadn't just agreed to the column on social diseases.

"I really ought to be going," he said abruptly, and several of the various Mergansers looked surprised, but Abby's smile seemed full of relief. "I really am sorry to eat and run like this, but I did want to see the Denton boy this evening and it looks a bit like snow out there and . . ."

"I was expecting that we'd have a talk," the reverend said. "Looking forward to it."

Abby jumped up, banging her knee on the table, and sending glasses splashing, silverware clattering. "I'll get your coat," she said, charging to the pegs near the door. "We don't want to keep you!"

"But I got cigars," Jed said, pulling them from his pocket and holding them aloft.

"He's got to go," Abby said, opening the door before he had even got his arms into his coat, and stepping out onto the porch so that he had little choice but to follow her.

"Some other time," he called back into the house, thanking Clarice Merganser as Abby all but yanked him through the open doorway.

"It's cold out here," he warned her.

"I'm all right," she said, crossing her arms over her chest and tucking her hands up into her armpits.

"You're freezing," he said. "Go on inside now."

"I'm sorry about them," she said softly, gesturing with her head toward her house while her shoulders sagged.

"They aren't the problem," he said, tipping her chin up with one finger so that her eyes would meet his. "This isn't to be, young lady." He said the words, but he couldn't seem to let go of her chin, let his hand fall, walk away.

"Who are you telling?" she asked him, pulling her head back just enough to break the spell and taking hold of the doorknob before adding, "Me, or yourself?"

Chapter Four

❧

SETH LEANED OVER JAMES LEROY DENTON'S LIT-tle body, shielding it from his mama as if she didn't know just how skinny her baby was getting. Just how much skinnier he was than the last time Seth had been out to their farm.

"He won't . . ." Caroline Denton began, looking down at herself shyly, as if it were somehow her fault that the boy was failing to thrive. "At first I was hurting some, but I'm afraid now that I might be drying up, Dr. Hendon, and soon there won't be anything for him to take."

There were tears in her voice and he put his stethoscope to the boy's chest, praying to hear something, anything that he might be able to treat, to put a name to, to cure. The boy was just fading away, failing to thrive. He lay in his little cradle like an old man, just waiting for death without putting up a fight.

"Will he take the sugar water?" Seth asked. His hope was to enrich the water, add cow's milk to it if Caroline ceased to produce. He could—

"Hardly any."

"Well, at least his breathing seems good. That's a good sign. He needs plenty of fresh air, but with the weather so cold, I wouldn't recommend taking him outside. Just keep the window open a bit for good ventilation."

She nodded, hanging on his every word, as if opening the window would save her son.

"No drafts on him, of course," he added.

"Of course," she repeated like the amen of a prayer.

"We're going to have to try to peptonize some modified cow's milk for him if he doesn't turn around in the next day or two," he said.

"Peptonize," she agreed, as if the word had any meaning to her, as if hydrolizing milk was something she did every day.

"I'm also going to stop by Mrs. Jenkin's place," he said. "Her Thomas is about weaned and she might be able to give James here some nourishment."

"I still do have milk," Caroline said, her hand between her breasts, rubbing unconsciously at the pain in her heart.

"Sometimes another woman's milk helps," he said, making sure not to imply that there was anything wrong with Caroline Denton's milk, that it wasn't her fault that the baby was wasting. "They call it marasmus," he told her. "A failure to thrive."

"Marasmus," she repeated. "Can you cure him?"

He shook his head. "I'll do what I can, but there's no organic disease to fight. And he's so very little."

She nodded, accepting. They were always accepting, it seemed to Seth. While he railed and shook his fist at the heavens, they lost their sons and daughters and husbands and wives and accepted it because he told them there was nothing else to do.

He washed his hands at the Denton's sink and took the towel that Caroline offered him. "Where's Mr. Denton?" he asked, not wanting to leave this poor young mother alone with her ailing baby.

If Seth had had a sick child he would want to be there with the child and for his wife, not off somewhere.

Now, there was a strange and errant thought—Seth Hendon with a wife and a son. A chill ran through him. He'd had sickness in his family. He'd had death. He'd buried his parents. He'd buried Sarrie. He'd attended the funerals of every patient that hadn't made it. That was more than enough, thank you. He was done.

"Horse threw a shoe and Jimmy had to take him in to town," Caroline said. They smiled sad smiles at each other, an acknowledgment that life had a way of going on.

Caroline took back the towel and poured them each a cup of tea. When she set the cups out on the table she seemed unnaturally calm.

Seth knew what was coming, wanted to race out of the house before she could ask it, wanted to jump into his buggy and be halfway to town before she could get the words out so that he wouldn't have to hear them, wouldn't have to answer them.

But instead he pulled out the chair and sat. And as he knew she would, she asked. Her eyes were clear and dry and except for the grip on her teacup between her hands, one would have thought the question had no more import than whether or not it was going to snow. "Is he gonna die?"

"A baby needs to eat," Seth answered. "An adult can go without for a while, but a baby has fewer reserves. . . ."

She closed her eyes tightly and sat as still as the prairie before a storm.

"His appetite might pick up," Seth said, though from all he'd read it didn't seem likely.

"I just don't understand," the woman said, fighting against tears now and barely winning. "He doesn't have so much as a sniffle. He's not warm to the touch, his tongue ain't dry. He just don't seem sick, and yet he's dying."

"He's *failing*," Seth corrected. "He's not flourishing as he should be—"

"Doc!" He heard the call at the same time he heard the buckboard come rattling up to the house. "Doc! You there?"

Seth squeezed Caroline Denton's shoulder as he stood up. "That was mighty good tea, Caroline," he said softly before going to the door and opening it enough to see that it was Jedediah Merganser shouting for him.

Panic seized his throat so that all he could do was nod, take his bag, and grab for his coat, which Caroline held out to him.

"Follow me," Jed said, bringing around the buckboard while Seth climbed up into his own buggy, released the brake, and gave the horses their head. Seth called after him, his voice lost to the clatter of the buckboard, the thump of horses' hooves, and the wind itself.

The boy drove the horses fast, urging them to go faster still, and Seth, without a choice, followed behind, choking on dust and praying that he wouldn't be too late.

But too late for what? he wondered. He'd left Abby with a headache, which she'd assured him was nothing. Had she fainted? Had she tripped and fallen somewhere? He told himself that it didn't have to be Abby he was racing to see, but that didn't ease the fear that it was.

And then they were racing down Ridder's Lane and unless Abby had gone walking down by the pond, it wasn't likely that it was she that they were rushing toward. The rush of relief he felt was followed hard upon by profound shame. Wasn't everyone in Eden's Grove his responsibility? Someone needed him desperately—and all he could do was be glad that it wasn't Abby.

They turned off Ridder's Lane at Joseph Panner's place and Seth couldn't help shaking his head. He was an idiot racing down here after Jed Merganser, who wouldn't know a medical emergency if he cut his own head off with one of his infernal inventions. Joe Panner's toes had looked to be healing just fine only a couple of days ago, but the man wanted daily assurances that he would be able to get back out to Ridder's Pond for that damn fish before the ice melted.

Serve the man right if he fell in again.

See? See? he thought to himself. It was time to give up medicine. A doctor wishing his own patients ill.

When he got back to his office he was going to write to Massachusetts General Hospital. It was a long shot, hoping someone from such a prestigious institution would consider coming to a little pit-of-the-peach town like Eden's Grove, but long shots were better than no shots, and he'd heard nothing yet from Philadelphia or Chicago.

"We're here," Jed yelled to Panner, as he came back to Seth's rig and took the reins from him. "Went right through the ice again," Jed told him. "But this time Pa wasn't wandering by to save him."

Seth felt himself grimace. Damn, but with all the real threats to a person's health, the germs and bugs and sicknesses, the accidents that couldn't be prevented, the injuries that couldn't be helped, it was really hard to work up any sympathy for a man who felt the need to tempt fate by going ice fishing on a frozen pond. Twice.

It was eerily quiet, and Ella Welsh, who could best be described in polite terms as Panner's lady friend, opened the door as they approached it. Tears tracked her face as she squinted out at them.

"He just kept saying to get the reverend," she said, "so I ran there, but no reverend."

"Prudence was supposed to find Pa while I came for you," Jed said. "I got the doc, like I said I would." And then the boy followed Seth like some lost puppy as he made his way to Panner's bedroom. Steam rose from the basins of water Ella had used to try to raise his temperature. In the middle of his bed, Joseph Panner looked wholly serene, if a bit gray. Beside him, in a puddle that was soaking into the bedding, lay the largest walleye Seth had ever seen, no doubt the one that Joseph Panner claimed was the largest in the world, the hook still protruding from his mouth.

"Stupid fool," Ella said.

"I don't think you're supposed to speak of the dead like that, Miss Welsh," Jed said, hanging in the doorway as if he were afraid to come into the room.

"He wouldn't be dead if he hadn't been so stupid," Ella said. "A goddamn fish. What kind of fool risks his life for a goddamn fish?"

Seth had to wonder the same thing. The man apparently had everything else. "Something about wanting what we can't have," he supposed aloud, lifting the fish and handing it to Jed. It was heavy, heavier than any fish Seth had ever caught. Panner might have been right about it being the world's biggest walleye.

"If only you'da gotten him here a little sooner," Ella said to Jed, her expression softening as she pushed Joe Panner's graying hair off his forehead.

"He was way over at the Dentons'," Jed said, clearly defending himself since it had taken so long to bring Seth there.

The town was too big, too sprawled out for one man to see to it. It was too much for one doctor.

At least it was too much for Seth.

"I thought I'd find you here," Abby said as she came into Seth's office with what was left of the dessert he hadn't stayed for. She put two pie halves on his desk, piling his papers neatly in the corner of it. "Massachusetts General Hospital," she said, pretending to be impressed.

Seth pulled the paper from her hand. "What are you doing here?" he demanded.

No retort, no joke or cute little answer came to mind, so she told him the truth. "I was worried about you. Jed came home and told us what happened and I thought you might need me."

"*Need you?*" He sneered at her, and she caught a whiff of whiskey on his breath. "Need *you?* When chickens talk, my dear Miss Merganser, relative of the loon, that's when I'll need you. *If* then."

"Tea or coffee?" she asked, walking past him and heading for the small utility kitchen with the little stove meant really for heating up poultices and the like.

"Go home, Miss Loon!" he shouted at her. His words were just a little slurred. Abby thought that he carried his drunkenness well. But then she thought he did everything well.

"Tea, then," she said. "I like how that goes with quince pie."

"I hate quince pie," he said. "And I sure as hell don't feel like celebrating tonight." He stood and took the pies over to the door, where he placed them on the seat of a chair.

"Of course you don't. I don't blame you."

"Well, I blame me. Who's fault was it, if it wasn't mine? Did I make it clear enough to Joe Panner that his penchant for walking on thin ice was going to kill him? You were there. I never even said—"

"Said what, Seth? That if he fell into a frozen lake he'd likely die?"

"I was way the hell across town," he said, coming to lean against the doorjamb while she fussed in his kitchen.

"You say *hell* a lot when you're drunk," she said, throwing him a quick look while she strained their tea.

"I'm not drunk," he said, coming closer to her, close enough for her to smell the starch in his white shirt. "You want to know how I know I'm not drunk?" he asked, and put his hands on her shoulders, turning her around so that she faced him.

"How?" she asked, tipping back her head so that she could see his face, his sad dark eyes with the lines that radiated from them, reminding her of how he used to smile.

"Because if I were drunk, I'd take you in my arms and kiss those soft lips of yours," he said, and he pulled her closer against him. "I'd drop kisses on the top of your head," he said, doing just that. "I'd tip your head back until you were just at the right angle"—he tipped her head just so, until her lips were inches from his, until she could feel his breath on her face—"and I would kiss the hell out of you—"

He dipped his lips to hers, gently, just barely brushing one against the other, pulling back slightly, coming at her a little harder then, pressing his lips against hers, easing hers open so that his tongue could play against the inside of her bottom lip, so that it could sneak into her mouth and do wicked things to her insides.

"*If* I were drunk." He stood up straight and made sure she was steady on her feet. "Is that how your friend in St. Louis kissed you?" he asked, folding his arms against his chest.

"Like that?" she asked when she could talk again, when she could drag in a breath and push the words past the lips he had kissed. She leaned closer to him, wishing he would open up his arms and drag her against the length of him. "I'm not sure. Could you show me again?"

And then she saw where his laugh lines came from. Tipping his head back he all but roared at her. "Your father ought to lock you up and throw away the key, young lady!" he said, and then the man who had kissed her seemed to vanish, and in his place was Dr. Hendon, cool, calm, collected.

"To protect me from you?" she asked, but before she could add *I think not*, he shook his head.

"Not me. I'm on my way out of this town, Abby dear, just as fast as I can find someone to take over this practice."

"And what will you do with yourself, Dr. Hendon? Or should I call you Seth, now that you'll be giving up doctoring?"

He seemed to give the matter more thought than it deserved. "You should continue to call me Doctor since I am your elder." He took one of the teacups she had filled and went back to his desk. "Thanks for the tea. You ought to go on home now."

"You didn't answer my question," she said. "What will you do with the rest of your life?"

"Maybe I'll go pan for gold in Nome," he said, and she let out a breath she hadn't even realized she was holding. So he didn't have a plan. There was nothing, and no *one* calling to him. Nothing and no one but her.

"I read about a gold strike up there in your paper, Miss Newspaperwoman."

"Well, that sounds wonderful. No responsibilities. No one depending on you. Just what you've always wanted," she agreed.

His smile wasn't all that bright, as if she weren't supposed to have taken his suggestion so seriously. Well, she'd be just as serious about all of this as he was.

"You won't be leaving before the summer, will you?" she asked. "Emily is expecting again, and since you delivered Suellen—well, gosh, I guess you delivered everyone in this town under the age of twelve, huh?"

"Eleven," he corrected. He got a wistful look on his face, and shameless as she was, she meant to exploit it.

"Remember when the Rogan boys were born? Three babies at once! Of course, no one expected them to live, being so tiny and all. They sure are little terrors now!"

He smiled. Abby was sure that he knew just what she was doing, but for some reason he let her do it anyway. Maybe sometimes a body just needed to hear that things were better than they were thinking.

She gasped. "Did you hear about little Stevie Solomon? Seems he wrote some dirty words on his slate at school and Miss Kearny caught him and threatened to wash his mouth out with soap!"

"Why wash his mouth?" Seth asked. "Did he say them, too?"

"Well, I don't think she wanted to smack that boy's

hand when it really is a miracle that he can use it at all, what with how bad it got mangled up in his pa's reaper. Of course, I suppose if you hadn't been here and his father had just wrapped it up good, it'd be just as fine today, don't you think?"

"I get your point, Abidance. You don't have to lay it on quite so thick," he said, taking a second helping of the quince pie he supposedly hated.

"I have apple, too, if you prefer. I know I want my fill before I give up sweets for Lent," she said, opening the top of the pie keep and popping a bit of crust into her mouth. It didn't taste as good as her best pies, but she surely liked the way Seth watched her eat it, liked the warmth that spread inside her under his gaze. She took a bit of the crumb topping and put it carefully into her mouth, then licked her finger, her eyes locked with his.

"I remember things too, Abby," he said softly. "I remember a little girl coming to me in tears because her baby doll had lost her arm and wanting to know if I could fix her. I remember you and Sarrie hiding in my examining room so that you could see if the pictures in my medical books were for real."

"I've grown up, Seth," she said, reaching out and running her finger down the side of his face, feeling the stubble on his jaw that came with the night.

"And while you were doing that, I grew old," he said sadly, taking her hand in his and putting it back down on the desk. "Much too old and sad for someone like you."

"Maybe you're right," she said thoughtfully. "About

medicine, I mean. Maybe it makes you too sad. Maybe you could love me if you were a prospector."

"But I'm not a prospector," he said with a sad smile. "Am I?"

"Not yet," she said, "but maybe you will be."

Chapter Five

M Y DEAREST ABIDANCE," ABBY'S COUSIN ANNA
Lisa had written.

*It has finally happened! Our own dear Armand,
whose cause you have always championed, has
asked me to marry him! You can imagine how
he laughed when I told him you and I had
pledged never to marry but to grow old together
in a grand run-down old house with tattered
lace hanging in the windows! I trust, knowing
your feelings for your darling doctor, that you
will not hold me to our childhood promises.
And I expect your help at every turn in
planning my nuptials.*

The paper crinkled in her pocket and Abby's mother
frowned at her as if the tiny noise would disrupt the
dignity of Joseph Panner's funeral. As if there were any
dignity to Joseph Panner's funeral! Had it not been that
he'd drowned in frozen waters, she'd be tempted to say

that they'd be fighting over his legacy before the man's body was cold.

"A man of honor, a devout man, known to all of us for the ability to live up to his shortcomings . . ." her father was saying, while behind her Ansel snickered at her father's words.

But her father's words, as he always complained, were going in one of Abby's ears and out the other, no matter how hard she tried to work up some sorrow at Joseph Panner's passing. It wasn't that she didn't like Mr. Panner, it was just that she couldn't forget the letter in her pocket. *Married.* Her cousin was going to be married. And Abby was happy for her. Delirious. Why, she couldn't be happier if . . . She looked over at Seth, next to Ella Welsh, decked out in more black crepe than they'd hung on the firehouse when the old chief had died.

Seth stood solemnly, respectfully. But she could see his fingers curling and uncurling, and she was sure that all he could think about was getting away from the cemetery. Only twenty or thirty feet away, Sarrie lay still and cold beneath the hard earth. Despite Abby's trying, the winter weather had made it impossible for anything to grow over her grave. The ground was still as raw as Seth's pain.

He looked tired. She'd heard that Mr. Youtt's oldest son, John, had awakened in the night with a horrible pain in his stomach. They'd run for Seth and he'd spent the night there, packing Johnnie's stomach in ice and trying to keep him calm. Mrs. Youtt was home with the boy now, and she knew that Seth would be hurrying back to him as soon as the funeral was over—sooner if little Jenny Youtt came running for him.

She wondered about the last time Seth had taken a day for himself, gone fishing or sat by the fire with a good book. When Sarrie was alive he had always taken time to sit with her. Sometimes he would read to her, Sarrie said. Sometimes he would take out his violin and play one of the tunes that Sarah loved.

Abby had heard him playing once. She'd been bringing Sarrie the latest issue of *Demorest's Magazine* and they hadn't heard her come in. The moment Seth saw her, he'd stopped. She'd bet anything that he hadn't played a note, read a chapter, even gone for a walk to stretch his legs, since Sarrie's death.

Her father was eulogizing Joseph Panner, praising his generosity and tactfully skipping over the source of his funds. The way her father put it, it sounded a lot like Mr. Panner had very wisely, in his last moments, bought his place in heaven.

"And a church shall stand testament to the good in his heart and the purity in his soul," her father said, and even at a distance she could see Seth's eyebrows rise. Purity of his soul indeed! The man drank, swore, and caroused enough to keep two taverns in business and Miss Ella Welsh in silk.

"I suppose this isn't the right time or place," Mr. Youtt, the town's only lawyer said, clearing his throat before interrupting her father. "But before you start building that church, Reverend Merganser, you ought to know that there isn't all that much money left, and what there is he left in bulk to the town of Eden's Grove to do with as they see fit."

Ella Welsh all but collapsed against Seth, who steadied her more solicitously than Abby thought she deserved. Of course, Seth was a gentleman and a doctor. She couldn't expect him to just let the woman fall down, could she?

"Would you look at Ella Welsh!" Prudence whispered against Abby's neck. "It looks like she's already staking out her next victim!"

"And it's *your* victim . . . I mean your man," Patience added. At least she had the good sense to keep her voice down, but then with their father being a reverend, they'd all pretty much been raised on funerals and solemn events.

"He's not *my* anything," Abby hissed at her sister as her father spoke to the assembled group about Joseph Panner's money and the man's intentions as if they'd been written in stone and handed down to him.

"They say a zebra can't change his stripes, but Joseph Panner did just that, and as we lower his body into the ground, there is solace in the fact that a church will grow from it where all of Eden's Grove's citizens can worship as one and sing their own joyful songs unto the Lord—songs of thanksgiving—"

"I think we ought to just split the money between us," Mr. Ellenberg, the new butcher, said. "I mean, we aren't all of the same faith and those who want a new church could contribute their portion to that church, and those who don't—"

"I think we ought to install streetlights," Mrs. Winston, the milliner, said. "A body isn't safe at night walking about in the dark."

Six men stood holding the sturdy leather straps slung

beneath the heavy coffin of Joseph Panner. Each of them kept their eyes glued to the reverend, waiting for the signal to lower the coffin.

"Only heathens don't want a church," her father said, his cheeks reddening. "Why, what kind of a town hasn't got a church? I'm not even sure it is a town without a church to unify it. Maybe it's just a collection of houses and businesses that only have a postal address in common?"

One of the men holding the leather straps shifted his weight and coughed. Her father didn't seem to notice.

"Meaning no disrespect, Reverend Merganser, but there are people who don't worship the Son and the Holy Ghost, but only our Father. I don't need your church to pray to my God, so why should I put my share—"

"There are no shares," Mr. Youtt said. "And before we pick his bones clean, it would be nice if we laid Joseph Panner to rest, don't you think, Reverend? I have a sick child at home and I—"

"Oh, yes! Yes! Lower it!" her father all but shouted. "It's not as if there is anything to discuss anyway. Joseph Panner meant for there to be a grand church— a cathedral—here in Eden's Grove, and by God, there will be."

As he said the last, Joseph Panner's casket hit bottom with a clunk, as if to put an exclamation point on her father's declaration. What an article this would make for *The Weekly Herald:* "Argument Breaks Out at Funeral of Eden's Grove's Richest Man. Will the Town Get Its Church?"

She was halfway through writing the first paragraph in her head when she heard Seth's soft voice.

"Before one dime of Panner's legacy is spent, I think we need to have a good deal of discussion about what the people of this town really need. Obviously this is not the time or the place. I propose that we meet in the grange hall tonight and—"

"Is there really anything to discuss?" her father asked. "We need a church more than we need anything else on God's green earth and that is—"

"We need a hospital. If not a hospital, then a clinic. We need someplace that can be kept sterile. I have only one examining room, and I can't purify it between each patient. Johnnie Youtt's got appendicitis. If I can't get the inflammation to subside, I'm going to need to operate on that boy. And once I open him up, one little germ, something left from a previous patient, can lead to his death—"

"But surely you don't believe that could be more important than a church. Why, where will his family go to pray?" her father asked. "Where will they find God and ask that the kingdom of heaven be—"

Abby listened to her father. She'd listened to him all her life, and knew that he had a heart as good as any, knew that the church was not a tribute to himself but to God. Good as her father was, well as he meant, he was missing something so essential here that Abby found it impossible to hold her tongue.

"Dr. Hendon is talking about saving lives," she said, and she could see the hurt cross her father's face as surely as if she had struck him with her hand. And she could see that it was true, what Shakespeare said about how an ungrateful child's words could be sharper than a serpent's tooth, because her father's soul was bleeding for everyone to see.

In the quiet, her father said softly, "And I am talking about saving souls."

She waited for someone else to say it, but no one did, despite how obvious it was to Abby. Finally, reluctantly, she laid a hand on her father's arm, and said, "Papa, you don't need a building to save souls. You just need faith. Seth needs a physical place to do his work."

She felt Ansel's arm come around her, hug her against him in silent praise.

"Dr. Hendon is doing *his* work, but my 'his' has a capital *H*. It's the Lord's work that I am doing," her father said, so clearly wounded by her betrayal.

"I like to think that I am too," Seth said softly.

"You?" her father asked, his voice sharp with anger, and Abby held her breath, sensing that battle lines were being drawn, that things would be said in another moment that could never be taken back. "You don't even attend church. Of course you want a hospital so you have a place to spend your Sundays while the rest of us are on the street. You—"

"Well, this is some fine eulogy," Ella Welsh said with a humph for punctuation. "Joe'd have gotten a good laugh over how you all can't get him in the ground before you're fighting over his money."

"You're right, of course," her father said. "It's just that I think that a fine church is a more than fitting memorial to Joseph Panner."

"As would be a hospital," Seth said under his breath.

"Well, Joe never talked much about dying, but I

don't think he'd much fancy a church or any sort of hospital," Ella said, wrapping her cloak more tightly around a body that had apparently denied itself nothing. "I think a statue of him in the square would be something that he would've liked. Perhaps—"

"We don't have a square," someone said, and everyone began to move away from the grave site toward the cemetery gates. "Or a village green, like we had back East when I was growing up. Wouldn't it be nice to have a—"

Whoever it was that was talking—Abby couldn't see her—stopped suddenly as Jenny Youtt came running toward the cemetery as fast as her little legs would carry her.

"Where's the doc?" she asked, and the sea of people parted leaving Seth in the girl's vision. "Ma wants to know if Johnnie can eat. He's powerful hungry and—"

Seth looked relieved. Abby thought she even saw the hint of a smile on his face as he took the little girl's hand and suggested they go back to her house to have a look at her brother.

And as Seth relaxed, so did she. The muscles in her neck seemed to ease. Even the throbbing in her head seemed to lessen when she saw him smile.

"Eight o'clock at the grange hall," Ansel called out. "If you can't make it, Doc, send word." To Abby he said, "We'd better get over to the office and make some bills to post around town. I'll stop home and tell Emily to spread the word. You stop in at Walker's Mercantile and tell Frank to let all his customers know."

She almost felt excited at the prospect, and then she

saw her father. He was headed right for her, and if he
was excited too, it was certainly not in the same way.

"I am sorry we let that man into our house," she
heard him tell her mother. "I am sorry he broke our
bread and that I let him look at my toes. That poor man
is sick in his heart and soul and I'm afraid that he truly
intends to stand in the way of our church!"

"Papa, he wants to save people, same as you," Abby
said, trying to take her father's arm, only to have him
pull it away from her. "You are on the same side, you
two. You both want to—"

"The same thing! Why, I want what's best for everybody—even the Baptists'—souls, and that doctor
friend of yours only wants what's best for their bodies.
Imagine! Interrupting a funeral like that! Bringing up
the man's gift to the church like that, causing controversy—"

"Seth didn't cause the controversy. *You*—" Abby began to correct, only to feel the point of her mother's
boot against her calf, and catch the warning look her
mother gave her. "Well, anyway, I think everything will
depend on how much money Mr. Panner actually left
us. Maybe there'll be enough for both of you." *For
both my men,* she thought. And if there wasn't, she
knew, as "Dear Miss Winnie" said, just where her allegiance lay.

Seth considered skipping the meeting at the grange
hall now that it was clear Johnny Youtt was all right. Of
course, he'd have to watch for any swelling on the right

side of the boy's abdomen. The appendix might get inflamed again and he'd have to consider surgery again.

Which was why, despite how tired he was, how committed he was to leaving Eden's Grove anyway, and how reluctant he was to go head to head with the reverend, he planned to go over to the grange hall just as soon as he checked back at his office and made sure that there were no emergencies posted on his door. He'd worked out a system with the folks in Eden's Grove. He'd leave a note. on the front door saying where he could be found, and if they felt that they could wait until he was done wherever he was, they'd leave a note explaining the nature of the problem and go on home to wait for his return.

Of course, Abby left him all sorts of notes. Notes that said "Don't forget to eat supper! Mr. Woo left your shirts with me at the *Herald*. Take a deep breath and smile!"

Tonight there was no note on the door. Well, good, he told himself. Good, and good again. There were no emergencies, and surely he could not have been looking forward to another of Abidance Merganser's loony notes.

He had to admit, though, that Abby had surely surprised and impressed him at Panner's funeral. When had she gotten so insightful? Was she really the same Abby who had left him a bag of black licorice nibs with instructions to put one over his front tooth to see if any of his patients noticed? Such a funny little girl. Frivolous. It was as if she just refused to see the seriousness of life itself.

He checked his watch. He had just enough time to

take a cup of tea before heading over to the grange hall. As he opened the door to his office he heard a noise, which was quickly followed by a clattering that he had somehow caused himself by kicking whatever was lying in wait for him in his doorway.

"Seth?"

Oh, great. Instead of a note, he had the loon in the flesh.

"What are you doing here in the dark?" he asked, turning up the light and looking at an array of pans and picks on the floor. "What is this stuff?"

"Oh," she said, stretching and yawning and causing his insides to turn over as he watched her innocently come awake in the chair behind his desk. "I guess I fell asleep while I was waiting for you. Do you like your presents?" She gestured at the mess he'd tripped over as if it were something precious. He stared at the various pieces. A pick, a pan, a mattock, and a miner's bandanna.

And try as he did, he couldn't keep the laughter tamped down, couldn't keep the smile from his lips.

"Where's my mule?" he demanded. "Every good prospector has to have an old mule."

"Old Bessy's out front. Didn't you see her?" Abby asked, and for a second he almost turned around and looked, but then he saw the tiny shake of her head before her smile dazzled him, made him dizzy with its brightness.

"What am I going to do with you?" he asked, poking at the gold pan with his boot toe. "You're nothing short of incorrigible."

"Isn't it awful?" she asked him, stretching once

again, this time with her arms up over her head, guilelessly revealing a figure that had blossomed a good deal since the last time he'd pressed a stethoscope to her chest.

"It is," he agreed, but he wasn't talking about her incorrigibility that was awful anymore. What was awful was the way his body reacted to hers, as if he didn't know better, as if he and she were two hands on the clock and it was a minute to noon.

"I'd better get over to the grange hall," he said, when he was sure that staying alone with her in his office was as dangerous as a stroll on Ridder's Pond.

"So how is Johnnie doing?" she asked, not budging from his chair any faster than it appeared she'd budge from his thoughts or his life.

"Better," he admitted cautiously. Sometimes, miraculously, the flare-up of an appendix was an isolated event, never to be repeated. In his experience this was rarely the case, but as he'd told the Youtts, it was possible. Except for his announcement at Panner's funeral, he hadn't told them how dangerous an operation would be in the confines of his office. "I've got to get to the grange hall, Abby. Will you be all right getting home yourself?"

It was an odd question for him to ask. Abby came and went as she pleased. Before he could retract it, take back the caring that had seeped into his voice, she told him that she was going to the grange hall with him. "I have to cover it for the paper," she explained, though they were both well aware that Ansel would be there and would no doubt write the story and the editorial that would accompany it.

"I appreciated what you said at Panner's funeral," he admitted, albeit grudgingly. He could feel himself at the top of the slippery slope, the toe of one foot already on the mire. "I don't imagine your father was very pleased with you."

"I didn't say those things because of my feelings for you, Seth. I said them because they are true."

"Don't," he said, picking up the mining tools on the floor. "Don't think yourself in love with me, Abby. It isn't so." He didn't dare let her believe it, or he might start to believe it too, to return the feelings, to forget about leaving medicine and Eden's Grove and everything behind him. He might start to think about dinners at a table surrounded by his family, his loving wife, babies.

Babies! Abby herself was a baby, he thought as he piled the picks and pans beside the door. She was full of childish dreams he could never take part in. And if he had any dreams himself, they were too sad, too dull for the woman with the radiant smile and the too-bright eyes.

"You can tell me all you want that *you* don't love *me*," she said, rising finally from his chair and heading straight for him, not stopping or completing her sentence until she was close enough for him to smell the lemon she rinsed her hair in. "But don't tell me that *I* don't love *you*. You may not like it, you may not want it, but it is the way it is and the way it will always be." She put her hands on his chest and he made no effort to stop her. "And there is nothing you can do about it."

Was it simply that he was flattered by the attentions of a beautiful, intelligent young woman? Whatever it was, he didn't want to stop Abidance Merganser from loving him, from moving her hands up his chest and around his shoulders, from pressing her body closer to his and tilting her head at just the right angle so that kissing her would take less effort than pushing her away?

"You know I don't love you," he said as he lowered his head and tasted first her temple, then her cheek.

"I know," she said, tipping her head back farther so that her lips brushed against his as she waited for him to take possession of those lips.

"And that I won't ever love you," he murmured against the softness he could taste.

"Of course not," she agreed, leaving her lips parted slightly so that he had no choice but to kiss her fully, soundly, to take her head in one hand and her back in the other and pull her against him until he could feel her heart beating against his chest, feel the crazy throbbing of her pulse as it matched his own.

"Just so there isn't any misunderstanding later, Abidance, I am leaving Eden's Grove," he warned her, his fingers lost in the waves of hair piled on her head.

"I could go with you," she whispered, leaning back so that he could kiss her neck. "Anywhere you want to go," she added, sighing, her eyes closed, as ready for bedding as he had ever seen a woman.

This was madness. Insanity. If he weren't a man of medicine, he'd think he'd been bewitched by some magician with a very strange sense of humor. He felt as if he'd come in through the door and onto some Shakespearean stage—one of the bard's comedies with mistaken identities and gods that played tricks on man.

And with every ounce of strength he had, he fought against the urge to just give in to it all—that it was all too big to fight, too strong.

"Abby, look at me," he said, setting her away from him with his hands circling her upper arms. "I am not going to marry you. Consequently, I am not going to bed you. Which means that kissing, which leads to touching and holding and wanting, is now out of the question. Understood?"

She raised one delicate finger and rubbed her bottom lip, making his insides do flips. Then she shook her head slightly. "No, I don't understand. Because you don't now have plans to marry me someday, you can't kiss me today, is that right? I think you see everything backward. You think, 'I like kissing you, but I don't want to marry you,' so then you can't. Why can't it be 'I don't want to marry you, but I like kissing you,' and then you could?"

His mind turned to mush around her. "I have to get to the grange hall," he said when he could think of no answer for her, no good reason not to go on kissing her all night and all the next day.

"Let me just get my coat on," she said, but he put a hand on her arm as she walked past him.

"You better go freshen up some first," he said, winding one of her curls around his finger.

"Do I look as if I've been well kissed?" she asked him. He didn't know how she did it, this woman child who was red-hot innocence—a paradox if ever there was one.

He leaned down slightly, lifting her chin with just one finger, and answered, "Almost." Then he dipped his head and took one long draft of all that was Abby, swearing to himself that it would be the last draft, the last time that he took her into his arms, that he kissed her, that he let his heart wish that maybe, just maybe it could be.

When he was done he had to steady her on her feet and couldn't help laughing at his little siren.

"Didn't that man in St. Louis kiss you like that?" he asked.

"What man in—" she began, little phony that she was, playing games with him. She looked thoughtful, then finally said, "Oh, Armand! You must think I'm a faithless hussy, but kissing him was just so different. *So* different!" She looked in the little framed mirror on his wall and patted at her hair. "Well, we'd best get going, or we'll be late."

So then, had she, or hadn't she? Was she just pretending about Armand? One of her infinite fabrications? If so, where had she learned to kiss like that? Where had she learned the art of seduction? "Different how?"

"Well," she said, turning and giving him that damn bright smile of hers. "In between kisses he told me he *did* love me."

"And did that make you as dizzy as I did?" he asked, as if he were in some sort of competition with some man he didn't know for the hand of a woman he didn't want. Well, he wanted the woman, but not the . . . she really did tie his brain into a knot!

"Kissing him was a dream," she said with a great sigh as she wrapped her cloak around herself.

"*He* kissed you. *I* kissed you. How many others are

there?" he asked, crossing his arms over his chest while she took one last look in the mirror, examined her lips and apparently found them satisfactory.

When she finally turned to present herself to him, she laughed, and said, "Why, Seth Hendon! And I thought you knew everything about me." And then she reached around him for the doorknob, brushing against him as she did.

He'd thought he knew everything about her, too. He was sure of it.

But that was before he'd kissed her.

Chapter Six

&B&

*H*E IS NOT ALLOWED IN THIS HOUSE!" HER FATHER grumbled when they finally got home after the meeting at the grange hall. "Add that to my list!"

So far Seth wasn't allowed on their street, in their garden, on their porch. He wasn't welcome to Sunday dinner, he wasn't invited to any future parties they would ever host, and Abby's father didn't even want Seth to attend his funeral, whenever that happened to be.

"And you are not to speak to him, to dine with him, and needless to say, keep company, kiss, or marry him, young lady!"

Too late Abby thought, smiling to herself. Much too late. Oh, could Seth Hendon kiss! She was positively weak in the knees at just the thought. Had he not held her up, she'd have been a melted puddle of woman on his office floor.

"I should send you to your room," her father continued, while her sisters came to see what all the commotion was about and her mother took off her coat and headed for the kitchen, no doubt to put up some tea to calm her husband down. "But then you wouldn't hear me yelling from there. I should probably disown you, but then I couldn't tell you what to do anymore. . . ."

"She only spoke her mind," Jedediah said.

"A woman's mind belongs to her father until she is married and to her husband after that. Did I say already that you won't be marrying him?" he asked.

" 'A woman's mind belongs to' . . . you can't be serious, Father. A woman has enough curses in life, bears enough burdens—"

"That her mind shouldn't be one of them," her father cut in. "Do you think that your mother would ever voice an opinion that wasn't mine?"

"Well, I'd certainly like to think so," Abby said. "Otherwise why not just cut out our tongues when we're born? That way we'd never say anything that'd displease you."

Her mother had come back into the room. With her sisters there, they stood four women to two men, and Jed certainly seemed to be on their side.

"It's just like a woman to be as silly as all that," her father said. "You know quite well that I think women have a lot to say—some of it even worth listening to, especially in the house and in the garden. But what to do with Joseph Panner's money, well, that's just not their business. They can't possibly understand—"

"I understood everything that was said at that meeting, Ezra," her mother said firmly. "And I didn't raise five children so that three of them could stand mute while matters that affect them were being decided."

"Now look! You've turned your mother against me,"

her father roared, wagging a finger in her face. "I always listen when your mother is thinking. But it's something we do in private. When we're outside of this house, in a public place, for you to side against me—"

"I didn't side against you," Abby said. "You know I never would. I simply said that it was a matter of priorities. You could hold services in the grange hall, but Dr. Hendon could not operate on Johnnie Youtt there, now could he?"

"I heard you in the grange hall, Abidance," her father said, sitting down in his chair with a huff and crossing his arms over his chest. "Mother, we named all of our children wrong. Well, all the girls. The boys we gave real names to, but Patience isn't, Prudence wasn't, and Abidance won't!"

Her mother smiled that indulgent smile reserved for those she loved. "If one of my children needed an operation, Ezra, I'd want Dr. Hendon to have a safe place to do it. And it isn't as if he's asking for himself. He's asking for all of us."

"Thank you, Mother," Abby said. Finally a voice of reason.

"And I'm asking for myself?" her father asked petulantly. "Is that what you're saying?"

She let out a big sigh. There was obviously no use. Tomorrow she would write an editorial for the paper advocating the use of the funds from Joseph Panner's estate to build a medical facility. Her father had been invited by Ansel to write an opposing editorial urging the erection of a new church. It had been agreed that in two weeks, at the town's regular meeting, a motion would be made, a discussion would follow, and ultimately a vote would be taken on the disposition of the funds.

Obviously her father did not think there was anything to discuss. "A waste of everybody's free time," he said. "How can there even be a question? As I told everybody, Dr. Hendon's been practicing here for ten years in the same house that Doc Spinner practiced in for twenty before that. I've been supporting the doctor for years. Didn't I have a bowl at the back of the church for the sick? Without the church where would we put that bowl? The town needs a church with that money and that is how this family will vote."

"Not me," Abby said. "I will vote—"

"You won't vote at all, young lady. This is a matter for the town council—"

"All men," Abby cried. "Oh, no. This is going to affect every single citizen in this town. And therefore it should be voted on by every citizen." Now she had two editorials to write. And a headache that throbbed with every deep breath she took, not to mention all the shouting.

"We've always voted before," her mother said. "At least, *I* have, and now that the girls are young women, I think that they are entitled to vote, too."

Her father looked as if her mother had plunged a dagger into his heart.

"I'm going to bed," Abby said softly so that she wouldn't hurt her head any more than it already hurt. She supposed that her pain was nothing compared to her father's.

And she couldn't help but wonder, as she crawled

under the covers, what Seth was thinking alone in his room above his office. Was he thinking about how she had stood up for him at the meeting, said that a doctor's hands were as good as tied if he couldn't operate safely? Said that there could come a time when each and every one of them would regret not building for Seth exactly what he needed?

Or was he thinking of earlier in the evening, when he'd kissed her? Smiling in the darkness she thought of the feel of his lips pressed against hers. He'd closed his eyes while he'd kissed her—a kiss that was the stuff of dreams.

Seth still had Miss Ella Welsh on his mind the next day when he scrawled a hasty note on his blackboard and headed for *The Weekly Herald*'s office. The woman had come to him complaining of chest pains, and was quick to show him a chest that certainly explained Joseph Panner's interest in her. She was vague about her pains, but clear as a bell about her intentions. She wanted him to know that Joseph had left her his house. And she was lonely in it.

He suspected she wouldn't be lonely for long, but didn't volunteer to make any house calls anytime soon. She'd looked pretty disappointed, but, like all the women he'd ever met, she made it clear that while he might be saying no, she wasn't hearing it.

He pushed open the door to the newspaper office and stepped in out of the cold to hear Ansel asking Abby, "Well, that's not so bad. So now he won't even recite the Gospel to you?"

"Ssh!" he heard Abby say as she pulled the glasses from her nose and smiled at him.

"For heaven's sake, put them back on," Seth told her, "before you have people boycotting that sweet Mrs. Winston's millinery because of the new, larger bats that can be found filling her front room!"

"I never wrote that!" she cried indignantly before casting a glance at Ansel. "Did I?"

Ansel merely shrugged, apparently not in the mood for light talk. "Can I help you, Dr. Hendon?" he asked, and rather formally, it seemed to Seth.

"I brought over the article on frostbite," Seth said, taking it from his inside coat pocket. "According to the almanac, we're in for one last cold snap that could be pretty severe."

Ansel made no response.

"It's already pretty cold in here," Seth said. "Have I done something . . ." He let the words trail off. Had Abby told Ansel that he'd kissed her?

"It's not you," Ansel said, staring at Abby and shaking his head.

"I spoke my mind. I thought you would applaud me for that," she said.

"I do applaud you. And I applaud Doc, here, too. And I'd probably applaud a trained monkey, but that doesn't help anything, does it?"

"What exactly needs helping?" Seth asked, an uneasy feeling creeping up his spine.

"My father is angry that I have a thought in my head that doesn't come straight from him. He doesn't feel I should have an opinion if it differs from his. I suppose I'm fortunate that they don't ordain women in the

Methodist Church or I'd have to be a reverend just because he is . . . which reminds me, Ansel, that you went up against him yourself and now you're telling me—"

"Abby, much as you hate to recognize this, you are a woman. I could just move out of the house, take a wife, make a life for myself. You—"

"I could move out of that house tomorrow," Abby said, taking off the printer's apron she wore. "And I don't need a husband to do my thinking for me. I don't have to be at that man's mercy, or any man's mercy, and—"

"Don't be an idiot, Abidance," Ansel said. "Where would you go? I don't think you've saved ten dollars that I've paid you—"

"For now, I could move in with you and Emily," she said, but the look on Ansel's face seemed to say that wasn't even a remote possibility.

"Then I could move into Seth's spare room," she said.

Now she had Ansel looking at him accusingly, as if he'd ever offered such a thing, as if he'd ever allow it. He didn't even consider Sarrie's room a *spare* and putting everything else aside, which he certainly wasn't, he couldn't possibly bear the thought of Abby in Sarrie's bed. "You aren't moving anywhere," he told Abidance, and the words rang familiarly to him from some dark corner of his mind. Ah, yes. All those years ago when he'd found Sarrie and Abby at the train station, tickets in hand, the two of them vowing to move to St. Louis.

"You aren't moving anywhere," he had said then, and he repeated it now. Why was it that every time he began to think of Abby as a grown woman, a very kissable grown woman, something had to remind him that she was the same little girl who had stolen all of his bandages to wrap his sister in when they were playing nurse.

"They won't talk to her," Ansel said. "At least *he* won't, and they won't cross him, so if he's around, they won't talk to her either."

"Your family?" Seth asked incredulously. "Your father? He's that angry about my wanting to build a hospital?"

Abby shrugged, and Ansel said, "He feels she betrayed him, speaking out against the church last night. He's declared you the enemy and he's forbidden her to see you or—"

"Ansel!" she shouted at him. Clearly this was something he had been asked not to reveal. She looked at Seth with her chin raised proudly. "He can't tell me what to do."

All Seth wanted was a place to do some simple procedures safely. He didn't want Massachusetts General Hospital, for heaven's sake. It wasn't even as if he planned to stay in Eden's Grove. But a first-rate clinic with modern equipment would make finding a replacement so much easier. Still, he didn't think the clinic was worth Abby's having a falling-out with her family. When he moved away, they would be all she had left.

But he didn't say any of that. Instead he put the article on the desk that separated him from Abby and Ansel and rebuttoned his top coat.

"I have no intention of listening to a word he says," Abby said.

"Especially if he isn't talking to you," Ansel added on.

"Maybe not," Seth said, picking up her glasses and placing them on her nose, tucking the wires over her ears as if she were a china doll. "But *I* do."

"You're giving in? You want to vote to use the money for a new church, when the grange hall accommodates everyone for Sunday services?"

"No, I'm adamant about the clinic," he said as he turned to leave. "But if your father doesn't want you talking to me, I guess I have to respect his wishes. A father does have—"

"—Rocks in his head if he thinks he can tell me what to think, how to vote, or who to talk to," she said with a huff, banging her hand down on the table and then yelping in pain.

She grabbed the hand she'd hit with her good one and clutched it to her body. She took a deep uneven breath with her mouth wide open.

"Jeez, did you break it?" Ansel asked, laying down the tray of type he was holding.

Seth saw the blood oozing out between her fingers. He saw the short spike on the countertop and for the first time in his medical career, he felt weak in the stomach.

"Damn it!" he shouted, pulling out his handkerchief and grabbing her hand to have a look at it. "You're going to need stitches. Two. Maybe three."

"I'm fine," she said, trying to take her hand back as if she could just will herself well. He'd been standing right there. If only he hadn't made her mad, if only he'd noticed the spike, if only he'd done something, *anything*, to stop this from happening.

"You are not fine," he heard himself saying more loudly than necessary. "You are bleeding profusely. Do you feel faint?"

"No," she said as if she were afraid that he'd yell at her if she was.

"Damn," he said again. "This is deep. Do you think you can walk to my office?"

"Yes," she said stoically, not *Of course I can*. Not *Certainly*. He didn't know if she was afraid of him or the blood or what, but when she came around the counter he didn't like the color of her face. Scooping her up in his arms, he told Ansel to get the door, and he carried her—with no objection from her, which scared him more—to his office, where Ansel once again opened the door and got out of Seth's way.

Gently he laid her down on the examining room table and lit the lamp beside it so that he could see the damage clearly. He showed Ansel how to apply pressure to Abby's hand and then with a squeeze to her shoulder he assured her he just needed to get a few things and that he would be right back.

His brain refused to work. The office he'd worked in for eleven years appeared rearranged, so that now, when he needed them, he could find neither his needle nor his boiled silk thread. Someone had hidden his bottle of carbolic acid.

"Does it hurt much?" he heard Ansel ask Abby, and he grabbed the things he needed, which by some miracle now seemed to appear in the exact places he'd already looked for them.

He came back to her side, apologizing for how long he'd taken, apologizing for how much it would hurt. At least, he thought he was apologizing until Ansel insisted that he stop yelling at her, and Seth realized he'd raised his voice again, even while he was trying to tell her how sorry he was that he would have to cause her pain.

"What's the matter with you?" Ansel asked. "Do you treat all your patients like this?"

Only the ones I love, he thought. *Because I couldn't stop the accident from happening, because I can't make it just go away, and that makes me angry.* He closed his eyes for a moment and shut out the thoughts. He had work to do.

"Ansel, go around to the other side and hold her other hand. Abby, you keep your eyes on Ansel." He glanced quickly at her face, willing her to look at her brother, and then bent to the task.

"Don't you think the weather's getting warmer," she asked suddenly, breaking the silence in the room. "I think spring is just around the corner."

"I think your father's probably around the corner and not likely to be pleased that you're here in my care," Seth said, reminding himself that there were a million reasons why he couldn't love Abidance Merganser.

"I don't care what my father—" Her words stopped abruptly as the needle pierced her skin. Seth felt the pain as surely as if he had stuck the needle into himself.

"Squeeze Ansel's hand," he told her. "As hard as you can. Ansel, talk to her!"

"So Emily wants to pick the name for the new baby," Ansel said, obviously fishing for a topic that would engage his sister. "Whether I like it or not."

"When you carry a child in your stomach for nine months, Ansel, then you can—"

Within Seth's grasp, Abby's hand was twitching wildly. He tied the final knot and told her it was over.

"Just two little stitches," he told her. "Nice and clean, and see that you keep it that way. I'll bandage it up, but you aren't to get the bandages wet or dirty. And I want to see you tomorrow—"

"I want to see you, too," she said, turning those big brights on him.

"I meant your hand," he said, feeling himself color under Ansel's scrutiny.

"You want my hand?" She was teasing him, right out in the open in front of her brother.

"Yes. Just send it over with Ansel tomorrow," he joked back. It fell flat. Ansel was studying his face and Seth felt as if everything he felt for Abby was suddenly written there—the love, the doubts, the regrets. "I heard from a doctor at Massachusetts General," he told them both. Best to get it all out on the table.

Abby tried to sit up, and he assisted her, the same as he would assist any patient, a hand behind her back, the other helping her with her legs as she swung about on the table.

"You should just sit here for a few minutes and rest," he said. "I wouldn't plan on doing anything with that hand for a while."

"What about the doctor from Massachusetts?" Abby asked him. "What did he say?"

"He wanted to know about the town, the usual ailments, the facilities. . . ." He had a hard time looking at her.

"He'd be interested in taking over your practice?" Ansel asked.

"Possibly. Not likely. It seems he's a pretty important doctor at Mass. General. A senior resident. Maybe he just had a bad day and was looking for a way out. I'm sure the feeling will pass. . . ."

"Will it?" Abby asked him, and it was clear that once again she'd turned things around on him. Having feelings for Abidance Merganser was like being in the eye of a cyclone—one felt perfectly calm, but everything just kept whirling around and winding up somewhere else.

"Maybe I'll write your editorial for you," Ansel said to Abby. "I could put in something about attracting a better quality of physician here with better facilities."

"I could just dictate it and Jedediah could take it down for me," Abby said softly.

"Yeah, and he could fly it over," Ansel said sarcastically. "I don't think it would be a good idea to get him involved in this, Abby. Pa's already feeling ganged up on."

"Doc? You in?" someone yelled from the outer office. Seth poked his head out the examining room door. "It's Callie Jean. Her time's come."

"I'll be right out there, William," he said. "Tell her not to have it without me!"

"She wouldn't want to Doc," William said, his cheeks red, "but these babies of hers sure do have a way of hurrying into the world!"

"He'll have to be pretty damn fast to beat me," Seth said. With a quick nod at Abby and Ansel he grabbed up his bag and was on his way.

Abby watched him leave. He looked back at her as he hurried through the doorway, as if there were something he wanted to say to her, and then thought better of it.

"He's going, Abby," Ansel said softly, coming to lean against the examining table beside her. "If not now, soon."

"And I'm going with him," she said weakly. "I would follow him to the ends of the earth."

"And would just following him be enough? He surely has no intention of taking you."

Maybe he hadn't now, but he would. She would make him want to take her with him. Somehow, she would make him.

"What makes a man love a woman, Ansel? What makes him want to own her, possess her, keep her for himself?"

"I suppose it's different for every man," Ansel answered.

She supposed it was. Ansel had married to get the newspaper, but she had nothing of value to offer Seth. Her mama's father had run the best still in Iowa way back when her father had come to town. That had surely been inducement enough for him. Maybe she could become a nurse. But not before Seth was long gone.

"Love's a funny thing," Ansel said, his eyes focused somewhere beyond the room in which they sat together. "Sometimes, no matter how hard you try, you just can't make it happen. And sometimes it doesn't really hit you until it's out of your grasp."

She knew the prospect of losing Seth made her want him all the more. Why couldn't it work the other way?

"Would you help me write a short note to Armand Whiting?" Abby asked her brother. "I just want to congratulate him on finally winning Anna Lisa's hand."

"I have an awful lot to do," Ansel said. "And you'll be needing a bit of time off, it seems." He almost seemed relieved at the prospect.

Abby got down from the table, cradling her bandaged hand. Pathetically she said she understood.

"All right, Abidance," her brother agreed. "A quick note. And then I want you to go home and rest and I'll come by later and see how you're doing."

Dear Armand, she wrote in her head. *How wonderful for you and Anna Lisa! To think that our childish promises have finally come to fruition. To think of you in terms of love and marriage warms my heart and soul. You must write me back and tell me all about the plans for the wedding. How I would dearly love to get a letter from Mr. A. J. Whiting in St. Louis, Missouri!*

And how much more wonderful it would be if Seth were around when it arrived!

Chapter Seven

As far as Seth was concerned, there was nothing that compared to delivering a healthy baby into the world. It was the one thing he would miss about medicine, he thought as he strolled back to his office, his coat open to better enjoy the first spring breezes and the warm late-afternoon sun.

He went straight to *The Weekly Herald* to check on Abby's hand. Strictly as her doctor, of course. It was his responsibility—as her doctor—to make sure that she was doing all right.

Ansel was busy setting type. There was no sign of Abby.

"She went home, then?" Seth asked, some small piece of him hoping that maybe she was waiting for him in his office, another piece praying she was not.

"Not much help to me here one-handed," Ansel answered. "And she was looking kinda done in, so I sent her on home."

"She get there okay?" Seth asked.

"You care?" Ansel answered.

So it was to be out in the open. So be it.

"I got the feeling you were annoyed just to be treating her this morning."

"Don't be silly," Seth said. He remembered Abby herself chiding him for the way he would sometimes yell at Sarrie when she'd gotten out of bed, or done too much. And here he was, doing it again, this time to Abby. "I was happy to treat her. I mean, I was glad that I was here when it happened so that I could . . ."

"It never would have happened if you weren't here, Doc," Ansel said.

"Really? It seems to me with Abby's vision being what it is, it's amazing she doesn't have accidents more often."

"She wears her spectacles when you aren't around," Ansel said. He hadn't for a moment stopped what he was doing. Apparently Seth wasn't worth his full attention.

"And that's my fault?" Seth asked. "You seem to be holding me responsible for everything today."

"When it comes to my sister, I think you are." Now he put down the tray of type, and set the rollers of the press in motion. "And I know you know it."

"I know your sister's sweet on me, if that's what you mean," he said.

"My sister fancies herself in love with you, though it beats me why. Still, she does, and I get the distinct feeling that you're feeding that fancy just enough to keep it alive." Ansel cranked something on the printing press that made a good deal of noise and Seth had to raise his voice to be heard over it.

"I have told your sister repeatedly that I am not interested in her as anything but a patient and a good friend of Sarrie's," he shouted over the noise of the press.

"Well, pardon me for pointing this out to you, Seth," Ansel shouted back, "but Sarah is dead. And Abby is still going over to your place, still cooking for you, still making the same goo-goo eyes at you she was when Sarah was alive. And don't pretend you don't know it."

As if out of spite, the press became noisier still when Ansel fiddled with it. Seth raised his voice another notch.

"Not that this is any of your business, but I have told your sister repeatedly that I do not return the feelings that she thinks she has for me—that I—"

"Thinks she has for you!" Ansel was red in the face from shouting, and now he added a wagging finger to his arsenal. "You really are an ass, Seth Hendon. How could you be so condescending to that girl? A girl who saw you through your toughest time, who held your sister's hand day after day as she faded away? Can you imagine what that makes her feel like?"

"No, but I imagine *you* can," Seth shouted back. "And it seemed to work just fine for you." It was something that he supposed he'd never forgive Ansel for. And now Ansel would probably never forgive him.

"Well, maybe it's a Hendon family trait. Make a Merganser fall in love with you and then cut them loose. Let them go off somewhere to lick their wounds—"

"It didn't take you long to rebound. You had Emily wedded, bedded, and carrying before Sarrie's tears were dry."

He could see Ansel's Adam's apple bob furiously as

he swallowed years of regrets. Behind Ansel, the machine quieted. After all the noise, the silence felt unnatural, and Seth found himself lowering his voice to a whisper.

"I'm sorry. That was unnecessarily cruel." Saying the words hadn't felt nearly as good as he'd anticipated it would all this time.

"Are you getting back at me through Abby?" Ansel asked. "Because she doesn't deserve that, Hendon."

Seth shook his head slowly. "I don't want to hurt your sister. The truth is I'm more than fond of her. If I thought there was a chance, I'd . . . Look at her, Ansel, and then look at me. She's full of life, full of youth, full of potential. I'm thirty-six years old. I'm—"

"You sound too much like Sarrie. Only she was dying, Doc. I knew what I was seeing when I looked at her. But when I look at you, I see a man who is good, kind, and according to Emily, devastatingly handsome."

"I'm nearly twice her age. I can only disappoint her. . . ."

"You mean you can't . . ." Ansel let his words trail off.

"I'm talking about her joie de vivre, her ability to see the best in everything while I rout out the worst."

"But you can make love to a woman? . . ." Ansel asked.

"Yes, Ansel, of course I can. I'm only a few years older than you, and around Abby, well . . ." He realized a man didn't want to hear his sister thought of in that way, and he didn't want to discuss how Abby had put him in what appeared to be a permanent state of arousal at just the mention of her name, and so he moved on quickly to the heart of the matter.

"Ansel, I would destroy everything wonderful, *wondrous,* about her. I can't bear to think what being with me would do to her. I don't want my life to touch her—the things I see, the—"

"For all your schooling, you're still an idiot, do you know that?"

Seth had no response, and after what seemed like hours, Ansel repeated himself. "A goddamned idiot."

"Maybe," Seth allowed.

"Abby tells me you are trying to find someone to take over your practice?"

Seth nodded.

"You're leaving Eden's Grove?"

Seth nodded again.

"There's no chance that you'll marry Abby and take her with you?"

Seth shook his head.

"Then stay the hell away from her." Ansel, fairer than Abby, had turned red in the face and the pulse in his neck was throbbing.

Seth nodded.

"I'll bring her by tomorrow so you can check her hand," Ansel said, clearly meaning that there would be no opportunity for Seth to see her alone.

If Ansel thought that, he didn't know his sister very well. Seth figured it wouldn't take Abby long to find a way to defy her brother, her father, convention, and Seth himself.

And a tiny piece of him was full of anticipation at the thought. Several of his journals had been reporting on something called masochism lately—all part of the new field called psychiatry. In addition to a host of sexual implications, it described a person with a taste for suffering.

He seemed to fit the profile all too well.

Ansel was a pain in the neck. A royal pain. It seemed to Abby that it had become his mission in life to keep her from Seth, to point out every time Miss Ella Welsh went into Seth's office (twice in as many days), and to repeatedly send her on errands (since she couldn't write or set type, he said) to Frank Walker's store and Emmet Sommer's farm.

It was a good thing that Frank and Emmet were the only eligible bachelors in town, or her feet would have been too blistered to get into her boots.

Just the same, after reading "Dear Miss Winnie's" latest column, she managed to slip in a visit to Seth on Friday. After all, she did want to see what he thought of her editorial.

"It was good," he said. She noticed he didn't stop what he was doing to talk to her.

"Would you like me to help with your inventory?" she offered, watching him count bottles and jars and bundles and mark down the totals on a sheet of paper he had clipped to a board.

"You aren't supposed to write," he said, still not looking at her.

"I can count without even using my fingers, I'm that clever," she said, coming over to where he was and looking into the medicine cabinet with him. She heard him inhale and then move away.

"I'm done here," he said. "Guess I better take a look at that hand."

"Mmm," she agreed. It was time to put Miss Winnie to the test. She cleared her throat. She crossed the fingers on her good hand. "Seth, do you think you might have a minute to write a letter for me? I don't want to ask Ansel, and the rest of my family isn't, well—"

"They still aren't speaking to you?" he asked, apparently surprised. Well, he didn't know how stubborn the Mergansers could be. And she was the stubbornest of all, she thought with just a hint of pride.

"At least this way I don't have to hear what they think of my editorial," she said with a shrug.

He finally met her eyes. "Your editorial was brilliant," he said, and his words washed over her like a chorus of robins on the first day of spring. "You advanced arguments I hadn't even thought of."

"So then you don't subscribe to my father's theory that women shouldn't have thoughts of their own?" she asked, drinking in those incredibly blue eyes, that nearly black hair with two stray gray hairs by his left temple. The dimples that appeared so infrequently, showed up and then were gone in a flash, like a peek of sun between the clouds.

"I'd make an exception for you," he said, taking her hand into his and examining the bandages he'd replaced yesterday. Clean, clean, clean. Keep a cut clean, he'd said, and it'll heal properly.

"Vegetable soup?" he asked, noting the stains on the edge of the bandage.

"I could bring you some," she offered. "Patience says its better than what I brought you last week."

"You aren't supposed to be using this hand," he chided her, carefully unwrapping the dressing. "You're a slow healer. It doesn't suit your personality, Miss Quick-to-Leap-without-Looking Merganser."

"But it is healing all right, isn't it?" she asked, examining her hand. It looked all right to her, even when she kept her spectacles on to inspect it. "I could stop by twice a day, like Miss Welsh. . . ."

He shook his head at her, but there was a smile on his face. More and more he smiled at her, and each time her heart felt as though it would leap from her chest if her shirtwaist weren't so tight.

"Your hand is healing just fine. Slowly, but well."

"Will it be all better before you take off for Nome?" she asked.

"I've decided against prospecting," he said, but before she could get her hopes up, he added, "in favor of fur trapping."

She supposed she sighed, because he looked up at her and his smile melted. "Are you feeling all right?"

No, she thought. Her headaches were worse, despite her wearing her glasses for two days straight except for the short moments she was with Seth. And this morning she'd actually lost her balance the pain was so severe. But the headache powder she'd bought at Walker's Mercantile had helped some, and she always felt better in the afternoon. "Oh, I bet I'm every bit as sick as Ella Welsh," she teased.

"You look pale," he said, tipping her chin slightly.

"It's nothing," she said, knowing that he would take her shyness to mean that it was just the time of the month that made her look pale.

He nodded as if he understood. It was tempting to tell him how awful she was feeling, but once she opened that door, she was afraid she might not be able to close it, and so she asked him about the Denton baby instead.

His shoulders sagged and his frown became a grimace. "I've got him on a mixture of cow's milk and water. He's not done well with his mother's milk, nor with sugar water. I'm running out of things to try."

"It must be hard for Caroline Denton," Abby said. She couldn't imagine what it would be like to have a baby wasting away and not be able to stop it.

"She's bearing up all right."

"And you?"

"Me? A piece of me dies with everyone I've ever lost. There's not much left."

"You can be so morbid, Seth!" she scolded. "On a brighter note, I heard that Callie Jean Evans had a little girl. I don't suppose you get reborn with every child you deliver, do you? No, that would be too cheerful for you."

"I told you I wasn't a cheerful man," he said.

"Well, do something about it," she said.

"All right. I'm very happy that Mrs. Evans has another healthy baby, but I can't help hurting for Mrs. Denton. Let me wrap this hand back up in clean gauze."

"Backward again," she said, thrusting her hand out

so that he could see to it. "It goes: 'While I can't help hurting for Caroline Denton, it is wonderful that Callie Jean has another healthy baby. And this one a girl! With two big brothers she'll surely be a pampered little thing, won't she?' "

"I suppose," he said, concentrating on squeezing her hand just so and then wrapping it so that it would stay that way.

"About that letter, Seth?" she asked. "It would only take a minute. I'd do it myself but—" She held up the hand he had just bandaged.

"All right," he agreed. "I suppose you've written down a few things for me over the years. It won't kill me to write one letter for you."

She smiled at him. It might, she thought. If Miss Winnie was right, it just might hurt like the dickens.

"It's to Armand," she said when they'd settled at his desk and he had taken out a clean sheet of paper and dipped his pen and stood at the ready.

"The boy you know from St. Louis?" he asked.

She laughed politely. "He's not exactly a boy, Seth. He's nearly as old as you. Well, a little younger."

Seth grimaced.

Abby's toes curled with pleasure.

"And the man isn't married yet?" Seth asked.

"Tragically," she said quickly, "his first wife died. It took him two years to get over it, but when we met again, he says the darkness lifted for him."

Seth grunted.

Abby tapped her boots together.

"Dear Armand," she dictated. "It's a French name,

you know. I do so love French. Everything sounds so romantic in French, *n'est-ce pas?*"

"*C'est possible.*"

"Why, I had no idea you spoke French, too," she said. "Okay, so then do a fancy flourish after his name. I usually turn it into a rose, but . . . well, just a line like you put there will be fine."

Seth tapped the end of the pen against the desktop. Abby tried not to wiggle victoriously in her seat.

"My good friend Dr. Hendon is writing this down for me because I have injured my—"

"I'm not a secretary," he interrupted her. "You'll have to go slower."

"My . . . good . . . friend . . . Dr. . . . Hendon . . ."

"I got that part," he said. " 'I've injured my—' "

"Foot. Just kidding. You know what I did. Why don't you just tell him and tell him not to worry, I will surely be fine."

A definite *humph* escaped his lips.

"Do you mind doing this?" she asked innocently. "I mean because Armond is interested in me?"

"Are you interested in him?" He didn't look at her but played with his inkwell and pen as if it weren't working perfectly fine.

"Oh, I was before he got married, you know," she said. "Now? Well, he is quite a kisser, and I am twenty years old and a woman does need to make plans. Especially a woman whose family refuses to talk to her because she—"

"Are you saying that it's my fault, and out of some sense of obligation or responsibility, I—"

"Fine. Write that I miss him terribly," she snapped back. "And underline 'terribly.' Tell him that no other man has ever made me feel as cherished as he has and that through the long cold days of winter the memory of his kiss has—"

His hand stopped and he looked up at her. "Don't you think that's laying it on a bit thick?"

"When *you* write a love letter, *you* write what *you* want, all right?"

"Are you writing a love letter?" he asked. "With me holding the pen?"

"Would you rather I didn't?" she asked, praying that he would say so, holding her breath for his answer.

"Write whatever you like," he said. "I'm up to 'No other man.' What came after that?"

"No other man has ever made me feel cherished, wanted, held dear—"

"That's not fair," Seth said. "I do hold you dear. Just not in a way that could lead to—"

"Marriage. Yes, you've made that very clear." She pretended it didn't matter, but knew he was probably seeing right through her, and so she added, "I don't like it. What I'm doing to Armand, allowing him to be my second choice, is not admirable. But then I suppose that I'm really his second choice, and unless you've changed your mind . . ."

"Does he really make you happy?" Seth asked her, leaning over the desk to put his hand atop hers. "Do you smile with him and laugh and go for walks in the park and talk about children and—"

He seemed to wish it so, even though it meant that

he would lose her. And if he wanted so much to lose her, then so be it.

"Yes," she said. "He's actually very glad I'm so young so that if things work out between us we can have lots and lots of children. And it's good that he's already sown his wild oats and gotten over his wife's death and that he likes to laugh along with me.

"Of course, it wasn't easy for him at first, but seeing him smile, knowing I'm the one who can bring that smile to his lips and take away his pain—"

"Then I'm happy for you, Abidance," Seth said solemnly.

"Me, too," she said. "Though I do wish it could have been you," she admitted softly.

He looked beaten and tired, but he smiled at her all the same, those two dimples of his twinkling sadly at her. "So do I," he said, patting her hand. "So do I."

Ansel's pity was written all over his face when Abby got back to the *Herald*. He shook his head at her as if to tell her that the smile on her face didn't fool him one bit.

"I see you've a clean bandage," he said, coming to help her off with her coat.

"I stopped in at Dr. Hendon's and he took a look at it. He says I'm healing slowly. It feels as if I'm doing everything slowly these days," she added as she fished her glasses out of her pocket and awkwardly attempted to get them in place with only her good hand.

"Let me help you," he said, hooking the wires over

her ears and looking into her pale face. "You look awful, Abby. Not that I'm surprised. This whole thing with the doc is taking too big a toll on you. I believe it's making you sick."

"I'm fine," she said. "Actually better than fine." After all, she had a plan in motion, and nothing made a body feel better than a plan.

"Are you eating?" he asked. "You look skinny as a quill pen to me. And what about sleeping? You've got smudges beneath your eyes."

"Ansel, stop it now. I am eating, I am sleeping, I am feeling just fine." Her words probably would have been more convincing if she'd been able to resist sighing after them.

"Are you still having those headaches?" he asked, like a dog with a bone who just wouldn't let go.

"My head doesn't hurt nearly as much as my heart," she said. "I suppose my conscience is pinching, too. And all of it serves me right, as usual."

"What have you done now?" he asked, chucking her under the chin affectionately, as if he'd forgive her anything.

"Can you keep a secret? And pinkie-swear you won't tell a soul, especially Seth?"

He leaned back against the counter and gave her a long stare before saying, "It's been a long time since I pinkie-swore." With a smile on his lips, he kissed his pinkie finger and held it up in the air. "What have you done now?"

"I told Seth I had a beau in St. Louis who was madly in love with me."

Ansel's lips were trembling as he tried to hold in his laugh.

"I *could* have," she said defensively. "Anyway, I made him write a love letter for me since I couldn't write it myself." She dug into her reticule and produced the letter, which she tossed into the wastebasket beside the counter.

Ansel fished it out. "But this is to Armand," he said, looking at the address.

Abby shrugged. "I don't know any other men in St. Louis," she explained. "So I borrowed him."

"*Borrowed?*" Ansel asked, his eyebrow rising.

"Well, I'll give him back to Anna Lisa when I'm done with him," she said. "Or I'll just say it's an incredible coincidence that both her fiancé and mine are named Armand."

"Both Armand Whiting? That would be quite a coincidence," he said, trying not to smile.

"Oh, no. Mine is Whitiny," she said so seriously she thought he almost believed her. "That's not a *g* there, though I can see how you'd make that mistake."

"Really, Abby, who is going to believe that?" he demanded.

"Who has to?" she asked. "I'll just drop his name now and again, just with Seth, who won't know any better, and then he'll fall in love with me and I can give Armand the boot."

"You're as crazy as the rest of the family," he said, but it seemed less an accusation than permission to go on with her plan.

"I had to do something," she said. "Or he'll never realize that he loves me, Ansel."

"Well, at least that explains that very strange note of congratulations you had me write to poor Armand. '*I won't believe that you know how happy I am for the both of you if you fail to write me back right away!*' I thought you were just being your eccentric little self."

She put her hands against her temples and pressed. "Please don't call me little, Ansel. I feel older than ma's bedroom slippers and just as worn out. He pushed me so, I just had to tell him that I'm practically engaged! And was he jealous? No, he was just sad, as usual. Sometimes I wonder why I love him at all. I see stars and he sees clouds." She gave Ansel an apologetic little smile, and added, "Oh, but when I do make him smile, make him see the sun and the stars, oh, Ansel, I feel as if I've moved mountains, I've conquered foreign lands."

"Your Dr. Hendon is a mountain, all right. He's immovable. And you're right about foreign, too. Sometimes I wonder if we speak the same language."

"Well, I'm not giving up. I intend to tickle every jealous bone in his body."

"Abby, he just may not want to love you," Ansel warned her, putting his hand on her shoulder.

"Well, aren't you the brightest flame in the candelabra?" she asked, shrugging him off. "Of course he doesn't want to love me. But I aim to make him do it anyway, or die trying."

"You could be just setting yourself up for heartbreak. Why go trying to attract some hornet to your hive when you've got two honeybees buzzing around?"

"I'm not looking for honeybees. I'm not some flower, Ansel, and I don't need some bee to come around and pollinate me, for heaven's sake! I want Seth, not just any man."

"Well, you may not be looking for an alternative, but one wouldn't be so bad, you know. Get your mind off the good doctor and all."

"I don't want my mind taken off Seth, and if I did, I could do it myself. I don't need some—"

"Don't look now, but whether you need one or not, there's one headed your way."

Abby spun around just in time to see Frank Walker come into the office, a bunch of leeks in his hand. He held them out to her like a bouquet.

"Know how you like these for your soup, Miss Abby," he said politely, nodding at her and looking over at Ansel for encouragement.

"That sure was nice of you," Ansel said, glaring at Abby until she repeated his words. "Have you ever had Abby's potato-leek soup?"

"I can't say as I've had the pleasure," he said, just as Seth walked in the door. The *Herald* was getting busier these days than Walker's Mercantile after the fruit train arrived from down South. "But I do hear it is as special as . . . well . . . as . . ."

"Dr. Hendon," Abby said as icily as she could. "To what do we owe the honor?"

"I think you ought to make some of that soup for Frank," Ansel said as though Seth hadn't even come in the door. "For one thing, he did bring you the leeks, and for another, he'll be sure to save you the best ones off the train if he gets a taste of your cooking."

"Abby's potato-leek soup?" Seth asked. She could almost see his mouth water.

"Frank here brought me some leeks," Abby said sweetly. "So I thought I might make him some soup."

"You gonna start giving out numbers, like at the butcher shop on Fridays?" Seth asked.

"We don't have to give out numbers," Frank answered, though Abby was quite certain the question was not for him. "And Miss Abby'd never need one," he added shyly.

"She still can't use her hand." Seth lifted Abby's hand as if he owned it and pointed out the bandages to Frank, though anyone could spot them from half a block away.

"That healing okay, Doc?" Frank asked, and Abby could see Ansel eyeing Frank approvingly. Oh Frank was nice and good and kind, and not bad looking in a gangly sort of way, even missing his front tooth. But he didn't make her heart race, didn't make her knees weak, didn't make her breath stop right in her chest at the very sight of him. And when he touched her, like helping her out of a buggy, or down some icy steps, it was like her pa or Ansel helping her—she was never sorry when he let her go.

As Ansel, Seth, and Frank discussed how her hand was healing, Abby studied each of them, one after the other. In fact, she couldn't seem to get more than one of them in her line of vision. There was no question she was going to need new glasses, she thought, and quickly took them off to look, if not see, her best.

"Put your glasses back on," Seth said with a shake of his head, as if she were a foolish child.

"Abby, you need them," Ansel said. "You look just fine in them."

After she complied, Frank dipped his head back some and studied her in her awful wire rims. "They make your eyes look even bigger, Miss Abby. A body could get lost in eyes that big." And then, because with her glasses back on she could see it quite clearly, she watched Frank Walker blush.

And she didn't miss, either, Seth's obvious discomfort as he went digging in his overcoat pockets and then finally found what he was looking for in his inner pocket.

"Next week's column," he said. " 'Household Emergencies.' "

He held it out to her, but Ansel reached over and took it. "I'll have to set it, with Abby's hand still not healed."

"It certainly is taking a long time," Frank Walker said, looking accusingly at Seth. "Didn't you sew it good?"

Abby had to cover her mouth with her good hand not to laugh at the indignant look Seth gave Frank.

"Well," she said, deciding that having three men concerned about her welfare was a lot more enjoyable than she would have suspected, "if you gentlemen will excuse me, I've got to bring an ad over to Emmet Sommers and make sure I've got the wording right."

She took her coat, but only threw it over her arm. The looks she got from the three men in the newspaper office would surely keep her warm halfway to Emmet Sommers's farm.

· · ·

Seth hated mollycoddling his patients. Not the truly sick ones, of course. Those he would stay up with all night, if necessary.

"There is simply nothing wrong with your chest," Seth said to Ella Welsh. "Not as far as I can see."

Ella's laugh was throaty and inviting. "Well, it ain't flowery, but I'll still take it as a compliment."

"I meant medically," Seth said.

"Then why do I feel such a pain over here?" she asked, toying with her left breast and looking at him with big round eyes that he supposed were meant to look innocent. "Is it just heartache?"

He nodded. "I suppose that's it," he agreed, turning away from her and writing something in her file to signify that the examination was over. "You can close up your buttons now."

"What would you suggest I do for my heartache?" she asked, and the muscles in his neck tightened and he rolled his shoulders to ease the cramp.

"I'd suggest that you go on home and give yourself a few more days to get over Mr. Panner's death. Treat yourself to a nice warm bath. Sleep late. Let yourself grieve a bit. It's hard, and it takes a long time to get over someone's death."

"You still missing that sweet little sister of yours?" Ella asked.

"I'm over my grieving," he said.

"Sure you are," she said, sounding unconvinced. "But if you ever need to grieve with someone else, Doc, come on out to the house."

Hold your breath till I get there, he thought unkindly. But all he said was that he thought he heard someone out in the waiting room. He opened the door just in time to see the flash of skirt exiting his outer door. He had no time or need to wonder who she'd been—there, on his desk, were a pair of snow shoes and a rifle rustier than an old gate.

"Something funny, Doc?" Ella asked, and Seth realized that he had laughed out loud.

"Not at all," he said, shaking his head.

He'd have to be careful what he said to Abidance Merganser. First the gold-panning supplies, and now the trapper's goods. Apparently she was making a habit of taking him at his word.

Chapter Eight

ANSEL HAD HIS ARM AROUND EMILY'S WAIST AS he escorted her into the grange hall. A pang of jealousy hit Abby right in the pit of her stomach. Maybe she was wrong to pursue a relationship with Seth Hendon. Maybe she was wrong about the importance of love. After all, Ansel wasn't in love, yet he had a mate for life, a partner, someone to share the good things and the bad with, someone to grow old with, someone to dote on.

Frank Walker was willing. Emmet Sommers was willing. Well, Emmet Sommers was willing to be someone's partner all right, but it looked like it was Patience who might be parking her slippers next to Emmet's one day, if the way they were sitting beside each other on the back bench was any indication. And that was just fine with Abby.

Still, life was passing her by. "Mind if I sit here?" Frank Walker asked. She looked up at him and tried to smile, gathering her skirt closer so that he could fill the seat beside her.

"Would you mind moving down there, Frank?" a familiar voice asked.

No, life wasn't passing her by—it was whirling around her, out of control, as Frank eased his way beyond her knees and sat to her left and Seth took the seat to her right.

"You didn't show up to have your bandage changed today," he said. Not *Hello.* Not *How are you, Abby?* No, strictly doctor/patient.

"It looks clean to me," she said, holding out the hand her mother had rebandaged.

"I was going to take the stitches out today," he said. "But you never came by."

"I'll stop by tomorrow morning," Abby said. "If that's all right."

"Of course it's all right," Seth said. "I can write another letter for you, if you like." He looked past her at Frank.

"Once you take the stitches out, I should be able to write myself, don't you think?"

He sat back in his seat, stretching his arms over his head and then leaving one on the back of her chair. Then Frank asked if she was cold, and adjusted her shawl, trying to pull it out from beneath Seth's arm. When Seth finally lifted his, Frank quickly replaced it with his own.

"I'd like to call this meeting to order," Horace Parks, the mayor of Eden's Grove, said. He'd been strangely silent on the question of whether the money should be spent on a church or a hospital, and Abby figured that he was probably waiting to see which way the wind was blowing before taking a position firmly on the fence.

"I figure that the fairest way to do this is to let Reverend Merganser speak first, then Dr. Hendon, and then let anyone speak their piece who's got a mind to."

"People without minds should remain silent," Seth whispered to her. She smiled politely, but refused to laugh. He could be her doctor or he could be her intended, but she wasn't going to settle for anything in between.

"As to the question of the ladies voting—" the mayor said, stopping to blink several times at the clamor. "I can't for the life of me figure out how to take a vote on that. Do the ladies vote on the ladies voting?" he asked Mr. Youtt, who was seated in one of the chairs at the front that faced the audience. Her father was seated in another. The fourth was empty and she ordered her toes to uncurl. So Seth Hendon was sitting next to her instead of up at the front. He probably just didn't want to be such a clear target for tomatoes.

"Women have always voted in Eden's Grove," Mr. Youtt said. "There were times when the town was so small that they were needed for a quorum. Women in this town have fought fires beside their men. There probably isn't a barn in Eden's Grove, or all of Iowa, for that matter, that'd be standing but for some woman's help. Miss Rachel Kearney has taught a good half of us how to read. Miss Abidance Merganser writes a fine column in our paper. Mrs. Walter Waitte mans our only phone. Or should I say *ladies* it?" he asked to a good deal of laughter.

"To now turn and say, 'Thanks for everything, but we'll take it from here on out,' seems ungrateful and unwise. I know that I want to hear anything these ladies have to say. I know that my wife's opinion differs from my own and is no less valid than mine."

"Well," the mayor said, "anyone brave enough after that to oppose the ladies voting?"

Abidance watched her father squirm in his chair.

"Reverend Merganser?" the mayor asked.

"Me? I got nothing to say," her father replied. "And I'm only gonna say it once. Eleven months a year the ladies in this town are busy with their husbands and families and making sure that they all come to church to say their prayers. And the other two months they're busier than ever what with Easter and Christmas. So since it's not any of those, and even if it was, I don't see why they can't vote if they don't want to not do that."

Abby covered her mouth with her hand. Snickering at the reverend, especially when the reverend was her father, was just not acceptable.

"Then that's settled, isn't it?" the mayor asked Mr. Youtt.

"I suppose," Mr. Youtt said, shaking his head at Abby's father. "He did say they ought to vote, didn't he?"

Several women in the audience yelled that indeed that was what her father said, or at least what he meant.

"Anyone object to the ladies voting?" the mayor began, but then before anyone had a chance to, he added, "'Cause you're in the minority here and I wouldn't expect a decent meal till kingdom come if you do!"

Seth shifted in his seat, claiming he was having difficulty seeing, and pressed up against Abby's side.

"You hear anything from that friend of yours you had me write to in St. Louis?" he whispered, an eyebrow raised as if he thought she'd just dreamed him up out of thin air.

"I will," she said confidently. And if Ansel had told Seth that Armand was not really her beau, she was going to chop him in little pieces and feed his heart to Disciple, the cat.

"Why bother with St. Louis?" he whispered, raising his eyes to Frank.

With a less than gentle shove she pushed him away from her, then pretended that her boot needed tying. When Seth, too, lowered his head, she said, with a sweet smile that never wavered though her insides were mush with his breath on her cheek, "I'm not looking for a husband. I'm looking for love."

And then she directed her attention to her father, who had just been given the floor after the mayor had thanked each and every person nearly by name for coming, for bringing pies, for seeing to the coffee and tea, and so on and so forth.

"Well, I always like to wait until I see the final vote before I anticipate what this town is likely to do, but the days ahead lie ahead of us just as they always have and they always will, and so it seems to me that we need to say God bless the Lord and show Him that we mean it each and every day that is still ahead of us.

"That's really all I have to say, except that I also want to say that while the Lord does work in mysterious ways, that's what He was doing when He sent me by Ridder's Pond the first time Joseph Panner drowned, so that God could tell him that He cared, and even though the second time was different, God still cared about Joseph Panner and we should care about God.

"And show we care with the biggest cathedral that Iowa ever saw. And then people would come to Eden's Grove and they could live here and worship the way they pleased at our church."

The worst part of her father's speech was that there wasn't a person in Eden's Grove who didn't know just what her father meant, and that it came from his heart and not his head. She looked over at Seth, figuring it was now his turn to speak.

Sitting beside Abby, Seth allowed himself to take a deep breath before rising. "Wish me luck," he whispered as he came to his feet. With the loony Reverend Merganser done giving the town the last piece of his mind, it was his turn to speak.

"I have nothing against churches," he said, figuring that he didn't want people thinking they were voting against God if they wanted a clinic in Eden's Grove. "I thank God every morning when I get up that He's seen me through another night. I pray for His help a hundred times a day, when I see a sick child, when I stitch together an open wound. And when—like the other day when a new little Hartley came slipping into my hands—He lets me share His miracles, I thank Him again.

"But I thank Him wherever I am. I pray to Him wherever I am. It doesn't take a church and a congregation for the Lord to do His work, but it takes a great deal of equipment for me to do mine."

He went on to explain to them all about asepsis and germs and the importance of a sterile operating facility.

By the time he got to the types of operations that required optimum conditions and the statistics of survival with and without, he knew he had lost them.

"Let's take the vote," someone shouted. "Alice left a pie cooling on the sill that's calling me all the way from home."

"I'd like to say something," Mrs. Youtt, the lawyer's wife, said, coming to a stand in the front row and turning toward the crowd. "I feel like I'm being ungrateful to Dr. Hendon, saying what I've got to say after he saved our boy, but the truth is, while some of us may get sick and a few of us might need that surgery that he keeps talking about, we're all of us gonna die sometime. And not to have a church service when we go . . . It's not like I think we won't be allowed in the heavenly kingdom or anything, it's just . . . well, it's fitting. A proper end to a decent life."

"Just like I said," the reverend said when she was finished, and all Seth could do was shake his head. He knew that in a way Mrs. Youtt was right—with luck and care there'd only be a handful of patients who would benefit from the clinic at any time, but the whole town would enjoy the church. There would be weddings and baptisms and communions. And there would be funerals.

Mr. Youtt spoke next, in favor of the clinic. It was nice for Seth to think that someone who wasn't in love with him agreed with him. Not that Abby was really in love with him, he thought.

He looked out at the crowd to where she sat beside Frank Walker and reluctantly admitted to himself that they made a rather handsome couple. Not that old one-tooth Frank was a good-looking man, but Abby more than made up for whatever he lacked. Seth doubted Frank was a day over twenty-three, and already he was managing the mercantile that belonged to his father.

Leeks. The man had brought her leeks and she hadn't thought it self-serving in the least. As if Frank wasn't planning on not only getting to taste Abby's soup but no doubt make an evening of it—he'd start with the soup and he'd move on to tasting Abidance Merganser's sweet, sweet lips.

"Dr. Hendon?" Horace Parks asked him, nudging his arm. "Did you want to say anything else?"

"I do," Abby said, rising to her feet while the words she spoke resounded in his mind. Oh, she'd say them in a church one day, but to someone who suited her better, someone who didn't suck the wind from her sails. And as she proceeded up the aisle between the chairs of the hall which also served as their church, he held his breath, imagining. Tamping down thoughts. Wishing. Tamping down hopes.

"I feel traitorous. And if I didn't right from the beginning, I certainly have in the last two weeks. I was brought up in the Eden's Grove Methodist Church. I love the church and I love its reverend." She smiled at her father. "But the Eden's Grove Methodist Church is not a building. It's not a place. It's a community.

"It didn't burn down in the fire. That was just wood and mortar. But the people who die leave this community and some of them might not have to go so soon if they get the proper medical attention. Maybe there will be only one person saved by Seth's clinic. But maybe that one person is the one you cherish most in the world. Maybe she's the one who would have given birth to our next mayor, or our next reverend, or the next president of the United States. Maybe he's the one who would have been there to pull you from the river, or catch you when you fell.

"Is one of us less valuable than all of us?"

There was silence in the grange hall, and Seth thought that his chest might burst with pride. Abidance Merganser was not a child, not some flippant little slip of a girl who didn't understand the seriousness of his work. As she had told him when his sister was dying and she insisted on buying Sarrie a fancy dress the girl would never wear, there was a difference between frivolity and happiness.

And he had been a fool not to see it before.

"No, Mr. Parks," he said softly in the quiet. "I have nothing else to say."

The voting took place by secret ballot. With very little talk people lined up in an orderly fashion and stood waiting for their turn to write either "hospital" or "church" on the small slips of paper waiting on the back table.

"You know a lot of them probably couldn't spell 'hospital,' " Abby said as she walked beside Seth back toward his office.

"Maybe we should have told them to just make a cross or an H," he said. "Or draw someone in pain. Or a tombstone."

"An awful lot of people did vote for the clinic," Abby

said. "If they all donated a bit, maybe you could at least—"

"Don't you have to go home?" he asked, looking at her as if she was the enemy.

"It wasn't my fault that they voted for the church, Seth. Don't take it out on me."

"I'm not taking it out on you," he said sharply. "I know you tried. You made a great case for the clinic. You were grand. Better surely than I was. I thank you, from the bottom of my heart, for all the good it did us. What more do you want from me, a jig?"

"I want you to pick up the pieces, Seth. I want you to figure out a way to get a clinic built without Joseph Panner's money. I want you to think that while we didn't win the vote, there were still a lot of people who understood the need for a clinic, instead of that while there were a lot of people who understood the need, we still didn't win the vote."

"I can't do it, Abby. I'd like to, but I just can't put a good face on it. Not even for you. You're so very lucky, walking around in those rose-colored glasses of yours, turning things around in a way I can't. I have to see things the way they really are."

"I see things the way they really are too. I see that while the Denton baby is failing, the Evans baby girl is hearty and hale. But you don't. You see that while the Evans baby is thriving, the Denton baby isn't. I see that while Joseph Panner may have died, your skill beat the frostbite. You see that even though you beat the frostbite, Joseph Panner died. I see that while you couldn't save Sarrie's life, you've saved the lives of countless others.

"And all you can see is that no matter how many lives you save, it doesn't matter because you lost Sarrie."

"You know me too well," he said, the hint of a laugh in his words. "How is it that when you know me as well as that you still always expect me to be happy in the face of disaster? Why haven't you learned yet who I am and why I will never be who you want me to be? Why do you keep expecting and wanting—"

"I don't expect anything of you," she said, stopping in her tracks. "I don't want anything of you. You're right. I should know better. I just keep remembering the man who wrote those silly affidavits for Sarrie and me, swearing that we would be friends forever, and then convincing Mr. Youtt to notarize them. I remember how you let me cry in your arms like a baby when Sarrie took a turn for the worse. I remember your teaching me to dance before the Springtime Ball that year when I was old enough to go.

"I remember your framing my first editorial and hanging it on the wall in your waiting room. I—"

"You were Sarrie's friend," he said, as if he didn't realize that she was much more than that to him. But she knew, she knew how he wished that things could be different as he fought his own feelings for her.

"I was your friend too, Seth. I still am, but you're shutting me out. This is not about the clinic, Seth. This is about us."

"Now who's turning things around? This is not just about us—and I've told you and told you that there is no 'us'—it's about the clinic. It's about my losing that vote and—"

"Do you really think that you are the only one who lost back at the grange hall? Do you really think that the world revolves around you and that everyone else is too stupid to understand? That the pain is yours alone?"

"People will die because I couldn't make them understand—"

"People will die, Seth, if you stand on your head and spit wooden nickels. Unless you sprout wings and figure out a way to convince God otherwise, people will keep dying. That's what life is all about."

"For some, but for others I'm their last hope, Abby," he said sadly.

"Well, maybe those people don't deserve a last hope. Maybe they just deserve nice funerals. And maybe you should just be happy that some of them—"

She touched the back of her hand to her head, hoping that the coolness would bring some relief to the unrelenting headache.

"I am so tired of your ownership of all the pain in Eden's Grove. I wanted that clinic. I can't do what you do, but I wanted to be a part of saving lives."

"I'm still the only one that will lose them," he said, having a pity party for himself while the night grew cold around them.

"I have to head on home, to where my family hates me and will have a fine time gloating over their wonderful victory. I only hope they don't come to regret it."

"Well, it'll be a fine funeral when they do, in a grand church, won't it?"

Her head was splitting apart. It hurt so much that it

made her dinner rise up her throat and threaten to spill into her mouth.

"I've got to go," she said, turning to look down the street and finding it hard to see into the darkness. She fished for her glasses and then decided she could find her way home blind. After all, it seemed as if she'd been leaving Seth and going home alone forever.

Chapter Nine

"FRANK WALKER WAS HERE EARLIER," ANSEL told Abby when she finally showed up at the *Herald* two days later. So she'd indulged herself in a little pity fest. Didn't broken hearts need as much tending as broken arms? "He was pretty concerned when I told him that you weren't feeling too well. You doing any better?"

She nodded. She really did feel better. She'd be darned if she'd let Dr. Seth Hendon rule her life. She'd be darned if she'd let him kiss her feet!

"You see the doctor?"

Oh, that would be a big help, she thought. "I don't need a doctor," she snapped at him. "I wasn't that kind of sick."

"Pru says—"

"Pru should mind her own business. Do I come telling you—"

"That you're biting everyone's head off?" he finished. "Obviously it's true."

"What do you all want?" she shouted at him. "When I'm little Mary Sunshine I don't understand the gravity of the situation. When I'm not all smiles and cheers I'm overemotional. Why don't you just tell me what you want me to say, and I'll say it?"

"I want you to say that you're over Seth Hendon and that you're ready to be treated nicely and well."

"It's over with Seth Hendon and I'm ready to be treated nicely and well."

"That was too easy," Ansel said.

"No," she corrected. "It was very, very hard. He didn't come to see me, he doesn't want me in his life, and I'm tired of pushing myself on him."

"Did he know you were feeling—" Ansel started, but apparently thought better of it. The last thing Ansel probably wanted to do was defend Seth Hendon.

"So what did Frank Walker want?" she asked. Ansel was as easy to read as last week's *Herald*. If she was over Seth, then Ansel thought he could just slot in poor Frank Walker. After all, in Ansel's eyes—heck, in everyone's eyes—a woman needed a man to take care of her and make her happy.

"He came by to bring you the first of the green peas. I told him you weren't feeling well and he—" Ansel began, then suddenly began hustling her toward the back office. "Go in the back. Take a rest in the chair, but leave the door open so I can hear if you need me."

"What?" she asked, pushing at his hands. "Ansel, stop—"

"Don't argue, for once in your life, Abby, please? You still look pale and I don't want you tiring yourself on your first day up and around." He put an arm around her and escorted her into the back office.

Before Abby could get herself up and back into the

main office, she heard Ansel's loud voice. "Frank! How have you been?"

"Busy," she heard Frank say. "I had to send wires to four different shops in Estherville before I could find some flowers and have them sent here on the train. But here they are."

"They're real nice looking. For Abidance?" her brother asked.

She supposed Frank nodded, smiling that shy smile of his that revealed his missing front tooth.

"Daffodils?"

"Tulips. My sister looked in one of those *Language of the Flowers* books we were selling last winter and she says that tulips mean beautiful eyes."

"You're pretty sweet on Abby, huh?" Ansel asked, obviously wanting Abby to hear the answer. Shamefully, when she really should have made her presence known, she waited to hear what Frank had to say.

"I'm not hiding it," was what he said. "A man can do that and someone else'll come along and whisk the woman of his dream right out from under his nose. I'm not about to let that happen to me. You think she's up to visitors? I could just leave the flowers with your mother if you think she won't want me seein' her indisposed."

"I'm fine, Frank," Abby said, coming out from the back room, her cheeks no doubt as red as cherries in June. "I was feeling very poorly, but I'm over it now. Oh, but those are lovely! I think tulips are my favorite flowers. They mean that spring is right around the corner and that everything will be fine again soon."

•   •   •

She hadn't seen Seth since he'd taken out her stitches. He'd acted as if she were just another person who'd voted against his stupid clinic, instead of the one who'd stood up and laid her heart on the table in front of the whole darn town.

She'd heard the snickers. Well, let them look at her now, out to dinner at the Eden's Grove Grand Hotel dining room with the very eligible Frank Walker.

"Aren't you hungry?" Frank asked, frowning at the barely picked-at food on her plate. "I could have them bring you something else if you don't like your lamb."

"It's wonderful," she said, though in truth it could have been sawdust she was eating. She supposed her heart just wasn't in it. Wasn't in anything. She barely had an appetite anymore. Nothing smelled good, tasted good, seemed appealing. It was just as Ansel had said. Loving Seth was making her physically ill.

But that was behind her. It was just taking a great deal of effort to let go.

"So tell me how things are going at the store. Are you carrying anything newsworthy I could write about?" She'd been pouring her heart into her writing, be it her work or her letters to Armand and Anna Lisa. Writing to them had become her release and she poured out her heart to them, telling them how hard it was to love someone who didn't love her back.

"Well, we've put in our order for the most wonderful new camera that anyone can afford. It's called a Brownie box camera and it'll sell for only a dollar when we can get them in. They're promising them in just a few months time." He took a pause and looked at her. "I surely would like to fill a whole album with pictures of you, Miss Abby. And the film will only cost ten or fifteen cents a roll."

"At that price why stop at just one roll?" Abby teased. Frank was a nice man. There was nothing wrong with Frank.

"Miss Abby, are you done? The waiter is—" Frank said, pointing toward her side.

"Oh, certainly," she said, smiling at the waiter she hadn't even seen.

"Weather sure is getting milder," Frank said. He put his hand over hers and patted it gently. "I thought maybe Saturday when I was finished with the inventory, if you weren't otherwise occupied, I could take you for a ride out east. There's a piece of land that my father's thinking of selling, and I was thinking of maybe buying it, building me a house out there and . . ."

She knew what he was asking. "I'd like that," she forced herself to say.

His eyes widened and instead of feeling flattered and wanted, she just felt empty and deceitful.

"Frank, you know that there is someone else, don't you?" she asked.

"I heard about the man in St. Louis," he said, nodding. "But I figure that being here I've got the inside track. I mean, he ain't taking you to see a pretty piece of land with the sweetest little brook running through it on Saturday, now, is he?"

"No," Abby agreed. "He isn't."

"I know it might take you a while to come to care for

me the way I care for you, but I'm a patient man, Miss Abby, and all I ask is that you do give it a try."

"That isn't asking very much," Abby agreed. It was no more than she'd asked of Seth, and he'd refused. "A babbling brook, did you say?"

Frank's eyes sparkled when he smiled, and it was easy to overlook his missing tooth. He had deep lines by the corners of his eyes despite the fact that he wasn't much older than Abby. Apparently he smiled a lot. "And oaks that touch the sky."

"I like oak trees," Abby said. "They bend for no one. My mother likes willows—every time there's a storm she looks out the window and says 'A reed before the wind lives on, while mighty oaks do fall.' I'd rather stand proud and tall for as long as I can than bend at every breath of hot air that comes my way."

"I do love to hear you talk," Frank said. "I always feel like I'm reading a book with lots of levels of meaning. I only wish sometimes that Mrs. Kearney was sitting at the next table so she could tell me what the author means."

It means that I have trouble compromising, she thought, *that I can't bow to someone else's wishes. . . .* "It means I'm too proud, according to my mama. And not very practical."

"There ain't nothing wrong with dreaming and wanting things to be perfect," Frank said, and took the little dessert menus from the waiter, handing her one. "What'll it be?"

There were seven offerings, each one more tempting than the one above it. There was *suedoise* of peaches, three kinds of pie, two types of gingerbreads, and plum duff with custard. Why was it that the sweetest things in life suddenly had no appeal?

"Maybe you'd just like me to take you home. You look kind of tired, if you don't mind my saying so," Frank said, closing the menu as if she were infinitely more interesting.

"I am awfully tired," she admitted.

Trying to fall in love was very hard work.

"I do believe your boat has sailed," Ansel told Seth when he stopped by the *Herald* on Saturday afternoon. "Abby is over at the mercantile picking up some things for the picnic lunch she's preparing for Frank tomorrow."

"Good," he said, an admirable response to having been kicked in the gut.

"He wants to show her some land he's thinking of buying," Ansel continued.

"Land," Seth said, nodding as if this was the natural course of events. "Frank seems a good man."

Now it was Ansel's turn to nod.

"Whatever happened to Mr. St. Louis?" he asked, expecting to hear that Abby had simply made up the man to make him jealous, just as she was making him jealous with Frank Walker, a man so far beneath her that he'd need binoculars to see the bottoms of her shoes.

"Heard from him again yesterday," Ansel said, fishing in the wastebasket and producing a letter from Mr. A. Whitiny of St. Louis.

"She doesn't save them?" he asked, getting some satisfaction at least from that.

"Only the insides," Ansel said, showing him the envelope was empty.

"Well, two suitors," Seth said, trying to sound impressed rather than judgmental.

"She's cared a great deal for Armand for a good long time," Ansel said, "but Frank Walker has been damn persistent and he is here, while Armand is in St. Louis."

"Well, I just came to drop off my next column," Seth said. He missed going over them with Abby. He missed seeing her smile. He missed hearing her laugh and he missed knowing that when he was at his lowest she'd turn up and make life worthwhile.

"What's this one on?" Ansel asked.

"Stomach pains," Seth said. He'd seen a dozen patients since the Youtt boy had come down with appendicitis, all sure they were in the throes of an attack themselves. Only Mrs. Waitte even had pain localized to the right side, and that turned out to be result of a stay poking through her corset cover.

"Next week chest pains and then on to the head," he said.

Ansel made no reference to Abby's headaches, as if they were no longer Seth's business. "You hear anything more from that doctor in Massachusetts?" Ansel asked him.

Amazingly the doctor had written with several dozen very specific questions, as if he were truly interested in taking over Seth's practice. What a relief that would be. No more avoiding Caroline Denton's eyes, no more worrying about Johnnie Youtt's appendix bursting. No more sleepless nights waiting for fevers to break, for babies to be born.

He was going to be free, free, free.

Maybe it had to actually happen before he felt good about it.

"So what do you think?" Frank Walker asked Abby as they sat in his very fine buggy looking over tall prairie grass as far as the eye could see. Off to the right was a stand of oaks that, if they didn't quite reach the sky, made an admirable attempt.

A mild breeze rippled the grass and it swayed and bowed as if it were showing off just for her. "It's incredibly lovely," she said, trying to imagine a fine house with a small porch, complete with a freshly painted swing.

"If you say to, I'll buy it," Frank said, putting his arm around her.

"Well, it's a beautiful piece of land," she said. "You could build a wonderful life here, Frank."

"Are you telling me to buy it?" he asked.

"I . . ." she began, but she wasn't sure what to say. Could she really let her dream go and settle for something much, much less? Ansel had done it. And at least Emily seemed happy. Probably half the women in Iowa had taken the best offer they expected to get. And if they got love, too, well, then they were luckier than most.

"Thought I could hang a rope from that littlest oak," Frank said, pointing. "For a swing for the children.

"Do you suppose you'd miss working at the *Herald*? I mean if you were to—I know I'd miss seeing you there in the middle of the day, but coming home to you, oh, Miss Abby! That would be—"

"Frank, I—" she began again.

"I know you had strong feelings for that other man, but if he valued you right, he'd have made his intentions known, and not taken no for an answer. The way I see it, someone's always gotta be the one to care more, and I don't mind it being me, for now."

"What if I never—I mean what if it wasn't just *for now*? What if—"

"What if you stopped worrying so much and let me paint you a picture of what being married to me would be like? What it would be like for us?"

"All right," she agreed, remembering how Seth had told her, and bluntly too, that there was no "us." With Frank there would always be an "us." *Convince me. Please, Frank, convince me.*

"In the morning I'd be looking at you when you woke up. I'd lean over you and kiss that little nose of yours," he leaned over then, and planted a soft kiss just below the bridge of her nose. "And then I'd demand a real kiss so that I could remember it all the day through while I was over in town and you were here raising a houseful of little hellions who all want to be oak trees and not willows. . . ."

And then he twisted her in her seat, and pulled her gently against him, and pressed his lips to hers.

Chapter Ten

❧ ❦

ABIDANCE MERGANSER DANCED AROUND SETH'S head all week, as surely as she always used to dance around his office. The harder he tried to wipe her from his thoughts, the more stubbornly she remained planted there. And things he'd never noticed became things that he couldn't forget—the worn toe on her new boots, the fancy stitching on her dress coat, the comb that held her hair. Oh, that hair! Dark curls that had felt like silk when he'd threaded his fingers through them.

And all he could think was how he wished he could love her, but she was too young. And he was so old. And how she was so full of the wonder of life and he so resigned to the sadness in it. She was better off with Frank Walker. Certainly he was a simple man, a shopkeeper, and Abby was—he wouldn't think about what Abby was, not again. He just might love her, but he was old and she . . . The words danced in his head, coming apart and together in a million different combinations until there was only one version he could hear and feel and own:

He was too old and she was too full of life—*but still he loved her.* He loved her despite it and because of it.

It stunned him how easy it was to look at life the way Abby did. Yes, he was older than she, but many men were older than their wives. Yes he could remember her as just a child, but it was a gift, not a burden, to have had the opportunity to watch her turn into the radiant woman that she had become.

The radiant woman he had pushed into Frank Walker's waiting arms.

Into Frank Walker's buggy, which still hadn't come back though it was dark enough to light the lamps in his office. Seth forced himself to sit down with the newest issue of the *New England Journal of Medicine*. Maybe this time he'd be able to read it without his mind wandering to two people riding around in a buggy until after dark. Of course, Frank might have brought her home and the loon family was holding him against his will and that explained why at nearly eight o'clock the buggy still hadn't come down the street past his office on the way to the livery.

By nine he figured Abby's family were toasting the happy couple and taking inventory of her hope chest. Well, it was probably for the best. After all, Frank was perfect for Abby—even if he wasn't nearly as bright as she was. Even if he had no greater plans than to figure out whether pink soap or yellow was likely to sell better in the spring, while his Abby was planning to save the world.

Not *his* Abby, not yet. But not Frank's yet, either.

Would Frank permit Abby to continue to write for

the paper as Seth would all but insist? It would be a damn shame if—

Well! And about time, he thought as he finally saw Frank's buggy come meandering up the street. With the carriage hood up he couldn't tell if the man was alone. It was late. It was dark. Frank Walker damn well better be alone!

He opened his door so that he could follow the course of the buggy with his eyes until it turned into the livery. A minute or two later Frank came out and headed farther up the block, alone.

Seth closed the door to the office and hurried down the street, his eyes on Frank, as the man went into McGinty's Tavern. Did that mean a celebration?

He opened the door and followed Frank in.

Walker took a seat at the far end of the bar. Seth took one by the door. They nodded at each other, and after the barkeep had served Walker his scotch, Seth asked for the same. He matched him shot for shot, beer for beer, until he wondered whether either of them would be able to walk home.

And still they said nothing to each other. But Seth did hear him tell the barkeep he was buying that piece of land they'd talked about, building a house. And he did say something about being a papa that Seth couldn't make out.

He didn't need to. He'd heard enough. Abby probably had Frank's head just as turned around as his own. He didn't blame Frank for falling in love with Abby, and it was damn hard to go blaming her when he'd told her there was no *"us."*

Was there a superlative beyond stupidest? Beyond

most moronic? deranged? Abby had left him deranged, like those poor, crazy patients in hospitals who surgeons felt free to operate upon to see just how the hell the brain worked.

With what little was left of the dignity he possessed, he slid from the barstool and looked around for his coat. It took him a couple of minutes to remember that he hadn't worn one, and without a good-bye to anyone he left a few crumpled bills on the bar and headed back to his office.

The lights were still burning when he got there, which was a damn good thing, because his vision was playing tricks on him. Through the window he could swear that Abby was sitting at his desk, her head down on her arms.

It was a sin, what a little bit of scotch and a lot of hope could do to a man. Make him see things that weren't there, feel things he wasn't supposed to feel.

He let the door swing open until it hit a chair, hoping to scare off the ghost of Abidance Merganser. Instead it awakened it. Eyes red from crying blinked up at him.

"What happened?" he asked, heading straight for the coffee pot and lighting a flame beneath it. The last time he had been drunk around Abby he'd kissed her. He was afraid of what he'd do this time if he didn't exert all of his willpower to control himself.

"He kissed me," Abby said. "I swear I was all right with it until then. I wasn't trying to spite you, or make you jealous, or anything. I was just going to go on with my life. Mine and Frank's." She sniffed and looked around his desk for a hankie. He reached in his pocket and tossed one to her. He was not going to get close enough to touch her until he was stone cold sober.

"So he kissed you," he said. "Who the hell hasn't?"

"Have you been drinking?" She hiccuped twice and sniffed some more.

"Try holding your breath. And what the hell makes you think I've been drinking?" he asked.

She raised an eyebrow at him.

"Your fiancé and I might have had a few at Mc-Ginty's," he admitted. "Or more than a few." The coffee was bitter. He swallowed it as if he'd been bitten by a rattler and it was the antidote.

"My fiancé?"

"Excuse me. One of your fianceés. The local one."

"Frank?"

"There are more? Did you tell Emmet you'd marry him, too?"

"Frank told you I said that I'd marry him?" she asked. Did she think a man would keep marrying a woman as beautiful, as brilliant, as wonderful, as Abby a secret?

"He said he was buying that puny piece of land and building a house on it." He took a swig of coffee and felt his head begin to clear some. "And he said something about children. Planning on a whole passel, Abby girl?"

"He is," she said. "Would you like me to make you a fresh pot?"

"This is killing me just fine," he said. "So when's the big day?"

"There isn't going to be one," she admitted. "I told him it was a beautiful piece of land and he should buy it and build a wonderful house with a porch and put a picket fence around it all and live happily ever after there. But not with me."

He poured the dregs of the coffee into his cup and swallowed it before he spoke. "Why not?"

"Because I don't love him. Because my heart doesn't skip a beat when he smiles, or race when I see him from half a block away. I know you don't want to hear this, don't want me to—"

"Do I do that to you?" he asked, giving her his most brilliant smile. "Is your heart skipping a beat?"

"Don't tease me, Seth. I'm going to be an old maid because I can't let someone hope for what they'll never get from me. Frank said that—"

"I don't care what the hell Frank said," he said. He put down the coffee cup and came over to crouch beside where she sat at the desk. "I want to know what you said."

"I told him he was too good a man to settle for what he could get from me. That he deserved to be loved and cherished by a woman that would give him her whole heart. And that I couldn't do that."

"Because of Armand?" he asked, making sure to get her entire regiment of beaux out of the way. "Has he written to you swearing undying love? Has he asked you to marry him?"

She shook her head.

"Has he told you *Je t'adore, chérie*? Has he sworn *la belle passion*?"

"Stop teasing me," she said, her lower lip quivering so that he could hardly resist it. "This is hard enough."

"Ah, then," he said, rising just enough so that his lips

could meet hers. "Let me make it easier. Let me make it very easy." And as he spoke, he stood with her, and pressed himself against her with the urgency of too many years and too much sorrow.

"Seth?" she asked when he pulled his lips from hers long enough to find the top button of her dress and loosen it. "Are you still drunk?"

"Not so much that I don't know what I'm doing," he said, playing with the bodice of her dress. "See, I can unbutton a button with just one hand. Two, even."

"You can break a heart with less than that," she said, gently pushing him away.

"I am the one you love, aren't I?" he asked, holding on to her arm as she backed away. Beneath the silly leg-o'-mutton sleeve was an arm so slender, so fragile he was afraid that a strong grip could break it in two. "Just tell me that and I'll see you home safely."

"Why?" she asked. "What does it matter?"

"You won't tell me? Hell. Then tell me this. If I had another pick and shovel, what would you say to going prospecting?"

"I'd say you and Frank Walker are going to have worse headaches than I do, come morning."

"Oh, Abby girl," he said, taking her face in his hands. "Is your head hurting you again? Come and we'll get you some powder for it."

Abby took his hand and followed him into the examining room. She loved the feel of her hand within his, just as she'd loved the feel of his lips against her own. And even if this sudden affection was the result of too much to drink, she loved every ounce of it. He drank whiskey, and she drank Seth. And both were intoxicating and could lead them into trouble.

But for tonight she didn't care about trouble. It had hurt her nearly as deeply as it had hurt Frank to tell him that she could never marry him, that she was in love with someone else. She'd saved face by letting him think it was Armand. After Frank was happily married, she figured she could let Armand catch the influenza and die and then she could mourn him and grieve for her lost love for the rest of her life.

Unless Seth had truly come to his senses. Of course, he'd have to be sober for that to mean anything.

What a prospect! Never to be truly and thoroughly loved. Never to find out what it must feel like to be one with the man you love, to hold his love inside you and carry his baby in your womb.

He put some headache powder in an envelope and sealed it. Then he took some more and spooned it into a glass, added water, and handed it to her to drink with a look of such concern on his face that he seemed to think she was dying.

"It's just a headache," she said, drinking the glassful of medicine and handing it back to him. "Don't look so glum. It's been so nice to see you smile tonight."

This time his smile was broad enough to send his dimples deep into his cheeks. "Is your heart racing?" he asked, putting his hand just above the swell of her breast. "Why, I believe it is."

She tried to calm herself, but when she couldn't simply will her heart to slow down, and Seth was all but snickering, she said, "It must just be the medicine."

"Maybe," he said. "But what accounts for mine?" He

took her hand and put it on his chest. As she felt the racing of his heart, he closed his eyes for a minute.

When he opened them again he took her hand and placed a kiss in her palm. "Looks all healed," he said, gently pressing on the tiny scar near the heel of her hand.

"I'm very resilient," she said, closing her fingers over her palm an order to keep his kiss there forever.

"Like a reed," he said, spanning her waist with his hands.

"No, like an oak. I just grow a burl around my injuries and don't let them fell me."

"I have a great fondness for oaks," he said. His hand cupped her breast and one finger ran over the fabric that covered her nipple. "And acorns," he added.

"You're drunk," she said, but she didn't remove his hand. Drunk or sober, in love with her or not, she wanted him, wanted to feel his hands on her body, his breath in her hair.

"Only with you. You intoxicate me, Abby girl." He played with the buttons between her breasts, opening one, opening another. "You intoxicate the hell out of me."

"Well, whatever the reason, you're very drunk, Dr. Hendon."

"Better me than you, Abby girl. After all, I wouldn't want to be accused of taking advantage of you." He slipped his hand within the bodice of her blouse, and his fingers found her nipple and did a dance of love against it.

But it wasn't love. It was scotch, or beer, or gin, and

she swallowed against her shame as her body responded nonetheless, as if it didn't care that he didn't love her. At least for the moment, he needed her.

"Oh, Lord, Abby!" he said, his lips against her cheek, his breath still smelling from McGinty's as he searched out her lips once again.

"We can't do this while you're still drunk," she said, finally coming unwillingly to her senses.

"Why not?" he asked, smiling a smile that said he was well aware of how much she was enjoying every kiss, every stroke, every touch. "Afraid you're taking advantage of me in my weakened condition?"

"Yes," she said, the word sounding choked when she got it out.

"Leave it to you to get things backward again. A man gets a woman drunk to have his way with her, not the other way around."

"Well, you know how I twist things," she said, straightening out her shirtwaist, buttoning up the buttons, unable to look him in the eye.

"All right. I'll see things your way from now on. And I'll do this right, just as you deserve." He bowed from the waist and took her hand. "Miss Abby, would you do me the honor of accompanying me on a buggy ride tomorrow after church?"

"Frank already showed me the prairie and the brook and the oaks," she said, playing on the jealousy that had gotten her this far. "What are you going to show me?"

"He showed you a tree," he said. "But was it a fig?" He winked at her, and when she stood there mutely, he added, "Cause you know what they do with fig leaves . . ."

She thought she did, and felt the red creep up from her throat until both cheeks burned.

"Wanna see what's hidden behind them?"

He'd thrown up twice before he'd been able to get up out of his bed. And the only thing that got him up was the sun. It was shining so brightly that he had to close the curtains to save his brain from bursting through his skull.

To drink is to die one death too many, he thought as he crawled back under his blankets and held his stomach because he didn't dare touch his head. Heaven help anyone who needed doctoring today. Anyone besides himself, that is.

And if the headache, the nausea, the sensation that the room was spinning around him, wasn't enough, there was the memory of what he'd said to sweet, innocent Abby to make him really sick to his stomach. *Wanna see what's behind a fig leaf?* No matter how drunk he was, he couldn't have said that, could he? To Abby?

It had all been a dream, maybe, or a nightmare. Except that he could remember the taste of her sweetness, the feel of soft skin and firm flesh against his palm, her nipple between his fingertips.

Did he really ask her if she wanted a private anatomy lesson? He groaned and rolled over onto his stomach, his head over the side of the bed, and heaved into the bowl he'd brought with him to bed one more time.

• • •

"Doesn't Abby look lovely?" Abby heard Emily whispering to Ansel as they took their places behind her in the second row of the grange hall and waited for Sunday services to begin.

She kept her head back as they got settled, pretending to adjust her shawl as she eavesdropped. "Pru told me she was out with Frank Walker until well past dark," Ansel said loudly enough for her to hear easily. "And very quiet when she came in."

Abby turned in her seat and smiled tentatively at him and at Emily and the baby, but her eyes were really searching for Seth. Ansel looked around, too, no doubt looking for Frank Walker. Abby didn't see him either, and they exchanged shrugs before she turned back and smiled at her father as he stood up in the pulpit.

"Well, she's not interested in Frank," Emily whispered as Abby's father nodded at several latecomers and waited for them to get settled.

"What do you call dinner and a buggy ride all in the same week?" Ansel asked her.

"A poor substitute," she answered loudly enough for Abby to be sure that Emily wanted her to hear. "I just pray she isn't desperate enough to marry him."

"He could make her a fine husband," Ansel said in Frank's defense, while Abby prayed her father would get started with the day's service. "And she'd never want for anything."

"Anything that can be bought or sold in the mercantile, anyway," Emily agreed, as if that were a terrible thing, as if Abby were even considering that anyway.

"She could make him a good wife," Ansel said, and

Abby sat all the straighter for her brother's defense. "She'd be an asset to the store, and—"

"Welcome to the fourth from last service we will hold in this building," her father finally said, raising his hands to his congregation. "Of course, not counting our Wednesday night services, since not all of you attend them. And then of course there's Maundy Thursday coming up, and Good Friday the next day, which too many of you also skip, and well, anyways, Mr. Youtt has purchased a money order for the plans for the new church, which are being mailed to us. Isn't that right, Mr. Youtt?"

Mr. Youtt stood and agreed that a money order had been cut for pre-drawn plans and sent to Peabody and Sterns in St. Louis.

"And Mr. Waitte has offered to go to Des Moines for any wood we need, and I expect that we'll be raising the rafters and frame in less than two weeks or even before that time. Right, Walt?"

"If I don't have what we need, I'll get it," Walter Waitte agreed.

"The steeple will be built from California redwoods, which reach as close to heaven as a tree can go, and the bell is going to be cast in Philadelphia and shipped here by rail. Then Frank Walker's going to arrange to get it here, right, Frank?"

There was silence in the grange hall, as heads turned this way and that, looking for Frank Walker. Most heads turned. But not Abby's.

"Frank's sleeping in this morning," Frank Walker, Sr., said, after rising and clearing his throat. "He wasn't feeling too good."

Abby sank a bit in her seat and put her hand to her head.

"Nothing serious, I hope," the reverend asked.

"McGinty's influenza," the elder Mr. Walker said with a grimace on his face.

"Maybe the doc's with him," someone said. "Don't see him here, neither."

Abby slid farther down in her seat.

"Well, he was with him last night in McGinty's," someone else hollered. "They just mighta given each other that flu!"

"Something else to pray for, then," Abby's father said. "Let us bow our heads and pray that McGinty's closes early on Saturdays so that we can have a full congregation on Sundays."

Abby joined the other women in loud prayer. The men had apparently elected for the silent variety, if they were praying at all.

When the service was finally over, Abby stood and took a deep breath before facing the congregation. There was always the chance that Seth had come in late. Turning around, she saw that she had clearly wasted a *Please God!* on Seth's being there, but it didn't stop her from casting a second silent prayer that he be waiting for her outside the grange hall in his buggy.

"Morning, Miss Abby," Emmet Sommers said, tipping his hat to her politely, the way Seth never did. Seth never treated her like a lady. In fact, last night Seth had treated her like the hussy she was. And there was no sign of him this morning.

"Morning, Emmet," Abby said, but Emmet had already moved on and was helping Abby's sister Patience into her spring cloak and offering to see her home. Her nephew Michael was climbing Abby's leg, and she lifted him up into her arms, hugging him so tightly that he pushed at her chest and complained.

"I'm sorry," she said, sitting back down in the chair with Michael on her lap. "I guess I needed a squeeze more than you did, huh?"

"Grandpa says we can love you again," Michael told her. Then he pushed the hair away from her ear and whispered so close to her that it was hard to understand, "Don't tell him, but I never stopped, Aunt Abby."

Again she hugged him, this time not so tightly that he would object. "Grandpa was mad at me, but he never stopped loving me."

"How did you know, Aunt Abby?" Michael asked her.

"How do you know that when you turn on the faucet in the bathroom, water is going to come out of the spout? It isn't there until you turn it on, but you know it's just waiting, don't you?"

"Why didn't you just turn it on?" he asked her. "Didn't you want to get loved?"

"Yes, I surely did," she answered him, ruffling his sandy hair. He looked a lot like her brother-in-law, Boone, and Abby couldn't help but wonder if someday he'd break a woman's heart just the way Boone had done when he'd run off and left Pru and the children. "But with love, it takes two to turn the faucets on," she said, floundering with her explanation as she looked around for Seth.

"Otherwise someone might get burned," Michael said wisely.

"Exactly," she told Michael. Despite the words of encouragement she'd repeated to herself over and over again in the night, there was no sign of a loving, sober Seth Hendon. "You're a very wise little boy."

And then Gwendolyn took one of her hands and Michael took the other and they pulled her out of her chair and led her down the aisle to the back of the grange hall.

Outside there were plenty of buggies and the day was glorious.

But Seth wasn't there, and it was raining in her heart.

Chapter Eleven

ON MONDAY MORNING SETH STOOD IN Walker's Mercantile with two oranges, a box of candy, some pink writing paper with little flowers down the edge, and two leeks. He dropped one of the oranges and it rolled several feet, coming to rest by Frank Walker's big toe.

"Need some help there, Dr. Hendon?" Frank asked. He seemed to have recovered more fully than Seth had, but then, at twenty-two, the body was more resilient. That was why the Lord made man wiser as he got older, to compensate for the body's shortcomings. Of course, it hadn't helped in Seth's case—he might have been wise enough to know that Saturday's drinking would lead to Sunday's puking, but it hadn't stopped him.

"You have any fresh flowers?" Seth asked, handing what he could to Frank and lifting up a bottle of perfume to take a whiff.

"You doing some courting, Doc?" Frank asked, pulling a bunch of half-dead tulips out of a tall tin can and rolling them in paper.

"Think I'm too old for that sort of thing?" Seth asked. Frank probably thought anyone over thirty had one foot in the grave. Still wet behind the ears, he'd probably lose his breakfast if he knew that his mother had come to see Seth yesterday afraid she was carrying again. No doubt he thought his mother and father had ceased to carry on as soon as his younger sister was conceived.

"Not at all," Frank said politely. "I'm sure the widow Draper will appreciate—"

"Helen Draper? What's Helen—" and then he realized what Frank meant. "I'm not seeing Mrs. Draper," he said softly. It had been months since he'd seen Helen. At least in that way. She'd come to see him with a cough in February and he'd prescribed a tonic for her. In March she'd had a splinter in her foot he'd had to remove. She'd offered to make him a home-cooked meal and he'd put her off.

"Really? She must be disappointed about that. Who's the lucky lady?" Frank asked, as if it were any of his business.

"These things look like they're for an *old* lady?" he asked, pointing at the array of things he'd collected as they lay on the counter. Helen Draper would like all of them. "Maybe you've a point there. You happen to have a prospector's pick?" he asked. "And a small shovel?"

Frank's eyes widened.

"And that two-seater you've got in the window—that tandem bicycle? I'll take that, too."

Frank's jaw dropped.

"Problem?" he asked the shopkeeper.

"Oh, no, sir!" Frank responded. "I've got the shovel out front and the pick down in the storage cellar," he said, his voice trailing behind him as he raced hither and yon collecting everything that Seth wanted.

And then Seth spotted it. He grabbed the flowers in one hand and the little bauble in the other and hurried past Frank on his way out.

"Charge this, too," he said, showing him the trinket as he nearly raced down the steps. "And send everything over to my office when you've got it all together. Put the food in the kitchen, would you? If you don't mind?"

Seth was out of breath when he barged into the *Herald*'s office shouting Abby's name as if he'd just discovered a cure for some rare and awful disease.

She was resting in the back room when she heard him call.

"She here, Ansel?" she heard him ask. "Abby? You here?"

Ansel must have gestured toward the back room because suddenly he was there, crouching beside her, holding out to her a glass ball with the world afloat in it. He shook it in front of her face. Inside the sphere, the globe spun slowly and little flakes of snow danced around it.

"The world upside down," he said, handing the globe to her. "Just the way you see it."

"Do you never get tired of making fun of me?" she asked.

"I'm not making fun of you," he said, putting a bouquet on the desk in front of her. "I'm showing you that I see what you see—the world the way you want me to see it."

She fingered the dying tulips.

"And I wanted to say I'm sorry about yesterday. I had a medical emergency."

She looked up at him, wanting to believe that was what had kept him away.

"My patient spent the day heaving," he said. "By the time the idiot could sit and hold his head up it was after three. By the time he ran to the grange hall everyone was gone."

"Why did he run to the grange hall?"

"There was someone very important he wanted to meet. Someone he didn't want to disappoint, ever again."

"I see," she said, a flicker of hope licking at her heart. "And he didn't know where this person lived?"

"Worse! The fool was too chicken to go there! You see, he'd have to apologize for missing their appointment, and for missing church, as well, and the reverend—did I mention the reverend was her father? Well, the reverend isn't too partial to this patient, and the patient didn't think he'd get the chance to apologize correctly, the way she—did I mention this was the woman of his dreams? Well, he thought she deserved better than the possibility of having her boots decorated with the remnants of his stomach."

"The woman of his dreams?" she asked, her toes curling, her insides jumping. "Has this fool of a patient ever told her that?"

"Didn't I tell you he was a fool?"

"Hey, Doc," Ansel said, coming to stand in the doorway. There's someone leaving a note on your office door."

"Let 'im," Seth said, but Abby shook her head.

"Better go see who needs you," she said softly.

"Will you come at lunchtime?" he asked, taking her hand in his, his blue eyes pleading with her to say yes. "So I can tell you all about how this fool patient expects to make it up to this girl? And maybe you can advise me about what to tell him. What it would take for a girl like, say you, for example, to forgive the idiot?"

"I think it's Mr. Denton," Ansel came back to the doorway to announce.

"Go," she told him.

"Will you come at lunchtime?" he asked again, rising to his full height. "And dinner, too? He has a lot to apologize for."

She smiled and he hurried past Ansel. She heard the bell over the door jingle as he left.

So it was true what they said about love . . . you did hear bells!

Life was beautiful, Seth thought as he got ready for Abby to show up. In the kitchen, where he and Abby and Sarrie had often shared meals when Sarrie was up to it, he set a fancy table, complete with a freshly laundered cloth he borrowed from his examining room.

Meticulously he arranged the plates so that every stain was hidden, a slight tear was under his water glass. He would have to remember to drink in only

Abby's beauty so she wouldn't know he hadn't had a tablecloth cleaned since Sarrie had passed away.

He almost set the table for three, he felt so strongly as if Sarrie was a part of his relationship with Abby. Memories flooded back of two giggling girls, of furtive glances, of whispers as he'd pass Sarrie's room in just his pajama bottoms. He remembered once just before Sarrie had taken to her bed for the last time, putting his arms around both of them, and the strange feeling that coursed through him at the feel of Abby's body pressed against his side.

"Seth?" he heard her voice out in the office, heard the fear in it that he had let her down again.

"Out in the kitchen," he called quickly. He looked around. Things looked nice, welcoming. It was a good place to say he was sorry. A good place to start anew.

She stood in the doorway as if she were afraid to step over the threshold.

"Remember when you and Sarrie used to bake me cookies and you'd drag me back here between patients to eat them?" he asked.

"You were very good about that," Abby admitted. "Even if you hated it, you never let Sarrie and me know."

"I never hated it. Tea with you two was the highlight of my week," he admitted. "I never told you two that, did I?"

"The highlight of your week! Oh, yes, I'm sure! We knew you had better things to do than sit sipping tea with us and—"

"I wish we'd done it every day," he said, meaning every word.

Abby looked sad and he wanted to kick himself in the ass. One more thing to add to his list of resolutions—never make Abby sad again.

"Do you still bake cookies? Or are you too busy at the paper?" he asked.

"Often I bake them on Sundays with Pru's children, and sometimes with Suellen, too," she said. "Lately we've been experimenting with baking crosses to give out on Easter. Well, not exactly give out. Jed is planning on throwing them down from his flying machine when he clears the church."

"Abby," he said, trying to warn her that the likelihood of Jed's flying over the church was as great as his ever attempting brain surgery in Eden's Grove.

"I know, but crosses are as good to eat as any other shaped cookies," she said. "And when they throw them out the window at me to see if they'll do damage when dropped from a distance, at least they won't hurt!"

"Well, next week do you think you might bake an extra batch for me and bring them on Monday for tea? I mean if you can take the time from the *Herald*?" he asked. He wanted her to know that he took her work seriously. He didn't expect her to just drop everything to be with him, no matter how much he'd like to hear her say that.

"I baked several extra batches yesterday," she said pointedly.

"I am really sorry about yesterday, Abby girl. But it was all your fault."

"Mine?" He loved it when she lifted her eyebrow as if she were asking whether he really expected her to believe what he was saying.

"You were the reason I got drunk in the first place, running around the county with Frank Walker until all hours of the night. . . ."

She said nothing, just stood there looking so lovely he could hardly breathe.

"And about that night," he said, dancing his way around an apology, "I think I said some things that were highly inappropriate."

Hard as it was to believe, she was even lovelier when she blushed.

"I did then, huh? I was hoping it had all been some sort of hallucination. Not the kiss, mind you, but . . ."

She fiddled nervously with the button at her neck.

"I really had no right," he said, "being drunk and all. And the truth of it is, watching your hand playing with that button of yours, stone cold sober, I'm having trouble not doing it again."

"Maybe we should eat lunch," she said, a bit of a titter in her voice.

He smiled, watching its effect on her and loving every moment of it. "What did you bring?"

She looked at him blankly.

"For lunch?" he reminded her.

"Me? You invited me to lunch, remember?"

Talk about a lovesick fool. He'd set the table, he'd put the out-to-lunch sign on his door. What had he supposed they'd feast on—other than each other? He thought about what he had in his ice box—a pitcher of milk, a half dozen eggs, and a little leftover ham that Mrs. Youtt had brought by. She was still trying to thank him for taking care of Johnny. And he thought she was feeling a little guilty about the vote.

"Wait!" he said. He picked through the carton that Frank had left in the corner. "Aha! Oranges, *ma chérie*. And chocolates for dessert. And a leek for the main course?" he asked jokingly, holding one up.

Abby took off her coat and rolled up her sleeves. "Fine luncheon you've invited me to, Dr. Hendon," she said as she found an apron in the bottom drawer and tied it about her tiny waist. "Inviting me to make my own meal."

He leaned against the counter and watched her rifle through his cabinets, his ice box, his larder. She murmured about omelettes and soufflés and quiche Lorraine. Pans and bowls and wire things he had no idea what to do with materialized on his counter. And a slow, self-satisfied smile crossed his lips. This was a glimpse of the future, and it was his.

She had the oven heating and was examining the knives in his block when he came up behind her. Reaching around her, he slid the meat knife from its holder and handed it to her. "You know you really have to be careful with knives," he said, her hair tickling his nose. "Maybe I better show you how it's done."

He reached around her, an arm on either side, his chin nearly resting on the top of her head. He put his hand over hers on the knife handle. "Like this," he said, drawing the knife blade down the length of the ham.

He shifted his body and turned the ham to begin dicing it. He hoped that was what she wanted to do with it, because he wasn't letting her go until it was in tiny pieces. With every stroke his inner arm brushed against her breast, and he hoped and prayed that the stupid bustle that was pressing against his groin hid from her the extent to which he was enjoying his cooking lesson.

"I need to cut the leeks," she said, but as she turned to get them, he trapped her in his embrace.

"Isn't cooking together fun?" he asked her.

She looked at him as if he'd lost his mind. Her breathing was rapid, her chest rising and falling against his own.

"I always knew you liked to cook, but now I see why," he said, taking the knife out of her hand and then lacing his fingers through hers.

"We cooked together once before," Abby said, and he tried to remember when. It came to him sadly. It was the day before Sarrie died and they'd been frantically trying to make her some pudding, anything she might find easy to swallow.

"You were very good to Sarrie and to me," he said, pressing against her until he knew he had her trapped against the counter. "I wish I had been better to you. But then I have the rest of my life to try, right?" he asked happily.

He could see she was suspicious.

"I mean it. I'm going to make it up to you. I'm going to devote myself to making you happy. I'm going to kiss . . . those . . . incredibly . . . soft . . ."

And then he was kissing her, and stone cold sober was better than any drunken kiss could ever have been. His senses reeled, his knees buckled. Like a starving man he lifted her and carried her to the table, pushing aside glasses and plates, not caring what fell to the floor or what broke, and set her down right on the table to feast his eyes upon.

His eyes were not enough, so he leaned over her and kissed her lips and fought with her shirtwaist until it gave in to his desires, and he opened it so that he could see the beauty that Abby had become. And once again, looking wasn't enough so he bent to kiss her breasts, and touch, and taste, and wonder if he could ever get enough of her.

If the button of his cuff hadn't gotten caught in her hair, he wasn't sure he'd have ever looked up and seen the fear in her eyes, mixing with the pleasure he knew she felt. *Too fast* he told himself. *You're rushing her too fast.*

He righted himself and carefully closed her shirtwaist, grateful that in his rush he hadn't ripped it. When he had her covered, he eased her back on her feet and mumbled how sorry he was, how she did things to him, how being around her he got carried away.

"The leek," he said, producing it and handing it over to her so that her hand came around it. Idiotically, he couldn't seem to let it go—whether it was the sight of her hand wrapped around its stalk, or the knowledge that she was going to chop its shaft to little pieces, he continued to hold it. And she moved her hand up on it, circling it, completely innocent and unaware of the implications of his standing there in the kitchen with her, moving the leek back and forth, up and down, within the confines of her grasp.

"I better get some more firewood," he said, hurrying to the door and opening it for a gulp of cool spring air.

"There's plenty here beside the stove," she called out to him, but he was halfway across the yard, walking oddly and praying for relief.

Later, when they were finished with lunch and she was washing the dishes, Seth came up behind her again. It was dangerous to turn her back on him, and she was obviously one of those women who enjoyed living dangerously.

"Left hand or right hand?" he asked.

"What?"

"Would you rather have what's in my left or my right hand?" he asked, obviously hiding something behind his back.

"Which one is better?" she asked.

"Left hand," he said, but before he could pull it out she demanded what was in his right. "Why the right?" he asked.

"I know you'll give me both and I want to save the best for last," she said, trying to peek around his back.

"My article, then," he said, handing it over to her.

" 'Pains of the Chest Region,' " she read.

"I was careful to mention that racing hearts can be caused by factors other than disease," he said, pointing to a paragraph near the end. "Like seeing someone half a block away, I think it was. . . ."

"You did not put that in there, did you?" she asked, searching the paragraph he'd pointed to.

In many instances, emotions can affect a body's physical reaction. Just as embarrassment can

*cause blood to rush to the head and cause a
person to blush, fear, anger, and sadness can all
cause tremors within the chest cavity. It has
been reported by some that pleasant emotions
such as excitement, joy, and affection can also
cause the heart to feel as if it is racing, and
indeed it does temporarily affect the speed of
the heart.*

"I left out the part about holding my hand over your bosom to check the effect," he said with a wink.

"You could have left it in," she said with a shrug.

"And scandalized all your readers?" he asked, pretending to be shocked.

"Of course," she said, knowing full well she would be the one to set the type and would have edited it out anyway.

"I'll remember that next week when I do headaches. I'll be sure to explain that when you're sick with love you can give yourself a doozy of a headache with too much scotch and beer."

At least, that was what she thought he said. It was hard to concentrate past "sick with love."

"Don't you want to know what's in the other hand?" he asked and she tried to care, when the truth was that he had already given her, with just a few words, more than she had even dared to hope for.

He held out a pretty flowered box and lifted the lid for her. Inside was lovely pink stationery.

"For writing to Armand," he said. Before her heart could sink too far, he added, "to say good-bye."

" 'Dear Winnie' says that it's easy for a man to become too sure of himself, and that the minute he does—"

"I hear that she's an old spinster who's never even been kissed," he said. "You want to take her advice, or mine?" He held the box out to her and waited patiently for her to take it.

"About Armand," she started, but he put a finger over her lips and she had all she could do not to kiss it.

"I know," he said softly. "You mean a lot to him. It's not surprising. So let him down easy, Abby girl. Just so that you let him down."

"Doc? You here? I got that bicycle out of the window, and the pick you wanted from the cellar!"

"I'm back here," Seth called out to Frank while Abby looked frantically for a place to hide. Just a couple of days ago she was kissing Frank. Now here she was in Seth's kitchen, her shirtwaist only half tucked in, her lips no doubt red from kissing.

She opened the back door and took a quick step out onto the porch and then a second one.

And then somehow she was on the ground, her elbow smarting, and before she could get up, there were Seth and Frank, both staring down at her, concern etched on both their faces.

"Jesus, Miss Abby!" Frank said. "Are you all right?"

She arched her back and felt a few other places hurt. She started to get up, cradling her elbow, but before she could even come to a full sitting position, Seth was crouching down beside her, feeling her arms, her legs, examining the scraped palms of her hands. "Anything hurt especially? Besides your elbow? That's probably just your ulnar nerve."

"Her ulnar nerve?" Frank asked, leaning over her as though he too had some proprietary interest.

"Her funny bone," Seth said with obvious superiority before turning his attention back to her. "What happened?"

"I don't know," she said, pressing the heel of her hand against her head to stop the pain there. "I just didn't see the steps, I guess."

"You didn't have your glasses on." Seth shook his head at her and grimaced. "How many times do I have to tell you about those damn glasses? You could have broken something."

He went on yelling at her while she looked around. The truth was, unless she turned her head, she couldn't see him squatting next to her. Unless she tilted her head, she couldn't see Frank standing above her. She stared at her fingers and moved her hand closer to her body until the fingers disappeared well before they touched her chest.

"Stop yelling at her," Frank demanded. "Can't you see you're upsetting her?" A handkerchief appeared in front of her. She tipped her head way back and saw that it was Frank holding it out to her. Everyone has to tip their head to see above them, she told herself. God put man's head on a neck so that he could turn it side to side and raise it up and down.

She touched her temple, but couldn't see her hand.

"And you've got a headache, again, don't you? If I prescribed medicine, you'd take it, right? So why, when an eye specialist prescribes glasses, don't you wear them? Does that ridiculous 'Dear Winnie' advise against ladies wearing spectacles?"

"Frank's right. You're yelling at me," Abby said, fishing around in her pocket for her glasses and pulling out their brown leather case. She snapped it open in silence.

"I'm sorry," he said finally when her glasses were on her nose. Again she tested her vision. There was nothing beyond the rims of her glasses, unlike when she'd first gotten them and she could see their edges clearly and what lay beyond was much less clear.

"You should be," Frank said, gingerly helping Abby up by her good elbow.

"You better come inside and let me clean your hands," Seth said. He looked two shades paler than he had while preparing lunch.

"I'm all right, Dr. Hendon," she said softly, trying to take the terror from his eyes. He had that same look he'd get whenever Sarrie took a turn for the worse. *He's angry that he can't stop the clock,* Sarrie would tell her. *He's angry that he can't change the results. He's angry that he can't kiss my forehead and make me all better. But he's not angry with me.*

How can you tell? she'd asked Sarrie.

His eyebrows, his eyes, the set of his mouth.

Now she knew.

He loved her.

Chapter Twelve

⟶ ⟵

S ETH MADE HIS DAILY TREK TO THE POST OFFICE
just after three. On his way, he walked past the
site of the new church and saw another fresh
load of supplies lying in wait for Saturday, when the
plans would arrive and the building would start in ear-
nest. Two men were covering the bundles with tarps,
and when he looked up, he saw the sky had darkened
with heavy clouds.

Over the last few days, several farmers had cleared
all the debris from the building site, evened it out,
made it ready for the framing to start. It had taken him
a while to realize it, but it wasn't Joseph Panner's
money that had really gotten the church going. It was
the fervent wishes of the townsfolk. His father used to
tell him, when he was a small boy, that if he wanted
something badly enough, if he wanted it long enough
and hard enough, he could make it come to pass.

A part of him had believed it long after his father
was gone, when he'd sat beside Sarrie's bed, grateful
that she'd been given another day, and he'd wished and

wanted and prayed with all his might that she would be spared.

He decided to make a short detour and turned toward where the old church had stood, the cemetery on the rise behind its ashes. It was past time to visit Sarrie, and today he felt he could do it.

"Oh, Sarrie! You should have seen the look on Abby's face when she saw that pick and shovel," he told his sister, standing over her grave with a half smile on his face. "And the tandem bicycle. Well, I don't know what I thought when I saw it, except that it seemed youthful and fun and all the things that Abby is, and so I bought it.

"I took it out back and tried to ride the crazy contraption for the better part of an hour." He raised his pant leg and looked at the ugly black-and-blue mark on his shin. "Seems I have a lot to learn about being young that I missed the first time around.

"You were right about Abby, Sarrie. She is life itself. I only hope . . ." He wanted to say that he hoped he wouldn't destroy that, but the words wouldn't pass his lips. Some things were better left unsaid, he supposed, and he took a pebble from the ground and put it on the lower edge of Sarrie's headstone to show that someone had been there, someone had cared.

And then he headed for the post office. He'd heard precious little in the way of interest from the doctors he'd written to, and he wondered if he had been just a little too honest in his portrayal of Eden's Grove, and a little too stringent about the requirements for the doctor to whom he would entrust the care of all the people who depended upon him. So many babies he'd brought into the world, so many bones he'd set, gashes he'd sewn—he had such a stake in so many people's lives that it would be hard to turn his back on them without being sure that they were in the best of hands, hands better than his own.

Seth had barely crossed the threshold of the post office when Mr. Norman, leafing through the stack on his counter, looked up at him, and said, "Got a letter for you from Massachusetts General Hospital. You giving those guys over there more of your good advice?"

"Gotta keep reminding them to take out all the sponges before they sew those patients closed," Seth told him.

"I like that new column of yours in the *Herald*," Mr. Norman said, continuing to go through the stack. "Bicarb did the trick for me after Sunday dinner, just like you said. Good idea, that one."

"Actually, it was Abidance Merganser's idea," he said, giving credit where it was due, and liking the sound of Abby's name on his lips.

"Missy Smiles did that? Well, so she's got a brain in that pretty head, does she?" He pulled out two letters and set them aside. "Doesn't surprise me at all."

" 'Missy Smiles'?"

"Watch anyone as that girl passes, Doc," Mr. Norman said with a wink. "Young, old, even the crotchety ones. You'd need a pretty big basket to hold all the smiles that girl gets in return for one of hers."

Seth nodded, but said nothing. It would be damn hard sharing Abby with the whole town, once she was his. Of course, that was if they stayed in Eden's Grove.

He looked down at the envelope in his hand and wondered what he hoped it contained.

"Mind taking these in to the *Herald*, it being right next door? Save Miss Abidance the trip over later," Mr. Norman asked, holding out two letters to Seth. "She'll be happy to get that one from St. Louis, I'll betcha. 'Course she's always happy, that girl."

Seth took the letters and shoved them into his coat pocket.

"Something wrong, Doc?" the postmaster asked.

"Nothing at all," Seth said, noticing that the clouds had let loose and heavy drops were beginning to pelt the window. He put up his collar and opened the door to a rain-soaked gust. "Great day," he grumbled, not happy at all to be carrying a letter from A. Whitiny in St. Louis to the woman they both loved. "Just an all-around great day."

Inside the offices of *The Weekly Herald*, with the rain running down the windows and trying to put a damper on her mood, Abby was hunched over the type cases looking for the fancy letters they stocked for advertisements. If she were to order some fine paper, like the salesman had left samples of, they could print all sorts of elegant things they'd never considered printing before. All right, maybe she hadn't mentioned to Ansel that she had wedding invitations in mind, maybe she'd just said that she wanted to try making a gift of personalized notes for Anna Lisa and Armand. . . .

She had pulled out most of the letters that she needed to print the newlyweds' names when the little bell over the door rang and she saw Seth standing in the open door looking like a drowned rat.

"Oh, my heavens!" she said, her hands flying to her cheeks. "What a mess you are!"

"I got your mail," he said testily. He fished in his pocket and pulled out several soggy envelopes.

"Take off your coat. Come by the stove and dry out," she said, wiping her hands on her apron and pulling off her glasses.

"Abidance," he said, drawing out her name until she reluctantly put the glasses back on.

"Happy now?" she asked him.

"Should I be?" he asked, tossing a letter onto the counter.

She looked down at the dripping ink and recognized the sender. The name matched the one she had nearly finished spelling out on her worktable in plain sight, with "Mr. and Mrs." preceding it. Awkwardly she leaned an arm over her writing and the type that corresponded to it, fumbled with her apron strings and managed to casually throw the apron over her work, forgetting about the letter entirely.

"Aren't you going to read it?" he asked.

"Sure I will," she agreed. "Later. Right now I want to hear about you. How was your day?"

"Don't you want to see how your beau took the news?" It seemed more a dare than a question.

"I'd rather read it when I'm alone," she said, afraid he'd insist that she read it aloud, or worse, look over her shoulder. She could just imagine what it said. *For heaven's sake, Abidance! Go see a doctor about those headaches. And tell that Seth Hendon he's a fool if he doesn't scoop you up before Frank Walker turns your head.*

"As you wish," he said, but he was oh so clearly annoyed. He tossed two more envelopes onto the counter. "There's something for Ansel, too. Where is he?"

"Long gone," she said. "It's late. I should be getting on home myself."

She looked at the envelopes on the table and her breath caught in her throat. She picked up one of them and handed it to Seth. "It's from Massachusetts General Hospital."

He nodded and took it from her, stuffing it back into his pocket.

"Aren't you going to read it?" she asked. He'd been hoping for weeks to hear from the doctor there, and now the man's answer sat drowning in his pocket.

"Sure I will," he said. "Later. Now I'd like to hear about your day."

For a second she didn't get it. Then she realized he was merely parroting her words. He could tease the nap off wool, if he had a mind to. But she'd be darned if she'd play the game by his rules. "Well, I had a very nice day, actually. Things here have been very quiet and Ansel left early and I was just playing with some of our fancy lettering and daydreaming."

"That's nice," he said, but his fingers were playing with the edge of his pocket. "Massachusetts General Hospital. Hmmm."

"Go ahead and read it, Seth," she said. "No reason to be stubborn on my account."

"I'll just take it back to my office," he said, eyeing

her counter and moving her apron just a tad so that "Mr. and Mrs." was now in full view.

"Why don't you do that?" she said, leaning against the table so that he couldn't move the apron another inch. "I'll clean up here and stop by to say good night before I head for home."

"Don't go walking in this rain," he said, touching the tip of her nose. "I'll take you home in the buggy."

"I love buggies in the rain," she admitted, licking her lips seductively—she hoped—before remembering how he'd told her she ought to use pomade.

"Then I'll have to take the long way," he said, apparently in no hurry to get going. "So Ansel's not here, huh?"

She shook her head.

"How are those hands of yours? Those scrapes healing all right?"

"They're fine," she said, holding them out to him. In an instant the apron was gone from the counter and he was staring at "Mr. and Mrs. Armand Whiting" as type flew around them.

"That's quite a daydream you were having," he said.

"It's not what you think," she said weakly. "It was never the way I said it was. I mean—"

"Tell me this, and tell me the God's honest truth. Did you tell him that it's over between the two of you?"

"No. But that's because there never really was anything between us."

Seth raised one eyebrow the way he always did when she tried to tell him anything. "Does the man still think that you're going to marry him, Abidance?"

"No. I swear on my nieces and nephews and the family cat. Armand never even asked me to marry him, Seth."

"And this?" he asked, gesturing to the words on the paper-covered counter.

"Nothing," she said. "It has nothing to do with me, with us."

"What if," Seth asked, tapping the envelope with his finger, "in this letter, this Armand fellow asks you to marry him? What will you say then?"

"I know what I'd like to say, Seth."

"And what's that, Abby girl?" He was kissing her hand now, kissing her third finger where it met her hand, where a ring should go. Funny how one minute she could be Abidance and the next she was Abby girl, and all because she was throwing over a beau who didn't even exist.

"I'd like to tell him he's too late." There, she'd said it. Brazen hussy that she was, she'd all but asked Seth to marry her.

"He is," Seth said, reaching over for the brayer and rubbing out Armand's name with residue ink before coming around the counter and opening the door to the back room and motioning her to follow him.

Well, a brazen hussy once, it was hard to draw the line now. Especially when all she wanted was to be in Seth's arms anyway. And so she followed him into the back office, let him shut the door, let him take off his soggy coat with their future sitting in his pocket, let him take her face in his hands and kiss her cheeks and her nose and her chin and throat before coming back to settle on her lips.

"Is that how Armand kissed you?" he demanded.

"Never," she said, tipping back her head so that he could fumble with the top button on her shirtwaist. "He was a gentleman."

"And I'm not?" Seth asked, so hungry for her that he had backed her against the wall and pressed himself against her while he continued to work at her blouse.

"No," she admitted softly, loving the difference between all she'd ever imagined and what was the truth of it all. "You're simply a man."

"A man in love," he said, kissing her collarbone as he worked her shirt over her shoulder.

"Do you love me?" she asked, pushing him away slightly just to hear the answer, not to lose it in the passion, but to let the moment stand by itself.

He seemed to understand her need, and he stepped back, caught his breath, ran his fingers through his hair to straighten it. "I keep pawing at you in back rooms and compromising you in one way or another when I should be honoring you. When I don't see you, I have all these high ideas—things I'll say to you, things I'll do, like presenting you with a rose and kissing the back of your hand and asking if you'll do me the honor of dining with me.

"And then I see you, and all I can think is how much I want to hold you in my arms and taste your sweet lips and—"

"The question was do you love me," she pressed, feeling his hands wander over her hips.

"Without doubt or reservation," he said, letting her go and standing with his arms at his side, waiting for her to welcome him back to where they both knew he belonged.

"Will you marry me, Seth?" she asked as she slid into his arms and fought the buttons on his shirt until she could touch his skin.

"Leave it to you to have no respect for the proprieties. I'm supposed to do the asking," Seth said.

"So ask," she ordered him, allowing him to slip her blouse down over her arms, toss it behind her somewhere, and untie the pink silk ribbon that held her camisole closed.

He pushed the camisole off her shoulders too, so that it hung limply around her elbows and she rose from it the way the pistil of a flower rises within the petals. It was cold in the room, and silent as she waited for him to say the words she needed to hear.

He unbuttoned her waistband and pushed her skirt to the floor. He muttered something about ridiculous bustles, untied it, and flung it only the Lord knew where. "My God, you're beautiful," he said, which, while it was nice to hear, was not what she was waiting for.

She crossed her arms, returned the camisole straps to her shoulders and rubbed at her upper arms, trying to keep away the cold, the fear. And when he sat in the big leather chair and pulled her onto his lap, she tried to pretend he'd said more than he had.

"I didn't want to love you," he said, shifting her so that she could feel a hardness beneath her that she could only guess about. "I didn't want to sully you with my misery, and now look at me. I should make you get dressed, take you for a fine dinner, escort you home safely. . . ."

She made a move to get up, but he caught her and held her closer against him.

"And then I should ask your father for your hand."

She closed her eyes and let out the breath she'd been holding.

"I want to do this right," he said, but his hands were everywhere, and she sighed and gasped and encouraged his explorations.

"Believe me, you are," she said, shocking herself as much as him, raising a chuckle between the deeper breaths.

There was a small cot in the corner of the room. Ansel said that there were times when his father-in-law, Morton Cotter, had been so dedicated that he spent the night at the office. Mostly the kittens slept there now, but she rose and led him over to it.

Seth followed her reluctantly, looking down at the pathetic little cot and feeling himself grimace. His Abby was so fine, and he wanted so to do right by her and not take her here, her first time, on this dingy little cot in this awful little room. While he stood there mutely, trying to tamp down his hunger for her, his need, she pulled a fancy quilt from the bottom drawer of the tall oak filing cabinet and spread it on the cot. Then from the top drawer she pulled two mining candles they obviously kept for emergencies and set them on the little table beside the cot.

"Is this an emergency?" he asked her, trying to take away the seriousness of what they were doing, trying to stop themselves before they went too far.

"I've been waiting my whole life for this night, Seth. For this moment. I don't want to wait any longer. I don't want to risk waiting."

"Risk waiting?"

"Nobody knows what tomorrow will bring. Love me now, Seth. Hurry, before I—"

"Change your mind?" he asked, his wanting nearly painful as he watched her make a bed for them to share, her back strong and almost bare, her shoulders glowing in the candlelight.

She shook her head at him. "I would make love to you, Seth, if I knew how. Please don't make me look foolish."

Dear God, what good had he ever done to deserve Abidance Merganser offering herself to him, body and soul, heart and hand?

"You could never look foolish," he said, going back to check the little office door and finding to his relief that there was a lock on it. He snapped it shut.

"I'm the fool," he said when he was back at her side, taking off his trousers and somehow wrapping both of them in the quilt on the tiny bed. "Lie on top of me," he told her, positioning her so that he could kiss her breasts, could reach her so that he could ready her for what was to come.

She moaned and arched and ground against his touch until he thought he might go mad, and still he prepared her, tried to prepare her, despite her tightness, her innocence.

"Please Seth," she begged him, clutching at his chest, tears choking her voice. "Please."

"You'll marry me?" he asked her, rolling her onto

her back and poising himself above her. "You'll be mine?"

"I've always been yours," she said softly, her hand tracing his arm, running up his neck, pulling him down toward her.

Beneath him, her body relaxed and she spread herself for him as if all was right in the world.

And he slipped inside her, carefully, slowly, as gently as he could. And she rocked against him, each movement deepening their hold on each other, deepening their commitment, deepening their love.

And when it was over, she lay still in his arms.

"I can die happy now," she said softly, and the world stopped in its tracks. His head shot up and he looked down at her knowing that he would fight the devil himself before he'd let her go.

"What?" he asked her, fear rising in his throat.

"Not that I expect to," she said, waving away his worry. "It's just that a woman is always afraid that she'll die without knowing the secret—she'll wind up an old maid who's never known passion."

"You? What about Frank Walker? What about Armand what's-his-name?"

And beneath him she laughed, a beatific smile on her face as she stretched and arched her back, two glorious breasts rising up to pique his desire yet again. "Who?"

And he kissed her quiet, and took her slowly, and this time there was no pain.

There was only joy.

Chapter Thirteen

⚜

*H*OLY *MOTHER OF GOD. WHAT HAD HE DONE?*
And could it have been as good as it seemed,
as right, even after he'd taken her home last
night? Afterward he'd come back and flung himself
into his chair in a haze of satisfaction, pulled the letter
from Dr. Bartlett from his coat pocket and stood ready
to face the fact that he would be stuck in Eden's Grove
forever. And it had been so wondrous that he didn't
care, as long as he would be with the woman he loved.

Well, for the moment he hadn't cared. It had been
wondrous. It had been sublime. Abby had felt so right
in his arms that he was amazed that he could have
waited so long to make her his own, and he wanted her
again. Now. Always.

Only now there was a tiny wrinkle in his plan. How
could he have known that Dr. Ephraim Bartlett would
agree to come take over his practice? No one in his
right mind would want to leave Massachusetts General,
leave Boston and the civilized, advanced East to come
to some two-bit town that, as Reverend Merganser

was quick to point out, didn't even have a goddamn church?

And not only did the fool want to come, he *was* coming! Stopping to visit family along the way, the good doctor would be in Eden's Grove in just over a fortnight.

Well, Abby had said she'd follow him anywhere, hadn't she? Would she really leave her family, her home, and go . . .

Go where? He had no plan. In a fortnight's time he'd have no job. A fine husband he'd make Abby, to whom he wanted to give the world.

He wondered if she was next door at the *Herald* yet, and was willing to bet that she wasn't. She'd have poked her head into his office first, he was sure. She'd have brought him some fresh-baked muffins and a warm smile. And no matter how uncertain the future was, as long as she was in it, it'd be just fine, he was sure.

He heard the footsteps on the sidewalk, but he knew they weren't hers, and he knew they weren't bringing good news, so when James Denton opened his door, he had more to worry about than how he would support Abidance.

"Jim?" he asked. "There been some change?" He couldn't bear to ask if the baby was dead, didn't figure Jim would come to him but to Mr. Liming, the undertaker, if the news was that bad.

"He won't take nothing, Doc," the man said, the stoic facade that he'd kept for Seth crumbling there in his office, falling away and leaving a broken man standing with his arms stretched out toward Seth for help.

"I'll get my bag," was all he could say. *I'll come and look, and I'll see to Caroline. And then I'll tell you both to pray for a miracle, and I'll come back here and I'll pray, too.*

"Appreciate it, Doc," Jim said, as if he were doing the Dentons any sort of favor at all. "I know you got others to see, and . . ."

"I'll follow you in my buggy," he said, grabbing his hat and bag and hurrying Jim out of the office, glancing through the windows of the *Herald* and wishing he could see a sign of Abby to keep him going.

He had lost so much in this life—his whole family— and his faith. And one little slip of a girl had the power to give him back all of it—a family, with a bunch of kids who would climb his legs and sit on his shoulders and who he could tuck in at night; and the belief that with her in his life everything would somehow be all right.

He followed Jim Denton out to his farm, wishing he could make it all right for the Dentons, and for everyone else in Eden's Grove, knowing he couldn't, and praying that maybe Dr. Bartlett could.

"So how are you feeling?" Abby asked Emily after she'd taken off her coat and made herself comfortable—as comfortable as she could be on the settee in Emily's parlor.

"Excited," Emily admitted, her face a little flushed. "A new baby is always exciting, don't you think? I mean, inside me right now might be the next president of the United States!"

"Or at least the next editor of the *Herald*," Abby said, working on a smile.

"Are you all right?" Emily asked, her eyebrows lowering in concern. "You're looking like I was feeling when I woke up—like I feel every morning these days."

Oh, dear God! She'd wanted an answer and now she had it.

Emily put her hand over Abby's. "Are you feeling all right?"

"How soon after . . ." How did one ask a question like this? She should have asked her mother. Or Prudence. Prudence would know. But Pru and her mother would be horrified, and Abby was not about to risk her father's finding out. She fiddled with her skirt, balling it up until Emily stilled her hand.

"Abby, honey, whatever is wrong?"

Abby took a deep breath. "How soon after you and Ansel . . . made your baby," she said with her eyes closed because she just couldn't look at Emily and ask, ". . . did you start losing your breakfast?"

Emily was really quiet. So quiet that Abby could hear the clock ticking on the mantel, counting off the seconds.

"Well," Emily finally said slowly. "I can't really say for sure. It's hard to know exactly when the baby began, if you know what I mean, which I'm guessing you don't. Contrary to what your mama probably told you, every time you let your husband have his way, doesn't mean you wind up with a baby, you know."

"I know that," Abby said, trying not to sound testy.

"But how soon . . ." She covered her mouth as the nausea rose again as it had in the morning.

"Abby! You don't think you're . . . honey, you know you have to do more than just kiss a man to—"

"Emily, I've been sheltered, not cloistered!"

"Are you saying that Frank . . ." Emily asked.

"No! Of course not! I'm simply asking how you know if you're pregnant," Abby finally managed to say.

"Well, whoever it is that thinks she's pregnant ought to go see Dr. Hendon and—"

"How hard is it for you to tell me how soon you started heaving up your eggs, Emily? Is this some secret that women aren't supposed to share? I need to know if I could be with child. And I need you to tell me."

Emily got up and drew the drapes closed. She shut the parlor doors and put a chair in front of them before she came back to sit beside Abby on the settee.

"Abidance, listen to me. For a woman to become pregnant she has to be intimate with a man. Not just kiss, not just touch. They have to lie naked together and he has to—"

"I know what he has to do, Emily. I know what it feels like and I know I'll be doing it again, but I didn't think that I could get into trouble on the first time."

"Don't cry, honey," Emily said, wiping tears from Abby's cheeks, tears that Abby hadn't even felt. "You haven't done it again, not since the first time?"

Not since the first time? It had only been twelve hours or so, and she had had to go on home.

"How long ago was that? Have you missed your

monthly yet?" Emily asked. "Did Frank hurt you? Did he make you—"

"Last night," Abby said. "And it wasn't Frank, and I threw up this morning and my headache's worse than ever."

"Last night? Oh, Abby! You've probably just made yourself sick with worry. And well you should be." And then the shock at what she'd said set in. "What do you mean, it wasn't Frank?"

"I'm marrying Seth," she said, and suddenly the idea that she might be carrying his child wasn't such a scary thought, wasn't scary at all, in fact.

Emily crossed her arms and tapped at her forearm with perfectly manicured fingers. "Seth! Seth compromised you? He took advantage of you? Dr. Hendon?"

"He didn't take advantage of me, Em. It was more like the other way round. He's going to marry me."

"And does *Seth* know that?"

"He asked me before we—" Abby made a futile gesture with her hand. There were certainly nice words for what they had done on that little cot in the back room at the *Herald* but she couldn't think of any, sitting there with Emily in her lovely parlor with the fancy satin couch and the bone china tea set.

"Oh, I'll just bet he did," Emily said. "I bet he told you that he loved you, too."

Abby smiled and squeezed her shoulders up as if she were hugging herself.

"And where is he this morning?" Emily asked. "And did he make sure you wouldn't get pregnant?" she demanded.

Abby looked at her sister-in-law. If Seth had, she

wasn't aware of it, didn't know how that was accomplished, and didn't really care. "Will you help me plan the wedding? Mother will want to have some sort of potluck thing and Seth deserves something elegant, don't you think?"

"I think he doesn't deserve the right time of day," Emily said. "He certainly didn't deserve what he got last night."

"Emily, I have loved Seth Hendon for years. And now he loves me back. Please be happy for me. We have to plan this wedding right away, before I begin to show. I wouldn't have anyone saying nasty things about my son."

"A son now," Emily said, grimacing. "But then, I suppose the wonderful Dr. Hendon shouldn't have to settle for a girl, should he?"

Abby put her hands on her stomach. "I'm sure he'll love whatever—"

"Abidance, you aren't pregnant. Or if you are, you can't know it yet. You have to miss your monthly first, and even then you can't be sure. The only thing you can be sure of is that if Seth Hendon doesn't marry you, you're going to have some fancy explaining to do to the man who does. They don't believe that story about it happening when you were riding astride a horse, you know."

"I'm not pregnant?" Abby asked, feeling empty instead of relieved. "But I couldn't hold down my breakfast, Em."

"Didn't you read 'Ask the Doctor'? It was probably something you ate last night that your system couldn't digest. Of course, you could always ask your beau," Emily added with some disdain.

"Just because you and Ansel could wait," Abby said, and watched as a deep red flush crawled up Emily's neck and settled into her cheeks.

"You aren't the first woman who hoped to catch a man that way, Abidance, but not all men are so . . . You can have the wedding reception here, if you want," Emily said, unable to look her straight in the eye. "But Dr. Hendon had better talk to Ansel and tell him he means to marry you. And he better go ask your father for your hand—right away, before you find yourself in trouble."

"I'm sure he will," she said, wishing that she meant it. Seth didn't like to do things by the book. He'd probably think it was old-fashioned to ask for her father's permission. He might not even want a wedding. He might just want to go to Sioux City and get married by a justice of the peace.

"You do look like you're coming down with something," Emily said, frowning at her.

"I'm fine," Abby said. She said it then, she'd said it in the morning, she said it all the time. "Really," she added, and realized that she always said that, too.

"Listen to the voice of experience," Emily said, leaning close to her and keeping her voice low. "It gets better."

Abby covered the flush in her cheeks with her hands. *Better?* How could it ever be better?

"Getting to know another person takes time," she said softly. "You think you're in love now—just wait until you're married!"

• • •

"This is ridiculous," Seth told himself as he hurriedly finished the article on headaches for the *Herald*. He didn't need an excuse to go next door and see Abidance. And if he did, setting a date would be excuse enough.

Still, he felt awkward, like some kid. How was he supposed to have a normal conversation with her in front of Ansel when he'd held her naked in his arms and poured himself into her?

He ended the article on a hopeless note and knew he'd get the dickens from Abby about his gloom. She wanted everything curable, everything fixable. Put a bandage on it and make it better, even if it was something pernicious eating away at someone's very life.

He'd convinced Mrs. Thomas to nurse the Denton baby, and had set himself the smallest of goals. Just keep the child alive until Dr. Bartlett arrived and maybe *he'd* be able to save the baby.

Dr. Bartlett. Now, there was another subject he could discuss with Abby. He grabbed his hat and article and headed next door.

Ansel's back was to him, his sleeves rolled up past his elbows. On his right arm was a slash of black ink. When he turned to see that it was Seth who'd come in, he brushed the hair out of his eyes with his forearm and left a thick black mark there, as well.

"Slipped a gear," he said, looking down at his blackened hands. "You need something?"

"Abby around?" he asked, feeling his heart quicken at the thought of seeing her.

"Went to see Emily," Ansel said. "She seemed kind of upset. You know anything about that?"

"No," he said honestly. "I surely don't." If he were Abby and he hadn't gotten a letter from Dr. Ephraim Bartlett, hadn't had to go see to Jimmy Denton failing, he'd have still been flying high as a kite after the time they'd spent together last night.

"Knowing Emily, she'll make her stay for lunch. I expect she'll be in this afternoon."

Seth nodded. He wanted to see her now. Wanted to hold her now. "I'll just leave the next column on her desk," he said, passing Ansel and going into the back room, where the cot lay empty except for a stray cat, and the candles were nowhere to be seen.

He heard her footsteps on his porch and felt the smile come naturally to his lips. What a joy not to have to fight happiness anymore, to allow himself the pleasures that Abby, and life, had to offer.

He rose as she entered his office, watched as she waited for her eyes to adjust to the dimness inside after the bright sunshine of the glorious day. If he believed in messages from heaven, he'd imagine that the day was a blessing. *If* he believed . . .

"Oh, but it's dark in here!" Abby said, removing her hat and shaking out the curls he longed to run his fingers through. "I can hardly see a thing."

"Feel your way," he teased, standing in front of her and raising her hands to rest on his chest. Up they inched, making their way to his collar, near the nick by his Adam's apple, his jaw, until they rested on either side of his lips.

"Found you," she said, coming up on her toes and touching her lips to his own. It was the merest of brushes, not more than a taste, and when he tried to deepen it, she nearly lost her balance. He made sure she was on solid footing before asking if she wanted to go looking for any other parts of him, raising her hand to him again and sensing a shyness that was new between them.

He let his hands wander down her shoulders as if he were actually helping her with her cape, and stopped when she gave a little shake to her head.

"What is it?" he asked.

"Nothing," she replied, sounding like a typical female, but not like his Abby at all.

He took a step back and looked at her hard, seeing the blush on her face and the quick blinking of her eyes. "Nothing? You're obviously upset about something, Abby. Why not tell me?"

"Last night changed things, Seth," she said softly, as if she were embarrassed by what had happened between them.

"They did indeed," he agreed, trying to pull her into his arms and finding her body willing, but her manner nervous. "Are you afraid my feelings have changed?" he asked, assuring her with kisses against the top of her head that they hadn't. "That now that I've been with you . . ."

"Say it," she demanded of him, pulling her head back so that she could look into his eyes.

"Say what?" he teased, toying with her curls, his fingers brushing her neck and feeling her body melt against his.

"I need to hear it," she said, "to know that I didn't just imagine what you said last night."

"You silly girl," he said, feeling the effects of holding her too closely, inhaling her scent too deeply. "There aren't words," he murmured, holding her head in his hands, tipping it back, stopping her from pulling away while he kissed her as deeply as he needed to.

And she kissed him back, hostage to the same desires he felt, wanting just what he wanted, wishing as hard as he was that it was night and they could sneak away upstairs so he could show her instead of tell her just how much he felt.

"The words don't exist," he told her, feeling the soft warmth of her breast through her shirtwaist and wishing he could strip her naked in the light and see the beauty and the glory that was meant for him alone.

"Find some," she demanded, putting her arms between them within his embrace, trying to recover her breath and her dignity.

"I love you, Abidance Merganser. With this meager heart and this pitiful soul, I love every blessed thing about you."

"And you'll talk to my father?" she asked timidly.

"Absolutely," he said, unbuttoning her top button and kissing the hollow at the base of her neck. "But later. Not at this moment, Abby girl."

"But you will?" she pressed, as if she didn't believe his intentions were honorable in the least.

Over her head he could see Jim Denton wiping his

cheeks with the back of his hand as he came down the street heading for Seth's office. With more regret than he could put into words, he set Abby from him and straightened his tie. "I've got patients," he said, nodding toward the door.

"I'm sure you do," she said. "But you're exhausting mine!"

"You better get going now," he said, wrapping her shawl around her. "I left a column for you at the *Herald.*"

She nodded and looked at him wistfully, as if there were more she wanted to say, but Jim Denton was opening the door and before Seth had the chance to tell her that he was looking forward to seeing her later, she was out the door and gone.

She'd gone to the mercantile and flipped through the latest magazines, looking for wedding dress patterns. Then she'd stopped by the milliner's and tried on hats. Since she and Seth hadn't set a date, she'd said nothing to Mrs. Winston, nor to Frank, but they both knew why that silly smile was plastered on her face. She whiled away several hours before returning to the *Herald*, where Ansel gave her little more than a nod as he tinkered with a balking press.

And then she read Seth's column. And then she read it again, just to be sure she hadn't missed some small word that would change everything back to the way the world had been before she'd walked into the back room at the *Herald*.

The last paragraph refused to change, no matter how

hard she squinted at it, with her glasses on or without them, through her tears or when she wiped them momentarily away:

> *Headaches of an unrelenting nature can be caused by a growth on the brain called a tumor. These headaches worsen in severity over time and eventually are accompanied by nausea and an ever-increasing reduction in peripheral vision. Depending on the location of the tumor the patient may suffer from partial epilepsy, hemianopsia, disturbances in hearing, taste, and smell. Often a patient's sense of balance is affected. Over time the patient is incapacitated, loses his ability to reason, loses control over bodily functions and eventually falls into a fatal coma. New surgical techniques offer only the smallest hope to these patients, a mere 7 percent surviving the operation and going on to recover.*

Abby pressed against the pain in her forehead, feeling with her fingertips for what she knew must be there. She couldn't see her hand, resting just above her eyes. She couldn't see it until she moved it to nearly in front of her face. She remembered tripping down Seth's steps, falling two days ago when she got up suddenly from bed. *Sense of balance is affected.*

Seven percent surviving!

Disturbances in taste. This morning Emily's biscuits had tasted like sawdust to her. She couldn't remember the last time something had tasted good to her. Except Seth's kisses.

Seth.

She swallowed hard, willing her tears away. This would kill him as surely and as finally as it would kill her.

"You check that column of Seth's yet?" Ansel asked her, poking his head into her office.

"Yes," she said, her voice nearly failing her.

"Something wrong with it?" Ansel asked, not even looking up at her, which she was grateful for.

"No, just typical Dr. Hendon," she said, turning her back to him before he might raise his eyes. "Full of depressing news."

"What else is new?" Ansel asked.

What else indeed, Abby thought. *Well, your sister is going to die.*

"Well, if you want to see him about it, his buggy's pulling up."

Abby took the column with her, passing Ansel, passing the press and the counter and opening the door. She had no idea what she would say to Seth, she just knew that she needed to be held tightly to keep everything from falling apart.

She tripped on the steps up to his office and fumbled with the handle on his door. What once seemed insignificant now took on monumental import as she fought to control her hands and manage something as simple as a doorknob.

Seth was sitting behind his desk, his head in his hands. When he looked up at her, she could see the tears in his eyes. "I lost him," he said, and his voice broke and his sob shook in her own chest. "All I had to do was keep him alive another couple of days and maybe Bartlett would have known what to do. A matter of days, and I couldn't do it."

"Who?" she asked, watching him suffer from across the room, wondering if her own news would finish him off.

He looked up at her, surprised, as if he didn't know she were there, or as if she should be able to read his mind.

"Dr. Ephraim Bartlett of Massachusetts General Hospital. The man who is coming to take over my practice."

"Was it the new Denton baby who died, Seth? Is that who—"

"Just another in a string of failures," he said. "Better luck to Bartlett."

"Are you really serious about giving up medicine? Even when people need you so desperately?"

"Serious? I'd give my right arm not to have to see to one more patient."

"Not one?" she asked, fingering the column that rested in her lap. *Not me?*

"I shouldn't have to tell you this, Abby. You know me better than anyone. You know what it takes out of me. I've little enough left for you. Bartlett can't get here soon enough for me."

"Well, if that's the way you feel," she said, knowing what she had to do, understanding so completely in the pit of her stomach just what he meant about giving his right arm not to have to do it. "I guess then you ought to do it."

"So where would you like to live, Abby girl?" he

asked, obviously trying to put on a happy face for her. "By the ocean? In a big city? You name it and we—"

"We?" she said, pretending that she hadn't promised him her heart and soul and hand.

"Well, of course *we*. You don't think I'd seduce and abandon you, do you?"

"You mean last night?" she asked, trying to make it sound as if it had meant nothing to her.

"Abby? What is it? Why are you acting as if this is all news to you? You've known every step of the way that I was leaving. You knew I was in love with you before I knew it myself, and last night you agreed to marry me.

"So what is this now? Are you afraid to leave your family? Is that it? Are you afraid of leaving Eden's Grove?"

"I'm not afraid of anything," she said, wishing it were true. "I just feel as if you're rushing me, that's all."

"Rushing you?" He looked at her with utter disbelief. "*I'm* rushing *you*? Did I miss something here? Did you not, just hours ago, ask me to go see your father?"

Abby took a deep shuddering breath. *Get on with it*, she told herself. *For Seth's sake, get on with it.*

"I'm getting a really funny feeling here, Abidance. And I don't need this on top of losing that baby today. Now, I asked you where you want to live, and I think that's pretty damn fair of me, considering I'll be the one having to make a living for us there."

"I don't need you to make a living for me, Seth Hendon," she said, wishing that the words were not quite so true. "I don't need you taking that tone with me, and

I don't think I very much like the true colors I'm seeing in front of my eyes."

"What?" He looked at her as if she'd lost her mind.

Of course, that would come later, she thought to herself, screwing up courage that she'd never known she had.

"What? Are you having second thoughts now?" he demanded, pulling open his desk drawer and yanking out papers and forms and files, spreading them on his desk and letting bunches of them fall to the floor, not even bothering to look at her as he did.

"Yes."

Now he looked at her. Now all his shuffling stopped, now the world stood still.

"What?"

"I am," she agreed. "Second thoughts. I'm having them."

"Now? After last night? Is that what all the hemming and hawing was about earlier? I thought you were afraid I wouldn't marry you, not that I would, for heaven's sake! I'm sorry, Abby girl, but you can't have second thoughts after last night. You gave yourself to me—"

"I gave my innocence to you, Seth Hendon. Nothing more. You have no more claim on me today than you did yesterday. I don't have to marry you."

If she'd slapped him, if she'd taken out a rifle and shot him, if she'd lifted her skirts, pulled a dagger from her thigh and run it through him, he couldn't have looked more surprised. Or more wounded.

"Don't you want to marry me?" he asked after a

silence that seemed to go on forever. "You did last night. I thought you did just hours ago."

"Well, things have changed," she said, and wanted the words back the moment she'd said them.

"What's changed? What in God's name could have changed so much?"

"Everything's changed," she said, her left hand shaking so violently that she had to hide it behind her back. "I never thought you really meant to give up medicine. What would we live on? How would you support me?"

"I thought you said you didn't need a man to support you," he said angrily, now shoving papers back into his drawers as if what he was looking for wasn't there.

"I said I didn't need *you* to support me," she said.

"And by that you mean? . . ."

"Armand has asked me to marry him."

Seth's jaw dropped open.

"The letter? Last night you brought me the letter?" she said, floundering now at the sight of him, the bewilderment on his face.

"Armand asked you to marry him?" Seth asked, his brows furrowed, his head shaking slightly.

"He did," she said, stiffening her spine.

"And?" he asked, leaning over his desk toward her as if he was all ears. "So?"

"So you're not the only fish in the sea, Dr. Hendon," she said, now digging the nails of one hand into the palm of the other.

"I didn't realize you were trolling," he said softly.

"Neither did I," she said, wishing the pain in her head would relent just long enough for her to get this over with. But then, if there were no pain in her head, she'd be holding Seth tight, telling him how sorry she was about the Denton baby, and spinning him dreams of their future.

"You are considering his offer?" Seth asked, sitting back, more reserved, trying to save what was left of his pride, it seemed.

"Armand and I have been friends a long, long time," she said. "I've known him practically since I was a child."

"That has a familiar ring to it," Seth said.

"Perhaps," she agreed, "but it was very different. We actually thought we were in love almost from the start."

"Yet he married someone else," Seth supplied.

"I was hundreds of miles away. I was young. He had family obligations." She rather liked the way that sounded so she continued with it. "He'd been all but promised to her from birth. A merging of two family fortunes rather than a marriage of love."

"He sounds like a peach," Seth said sarcastically.

"There was family honor involved," she defended, almost forgetting that Armand was a figment of her imagination. "He had no choice but to marry her."

"I see. And now that she is dead you are considering his proposal, despite last night," Seth said, as if he needed to have it all spelled out for him to get it straight in his mind.

Forever and ever she'd wanted to see him jealous. It wasn't a pretty picture, and yet she had to go on with it. "Last night was wonderful, Seth. I'll never forget it. But we couldn't live on love alone, and since I'd never make you continue your practice . . ."

"This is about money? About whether you'll have enough to eat?" he asked, incredulous now.

"I have been poor my whole life. I've worn my sister's dresses and Sarrie's old shoes. I've left the table hungry and I've pined for things in Walker's window with no hope of getting them."

"Hence your fascination with Frank?" One of Seth's eyebrows was raised in what looked to Abby like contempt.

"I'm going to tell Armand that I'll marry him," Abby said softly, going to the door and standing so that her body hid her trembling hands as they fought with the latch.

"Just a minute," he said, his voice stopping her although he still sat behind his desk. "Last night changes things, Abby. It puts a bit of a monkey wrench in our plans. There could be lasting effects of last night. Beyond the explanation you'd have to give Armand."

Lasting effects. What a name to give a child that could have been conceived of their love. And what a terrible shame it would be if she was carrying his baby when she died. Then he would lose them both. "No," she said with complete certainty. "There are no 'lasting effects.'"

"You're sure?" he asked, obviously surprised.

"Yes," she lied, armed with knowledge from Emily. "It's impossible. Luckily my monthly started today. So you see, I'm not having your baby. And, hate me if you want, Seth, but I'm not going to be your wife."

The color drained from Seth's face as if she were killing him with her words. And what could she do that was softer, kinder, easier? Tell him she loved him and ask him to watch her die?

"Do you love him, at least?" he asked. "Or are you selling yourself to the highest bidder?"

"I'm sorry, Seth," she said softly, not bothering to answer his question, unsure which answer would hurt him less.

"What do you think that Armand fellow will say when he takes you to his bed and finds out I've been there first?" He was shaking as he stood up behind the desk.

"I'm counting on the fact that he'll love me no matter what," she said, feigning a confidence that didn't exist because Armand didn't really exist, not in the way she was pretending. "No matter what I've done, no matter what I do. In sickness and in health," she added, blinking back tears. "Until death do us part."

Seth just stood there, staring at her. He looked a hundred years old.

"I guess if I'm going to get married I'd better get over to Walker's and order a few things," she said. "You'll stop by the office to say good-bye before you leave Eden's Grove?"

"Wait!" he shouted, and she turned to see him shaking his head at her. "I'm just trying to understand. You gave yourself to me yesterday, and today you're engaged to someone else. Have I got that right?"

"Yes."

"What if you'd read the letter from St. Louis before? . . ." he asked.

She shook her head.

"I see," he said, the softness of his voice breaking her heart. "Well, I suppose I ought to say I'm sorry."

"For what?" she asked, sure now of only one thing. She would never, never be sorry for last night.

"For taking what didn't belong to me."

"You didn't take anything, Seth. I gave."

"And for that, I'm sorry, too," he said, and she could feel his eyes on her back even after she closed the door behind her.

After this, she thought, dying would be easy.

Chapter Fourteen

⊂❧❧⊃

*S*HE'D GONE BACK TO THE OFFICE ON *F*RIDAY AND told Ansel that she was ill. Oh, she didn't tell him she was dying, just that she had a sick headache and needed to go home. But she hadn't gone home—not directly.

She'd gone to Sarrie's grave and she'd poured out her heart and cried until she'd run out of tears. She wasn't afraid of dying, she assured Sarrie.

Her mama was a great one for saying that if life were fair Abby's father would be the bishop of Canterbury, and her mama would be the queen of Sheba. Jedediah always said it sounded like a chess game and said if life were fair, he'd be the white knight.

Clearly, Abby was a pawn.

Now Saturday morning bloomed like the first crocus of spring, bright and yellow and full of promise. She could hear the commotion downstairs and her father hurrying her mama with instructions for her to bring plenty of food and water to the new church site by ten o'clock, when the first shift of men would be ready for a break.

"Guess we better get stirring," Patience said, stretching in the bed beside Abby's, where she had slept since they were little girls. "Papa will be cross as two sticks if we're not there to set a good example."

"I'm coming," Abby said as she tested how far she could see this morning. No window without turning her head. No door.

"He's gonna think you still don't want that church, Abby," her sister warned as she sat on the edge of her bed, feeling for her slippers.

"Well, he'd be wrong then," Abby said. Though she had spoken against it, a part of her had wanted the church so that she and Seth could have had a beautiful wedding. Now . . . well, now she needed the church more than ever.

"I'd like to be the first bride in the new church," Patience said. "Don't you think that would be a really special honor?"

Abby agreed it would.

"And I want my babies baptized there," Patience continued.

Abby bit at the inside of her lip. She wondered how long she had. Would she see Emily's baby?

"And I want my daughter to be the first bride to be married there who was baptized there," Patience went on. "And when I die—"

"Well, at least you don't want to be the first person to have their funeral service there," Abby said, hoping to end the discussion as she fought the nausea that had become as constant as her headaches.

"Well, that's maudlin," Patience said. "I think that

Dr. Hendon must be rubbing off on you. Is he a good kisser, Ab? Better than Frank Walker? When Emmet kisses me I turn to goo inside."

Abby reached for her robe. "I'm very happy for you."

"So then he isn't a good kisser?" Patience asked.

"Who?"

"Who? Why, Dr. Hendon, of course! Everyone knows you're crazy about him, Abidance."

"I'm not interested in Dr. Hendon," Abby said, opening the door to their room. "I don't know where you get your crazy ideas! Seth Hendon! Why, I'd rather you didn't even say his name."

"Oooh," Patience said, as if she'd learned a secret, as if Abby and Seth had just had some little tiff that now Patience was privy to.

"It's not what you think," Abby said, the door now wide open so that anyone else might hear her. "I'm marrying someone else. Someone from St. Louis."

"What?" Patience asked.

"What's that, dear?" her mother said.

"What did she say?" Pru called up from downstairs.

She'd done it now. She surely hoped that God forgave lies born of compassion, because she was going to meet her Maker with a whopper on her lips.

An hour later she doubted there was a soul in Eden's Grove who hadn't heard about her impending marriage to Armand Whitiny. Frank Walker, supplying all the nails for the new church and going from man to man as needed to make sure their aprons were full, appeared to take great pride in admitting that it was no surprise to him. He'd heard it straight from Abidance herself weeks ago.

"We got in some mighty pretty white moiré this week," Frank told her when he came by the refreshment table for a quick drink. "I had in mind something else when I ordered it. That is, I had hoped . . ." he said with the hint of a smile.

"I'll come see it on Monday," she agreed. Oh, fine. Things. weren't awful enough. Now she was making a wedding dress she would never get to wear.

"Sorry I'm late," Emily said, coming up behind Abby and giving her shoulders a squeeze. "Had to do my morning worshiping at the porcelain bowl. Why is it, I wonder, that babies hate mornings until you can't see your toes?"

"Good morning, Emily," Abby said, turning and hugging her sister-in-law tightly. "It's so good to see you."

"Did you hear that Abby's getting married?" her mother asked, coming over to lay a gentle hand on Emily's belly as if she were saying good morning to her newest grandchild.

Emily's eyes sparkled. "I certainly did," she said, and winked at Abby. "We had quite a lengthy discussion about it yesterday."

"Imagine!" her mother exclaimed. "Just like her to be so sudden! Just like her to keep me in the dark! Well, if I'd known she was carrying on down in St. Louis, I'd have been sure to have gone with her. I mean as a chaperone, of course. But when she mentioned Armand, I always thought she was referring to that sweet boy Anna Lisa is marrying. Now it seems they're both marrying Armands! Isn't that the most wonderful coincidence?"

"Armand in St. Louis?" Emily asked, clearly confused.

And why shouldn't she be? Abby thought.

"Yes," she said, holding Emily's arm very tightly. "Where my fiancé lives, remember?"

"Armand in St. Louis?" Emily said again, trying to put together pieces of a puzzle that had yet to be created.

"Well, as I told Dr. Hendon, he's going to build a house here, too, but our primary residence will be in St. Louis," she said, still pinching Emily's arm. "Where he lives. Now."

Emily patted Abby's hand, the one that was no doubt cutting off any blood supply to Emily's left hand. "You know, I'm feeling just a little dizzy, out here in the sun. Would you mind taking me over to that bench by the mercantile?"

"Of course I wouldn't," Abby said solicitously. "Why don't I just help you over?"

They hadn't gone half a dozen steps when Emily yanked her arm out of Abby's grasp and demanded to know what was going on.

"Not here," Abby said, and then called back to her mother that she was taking Emily over to the *Herald* where she could have a little lie-down. That, of course, brought Ansel running and it took all she and Emily could do to get rid of him.

"Now, young lady, what is this all about?" Emily asked. "Dr. Hendon didn't remember asking you to marry him? Is that it? And now you're trying to get him to declare himself? That's a pretty tricky game you're playing."

"When we're inside," Abby said, and she could tell that Emily understood the import of her words, because now it was Emily who was clutching Abby's arm, and it felt as if she were holding on for dear life.

"So you've decided that you have a brain tumor," Emily said, her arms crossed over her chest and a frown on her face. "One article—no, one *paragraph*, and you're now sewing a dress to be buried in. Have I got that right?"

It sounded ridiculous when Emily said it. "You make it sound like I chose to have a tumor," Abby complained.

"And you didn't ask Dr. Hendon, am I right?"

"It would kill him if I went and died on him like Sarrie did," she said.

"And if you don't tell him, then you won't die? Abby this is the stupidest, most ill-conceived—"

"He'll be long gone by the time I die. He won't be here, watching me like he had to with Sarrie. He won't see me lose my mind and soil myself in my bed and—"

"Stop it!" Emily began pacing between the counter and the printing press. "You have to see Dr. Hendon immediately. We are going to go over there right now and—"

"If you tell him, Emily, I promise you that you'll never see me again."

That stopped her, but only for a beat. "Well, I'll just

have to live with you being mad at me. I am still going to—"

"I'll disappear," Abby said, already figuring out how she could take a train to St. Louis, borrow money there from Anna Lisa, and move on to somewhere no one would ever find her.

"That's ridiculous," Emily said, but it was clear that she was taking Abby seriously as she sat in Ansel's chair and opened and closed her fists in frustration. "You can't expect me not to do anything, Abby. I mean, you tell me that you think you're dying and expect me to say 'That's nice, dear? How can I help?' "

"Seth found someone to replace him—Dr. Ephraim Bartlett from Massachusetts General. He'll be here in a few days. All I'm asking is that you help me get Seth out of town and then I promise I will do everything Dr. Bartlett says. But I need you to help me convince Seth that he has no reason to stay."

Emily was quiet for a minute. "What if he's too late? I mean what if he tells you that you're fine and Seth is already gone? You have to see him before Seth leaves. Then you can just explain to Seth that you were an idiot and since he knows you so well he'll have no trouble believing you or forgiving you."

"Emily, the doctor won't say I'm fine."

Emily made a face. "Of course he will," she said. "Now, swear that you'll see the doctor before Seth leaves town. Or I'll go straight to Seth now."

Abby held up her hand as if she were taking an oath. But she didn't swear, instead she asked, "Do you see my hand?"

"Of course I do," Emily said. "Now, swear—"

"I don't," she said. She moved her hand closer and closer to her face until one finger came into view. And then she looked at poor sweet Emily, whose eyes were filling with tears. "I'll see the new doctor, I promise. But you have to help me convince Seth that I love someone else and that he should leave Eden's Grove."

"Oh, honey, he would want to—"

"No, he wouldn't. He'd do it, but it would take chunks of his soul. Please, Emily, help me do this one noble thing."

The bell over the door rang, and they both looked up.

"I didn't think you'd be here," Seth said. "I was just dropping off an ad for some of my furniture and things."

"Then you're really leaving?" Emily asked, doing a good job of hiding the tears that had gathered in her eyes.

"There's nothing to keep me here," Seth said, grimacing at Abby.

"I suppose not," Emily said. "Too bad you'll miss the wedding, but then you probably want to be gone before they finish the church anyway."

"There are some things that were Sarrie's," he said, his voice cracking as he said his sister's name. "I think she'd probably like you to have them, Abidance."

He stared at her, hurt, angry, waiting for her to say something, anything.

All she could manage was a nod.

•   •   •

He was getting used to things going from bad to worse. Even when he was already at the bottom of the well. But the little Denton baby was already dead, no one else was sick, and life had already kicked him in the teeth.

So it was hard to imagine that something else could go wrong on such a fine Saturday morning. Still, he supposed he should have expected that he'd have no time to himself to catch his breath, that someone would be waiting in his office when he came back. But even if he had, it wouldn't have been Ella Welsh he'd have anticipated.

"Dr. Hendon," she said, giving him a little cough so that he would know it wasn't a social call.

"Miss Welsh," he said, nodding his head at her. "Still not feeling well?" He'd given Ella enough cough medicine to fell a horse, or at least have it walking cross-eyed. He was surprised she was feeling anything at all.

"You see the church going up?" she asked, gesturing toward the window through which he could see more than he wanted.

"Seems like they're doing a fine job," Seth said. "It looks like they're leaving plenty of room for windows."

"Letting the Lord's light shine in, I heard the reverend say," she agreed.

"Well, he ought to know," Seth said. "You here for some more cough syrup?"

"I'm here to proposition you," she said with a wink.

Seth felt sick. He sat down in his chair. "I'm sorry I'm not interested. I can't tell you how sorry it makes me that I'm just not interested."

"It ain't that kind of proposition," she said, "but I am

cut to the quick that you won't take me up on that one. Looks to me like your heart is elsewhere."

"Heart? My heart? If I've still got one, it's hundreds of miles away. Thousands."

It was clear that she really didn't care. "I'm thinking of leaving Eden's Grove, and was hoping you might want to buy Joe's house to turn it into that clinic you wanted," she said.

"Where are you heading?" he asked, more interested in finding a direction than founding a clinic.

"South," she said. "To some big city where no one'll know nothing about me that I don't tell them myself."

It sounded like the right destination to Seth.

"So are you interested?" she asked. She wasn't a bad-looking woman. Clearly she had been a beauty in her day, but that day had been ripped from the calendar several years ago.

"I'm planning on leaving Eden's Grove myself," he said. He meant it to sound more enthusiastic, but somehow the words came out flat.

Just like his life.

"You wouldn't be going south, too, would you?" Ella asked.

"I don't know," Seth admitted. "Maybe."

"Well, if you're looking for a traveling companion . . ." Seth could see the loneliness on her face. He understood loneliness all too well.

"I'll keep it in mind," he said, though he doubted he would.

She nodded, pulled her cloak around her, and stood. When she was nearly to the door she turned.

"I suppose some more of that cough syrup wouldn't hurt," she said.

He pushed his chair back from the desk and went to get her some. It wouldn't solve her problem, but it just might ease the pain.

Chapter Fifteen

⚜

*T*HE FUNERAL FOR POOR JAMES DENTON, JR., WAS nearly as brief as the child's life. Abby had considered not going because she didn't want to see Seth there, see him hurting and know that some of that hurt was her fault. But in the end, she went, hung back from the crowd, and hurried home as quickly as she could.

She'd only seen Seth's back.

And that had been enough to rob her of breath.

At least no one else was home, and she could cry her heart out and be sick in the bathroom and all but feel her way down the stairs so that when they returned from the Dentons' place she'd have had time to pull herself together and be sitting in the living room as if all was right with the world.

Her mother would be so proud, if only she knew what a great actress her daughter had managed to become.

"You missed a nice spread," her mother said. "Did you work on your wedding list?"

"I meant to," she said, stretching as if she'd been

doing nothing at all. "But I fell asleep in this chair and got nothing done."

"Dr. Hendon was there," her mother said. "Poor man. He seemed to be taking the boy's death real hard."

"Yes," Patience agreed, looking at Abby suspiciously. "Something was really bothering him."

"The cross cookies are cool," Gwendolyn announced, coming from the kitchen with one in each hand. "Can I throw them out the window to see how it'll work from Uncle Jed's flying machine?"

"Go on up," Abby said. "I'll be there in a minute."

"Prudence and Michael stayed at the Dentons," her mother said, handing her the basket to carry up the stairs.

Abby nodded and trudged up the steps, one hand on the banister, hoping that her mother wasn't watching, ready to feign sleepiness still, if she was.

When she finally got to the attic, Gwendolyn was struggling to open the small window under the eaves, and Abby gave the child a hand.

"Will you hurry up and throw them?" Patience yelled up. "I've better things to do with my day than get hit by crosses, you know."

Abby examined the basketful of various kinds of candies and cookies shaped like crosses and wondered if prayers would do her any good now. Of course they would, she chastised herself. She would pray for Seth, who would go on to have a wonderful life.

"Please let him be happy," she said, kissing a taffy cross and tossing it out the window to Patience.

"Ow!"

No taffy.

"He's known such misery," she said to the short-bread cross as she let it go. "Let him find some peace."

"Ouch! And it broke in a million pieces," Patience called up.

"I think I've got it," her mother said, coming into the room, her hair dusted with flour, her skirt being held on to by Gwendolyn. "Try this."

Abby took the cross. It was small, fitting in the palm of her hand. It appeared to be meringue.

"We glued it to some paper," her mother said. "That way it won't crumble when it hits the ground."

"Here comes another one," Abby said, letting it go from the window. "Why are we bothering to do this when there is no chance that Jed's flying machine is going to work?"

"Got it!" Patience yelled. "It kinda floated and I caught it. Send down another and I'll let it hit the ground."

"Faith can move mountains, Abby dear," her mother said, handing her a second meringue cross. "Trust me. I've lived through miracles."

It was worth a shot, and so Abby silently prayed for the best and sent the cross out the window.

"Come on, hurry up," Patience said. "It's not so warm out here, you know."

"I threw it," Abby said.

"It must have landed in the bushes," Patience said, while Abby's mother looked at her knowingly as if they'd just witnessed some sort of miracle beyond Abby's bad aim. "Throw another."

"You throw it, Gwendolyn," Abby said, getting up and stretching out her back. She'd hardly done anything all day and she was so tired that all she wanted to do was crawl into her bed.

"Perfect!" Patience called. "All in one piece."

"Isn't that wonderful?" Abby's mother asked, as if the world was all peachy now.

"It sure is, Mom," Abby said. "Now all we need is a flying machine and we're all set."

"Well, then we're halfway there," her mother said, dusting off her hands and taking a bite of one of the crosses still in the basket, as if candy and cookie crosses and flying machines were equally difficult to invent.

"Can I throw more?" Gwendolyn asked, and reached for several crosses, tossing them out the window before her grandmother could stop her.

"Hey! Ow! Stop it!" Patience howled.

"Too much of a good thing," Abby said, patting her mother's shoulder and heading off to her room to lie down for a few moments before someone came looking for her.

"Why, dear, there's no such thing," her mother called after her.

But Abby figured her mother was wrong. She knew how much she loved Seth, and how much he loved her, and it was much too much of a good thing.

Seth had to give Abby credit for managing to avoid him for the better part of a week. He ran into her at Walker's Mercantile on the Friday that his article on headaches appeared in the *Herald*. It seemed to him that there was something fitting about that. It was just one more thing she'd roped him into and left in his lap—a column, a broken heart. To her it was all the same.

"It's one of the finest we have, Miss Abby," Frank was saying, the table linens he was showing her spread out over the length of the counter. "Twelve matching napkins come with it, of course."

"Lovely," Seth said, coming up behind her and standing just a little too close. He reached over her to touch the tablecloth as if he had even the slightest interest in it, brushing her arm as he did. "For your new home?"

She stiffened at his touch for just a second, then melted against his arms. For a fleeting moment he thought that just his voice, his touch, had changed her mind, and that she was nestling into the haven his arms ached to give her. But the body caught between the counter and his own was limp, and he caught hold of her as she collapsed against him.

He meant to pick her up and carry her over to his office, but he couldn't seem to order his body to be strong. Instead he eased her to the floor, cradling her against him, and ordered Frank to go over to his office and bring him his medical bag.

"What is it, Abby?" he asked, pushing the hair off her face, checking her pulse, feeling for fever, unbuttoning the top two buttons of her shirtwaist so that she could get more air. He did all the necessary things as if by rote, while his brain raced to places he couldn't bear to go. "What's happening to you?"

She blinked up at him, those huge eyes of hers unfocused at first, confused. She turned her head to check out her surroundings, and then brought her gaze back to him. "Did I faint?" she asked, rubbing at her forehead. "Already?"

"I'll take you over to my office," he said, trying to keep the gruffness from his voice. *Already?*

"I'm all right," she said, fighting his efforts to help her up. "I don't need to be examined, if that's what you have in mind."

She said it as if he'd suggested something improper, as if he were using it as an excuse to get his hands on her, to touch her again. "We can just talk," he said. "We *need* to talk."

"I've made my decision, Seth," she said as Frank came in and handed Seth his bag, hanging over him to stare at Abidance Merganser sprawled on his floor. Seth pulled the hem of her skirts down so that they covered her boots instead of showing the bit of flesh above her ankle. She was slow to slap his hand away, and she still hadn't even sat up.

"Why don't you help her up, Frank," he said, backing away from her to assure her that he had no ulterior motives. "Then we'll get her over to my office."

"You'd think a woman never fainted before," Abby said, but she wasn't convincing, especially when she didn't grasp the hand Frank offered her.

"You getting up or would you rather one of us carried you?" he asked. "I could—"

"I'm getting up," she snapped at him, letting Frank put an arm around her back and help her get to her feet. "I'm perfectly fine. I've really got to get back to the *Herald*."

"I'll walk you there," Seth said, taking her arm and steering her out of the store. "Just as soon as I'm done examining you."

He maneuvered her into his office and even got her into his examination room. She let him take her pulse, but she refused to let him do anything else, insisting she was fine.

"Do you really have your monthly?" he asked her directly, putting his stethoscope around his neck. "Honestly now, Abidance."

"I told you I did."

"You told me a lot of things, Abby. That you loved me, that you'd marry me. Now you go passing out in my arms and you say 'Already?' like you're expecting to faint. As your doctor I need to know, and as the man who shared your bed, I have a right to know. Could you be with child, Abidance?"

"No." There was regret in her voice, but he pretended not to hear it. And he strove to keep it out of his own.

"You still having headaches?" he asked, putting the stethoscope into his ears.

"No," she said again, color flooding her cheeks as he insinuated his hand within her blouse and pressed the cold metal disk to her breast. "I'm fine, Seth," she insisted, squirming beneath his touch.

"Hold still and just breathe normally," he said, listening to her heart race and wondering if it was any faster than his own.

"I skipped breakfast," she said as he checked the sounds of her lungs.

"That was stupid," he said, moving the stethoscope and trying to be professional about touching her this one last time. "Deep breaths now."

"I was trying to improve my figure some before the wedding," she said, then took a deep breath for him and continued. "The gown I'm making has the tiniest waist."

"Your waist is just right, Abby," he said, extricating his hand from her shirtwaist. "You seem awfully nervous."

"Well, I'm excited, if that's what you mean," she said. And then, just to make sure he didn't for a minute think she could be happy to see him, she added, "I mean about the wedding and Armand and all. And I haven't been eating all that well."

"And saying 'Already?'" he asked. What had she meant by that?

"Well, the diet and . . ." She looked around his office, tilting her head this way and that, as if things had been moved since the last time she'd been there. "I slept in my corset. There, go ahead and yell at me. I thought I could do it for a few nights before I'd . . . well, I'm sure that's why I fainted."

"I'm sure it is, too," he said, thoroughly disgusted. "Doesn't this Armand fellow like you the way you are? It's not as if you've an inch of fat on you. If the man loves you, I'd think he'd want more of you to love, not less."

"You think I'm too thin? Well, isn't it lucky for you that you don't have to marry me then."

"No more sleeping in that corset, Abidance. It has obviously cut off circulation to your brain. You are talking utter nonsense."

Damn it all! Now the little jezebel had tears in her eyes. He supposed if he wanted proof that she was having her monthly, here it was—she was emotional, irrational, and driving him crazy.

"That's a terrible thing to say," she sniffed.

"Abby, do you remember how skinny Sarrie was before she died? How she was skin and bones and big eyes and a smile?"

Abby closed her eyes, as if that would stop her from seeing Sarrie at the end, but she nodded and sniffed back still more tears.

"Was that attractive?" he asked, as if the question needed asking.

"No," she said grudgingly.

"Then no more diet," he warned her. "No more sleeping in your corset and no more passing on dessert."

She nodded.

"I'm sorry if I embarrassed you," he said, taking the stethoscope off his neck.

"Convinced I'm fine now?" she asked, coming down off his table and adjusting her clothing.

"Fit as a fiddle," he said. And oh, how he still wanted to tuck her under his chin, pluck her strings, and make beautiful music.

"It was awful," she told Emily later in the day. "Making up all kinds of excuses and—"

"How could you not tell him?" Emily demanded. "Is fainting one of the symptoms? Not that I think you have what you think you have."

"It's called a tumor, Em. And not saying the word won't change anything. And you know as well as I do that I've got one and that I'm going to die. I can't eat anymore—nothing has any taste. My head aches so bad sometimes that I can't even get out of bed, and now I'm going around town fainting."

"And you still expect me to keep my promise?" Emily demanded.

"If you want to see me again," Abby reminded her.

"Well, I think you're just lovesick," Emily said. "And scared and making yourself sicker. When I thought I didn't have a chance with Ansel, when he was still so in love with Sarrie that—"

"You knew he was in love with Sarrie?" Abby asked. "Ansel told you?"

Emily laughed. "Don't be silly. To this day he doesn't mention her name. But I knew, and I loved him all the more for his tender heart and his kind ways. Not every man could love so unselfishly. But my Ansel can."

"Unselfishly?"

"What do you suppose he got from his relationship with Sarah Hendon? Only pain, heartache. Not that she wasn't wonderful company, not that she didn't make him laugh and such. But he knew that loving her had no future, and still he loved her."

"But he married you. Weren't you . . . aren't you jealous?"

"Maybe at first. He'd go to see her, you know, behind my back. At least he thought it was behind my back. I'd tell him that I was spending the evening with my mother so that he could see her without having to lie to me. I never asked him how he spent those nights, and he never said."

"Why? I mean why did you share him with her? You could have married practically any man in Eden's Grove. Why choose one who was in love with someone else?"

"Abidance! How long did you love Seth before he noticed you were alive? And how many times did he tell you he could never love you? We don't choose love, it chooses us." Emily sighed and stretched out her back, then let her hands rest on her rounding belly.

"I told Seth that I was buying the table linens for my trousseau," she said. "I figured it would make sense if he saw them addressed to St. Louis."

"Very clever," Emily said.

"I have to be. He's got to go on to a new life before I get any worse. He has to be happy enough somewhere else that if he ever hears the news, I'll just be some fond memory."

"You remind me so much of your brother," Emily said. "So unselfish in your love. I know you're wrong about this condition of yours, I know that Dr. Bartlett will laugh when you tell him your fears and someday you and Seth and Ansel and I will all be happy and we'll know that Sarrie is looking down on us smiling."

Abby would have said something if her heart hadn't been stuck in her throat. She'd have told Emily how much she loved her and that she wouldn't know what to do without her. She'd have told her that she and Ansel deserved every happiness. But she'd have kept to herself the question of what would happen when Emily and Ansel and Sarrie were all together in heaven.

Well, she supposed she'd know soon enough.

"She sending that stuff down to St. Louis?" Seth asked Frank Walker when he got back to the mercantile.

Frank said she was. He was much more concerned about Abby's fainting spell than he was about her purchases.

"Keyed up about the wedding," Seth explained. He wondered if that was all it was. She'd certainly done an about-face with him, and now she was starving herself for some man whom Seth had never even heard about until a few months ago. The wonder wasn't that she was keyed up, it was that she was running off to marry some man she didn't love, couldn't love. He'd held her. He'd taken her. He knew.

"Suppose she'll be the one breaking in that new church altar?" Frank asked.

"I suppose she will," Seth agreed. Another reason not to build that church—one he hadn't even thought of when he'd opposed it.

"How's that bicycle working out for you, Doc?" Frank asked.

He'd forgotten all about the bike. Maybe he'd give it to Abby and Armand as a wedding gift. It was the first time he'd linked their names, even in his mind. He didn't like how well they fit.

He decided to give the bicycle to Jed. No doubt he'd turn it into something else, but that was just as well. The thought of two people pedaling in tandem through life hurt an inordinate amount. He'd be happy to be rid of it.

"You have a finer cloth than the one she was looking at?" Seth asked.

Frank pulled out a carefully wrapped cloth from behind the counter. "Out of her price range," he said. "Didn't even show it to her."

"Send it to the address she gave you," Seth said. "And charge it to my account."

"The napkins are extra," Frank told him.

"Twelve of them," Seth said. "I expect that she'll be throwing quite a few dinner parties once she has a home of her own."

"She strikes me that way too," Frank said. "You ever see anyone smile more than Miss Abby?"

"She is quite a smiler," Seth agreed. Except lately. Lately she'd hardly smiled at all. She'd hardly been herself. Maybe she was having trouble living with her choice. And maybe she deserved that trouble.

He took a few minutes to find some shaving soap, buying just a small bar of it since he'd be leaving Eden's Grove before too long, a new comb since he'd misplaced his good one, and a half a pound of black licorice nibs, though he hadn't a clue why he wanted them.

On his way out he ran into Emily Merganser. Everyone liked Emily, almost the way they liked Abby. Except that Emily was more reserved, had more common sense. Her manners were more refined—

"Oh, Dr. Hendon!" she said with a gasp. "Why are you here?"

"Just picking up a few things." He indicated the sack he was holding, surprised by her inquiry.

"Oh," she said with a tinkly little laugh that didn't suit her at all. "Of course you were. Of course."

So he'd been wrong about her. She was a good deal odder than he recalled, but then women were rapidly becoming a mystery to him. "Well, you take care of yourself now," he said, tipping his hat.

"Oh by the way, when exactly is that new doctor coming?" Her tone of voice was offhanded, as if she couldn't care less, but the anxious expression on her face told Seth that she did.

"Why? Aren't you feeling well? I haven't shut down my practice yet, Mrs. Merganser. I'll be happy to see you whenever you need."

She waved her hand in the air. "Me? I've never been better. Nothing like a bun in the oven to warm the heart, so to speak."

Seth had never heard Emily speak gibberish before, but he should have expected that, sooner or later, the Mergansers would rub off on her.

"I was just thinking about doing something to welcome the new doctor," she said, brightening as if she'd just decided it was a good idea, "and I need to know how soon he'll be here."

"I can't really say for sure," Seth said.

"Okay, then some idea? This week? Next?" She appeared almost desperate.

"Are you sure there isn't something I could help you

with? Everything fine with the baby? You having any difficulties?"

"You really are an impossible man," she said, her feathers obviously ruffled. "All I want to know is how soon Dr. Bartlett will be here."

"I'm not certain. A few days, I suppose. There will be plenty of time to plan your party after he gets here," Seth told her, trying to get past her and out the door.

"We may not have all that much time," she said. "I mean there's a lot of preparation involved. And we want to have the party before you leave. You will wait until after he's here and settled before you go on your grand adventure, won't you?"

"If it means you'll let me get back to work now, I'll say yes," he said, this time managing to get around her and get his hand on the doorknob.

"You'll be here another week? she called out to him. "'Two weeks? Three?"

Chapter Sixteen

❧

S ETH WAS STANDING IN THE HERALD'S OFFICE
looking like a lost puppy when Abby got there
Wednesday morning. Her heart leaped despite
the circumstances. She supposed that for as long as it
beat, it would leap at the sight of him.

"Sorry I'm late," she told Ansel before acknowledging him. "Hello, Seth. Something I can help you with?"

"He's worried about Emily," Ansel said, cracking his
knuckles the way he always did when he was nervous.

If she hadn't just come from Emily's, if Emily hadn't
told her all about her encounter with Seth and how
she'd given him the third degree about when the new
doctor was coming, Abby would be worried, too.

Of course, for Seth's sake she had to appear worried,
but not so much that Ansel would throw his fingers out
of joint. Never mind a tangled web—she was walking
on one thin strand of spider spinnings.

"I just saw her this morning, and she seemed very
well," she said. "What has you worried?"

"She kept asking about the new doctor," Ansel said

before Seth could answer, which was just as well because Abby didn't want Seth's voice melting her resolve and making her doubt her own decision.

"Oh, that," she said, as if that news was older than her papa's best pipe. "Of course she's worried about the new doctor coming. She's having a baby and this new doctor is going to . . . well, it's hard to explain to men. I mean, well, she's comfortable enough with Dr. Hendon, but—"

She fumbled around enough to make both Ansel and Seth uncomfortable and then just raised her hands as if she gave up trying to explain the vulnerability a woman felt when she climbed up on that examining table and let the doctor poke in places that were no man's business beside her husband's.

Seth blushed just a little. The sound of Ansel's knuckle cracking filled the room.

"So when *is* that new doctor coming?" Abby asked, taking out a pad of paper and a pencil as if what she was asking was hot news. "And how soon after he comes will he be taking over the practice? And how soon will you be leaving after he arrives?"

She looked at her pencil, poised over the paper and not at Seth, who had yet to say anything.

"And what about the doctor's credentials? I know that he's from Massachusetts General, and that you're very impressed with him. I presume he's a general practitioner and not one of those new specialty doctors, right?"

"He's a surgeon," Seth said quietly. "Or he was. Now he is interested in a general practice. He seems fascinated by colds and coughs, judging from his letters."

Her sight had diminished. She tasted nothing. Why couldn't her hearing fail her so that she didn't have to feel Seth's words slide over her skin like balm of Gilead? "And he'll be arriving? . . ." she asked, all professional, all newspaperwoman.

"I suspect by the end of the week," Seth said. "He'll miss tonight's prayer meeting, no doubt, but he'll probably be here in time for your father's sermon on Sunday."

"Oh, dear! Do you think we'll be able to convince him to stay after that?" she asked.

"You do expect to stay until he's made a commitment to Eden's Grove, don't you, Seth?" Ansel asked.

Abby stifled a groan. Emily had pleaded with her to let Ansel in on her secret, but she'd adamantly refused. There was nothing worse than long good-byes.

"Eden's Grove seems to be just what he's looking for," Seth said. "I expect I'll be leaving in less than a fortnight."

"Good," Abby said, though she hadn't meant to say the word aloud. Luckily she hadn't said *Thank God!* "I mean, good for you! Still planning to pan for gold?"

"I think I'm headed south," he said, obviously annoyed by her joy at his imminent departure. "Ella Welsh and I are—well, you don't need that for your article. What was it you wanted to know?"

Ella Welsh? That gold-digging, conniving, loose-moraled, over-the-hill concubine? That rouge-wearing, whispering hussy?

"His full name is Ephraim J. Bartlett. He's a senior

resident in surgery at Mass. General. Or he was. He took off the last several months and found he missed medicine, but not surgery, and so he has the notion that a small-town practice would be just what he's looking for."

Abby managed to write the man's name.

"He is widowed, and has grown children who live not too far from here, which played heavily in his decision, I would think."

Abby managed to write "dead" and "children."

"He won two grants, one on the use of something called X rays, and one in connection with some sort of research at the McLean Asylum in the field of surgical reversal of insanity. He was also one of the pioneers in the field of asepsis, but you might want to leave that out, since Eden's Grove has already shown that they have no interest in that subject."

She got down "surgical reversal of insanity."

"Anything else you want to know?" he asked.

"When did you say he was coming?" Ansel asked.

"Soon enough for Emily to get used to him before her time comes," Seth assured him.

"And Ella Welsh?" Abby asked. "Did you want to make some statement on that subject?"

"Ah, Abby! Let's leave that sort of thing for your 'Dear Miss Winnie' column, shall we?"

He had no idea he could be so petty, enjoy so much the look of dismay on Abby's face when he'd mentioned Ella Welsh. Oh, it was just fine for her to flaunt her marriage to some French gigolo who'd never even bothered to come up to Eden's Grove to meet her parents, but let him mention that he and Ella were leaving on the same train and the girl's hackles rose.

Maybe he and Ella ought to discuss just when it was she was planning to leave. And maybe he'd like to hear more about where she expected to wind up. And further, maybe it would be pleasant to have this discussion at the Eden's Grove Grand Hotel dining room, where everyone might see them.

And maybe tomorrow night, while all the men who were putting their backs into that new church were soaking their splinters out, he'd be feasting with Ella Welsh. Just maybe.

He'd hardly gotten the daydream started when he heard the cries and shouts from outside his already half-cleaned-out office, and opened the door in advance of the knock.

"Jed smashed his fingers," Paul Ivers said. "We were stacking up the wood for tomorrow, making piles for each man, and the wood slipped out of my hand and—"

"They're broken," Jed said, holding out his hands, one clutching the other, to show him.

"Could be," Seth agreed. "Or could just be banged up good. How many boards are we talking about?"

"One," Jed said. "But it was a long one." He cradled his hand until he was sure that Seth was taking his injury seriously enough. "And don't forget I've got my flying machine to work on."

Bending the finger ever so slightly, Seth could see that the bone was clearly broken, the tip of it protruding through the surface of Jed's skin.

"I'll have to wrap them in plaster," he told Jed. "But first I'll have to set them right and that's gonna hurt you quite a bit."

Jed nodded.

"How are things at home?" Seth asked, trying to distract him while he cleaned the injured skin. "We'll have to splint two of your fingers."

"Well, you'd think that no one ever got married before. Mama's all in a tizzy over Abby's wedding," Jed said before wincing and telling Seth that the carbolic acid burned.

"Just your mama? I'd think Prudence and Patience and Abidance would all be spinning, too."

"Well, Pru's not really speaking to Abby. Not singing at her, either. I think she's kinda jealous that Abby asked Emily Merganser—you know Emily?—and not Pru to help her with the wedding."

"I see," Seth said.

"And Patience? I think she's mad at Abby too, 'cause she wants to be the first to be married in the new church."

"And Abby?" Seth asked, warming up some water to make the plaster for the casts. "She excited?"

"Do women cry a lot when they are excited?" Jed asked. "It'd be amazing if that wedding dress she's sewing dries in time for the wedding with all the crying she's done over it."

Seth put out the splints and plaster and gauze next to Jed. He warned him that it was going to hurt, had him lie down, and asked Paul Ivers to hold Jed's shoulders against the table. "How come she's crying? Does she say?" he asked, then pulled on Jed's middle finger until the bones were back where they belonged, and wrapped the finger against the splint while he told Jed he was sorry he'd had to hurt him.

"I think she's worried."

"About what?" Seth asked. Not that he cared. She'd made her bed and—well, he wasn't going down that road.

"About my flying machine. I told her not to worry, that I'd get it going for Easter, but she keeps crying just the same. Mama says that women always cry when they're happy."

Sarrie had told him the same thing, but he hadn't believed it then and he didn't believe it now.

"They got the meringue crosses figured out. Now I just gotta find a way to power my flying machine."

"Might a bicycle help?" Seth asked. "I've one in the shed out back and—"

"Really?" Jed could hardly sit still while Seth set his other finger, and when he told Jed that the broken fingers would keep him from helping with the church building, Jed did not seem to be heartbroken at the news.

Seth considered trying to talk to Abby again and decided against it. She knew where he was, knew how he felt. And she'd caused him enough pain. He didn't think it wise to go looking for more.

"Eat something," Abby's mother said, and Abby dutifully put a forkful of something green in her mouth.

She didn't know what it was, didn't really care. Everything tasted the same and a good deal of it came back up later.

"I still haven't gotten a guest list from your Mr. Whitiny," her mother said, tapping her toe on the floor. "In fact, I haven't heard a word from him. Young people have no respect for the proprieties these days. Didn't even ask your father for your hand. No, just getting married with no by-your-leave!"

"He's away for a few weeks in Europe," Abby explained. "Family business, you know. Wine. So even if he's writing it'll take weeks to get here. And it's not as if we've set a date. There really isn't any rush with all this stuff, Mother. It might be best if we just waited until Armand got back."

"Wine?" her mother said. "Oh, my goodness. They won't want to serve wine at the wedding, will they? You know your father—"

"That's why he had to go to France," Abby said, pulling ideas from the air. "He's selling that business and getting into something else. Perfume, I think."

"Abidance Merganser, you are surely the luckiest girl on the face of the earth!" her mother exclaimed.

"Are you happy for me, Mama?" she asked.

"A man who loves you so much he'll give up his life's work for you? Change what he does just so that you can be proud of him? It's all I ever wished for you, Abidance. Not that I hoped for someone unsuitable who would reform, but—"

"I suppose I am the luckiest girl on the face of the earth," she said. "To have someone to love me."

"You know, this probably sounds just like your father, but while I surely do love all my children equally, I do have a special soft spot for you. Which isn't to say I love you more, which wouldn't be fair to your sisters, bless their hearts. The truth is that your sisters are simply not the brightest apples in the orchard. And anyone with two eyes can see that Ansel takes delight in hurting your father and that Jed . . . well, you know Jed. The boy can invent a butter churn that works on the new Victrola but he can't tie his bootlaces without an instruction manual.

"But you! You have always been my pride and joy. And to see you about to start a new life, well . . ." She sniffed and reached into her apron pocket for her hankie.

Abby sniffed, too.

And then Clarice Merganser bawled.

And Abby bawled, too.

And when it was over, her mother said that she had a terrible headache from all the crying and needed to take a lie-down.

And Abby did, too.

"I'd have met you at the station," Seth told Ephraim Bartlett when the man lumbered into his office unannounced and identified himself. "Had I known you were arriving today."

"No need," Dr. Bartlett said.

No need indeed, Seth thought. It was a wonder the man was able to carry his own suitcase from the train to

Seth's office. The man was seventy if he was a day. And used to city living. He probably wouldn't last a week.

"I'm older than you figured, I suppose," the doctor said.

"A bit," Seth admitted.

"My father practiced until he was ninety-seven," he said. "His father was an accountant until the day he died at a hundred and one. Try telling that to a hospital board when they're set to put you out to pasture."

Seth offered the man a chair, but tried to make it seem simply good manners and not that he thought the doctor was likely to fall down if he didn't sit down.

"Maybe I can't perform surgery anymore," he said, holding out a hand that shook so badly Seth had to wonder who had written the letters he'd received. "But there isn't a better diagnostician alive. I figured when you wrote me that there were no facilities here to operate, this was the place for me. Your folks can go to Sioux City or somewhere better if they need surgery, and to me for all the little things that poor diet, bad ventilation, and crowded quarters inflict upon them."

"The people in Eden's Grove eat well—most of them are farmers. They get plenty of good fresh air, and you're standing in the most crowded quarters in town," Seth said.

The doctor appeared unfazed. "Coughs, colds, the influenza. I've seen them all, I've cured them all," he said.

Seth couldn't resist. "You ever treat a child with marasmus?"

"Failure to thrive? Heartbreaker, isn't it?" he

replied, leaning forward across the desk. "You try changing the diet?"

"Cow's milk, wet nurse, supplements," Seth said.

"Once I saw it beaten," the doctor said. "But between you and me and not to be repeated to any patients, I'm quite sure it was God and not the doctor that cured that child."

"Well, I could have used Him for this one," Seth said. It wasn't as if he hadn't prayed his heart out.

"Too late, then?" Bartlett said.

Seth nodded.

"Don't be too hard on yourself, son. Sometimes our boss has plans we just can't understand. Did you do your best?"

"It wasn't enough," Seth admitted.

"Did you worry over him, run out to see him at all hours? Did you try everything you read, and grasp at straws beyond that?"

"I tried sugar water with mashed cooked egg. I thought the protein in that—"

"I never would have thought of that," Bartlett said. "That was a damn good try."

"It didn't work."

"Well, maybe you should just give up being a doctor and apply for God's job, seeing as how you're trying to do it anyway."

Seth had the sense that Ephraim had walked a good many miles in the same shoes that now pinched Seth's feet.

Seth extended his hand over the desk to Ephraim Bartlett. "Welcome to Eden's Grove," he said, a trifle ashamed at his first reaction to the doctor.

"I'll be sure to watch out for the apples," the doctor said with a grin. "Is there a hotel I could check into till I find a place of my own?"

"Stay here," Seth said, taking himself by surprise. "I've an extra room and you might as well get used to the place. The town voted down building anything better."

"It would give us a chance to go over some things," Seth added when Bartlett didn't immediately take him up on it. "There are a few patients I ought to see with you the first time or two. And we've got a mama-in-waiting who's a little nervous about a new doctor delivering her new baby."

"I think I remember how it's done." Bartlett replied wryly.

"Emily's kind of special," Seth said. "She's Abby's sister-in-law and—" He stopped abruptly, feeling as if he'd given himself away.

"Abby?"

He had.

"I'm sure you'll meet her," he said, rather than say *The woman I'm in love with, the woman I expected to grow old with, the woman I will miss until the day I die.* "She works just next door at *The Weekly Herald.*"

"Been in love with her your whole life, or is this a recent revelation?" Bartlett asked.

"She's just a neighbor," Seth said. "In fact, she's engaged to some fellow in St. Louis."

"Her loss," Bartlett said with a shrug. "You want to show me where I ought to put my things?"

•   •   •

Abby saw the elderly gentleman walk up the street and go directly to Seth's office. She had no doubt who he was. All she wondered was how she was going to get to see him without Seth finding out.

It turned out to be easier than she thought when she saw Seth leaving his house and climbing into his buggy alone.

"I'll be back in a little while," she told Ansel. "I need to take care of something."

"I thought I saw Seth leaving," Ansel said. For some reason he just couldn't seem to believe that she now had absolutely no interest in a man she had pined after for years. Maybe because he wasn't stupider than dirt.

"I think the new doctor's in his office," she said. "I want to get an interview for the paper."

"I'll go with you," Ansel said. "I'd like to meet him."

"Don't you think I can do the job?" she asked, taking off her printer's apron and throwing it on the counter in a ball. "Suddenly I can't write? It's bad enough you don't let me set type anymore. Now I can't even write the columns? Do you want my resignation, Ansel, because if you do, I'll be happy to set it in type and print it out for you myself. Of course, it's bound to be just riddled with errors."

Ansel's cheeks filled with air and he blew it out in a long huff that lifted the edges of the papers on the counter. He stared at her without saying anything.

Well, fine, at least she wouldn't have to argue with him about interviewing the doctor.

"I'll be back in a little while," she said, and she could feel him watch her leave, but she refused to turn around and meet his eyes.

With greater care than usual she navigated the sidewalk, stepping down the two steps that separated the *Herald*'s office from Seth's, and making sure her foot was solidly up on the doctor's threshold as she entered his office.

There was a pleasant humming coming from the examining room, and Abby called out the new doctor's name as she shut the door behind her.

Dr. Bartlett's face, eyes smiling above his beard, appeared around the doorframe. "That's me. Can I help you, young lady?" he asked, coming into the front room, wiping his hands on a towel.

"Hello," she said, suddenly tongue-tied and unsure what she wanted this man to tell her, what it was she needed to ask.

"I'm afraid you have the advantage," he said, extending his hand. "You're right that I am Dr. Bartlett. Who, pray tell, are you?"

"Abidance Merganser," she said, recovering herself and extending her hand, not as a woman would, but like a man, prepared to shake the doctor's hand. "I'm a reporter with the *Herald*."

"Ah," he said knowingly, as if she'd told him a great deal more than she had. "A pleasure to make your acquaintance, Miss Abby. They do call you Abby, don't they?"

"They do indeed," she agreed.

"Is there something I can help you with?" he asked, showing her to the chair that she always helped herself to, across from Seth's desk. She let go of a breath she hadn't realized she was holding when, instead of sitting in Seth's seat, the doctor perched on the edge of the desk.

"I'd like to interview you for the paper," she started, but then began to worry that Seth might come back before she'd gotten to ask the new doctor what she needed so desperately to know.

"Fire away," the doctor said amiably.

"Do you believe that what a patient tells a doctor is confidential?" she asked.

He looked surprised.

"You don't?"

"I certainly do. It's an odd first question, that's all. Do many of Dr. Hendon's patients have secret lives?"

"Just one," she said, rubbing at the printer's ink on her fingers. "And she needs to know, if she asked you something, that you would keep it to yourself."

"Of course I would, just as Dr. Hendon would," he said, folding his arms and looking at her as if he could see right through to her back collar buttons.

"And you wouldn't tell Dr. Hendon?" she asked, trying to appear calm, realizing that she should be writing this down, making it look like an interview.

"Anything you tell me, Miss Abby, will be strictly between us, if that's the way you want it." He raised an eyebrow at her as if to ask if they could stop playing games.

She breathed deeply, maybe the first good breath she'd taken in days, and gestured with her chin toward the examining room.

He nodded, opened the door for her and followed her in, closing the door behind him.

"If it's what I think," the doctor began, but she interrupted him.

"I wish it was," she said. They both knew that girls got in trouble all the time, and it was a good guess, she supposed. "I believe I'm dying."

"And why is that?" he asked, not making fun of her, not shocked, not anything but interested. "What would make a beautiful young girl like you think a terrible thing like that?"

"I believe I have a brain tumor," she said. Somehow it came out like a weather forecast. *I believe it's going to rain*, or like an order at the Grand Hotel. *I believe I'll have the roast venison*.

The doctor rubbed his beard as he studied her.

She told him about the headaches, about the nausea and vomiting and how hard it was to keep her balance. She told him about how she seemed to snap at people and finally she held up her fingers and showed him where it was that she could see her very own very shaky hand.

"If only you had an X-ray machine here in Eden's Grove," he said after a while.

"We don't," she said. "And no clinic for surgery."

"And no surgeon," he added.

"Then you do think that I do have a tumor," she asked, aware of every breath she took in, every breath she let out.

"I'd need to do a thorough examination," he said, but she could see that he was hedging. "There are tests that I can take, and other things I'd like to rule out, but—"

She looked deep into his sad eyes and wanted to

spare him, just as she wanted to spare Seth and Ansel and her mother. Without another word he put his thumbs against her forehead and pressed gently, making little clicks and tuts with his mouth as he did.

The outer door opened and closed, and Abby put her hand on the doctor's arm. "Remember that you promised to keep this a secret," she said.

"If you're right, it won't be a secret for very long," he said, taking her chin in his hand and looking deeply, sympathetically into her eyes.

"Long enough to let Seth leave Eden's Grove. That's all I ask."

"Dr. Bartlett? You here?" Seth called out.

"I'm giving an interview," the doctor yelled back. He left the door closed. To Abby he said, "If I were that man, I'd hate me for this even longer than I'd hate you."

It was still his office, Seth figured, and so while he offered a perfunctory knock, he didn't wait for anyone's okay to open the door to his examining room. Abby sat on the table, her legs hanging over the side, Ephraim Bartlett's hand on her arm, apparently helping her down.

"Odd place for an interview for the newspaper," he said, leaning against the doorframe while he waited for Abby to come up with one of her ridiculous excuses. Instead she all but ignored him, keeping her eyes on Ephraim.

"Thank you very much," she said, and Seth thought she seemed very subdued.

"I'm sure you'll want to continue this," Ephraim

said. "I know there's a good deal more to the story than I've already told you."

"Don't let me stop you," Seth said, but apparently they weren't, as neither took much notice of him.

"You don't think I have enough?" Abby asked.

"Maybe we could continue this later this afternoon?" Ephraim suggested.

"Well, I wouldn't want to be in Seth's—that is, Dr. Hendon's way," she said—for the first time in her life.

And for the first time in his, he wished she'd be underfoot forever.

"Don't be silly," Seth said. "I'd like to hear Dr. Bartlett's story, too. Why don't we go out into the—"

"I've got to get back to the paper," Abby said, as if the last thing she wanted to do was sit in the same room with him. "But I'd like to bring my sister-in-law over to meet you, Dr. Bartlett, or even better, perhaps you could visit her in her own home. I think she'd be more at ease there and she could get to know you so that when Dr. Hendon leaves you won't be a stranger."

She looked proud of herself for that one. If she was trying to make him feel bad for wanting a life of his own, for wanting to leave the small town where everyone needed a piece of him, she'd have to do better than Emily Merganser's reticence to allow a doctor to do his job.

"I could do that," Ephraim was agreeing. "I think the sooner the better in this case."

"Emily Merganser isn't expecting for another three months or so," Seth said. "There's plenty of time, and I have some other patients that—"

"My priorities are likely to be different from yours,"

Ephraim said, but there was clearly no malice intended. If anything he said it sadly, sympathetically. "Shall we?" he asked Abby, pointing for her to lead the way.

"Abidance, I need to talk to you," Seth heard himself say, though when she turned to him with those incredible eyes and waited for what it was he needed, he was almost struck dumb. "Sarah's things," he finally said, ashamed to be using Sarrie as an excuse to keep Abby a moment longer.

"I'll be back, Seth," she said. "We'll see each other again before you leave."

"Well, I should hope so," was all he could manage to say to her back as Ephraim Bartlett took his hat from the peg on the wall, put it on his head, and took Abby's arm to escort her out the door.

Ansel felt sick. The dinner Emily had allowed him to eat before telling him about his sister threatened to climb right up his throat.

"He's wrong," he said, wishing his words could make it so.

"He seemed almost as sure as she is," Emily told him, silent tears coursing down her cheeks. "I told him we could take her anywhere—Sioux City, Minneapolis—"

"Yes," he said, though a piece of him had already accepted the fact that Abby would die. So simply, just like that, a piece of his heart and his gut seemed to know, as if they'd known all along that his life was too good. "Even back East. The better doctors are back East."

Emily shook her head. "Too big a trip, Dr. Bartlett says. He's seen them do surgery for what she has, but he says that if she survived the trip it would take too much out of her to make her a 'good candidate,' he called it."

" 'If she survived'?" Ansel echoed, but Emily only shrugged.

"And if she doesn't go?" he asked.

"All she cares about, Ansel, is not letting Seth watch her die. She keeps saying how awful it was for him to watch Sarrie, and how she won't let him see her fade away when there's nothing he can do about it."

"How noble," Ansel said sarcastically. "What does she care how easy it is for him?"

"I think it is noble," Emily said. "I think it's a supreme act of love—quite like a woman who is dying forcing the man she loves into another woman's arms so that she'll know he'll be safe after she's gone."

There was silence in the room because Ansel had no idea what to say to that. Was he supposed to claim that he had always loved Emily when it was clear that she knew the truth?

"Can you grant Abby less than you granted Sarah?" Emily asked.

"What do you mean by that?"

"Dr. Bartlett says that only seven out of a hundred patients survive the surgery under the best of circumstances. As we all know, these aren't the best of circumstances. He says that she'll just get tireder and tireder and—"

She choked, but recovered herself as if she owed Abby more than tears.

"If we could even find someone to do the surgery, which Dr. Bartlett says we can't this side of the Mississippi, there is a good chance that—"

She put her knuckle into her mouth and bit on it, trying to control her breathing.

"She could lose her mind, Ansel. She could lie on a bed and be nothing for as long as she lives."

He hadn't realized he was pacing until he stopped and leaned his forehead against the doorframe.

"I promised her I wouldn't tell you," Emily said. "She wants to spare you all."

He'd loved his little sister from the moment his mother had let him hold her and she'd smiled up at him. He would love her till the day she died.

"Oh, dear Lord," he said, sinking against the wall until he was huddled on the floor in the doorway, Emily's arms around him.

"You gave Sarric peace," she said. "And I helped you. You'll do the same for Abidance."

"I can't," he said, shaking his head furiously. He couldn't watch his sister die. He couldn't be strong like Seth, and go on living. Not again.

"I'll help you," Emily said. "Like the last time."

He took several deep breaths and looked into Emily's face. It hurt him to see the love there, love for him that he had never earned, didn't deserve. "Just tell me what to do," he said softly, and let her cradle him against her belly, where a new life was waiting.

Chapter Seventeen

SETH PUT THE LAST OF SARRIE'S THINGS INTO ONE of the cartons that Frank had given him, and gently piled it on top of the others that he was setting aside for Abby. Lord, but it was hard not to hate her. Almost as hard as it was not to love her.

He left Sarrie's room, where Ephraim Bartlett had taken over one small dresser, and went back to his own, where he felt free to bang things about. His drawers lay open, his belongings strewn about, as he decided what to take with him when he left Eden's Grove forever. He kicked a full wastebasket out of his way, tumbling it, and swore, which he thought might help him feel better.

It didn't.

"Hendon? You all right?" Ephraim Bartlett called up the stairs.

"Never better," Seth called back, looking down at the mess he'd made and ignoring the throbbing in his big toe.

It should have been easy, hating Abby. She'd tricked him into falling in love with her, and then when she had him just where she wanted him, or where he thought she wanted him, she'd up and changed her mind.

Ephraim's heavy footfalls warned him that the good doctor was coming up to see for himself. The truth was, Seth actually liked Ephraim. He was a good doctor and a good man, and would take good care of Eden's Grove. Which meant that the minute Seth finished packing, he could head on out.

There was nothing to keep him there.

What had Sarrie always said about being careful what he wished for? That it just might come true. Right again, Sarrie. Right about so many things, like that Abby could light up the night with her smile.

He did not want to think about Abby at night. Not *that* night. Not *that* smile.

"I was figuring on the house being in one piece when you left it," Ephraim said, standing in Seth's doorway and surveying the damage a broken heart could do.

"Tripped," Seth said, which hardly explained the cyclone that had ripped pictures from the walls, broken a lamp, and left books scattered across his floor, their spines strained, their pages rent.

"Must have been quite a fall," Ephraim said. He didn't know the half of it, standing there with his sympathetic smile as if he had any idea what a woman's whim could do to a man's soul.

"You ever really been in love?" Seth asked, leaning over to pick up a copy of Dickens's *A Christmas Carol*. He flipped open the cover. There was Abby's inscription from several years back, her handwriting still childlike, her message—"See, it's never too late. Love, Abidance Merganser"—mocking him. He held the book out to Ephraim. "Here. I won't be needing this."

"Yes. For as long as I was married, and then some," Ephraim said, and opened the book to see what Seth had already read. "And I'll hold on to this for you, in case you ever change your mind."

"Your wife," Seth asked. "What happened to her?"

The doctor smiled one of those sad smiles, as if for just a moment he were worlds away. "Died. In her sleep, spooned up against me the way she was for forty-six years. I press a pillow against my chest now, or I'd never sleep."

"I'm sorry," Seth said, his assessment of Bartlett changing yet again as he imagined him as a younger man, in love, in loss. "How did you get over it?"

"Over it? I don't know that I'd put it quite that way. I'm a busy man—I work, I write to eight children, trying to be as wise as she would have been when they ask for advice and even when they don't. And at night, I have my memories. I pull them out and savor them— Evelyn dancing in my arms, Evelyn struggling to give birth to our first child.

"Time has been kind to me and has left me with only the good memories," he added, and cleared a spot on the bed to sit down.

"Evelyn. That's a lovely name," Seth said. But not as lovely as Abidance.

"Planning on leaving soon?" Ephraim asked him.

"That's my plan," he said. He didn't bother saying that there was nothing to keep him there.

"I'd like to go over some case histories before you

go," Ephraim said. "Patients with ongoing conditions, things like that."

"Of course," Seth agreed. He'd have to tell him about Johnnie Youtt's appendix, and Martha Reynolds's difficult pregnancies and a list as long as both his arms of symptoms and circumstances that he kept in his head.

"The newspaper woman—Abidance, isn't it?" Ephraim asked coyly, as if he didn't know about their relationship, as if he didn't know that Seth *knew* he knew.

"What about her?" Seth asked, figuring if the man wanted to go fishing, he'd have to bait his own hook.

"How's her health?" he asked, looking innocently at Seth as if to ask what else he could be interested in.

"Good enough to be making wedding plans," Seth said, unable to keep the bitterness from his voice. Good enough to have taken his breath away that night on the cot in the newspaper's back room.

"She's getting married?" Ephraim's hand gripped the rail of the footboard. "Abidance Merganser? Are you sure?"

"That's what she told me," Seth said, picking up more books and tossing them into a carton. If Ephraim Bartlett had any matchmaking plans, he had best drop them now. "Made quite a good match, actually."

"Do you know the gentleman?" Bartlett asked, looking at Seth as if he could see right through to his wounded, pathetic heart.

"He's not from around here," Seth said. "An old friend in St. Louis." he added.

"I see," Ephraim said, his death grip on the bed rail easing.

"I'm glad someone does," Seth said sarcastically.

"Not seeing this particular patient clearly?" the man asked, an eyebrow raised as he rose and shook out his legs.

"Clearer than she sees," Seth said. After all, he'd had a real close, *intimate* look. "Which reminds me, she's got terrible vision, and she doesn't like her glasses, so she's somewhat prone to headaches."

"So you attribute these headaches to her not wearing her spectacles?" Bartlett asked.

"She has no other symptoms that I am aware of," Seth said, trying to be as professional as Bartlett. "And she assures me that Garfield's headache powder works well on them, and if that junk helps, I've no reason to—"

"No, I didn't mean you should," Bartlett agreed. "Women tend to suffer from periodic headaches as well. What about her sister-in-law—Emily is it?"

"I did several tests on Abby when she first complained of the headaches," Seth continued. "Or at least when my sister, Sarrie, told me Abby was suffering. Abby never complains. Neither did Sarrie, when she was alive. Something for you to know if Abby ever needs your help, Ephraim. If she even comes to you, there's something wrong."

"I'll remember that," Bartlett said. "I'm sorry about your sister. Loss is hard. What about Emily Merganser? Does she complain much?"

"Emily? No. Normal pregnancy the first time.

Things seem to be progressing as they should. Now, Abby—"

"And the boy you wrote me about—was it appendicitis?"

"Johnnie Youtt," Seth agreed. "I'm hoping for it to have been an isolated incident. The truth about Abidance is that she's been more accident prone of late, so I'd suggest you tell her to keep those glasses on or she'll never make it down the aisle—"

"She started having these headaches when your sister was still alive?" Bartlett asked.

"Around the onset of puberty," Seth said, remembering how frightening the whole passage into womanhood had been for her. Apparently Clarice Merganser had done nothing to warn her and, like so many things about Abby's growing up it had fallen to him. Or maybe he'd sought them out, like when he'd taught her to dance. Maybe he'd been in love with her way back then and had just been waiting for her to grow up—

What good did all the wondering do him? Like drops of water on a stone, enough memories could wear him down, wear him away.

"Well, I didn't mean to interrupt your packing. I'm sure you're anxious to be moving on." The older doctor let the words peter out as he headed for the door. "Think I'll just look over some patient files downstairs if that's all right with you."

"If you think that perhaps I've missed something—" Seth began to say.

"Just want to have a look-see at what I'm up against, so to speak," Bartlett said.

There was nothing in Eden's Grove that belonged to Seth anymore.

"My goodness, but that is the loveliest dress I've ever seen," Abby's mother said, pulling the skirt away from Abby's legs and fluffing it out as Abby stood on the chair waiting for her to mark the hem. "You will be the most beautiful bride Eden's Grove has ever seen!"

"I was thinking, Mother, of perhaps going down to St. Louis to get married there. I could go down well in advance of the wedding and stay with Anna Lisa, and when the time comes she could send for you—"

"I don't understand," her mother said. "I thought that Emily was helping you arrange things here."

"It was just a thought," Abby said. Of course, it wouldn't work. Anna Lisa was preparing for her own wedding. How could Abby go there to die? "I was just hoping to spare everyone a lot of trouble on my account."

"Why, dear, whatever would make you think we want to be spared trouble on your account? We love you. We want to be part of whatever happens to you. That's why parents have children, dearest—to add knots to the cords that tie them to each other.

"You'll see," her mother added just as the room began to sway dangerously in front of Abby's eyes.

"Help me down," she said, hurrying to get off the chair before she fainted away.

•　•　•

"The doctor is on his way," Prudence was saying when Abby could finally make sense of the words. Prudence's lips moved again, but try as she could, Abby couldn't grasp what she was saying.

"I hope she didn't break anything." That was her father, his voice laced with concern.

"She looks so pale."

Her mother, maybe.

"Isn't that the loveliest dress? She looks like a bride." Ah, that was Patience, no doubt wanting her dress.

"Uncross her hands! She looks like a corpse!"

Pru again, Abby thought. Abby moved her hands herself and opened her eyes. "Oh, thank God!" Pru said, touching her hand to Abby's cheek.

"What happened?" her father asked, just as elephants came marching up the stairs.

"The doctor's here," Jed called. "Both of 'em."

"I tripped," Abby said, answering her father as Seth came into her line of vision. "My foot caught in the hem as Mother was marking it and—"

Seth was staring at her, warmth radiating as if he'd brought the sun inside with him. Her hand began to twitch and she hid it behind her head, burying it in the pillows.

"I'm fine now, really," she said, smiling at Seth and seeing Dr. Bartlett over Seth's shoulder.

"Why not let me be the judge of that?" he asked softly, and then his hands skimmed her arm, pressing here and there, taking her other arm out from behind her head and examining her hand. She gave a silent prayer of thanks that it had stopped trembling. "It's a lovely dress, Abidance."

His words were as gentle as his hands, and she tried to memorize his face, the soft lines by his eyes, the dimples in his cheeks that played peek-a-boo as he smiled at her.

"Armand will be breathless."

"Thank you," she said wishing everyone else in the room would disappear so that she could have these few cherished moments alone with Seth.

"He'll mistake you for a fairy princess," he said, touching the tip of her nose with his finger. "And want to carry you away to his castle."

"Legs all right?" Dr. Bartlett asked, clearing his throat before he did, as if to apologize for interrupting them.

"They're fine," she said, bending one knee and then the other. "See?"

"You'd best check for internal injuries," Dr. Bartlett said. "Why don't the rest of us go on downstairs and give this poor child a bit of room? You can tell me what happened while Dr. Hendon makes sure that Miss Abidance is fine. And perhaps she can let him know *exactly* what happened."

"I already told you what happened," Abby said. "I tripped on the hem of my gown. My wedding gown."

Dr. Bartlett humphed at her and shepherded her family out of the room, telling Jed he'd like to have a look at his fingers.

She knew she should ask Dr. Bartlett to do the examining. He'd promised to look in his books and report back to her with any positive information he might find. The fact that he didn't suggest it meant that he hadn't found anything that would help her. Still, she should stop him from leaving.

Being alone with Seth was not a good idea.

And yet she watched them all leave without uttering a word.

"You are exquisite, lying there, you know," he said.

"Maybe you shouldn't—" she began as he gently traced her bottom rib.

"Does it hurt you to breathe?" he asked, his own breathing shallow as his hands skimmed along her midriff. Did it hurt to breathe with him inches from her, with him touching her, with him close enough for her to take him into her arms and her confidence?

"No."

He checked the next rib, and the next. And then his hand was grazing the bottom of her breast and she was arching against it.

"Does that hurt?" he asked, stopping his exploration to study her face.

"I don't think this is a good idea," she said, scooting back on the bed.

"No? Why not? Can I still make your heart race? Or is it your impending nuptials that has you in this state?" he asked, his voice brittle. She almost believed that he hated her now, but his eyes were shining just a little too brightly, and his breathing was ragged.

Not a good idea was certainly an understatement.

"And while I'm at it, tell me this. Why did you make me fall in love with you? Why work at me, month after month, telling me you'd never get over me, that you loved me, only to turn away when I let myself love you back?"

"Things changed," she said, not having any better answer. "I had no way of knowing how it would all turn out. Please believe me that I just had no idea that it would come to this."

"Not good enough," he said. "You loved me as much as I loved you, that night on the cot. You gave to me, not to Armand, your most precious gift. If I stayed here, Abby? If I didn't give up my practice . . ."

Wasn't dying enough punishment? Did she have to bear this, too, for one night of passion?

"Seth, I . . ."

"I didn't say I would, Abby. I asked if it would have made a difference."

When she didn't answer, he rose from the bed. "I'm leaving in the morning. Unless you ask me not to go." His eyes pleaded with her and finally the expresion in them turned cold at her silence.

"I'm sorry, Seth," she said, trying to rise up on her elbows and finding it took too much effort.

"I expect you will be. You'll have to do some fancy dancing with your husband on your wedding night."

She closed her eyes. "I'll worry about that later," she whispered, and when she opened her eyes, he was gone.

Seth balanced the carton on his knee so that he could open the door to the *Herald*. The little bell rang out as Seth opened it, and Ansel, apparently proofreading Friday's paper, looked up and stared at him.

"Some of Sarrie's things she'd have wanted Abby to have," he said as he set the box on the counter.

"I'll see she gets them," he said. It looked as though he had a good deal more to say, but all that came out was, "So you're really going."

"Tell your sister to take it easy for a few days and—"

"Has something happened to Abby?" Ansel asked, jumping up from his seat. "Is she—"

"She fell off a chair this morning while your mother was helping her hem her wedding gown," Seth said calmly, motioning for him to relax. "She didn't break anything, as far as I can tell, but she was pretty shaken up. Out cold for a while, your mother says."

"Oh, God," Ansel said, as if Abby didn't seem to injure herself on a daily basis.

"I'm sure she'll be fine in a day or two," Seth said. "She always is."

"Is Bartlett with her?" Ansel asked. "Did she see him? What did he say?"

"I told you she's fine," Seth snapped, offended that Ansel already considered Bartlett his sister's doctor.

"Do you still resent that I married Emily?" Ansel asked him, maybe wondering if that was where his anger was coming from. "I mean, in light of Sarrie and all?"

The past was the past, and Seth had finally come to accept it. "No, you were just granting her her last wish when she could still see it come true," he said. "It must have been hard for you to do."

"It was the hardest thing I've ever done," Ansel said. "So far, that is." He sighed. "Do you think a person who is dying has the right to ask someone to do something they don't want to do? Just because they're dying?"

"Has Sarrie's request worked out so badly for you?" Seth asked. Ansel had a family, a home. It seemed to Seth that the man had no cause for complaints or second thoughts.

"She chose better for me than I might have for myself," he admitted. "It's taken me a while to see that."

"Well, you could have left town with Ella Welsh, like I am," Seth said with a laugh.

"Don't do anything stupid," Ansel warned him. "Don't do something that you'll live to regret."

"Would that involve leaving town, or leaving town with Ella?" Seth asked in return.

"Doc . . . Seth," Ansel started. "I wish . . . If I could . . ."

"Abby will be happy, Ansel," he said. "And that's what's important."

Ansel didn't seem to think so. His mouth was set in a grim expression. "Well, you take care of yourself," he said when there seemed nothing else to say.

"And you take care of your sister." He turned to leave but instead of walking away he finally gave in, and asked, "You know this Armand character she's marrying?"

Ansel cocked his head. "Armand? No, not very well."

"Well, will you give him a message from me?" Seth asked. "Will you tell him that if he doesn't do right by her, if he ever hurts her, or disappoints her, I'll find him and surgically remove his heart."

Ansel nodded. "I'll tell him."

"And tell Abby that I tucked a wedding gift in here,

as well," he said, pointing to the carton. "I don't think her new husband will appreciate it, but I wanted her to have it."

"I'll tell her," Ansel agreed again.

"Just one more thing," Seth said, still having trouble dragging himself from the *Herald's* office, from all that had been and all that might have been. "You have, finally, gotten over Sarrie, haven't you?"

"I'll love Sarrie until I die," Ansel said sadly, and then, maybe just to make Seth feel better, he added, "but I do love Emily, too."

Seth nodded. He was glad for Ansel that the man could move on.

He had no hope that he would do the same.

For him it would be only Abby forever.

Seth went out to the Dentons' place to tell them he was leaving. He stopped at the Youtts', the Marshalls', farm after farm, letting people know that he was leaving them in good hands. And then he headed back to his office, which soon wouldn't be his anymore, his home, which had been empty since Sarrie died.

With a sigh he opened the door to his office and found Emily Merganser waiting for him. She had a basket of things wrapped for traveling and waited patiently while he admonished her for carrying something so heavy while she was already carrying something so important.

"Ansel carried it over for me," she said. "But I didn't want to just leave it. I wanted to see you before you left."

"Are you having any problems?" Seth asked. Worry was written on her face like danger signs at a mine.

"I'm fine. At least Dr. Bartlett says I am." Her hand rested gently on the swell of belly that had become obvious overnight, it seemed. "I'm fairly certain this one's a boy. With all the heartburn that keeps me up at night, he's sure to have a beard along with a full head of hair!"

"You never struck me as someone who'd believe those old wives' tales," he teased her, realizing that she was yet another of the growing number of people he would miss. He wondered what she had really come about, but since he was in no rush to be alone, he waited for her to comment on the fine weather and the Merrimans' new cow and the lovely fabrics that Frank Walker was carrying in the mercantile now that he was the one making the purchases.

And finally she asked him where he was headed.

"I'm not sure," he said, trying to sound as if he had too many viable options to choose only one.

"Well, have you worked out some sort of itinerary?" she asked. "Some way that someone could reach you if they needed to?"

"You're in good hands, Mrs. Merganser. I promise you. Dr. Bartlett is—"

"It's not that," she said, looking uncomfortable. "What if something comes up that you'd want to know?"

"About anything in particular?" he asked, wondering if Abby had told Emily about their night together, wondering if Emily thought that he might be leaving something behind.

"No," she said, but something in her voice told him she was lying. "But wouldn't it be simply awful if you left and things changed and you didn't know it?"

What she meant was *What if Abby changes her mind?* and the truth was that he didn't think he could risk climbing that ladder and being pushed off the top rung again. "I'll write after I'm settled," he lied.

"What if that's too late?" Emily asked.

"If something's that important, I'm sure I'll read about it in the newspaper," he said.

"You aren't thinking of getting a subscription to *The Weekly Herald* are you?" Emily asked, worrying her lip.

Seth laughed. He'd miss Abby's articles and her mistakes, but no, when he cut ties, he cut them for good. There would be no suturing of this rupture, no setting of this break.

"What if I need to find you?" she demanded. "What if someone needs you desperately?"

"A matter of life or death?" Seth asked.

"Exactly," Emily agreed.

"Then they should see Dr. Bartlett," he said, taking his diploma down from the wall and throwing it into one of the still-open boxes that Ephraim had agreed to send on to him once he'd gotten settled.

"Is where you're going a secret?" Emily asked, clearly exasperated.

"Dr. Bartlett will know how to reach me once I've settled in. Does that help you any, Emily?"

"That helps me a great deal," she said. "How soon do you expect to be settled?"

Chapter Eighteen

THE FOLLOWING SUNDAY WAS GLORIOUS, IF THE weather was what mattered to a body. Abby tried to care, but the effort was too great. Rising, getting out of bed, getting dressed—all of it with her head splitting and her stomach rebelling—was as much as she could manage.

"What's the matter, Abby? Are you sick?" Patience asked, standing at the foot of her bed in her newest dress, all pink and pretty and ready to go. "I'd better tell Mama. Papa's already left for church."

"I'll be up in a minute," Abby said. "You go on down to breakfast and I'll—"

"You know you aren't fooling anyone."

Abby turned her head so that she could see Prudence, standing in the doorway, her arms crossed over her chest.

"She isn't?" Patience asked. Apparently Abby had managed to fool her, but then Patience had been conned into inviting the new neighbors to dinner with her father. And they were Baptists!

"She's scared to death to get married," Prudence

said. "Cold feet right up to her nose! Touch her hands," she egged Patience on. "I bet they're icicles!"

"They are!" Patience agreed after touching Abby's hand.

"It's no wonder," Prudence said, coming in and sitting at the end of Abby's bed. "You hardly know the man."

"*You* hardly know him," Abby corrected. "I've known him for years—"

"Oh, but you never mentioned him before?" Prudence asked skeptically. "Suddenly out of thin air, Mr. Right sends you a proposal through the mail, and you, on a whim, accept?"

"Something like that," Abby agreed, throwing back the covers and sitting up on the edge of the bed. She could feel the dry heaves working their way up her chest.

Today was not going to be a good day.

"It wasn't that different for you and Boone," Patience said. "He was just traveling through town and you took a fancy to him and two weeks later you two were camped out in the shed like it was the honeymoon suite at the Grand Hotel."

"Is that it, Abby? Are you afraid that you'll marry him and then he'll bolt, like Boone did?"

It was the first time there had been any sign that Prudence knew that Boone wasn't coming back, that he'd left her and Gwendolyn and Michael for good.

"Because this is different, Abby. Papa didn't find you and Armand—" Her face was crimson, and Abby wanted to spare her sister from having to relate the details that she hadn't known until now. So Boone had

had to marry Pru, and he'd made the best of it for as long as he could. It was harder to hate him for leaving when his reason for staying hadn't been true love to begin with.

"Girrrls! We're running laaate!" Her mother's song, the Sunday morning song that was as familiar to them as any hymn they sang in church, wended its way up the stairwell and into the room Abby shared with Patience.

Slowly she got up from the bed. Keeping her balance got trickier every day. Her vision got narrower and her hands shook more. But it was Sunday, and God and church offered a good deal more comfort than bed.

"Pick me out something cheerful," she told Patience, who had a wonderful sense of fashion—a blessing, since without that she would have no sense at all. "I'll be back."

And then she moved unsteadily down the hallway, lost whatever morsels were left in her stomach after last night's heaves, relieved herself, washed, and recovered.

With her sisters dressing her and getting her ready, the three were downstairs and at the table after only two more choruses of "We're going to be late and your father will be fuming." Her father didn't take his own family's tardiness well, and Abby much preferred hearing "Hosanna in the highest" over her mother's "late-late-late" hymn.

"Don't you all look so pretty?" her mother exclaimed just as Emily and Ansel and Suellen appeared at the back door with Emily's wonderful loaves of bread with the red eggs baked into them. "And look who's here!"

Her mother opened the door and Suellen came skipping in, greeted by Gwendolyn and Michael, who pulled her away to see the palm leaves that their grandpa had gotten for next Sunday's services.

If Abby felt awful, it was nothing compared to the way Emily looked to her, *at* her. It was, of course, to be expected. That was why, wasn't it, she was keeping her awful secret to herself? So that she didn't have to see the pain in everyone's eyes, the sadness that she could do nothing to erase?

So maybe the truth was that she wasn't being noble after all. Maybe she was just sparing herself that extra burden of guilt, and if that was really what it was about, well, she figured it wasn't so awful to indulge herself in this one tiny cushion against a whole sea of hopelessness.

"Dr. Hendon left Eden's Grove today," Emily announced, pretending that her news wasn't meant just for Abby's ears, for Abby's heart.

"Didn't look easy for him to go," Ansel added, and in a heartbeat Abby knew that Emily had told her husband. Just as well, she told herself. Emily was in no condition to bear the burden of Abby's secret alone. "I think he left a good chunk of his heart here," he added.

"Is he off to search for gold, then?" Abby asked in as light a voice as she could muster. Seth was gone. All the relief she had expected to flood over her—and nothing happened. All the joy for him, for his escape, that she had expected to feel—and she felt none of it.

"If he knew where he was going, he wouldn't say yesterday," Emily answered.

"Ella Welsh was headed for Kansas City, from what I

heard," Ansel said, while the family bustled around Abby, all getting ready to head over to the grange hall for one of the last Sunday services that would be held there, if her father was right about how soon the church would be finished.

"But he wasn't going there with her," Emily added quickly.

"Oh, no, I didn't mean to say he was," Ansel was quick to say, so Abby was pretty sure they were on the same train. Well, the man had a right to seek comfort where he could find it, she supposed.

Of course—un-Christian though it was, especially on a Sunday—she did hope and pray that all of Ella Welsh's teeth fell out while that floozy was on that train with Dr. Seth Hendon.

One teeny, tiny piece of her even wished that Seth found out—right in the midst of his flirtation with Miss Welsh—that Abby was dying. Oh, she didn't mean that! Not for a second. Not when she thought of the pain in his eyes when he'd offered to stay in Eden's Grove for her.

"Time we got over to the church," she said, watching her mother frantically finish taking one more cross off the baking sheet before they left. "Leave them, Mama. We've got to get going."

"What if we starched them?" her mother asked, holding up one of the small crosses she'd been crocheting since last Easter so that there would be plenty to give out at services. "There are already the palm leaves for next Sunday's services . . . what if we starched all these for Easter and then Jed could—"

"Could what?" Ansel asked sarcastically. "Throw

them from the sky when he gets that ridiculous contraption to fly? You don't actually believe he's going to—"

"Miracles can happen," Emily said. "That's what Easter is all about, isn't it?"

"If I were praying for a miracle," Ansel said, taking his wife's arm, but staring hard at Abby, "that wouldn't be what I was praying for."

"I brought some biscuits," Ella Welsh said, reaching into the basket on her lap and offering a shortcake to Seth.

"No, thank you," he said, shaking his head and looking out at the landscape, the rolling hills coming to life before his eyes.

"Why'd you leave, then?" Ella asked him as if he'd actually uttered what was inside his head and his heart.

"No reason to stay." He folded his arms over his chest and threw his head back against the seat, as if he might nap despite the early hour and the presence of a traveling companion.

"Men are idiots," Ella said, pulling her biscuit apart and popping a piece into her mouth. "Present company very definitely included."

"People in general are idiots," Seth said, checking his watch to find that they hadn't been out of Eden's Grove an hour and he was already worrying about Johnnie Youtt and Annesta Spencer, the church choir leader who seemed to be coming down with more than a cold when he'd seen her two days ago. And Emily Merganser too, who should have been the picture of health, glowing the way she had when she'd been carrying Suellen, but who'd instead looked pale and drawn. And the fact that Ephraim had had to see her twice worried Seth considerably.

Only Abby didn't worry him. He didn't even waste a thought on her. She was out of his head, expunged from his mind, gone from his heart. Yup, not a thought for the beautiful woman with the ready laugh and the quick wit. Not a second spent on remembering the way her eyes danced, the way she skipped across his threshold, the way she'd wound her way into his heart.

Nope, not a thought for the life they could have had together, doting on each other, raising a houseful of little Abidances who would light up the day like so many suns.

"I can't argue with you there," Ella said. "But by degree, men are far worse. It's a matter of intent. A woman has a good reason for being an idiot—love, family, hopes, dreams—they all make her do things any rational person can see won't work. But she can't help trying because she's got this ideal in her head."

"And what makes men worse than that?" Seth asked, agreeing sadly with her assessment of women and the things they would do to stop a dream from dying.

"Simple. Men don't have any hope. Oh, they have plans, they have schemes, they have arrangements. But they don't have that belief that—"

"That love can conquer all? Don't tell me you've been reading that 'Dear Miss Winnie' column, too. I'd have never pegged you for—"

"For what? A romantic? A believer? Miss Winnie understands something that you never will—because you're a man. She knows that every woman believes that the key to happiness is the same key that opens her front door—she said that, you know."

"She's obviously never met some of the patients I've had to treat after their husband's have gotten a little too drunk, a little too impatient, a little too angry."

"Sometimes a woman gives the wrong man the key, but a smart woman knows in her heart that all she has control over is her tiny piece of the world and that if she wants to be happy—"

"That's ridiculous. There's a much bigger world out there than a man and his wife. There's a war in Cuba, men are dying. There's poverty and hunger and—"

"And is that why you're so unhappy today, Dr. Hendon?" she asked, one perfectly plucked eyebrow raised as she assessed him boldly. "Is that why you want to bolt from this train at the very next stop? To enlist?"

"I was thinking about it," he said, sticking out his chin. He didn't add *As you were saying it, I thought of it.*

"I'm sure," she said sarcastically. She waited a beat or two and then stated, "You never married."

"I never joined the army or rode bareback either, and I'm inclined to try those first."

"And then will you be headed back to Eden's Grove, when you've gotten the itch out of your skin and the wanderlust out of your belly? Then will you head back with your tail between your legs looking for that girl to soothe the ruffles you've put in your feathers, the kinks you've put in your soul, and the bumps you've put in your life?"

He could have pretended he didn't know what girl

Ella meant. He could have denied until doomsday the notion that there was anything between himself and Abidance Merganser.

And Ella Welsh wouldn't have believed it.

Not any more than he would have himself.

"Our church," her father said, and added the most wistful sigh. "Our church is days away from completion. So many times I have asked you to stop and consider God's miracles—those over which we have no control—the rain, the budding of a flower, a hiccup.

"Now I ask you to consider the miracles that man has made. I mean those that man has helped God to accomplish. Or that God has helped man to accomplish—"

Ansel coughed loudly, encouraging his father to just get to the point. His father had a way of killing the bush he was beating around and then dragging it behind him until it was nothing but splinters.

"That church," his father said, raising up his arm so that the sleeve of his robe hung down like an angel's wing as he pointed across the street, "is a monument to the Lord. Well, all churches are monuments to the Lord, of course, but our church—the cooperation, the zeal, the commitment—it leaves me speechless, so all I can say is that I am proud of every member of this congregation for not doing what they were supposed to be doing so that they could do this, instead."

The choir seemed to take their cue from the lull in his father's talk and began singing "Jesus Keeps Me Near the Cross" with a zeal usually reserved for the last song—when they'd clearly rather be getting back to their cooking and on with their day.

And while they sang, Emily slipped her hand into Ansel's and squeezed it tightly. Her strength surprised him. Oh, not the strength of her hand, but the strength of her resolve. And the strength she loaned him to face his sister and pretend that this was just another Sunday, and not one of a precious few that were left to her.

Abby stood on Emily's other side, her voice pure and clear as she sang. He fought the urge to reach across his wife and pull his sister to him, to shout at the Lord that He had no right to take her from them, not Abby, not the girl that half of Eden's Grove called Miss Sunshine and the other half called Missy Smiles. Not the imp who made some of her typesetting mistakes on purpose, he was sure.

The children's choir, including Gwendolyn, sang "The Lord Is My Shepherd" and he saw Abby's toe tapping along with most of the others in the makeshift pew. "Let's make a picnic after church," he whispered to Emily. "A grand affair."

Emily nodded and whispered to Abby that they were planning a picnic for the afternoon. With one of her dazzling smiles, Abby leaned forward and nodded at him. She arched her brows in question, asking silently about the rest of the family, knowing that he'd rather be on the moon than spend a Sunday afternoon with his brother or his father.

But it wasn't his Sunday, and so he put his hand out, palm up, as if to say it was up to her.

"The cherubs will now come forward," his father announced. "And will sing 'Stand Up, Sit Down.'"

Ansel gave Suellen a little push out into the aisle, and bore Michael's feet treading upon his toes as the boy scampered across him to join his cousin. Annesta Spencer, the choir leader, collected the children and herded them to the front of the room, where she raised her hands and the babies stood at attention. At least Suellen did. Michael sat on the floor, and Eric Youtt pulled someone's braid and Miss Spencer had to stamp her feet a few times before the children were ready to sing. And then, like a choir of angels, their little voices rang out, and he turned to look at Emily and share a moment of pride.

But Emily wasn't looking back at him, or at Suellen in her pretty pink dress with the oversized bow. She had her arm around Abby and the two were whispering. He felt shut out, and a fire burned in his belly that his own sister had chosen not him but his wife to confide in, to share her fears and—

Emily was giggling. There was no doubting it. Something that Abby had said was so funny that Emily was covering her mouth with her hand to hide her laughter.

"What?" he asked Emily. "What's so funny?"

"Jed tried using some of the palm leaves for fuel," Emily whispered at him. "He figured if they raised the Lord . . ."

"They didn't—" he started, but Abby winked at him and patted Emily's back as if the only care she had in the world was making Emily smile.

She'd taken the news about Seth's leaving awfully well, almost as if it didn't even matter to her. Maybe he hadn't had a right to, but he'd poked about in the boxes that Seth had left for her and found the present he'd mentioned. And now, seeing her smile, seeing her laugh, he wondered if he should leave well enough alone, or if he should hand over to her the box of things Seth had wanted her to have.

Chapter Nineteen

∽

KANSAS CITY WAS BIGGER, BOLDER, BRASSIER, and louder than Seth had anticipated. He'd checked into the K. C. Park Hotel with Ella, still amused that she'd told the clerk that she was recently widowed and that Seth was her dear brother, come to help her get settled in a new life. The clerk had given them adjoining rooms, and Ella had opened her door in invitation, making Seth wonder just what kind of "new life" Ella was planning on.

"Now, you aren't planning on being faithful to a woman that dumped your sorry ass, are you?" Ella asked, standing in the doorway that divided their rooms.

He put his trunk up on the stand and opened it, ignoring Ella's question.

"You have been with a woman, haven't you?" Ella asked. "Wasn't there something between you and the widow Draper?"

"I've been with women," Seth said, shaking his head at Ella as she unfastened several buttons on her traveling suit. He'd been with women, and he'd been with

Abidance, and the first had had nothing to do with the other. Now he had the uneasy feeling that lying with Abby had changed all that, that the relief he'd found before, the physical release from too much caring, was going to be out of his reach. "I thought you were starting fresh here, Ella."

"Just don't want to get stale," she said with a wink. "Once we check out of here I'm gonna have to be on my best behavior if I want to find just the right kind of man to share my life with." She slipped out of her jacket and began unbuttoning her shirtwaist.

Ella Welsh was well endowed, and Seth thought it should have raised some interest to have her sashaying about losing pieces of her clothing as she went.

"You sure your equipment is still in working order?" she asked, eyeing his crotch, which showed no evidence of the interest he knew he should be feeling.

Every night since he'd been with Abby he'd been aware of his working parts, and cold showers, dull books, and even his anger hadn't dimmed the want he felt. So where was that desire now? Ella Welsh wasn't just built like an hourglass, she had dancing eyes and a warm smile. Sure, she sagged here and there, but Seth had more gray hairs than she had wrinkles. And if her bottom had spread, so had his middle.

"Is that a flicker of interest I see?" Ella asked. "Or did you pack your tongue depressors in your pocket?"

"Where'd you learn to talk like that?" Seth asked, sitting down on the bed and working at his bootlaces.

"You don't like it?" she asked, suddenly timid in her chemise and skirts. "Joe—"

"Is that the kind of man you're looking to hook up

with?" he asked, his tone reminding her that Joe Panner had never married her, never given her the respectability she talked about on the train.

"What'd *she* say?" she asked.

At first he thought she meant Abidance, and the thought of anyone knowing that Abby had allowed him to take her outside of marriage so burned his gut that he couldn't even look at Ella.

"The widow woman. If I'm going to be a widow, I ought to know the right thing to say." Her skirt puddled around her feet and she stepped daintily out of it. He kept his gaze glued to the floor.

"You don't really imagine that I would tell you such things, do you?" Seth asked. Helen Draper's words were no less privileged than Abby's, though they'd meant little to him, just as they'd meant little to her.

"All right, what does a *respectable* woman say then?" she asked, and he saw several layers of petticoat fall.

"*No.*"

"*She* says that?" Ella asked. "Or are you saying that?"

Seth got up from the bed and walked over to where Ella stood, rising from her skirts like the last shaft of wheat in a winter field. He bent over and picked up the skirts and petticoats, Ella stepping out of them so that he could. He gathered them into his arms and then pushed them at Ella, covering her chemise with the mass of fabric.

"I'm saying it," he admitted.

He didn't feel noble. He didn't feel pure or morally superior. He felt hollow and empty and adrift.

And he knew damn well that until he got back on

that train, took it to the end of the line, finished what he'd had a mind to do when he'd boarded it back in Eden's Grove, he'd have no peace.

Not that he expected much peace once he'd done what he needed to do. . . . He just wanted to put a period to this chapter of his life, and lying around in a hotel room in Kansas City with Ella Welsh wasn't going to do that.

He didn't know if anything would.

Jed begged off on the picnic, complaining about how his broken fingers were hampering him and muttering about not having much time to get his flying machine in working order. Abby couldn't help wishing him luck, despite Ansel's look of disgust at their brother's obvious foolishness.

The rest of the Mergansers headed out to gather up fixings for a picnic for six hungry grown-ups and three squealing-with-excitement children.

Abby offered to help Emily prepare her share, and headed off with her while her sisters and parents headed in the opposite direction with all three of the children in tow.

"I know that you know," Abby said to Ansel when she and Emily and Ansel were alone.

Ansel tried to look uncertain about what she was saying, but finally he just shrugged and nodded.

"Did you know before Seth left?" she asked, wondering how hard it had been for him to keep her secret.

"Yes," Ansel said. "And for that, you owe me."

"Ansel!" Emily said with a gasp.

"Owe you what?" Abby asked, as surprised as Emily that her brother would ask anything of her.

"I want to take you to another doctor," he said. "In Sioux City or in St. Louis, or wherever Bartlett thinks there might be someone who can help you."

"All right," she agreed, dreading the idea of a big trip, when just getting to church was exhausting. "After Easter, okay?"

Ansel seemed surprised that she would acquiesce. "Really?" he asked.

"I don't want to die," she said softly. It was the first time she'd uttered the words aloud. They choked her, and she had to stop walking and catch her breath while she fought against tears that she feared would never stop. "Oh, Ansel! I don't want to die!"

"Shh," she could hear him whispering over the top of her head as he cradled her against him and Emily somehow sandwiched up behind. "Shh, now. Crying can't be good for you," he added lamely.

"Maybe you all want to come on inside?" a voice asked, and Abby looked up into the kind dark eyes of Ephraim Bartlett, who stood in Seth's doorway.

Flanking her on either side, Emily and Ansel led her into the doctor's office where she had spent so many hours of her life.

"Why don't you help her into the examining room," Dr. Bartlett said. "Then it might be best if I see her alone."

"They know," Abby said.

"Tell me where I can take her," Ansel demanded, as if poor Dr. Bartlett had a secret he refused to tell. "Anywhere. Anywhere at all."

"There's a clinic in Minnesota," Dr. Bartlett said, but his tone was at odds with his words, a "but" hanging silently in the air.

"Minnesota," Ansel agreed, as if it were all settled.

"Have you heard anything from Seth?" Abby asked, then chided herself for even asking.

"He said good-bye only this morning," Dr. Bartlett said. "But I can tell you that he left with a heavy heart, my dear."

"Not as heavy as if he'd stayed," she answered, raising her chin proudly.

"He might have felt otherwise," Dr. Bartlett said, as though the good doctor had been around to see Seth die a little more each day as Sarrie faded away. As if he'd never read the medical text he'd loaned her that spelled out in detail how she wouldn't even know who Seth was in the end.

"He truly loved you," Emily said, in the past tense as if she were already gone. "Loves you," she corrected.

"When I hear from him, I can—" Dr. Bartlett began.

"No!" She'd made the right decision. Right for her, right for Seth. And it was her decision to make.

"Maybe this will change your mind," Ansel said, fishing in his suit coat pocket and pulling out an envelope with more than a note inside. "He left this for you."

"We have to get going or we'll be late for the picnic," Abby said. She made no move to take the letter.

"Aren't you going to read it?" Emily asked.

"No, I don't think so," she said softly, staring at the envelope in Ansel's hand with the small bulge in the corner. "Hold it a while longer, Ansel, won't you?"

"Afraid you'll change your mind?" Dr. Bartlett asked. Abby decided she didn't like Ephraim Bartlett after all. From the moment she'd met him, he'd known too much about her.

"If you don't open it, I will," Emily said, stunning not only Abby but apparently Ansel and the doctor as well. "You aren't the only one with rights here, Abidance. Seth Hendon trusted you with his heart and you owe him the courtesy of opening a letter from him, at least. Unless you're so unsure of what you're doing that you think it might change your mind?" she challenged.

"Nothing can change my mind," Abby said, reaching for the letter and feeling the shape of what was inside, knowing that Ansel knew it too, so there was little point in waiting until she was alone to open it.

Carefully she lifted the sealed edge and let the ring slip into her waiting palm. In her shaking hand the golden band danced wildly, and the tears she'd fought so hard not to shed overwhelmed her, until her breath came in gasps and they led her to a chair and guided her into it.

"Read it," she said, handing the envelope to Emily.

"I don't—" Emily began.

"I can't take much more," Abby admitted. "I will burn the letter unread if I don't hear it now."

"Ansel?" Emily asked, but it was Dr. Bartlett's voice that read her Seth's parting words.

"This was my mother's," he started, without preamble, so like Seth not to even say "Dear Abidence." "She told me to give it to the woman I would one day love."

"Go on," she said, staring at the sunlight glinting off the ring in her palm.

"That's it," Dr. Bartlett said.

"That's it?" Ansel asked, reaching for the note as if he didn't believe Dr. Bartlett. But Abby knew that Seth had written enough. What more was there to say?

With a great deal of difficulty, one hand shaking more than the other, she managed to slip the ring on her finger and smiled through her tears at Emily. "Leave it on when they bury me," she said.

"For God's sake!" Ansel shouted at her. "You are not going to die!"

"It really is too soon to give up all hope," Dr. Bartlett agreed, but Abby's eyes were on Emily, waiting. Finally Emily nodded.

"Now," Abby said, brushing away her tears with the palms of her hands. "It's time to go on a picnic. Wanna join us, Doc?"

Chapter Twenty

I T HAD BEEN A GOOD WEEK FOR ABBY, ALL THINGS considered. Oh, she'd had a bit of a time explaining the ring on her finger, but she'd claimed that Armand had foolishly sent it to her from France to be sure of the sizing and that since he wasn't at home yet, she dared not send it back down to St. Louis until he returned.

The same gullibility that allowed her mother to believe that cookies just disappeared from counters, and allowed her father to believe that the Lord had made Joseph Panner a gambler so that in the end Eden's Grove could have their church, allowed them both to accept her ridiculous story about a ring that clearly wasn't new. Maybe they were too busy to notice, or maybe they were minding their own business. It didn't matter to Abby, as long as they didn't know the truth.

Despite his fingers, Jed was still hellbent on flying over the church on Easter morning, and questioned nothing that wasn't related to speed versus wind drag or some such thing. And Abby's sisters, while they both looked skeptical, kept their doubts to themselves in a show of filial solidarity.

They'd spent the early part of the week baking crosses, acting as if Jed's plans would actually succeed, knowing that if they didn't, the crosses would be just as lovely given out by hand. And while they'd baked and cooled the cookies, her father had overseen the installation of the biggest windows Eden's Grove had ever seen, had organized men to finish plastering, to paint, to hang the twelve chandeliers that would light up the church against even the darkest forces of evil.

The palms had already been brought to the church, the children had rehearsed well for their songs, and the women had already met to begin organizing the flowers with which to decorate the new church come Easter Sunday.

There would, of course, be lilies, Abby thought as she made her way up the grange hall steps for services. She especially liked lilies, though at the moment she couldn't remember exactly what they looked like. And it was getting harder and harder to pretend that she was all right when she forgot simple things she'd known all her life that now only danced at the fringes of her mind.

Well, after Easter services in the new church, she'd tell her family that she was sick, that Dr. Bartlett had recommended that she go to Minnesota for treatment, and she'd put herself into Ansel's hands.

She tripped on the top step, knocking into Mrs. Denton, and blamed it on her new dress being too long. Easter, Abby thought, after a profuse apology, couldn't come soon enough.

Ansel took her arm and led her down the aisle. She hated it, the coddling, the caring, and chided herself for begrudging her brother this small thing that he could do.

"Mrs. Youtt!" she said, and stopped beside the woman's chair. "How are you? I heard that Johnnie will be lighting the candles for today's service."

Mrs. Youtt stood and kissed her cheek, nodding. "And just wait until next week's service! Have you seen the new church? Well, I suppose you have! I stopped in on my way here—just peeked in the windows, of course. I've never seen anything so magnificent in my life."

"I know," Abby agreed, trying to put aside her resentment at Mrs. Youtt's stance against the clinic Seth had wanted. What did it matter now, anyway? "It is a wonder!"

When Ansel again took her hand, she could feel the ring Seth had left for her hugging her finger inside the glove. She could tell, from the way in which Ansel held her, that he too, could feel it and their eyes met, his full of sympathy, hers, she hoped, serene.

As they filed into her family's pew, Abby stumbled yet again.

"Are you all right?" Ansel asked, his strong arms safely easing her into her seat.

She was so very tired of that question that all she could do was snap at him. "I'm clumsy. You haven't noticed that before?" And then she was sorry, looking at his kind face and knowing that he was thinking that she wasn't responsible for her own outbursts, which then made her madder, until her head throbbed and she looked away.

"We all know the stations of the cross," her father started, but she hardly heard him because her hands had begun to jump wildly in her lap. Emily, sitting beside her, took Abby's left hand and held it within her own. Ansel took hold of her right.

"All rise," her father said, and both Ansel and Emily tried to help her up as though she were some doddering old woman.

She pulled her hands from them and stood, sticking her chin out proudly, the same way she'd stood beside her brother in church from the day she was so small that she had to stand on the pew beside him.

It was a sad song, "Let Us Plead for Faith Alone," as all the songs were on Palm Sunday. And she sang it with all the sadness that was in her heart, sang it loud and clear.

"In Christ our—" the words went, and then it was as if the words were gone, all the words, and all she could mutter was a strangled "Oh" as she grabbed at the back of the bench in front of her and tried to stop the undertow.

"Oh, my Lord," someone behind her said, and she knew it would only be the beginning of all the prayers to come.

Seth had to tell himself over and over, as he sat in the railroad car that was slowly heading north, that there was nothing faster than the railroad, and even if he rented a horse—even if he remembered how to ride—this was the fastest way to get back to Eden's Grove, to Abidance, who needed him more than he had ever guessed.

What an idiot he was! If the whole thing hadn't been so deadly serious, it would have been funny, him standing at the door in St. Louis, demanding to see Armand Whitiny.

"You mean Armand Whiting," the lovely young woman corrected. *"He's out right now taking care of wedding plans."*

"I see. Is this his usual residence?" he asked casually. The little row house whose doorstep he stood on could fit in the hallway of the mansion Abby had described.

"May I ask who's inquiring?" the young woman asked, obviously affronted on Armand's behalf.

He removed his hat, chagrined that he hadn't had the presence of mind to do that as soon as she'd answered the door. Lose your heart, lose your manners, he supposed. *"Pardon me. Dr. Seth Hendon,"* he said, extending his hand.

"Oh, my Lord, no!" the woman said, going white and leaning against the doorframe. *"Please don't say she's dead. Please don't!"*

"Who?" he asked like some idiot owl. *"Who's dead?"*

"Your ticket, sir?" the conductor asked, standing beside his seat and rocking with the motion of the train.

"How much longer to Eden's Grove?" he asked, taking the ticket from his vest pocket and holding it out for the conductor to punch while Armand dug around in his own pocket for his and Anna Lisa's tickets.

"Gotta change at Kansas City," the conductor said. "Good two-hour layover there. Change again at Cedar Rapids. I'd say all told a good fifteen hours."

There was nothing good about it. He sat back in his seat and stared beyond the empty seat beside him at the landscape which seemed to fly by and get him nowhere.

Across from him, Anna Lisa—who it was hard to believe was the hellion that Abby had described over the years—looked at him sympathetically. It was a far cry from the look she'd given him when he'd demanded to see Armand Whitiny. Of course now that he knew the whole story, now that he knew that Armand Whitiny didn't even exist, it was surely no wonder she'd been so confused.

What kind of doctor was he? What kind of man, that he could be so inattentive to someone who mattered so much to him?

"So you think that if we took her to Boston," Anna Lisa started, and Seth watched as Armand took her hand within his and patted it.

"Boston would be the best place," Seth said, but now that all the pieces were fitting together he had to wonder if there would be time. At least Bartlett had connections there, he'd be able to cut through any red tape, grease any palms that needed greasing, find a bed for her, a doctor. . . . Did Bartlett know? Was he just imagining that he'd seen strange looks passing between Bartlett and Abby now that Anna Lisa had told him the truth?

He was ashamed to ask, to admit to being privy to so little, but his need to know was stronger than his pride, and so he said, "Does anyone else know? Her parents? Ansel?"

Before Armand said her name, Seth knew that Abby had told Emily, Emily who had all but begged him to tell her where he was going, how he could be reached.

It wasn't just some cliché, that pride goeth before a fall. The thought that Abby preferred someone over him had cut him so deeply that the only way to staunch the wound was to cut off the affected part. Of course, he couldn't live without his heart, but he had tried.

"She said that every time she looked at the pain in Emily's eyes she was convinced she had done the right thing in keeping it to herself. Dr. Hendon, I begged her to tell you," Anna Lisa said, and Armand handed her his hankie so she could dab at the tears in her eyes. "I told her that even if you couldn't help her—"

"She didn't want you to watch her deteriorate," Armand said, and it was clear that Anna Lisa wasn't the only one whose heart was breaking along with Seth's. "She has this notion that in the end . . . Well, I'm sure she's wrong, just as I'm sure she's wrong about the tumor and about dying," he said as if that could make it so. "No matter what that Dr. Bartlett might have said."

"Are you all right?" Anna Lisa asked him, reaching over and putting a hand on his knee.

"Fine," he said, as if he could be, would be, ever again. Had Bartlett told Abby what the end would bring? How she'd lose her balance? Hell, she was already past that if that fall off the stool when she'd tried on her wedding gown was any indication. When he thought about it, she'd been tripping for months, up the stoop in front of his office, off his back stairs. . . .

Then how she'd lose her vision as it narrowed—

He swallowed and looked out the window memorizing every detail as if he could save it for her, give it to her.

And how in the end she wouldn't know him. How, unaware, she would finally slip mercifully from their midst and they would have to be happy that she was at peace.

"No!" He hadn't meant to shout the word aloud, hadn't meant to come to his feet and need Armand and Anna Lisa to shush him and tug at him to sit calmly with them once again, checking his watch, wondering what was waiting for him back in Eden's Grove.

Abby was beating in the last bit of egg whites for the crosses when she heard Ansel's voice behind her. "What do you think you're doing?" he demanded. "You ought to be in—"

She turned as fast as she could and spoke loudly over her brother's words as her mother came in from the back porch. "Isn't it just a glorious day out?"

Ansel looked at their mother, and then he turned his attention back to Abby as if the woman who had brought them into the world wasn't even there. "Look, Abidance, we can do this the easy way or the hard way. You can go upstairs and lie down of your own volition or I can pick you up and carry you there and—"

"I'm just fine," Abby said, glaring at him. It was hard enough with Emily knowing, with Ansel knowing. Having her family know, watch her every move, wait for signs . . . well, she knew she'd never be able to bear it. "I'm sure it was just something I ate. Dr. Bartlett says—"

"He says rest is vital, Ab," Ansel said. "And you know it as well as I do."

Abby's mother sat down heavily in one of the kitchen chairs and stared hard at Abby. "Abby, darling, what is this about? Are you sick?"

"No," Abby said adamantly. "There is absolutely nothing wrong with me. Is there, Ansel?"

"It's just that you are looking a bit—" he began, trying to put the cat back in the bag now that he'd let it out.

"She looks more than a bit done in, Ansel. She looks like she's knocking at death's door. And here the two of you have seen Dr. Bartlett and kept me in the dark. Just like with this beau from St. Louis. I don't like this at all, Abidance. It's not like you!"

"Mother, I'm a grown woman now. That's all it is. I don't come running to you when I've a stomachache and am perfectly capable of taking myself to the doctor, who says I am just fine."

"Abidance," her mother said, shaking her head. "Don't you think I know you're throwing up every meal you manage to swallow? That you're falling asleep every time you sit down?"

"Well, making all these crosses is exhausting," she said defensively. "And this whole wedding business is, well, haven't you ever been tired?"

"The last time I was as tired as you seem, and looked as ill, I was carrying you," her mother said, and a look of pure terror came over her face. "Oh, my Lord!

Abby, you're not—I mean, Mr. Whitiny isn't even in the country! How could you—"

"Mother!"

"Compromising you! And your father's shotgun barely cool from Prudence's mistake! Where did I go wrong with you girls? Where did I—"

"For heaven's sake, Mother, there is no Mr. Whitiny!" Abby shouted at her mother's stunned face. "And there is no wedding, and there is no groom. In fact, there is no vineyard or perfumery or whatever else I told you." She turned and glared at Ansel. "Are you happy now?"

"Abby, calm down. This can't be good for you. Mother, would you excuse us for a few minutes?" he asked, trying to take Abby's arm.

"No, I will not! I want to know what everyone around here but me seems to know already," her mother said. "And I want to know now!"

"No, Mother, you don't," Abby said.

"Abby, could you be pregnant, too?" Ansel asked.

"What?" Abby demanded, not believing that Ansel would ask such a thing. And in front of their mother!

"Too?" her mother asked, seizing on Ansel's words. "What does he mean, 'too'?"

"Like Emily," Abby said quickly. "What else could he mean? And no, I am not having a baby. Not now, not ever! Are you happy? Would having a baby be the worst thing that could happen to me? Worse than dying?"

The room got oddly silent and Abby felt Ansel's arm come around her and hold her while she swayed, feeling almost as if she were being buffeted by a breeze.

"I mean a fate worse than death," she said, but it was too late. There was a hollowness in her mother's eyes, an emptiness.

"Goddamn you, Ansel Merganser," Abby shouted at him, pummeling her fists against his chest. "Look at her. And then ask me why I don't want anyone to know."

Ansel drew her against himself and patted her back rhythmically. "She has a right to know," he said softly. "They all do," he added, and Abby lifted her face to see Patience and Prudence standing in the doorway. She wasn't sure when they'd come in, but it was clear they'd been there long enough to get the gist of the conversation.

They had a right . . . "And my rights?" she demanded. "What of them? Or did you think I was simply being noble? Did it never occur to you that I wanted my last days on my terms? That I wanted to come and go as I pleased and—"

"Abby, maybe you should let us help you up to bed," Prudence said, coming and taking Abby's arm. "And then, maybe after you've had a little rest . . ."

"I'm perfectly fine," she said, fighting tears and swells of emotion that would drown her as she pulled her arm away from her sister and headed for the back door. "The egg whites are done anyway. I'm going to see how Jed is doing on his air carriage or whatever he's calling it today!"

She could hear her mother calling after her, but she stalked off all the same, leaving Ansel to answer their questions. Let him take their pain for a while.

She had more than enough of her own.

Chapter Twenty-one

ABBY LAY ON HER BED LISTENING TO THE SOUNDS of a somber household. Maundy Thursday was never a happy day, but never was it more solemn than this year. There was no arguing in her sisters' room about who was wearing whose favorite shirtwaist. There was no yelling up from the kitchen that no one was helping their mother with the preparations for Communion that night. Jed had made himself even scarcer and Pru's children were quieter than usual.

"All right if I come in?"

Abby propped herself up on her elbows and smiled at her father, wondering when he'd gotten so old. "Of course," she said, surprised by the tininess of her voice. And when had she gotten so meek? She cleared her throat. "I'll be getting up in a few minutes," she said in what she thought sounded like a much stronger voice.

"I could do Communion for you here if you aren't feeling up to it," he said before sitting on the edge of her bed and running a warm hand up and down her arm. "Or if you don't want to face them all."

Old, and wise. Who was this man who sat beside her

watching her with steady eyes that seemed to see into her soul? "Does everyone know?" she asked, reaching for the medicine that Dr. Bartlett had brought by just hours ago for the relentless pain in her head.

"I thought we could use all the prayers we could get," her father said gently.

"I don't think that'll do it in my case," she said, but because she needed to comfort him more than herself, she added, "I'm not scared." It was a bald-faced lie, but he accepted it, patting her hand and saying nothing for a good while.

"There is nothing to be afraid of," he said finally. It wasn't clear to her whether he was trying to deny that she would die, or that death was nothing to fear, but she didn't ask him because she didn't want to know.

"Do you expect the church to be ready by Sunday?" she asked instead.

"If only we'd built a hospital—" her father started, and she could see guilt cloud his eyes.

"Looks like I'll have better use for the church, personally," she said, surprised that she could still manage a chuckle.

"You were right to keep it a secret," he said finally. "It hurt me, but I can see that everyone's knowing is making it harder for you, and I would give the world to make it easier for you."

"Oh, Papa! And I would give the world to make it easier for you."

"The Lord sends tests, Abidance—"

"I don't think there's any passing this particular test, Papa."

"Maybe this test isn't yours, honey. Maybe it's mine,

or your mother's. Or maybe it's Dr. Hendon's," he said, looking at her for answers she didn't have.

"He's had so many tests, Papa. I had to spare him this last one."

"You really did love him then, I take it," he said, not so much a question as a statement of fact.

She nodded, too choked by the thought of Seth to utter his name.

"And that Armand Whitiny was just a fabrication so that you could send him away? That was very brave of you," he said, his eyes shining brightly despite the grimace on his lips.

"You always used to tell Jed there was a fine line between bravery and foolishness," she reminded him, wishing she had more to comfort her than her nobility.

"Have you crossed it?" he asked.

"No," she said, though Dr. Bartlett's words kept coming back to her about how Seth would hate them for keeping the truth from him. Maybe she'd just been a coward, unable to stand to see pity in his eyes. "And it doesn't matter now, does it?"

There'd been no one at the Mergansers when Seth had gotten there, out of breath, almost as winded as his horse, who'd pulled the buggy as quickly as its old bolts would allow. Now he and Anna Lisa and Armand stood on the steps of the grange hall listening to the voices raised in song to the Lord.

When the hymn was over, they slipped quietly into the last row in the hall and Seth searched the crowd with his eyes for the back of Abby's head. He finally found her, waiting between her sisters to take Communion, and his heart stopped beating. She was thinner, and she took Prudence's arm to mount the steps to her father's waiting hand.

And then, having received Communion, she turned toward the back of the church and he moved out into the aisle and opened his arms for her. He saw Patience whisper to her and watched her nod as if to say that she knew he was there. But she continued back to her seat and sat as if the whole world wasn't spinning out of control.

Only it was, and he'd be damned if he would just sit down and watch it do a death spiral out of his reach. He looked at Anna Lisa and Armand as they stared at him expectantly. He nodded at them, as if to say that they could count on him, for all that that was worth.

Marching up the aisle he was well aware of everyone's eyes on him. He could hear the whispers about Abby, someone hoping she wouldn't faint again, someone wondering why he had come back, someone wondering how he hadn't known. It seemed to take forever for him to reach the row in which she sat, but when he got there, he pushed his way to her side, where he stood with his hand out.

"I didn't think you attended church," she said attempting a haughtiness she couldn't pull off.

"I don't want to waste another minute," he answered her back. "Do you?"

"I don't know what you mean," she started, but his look stopped her. He didn't have to say *I know*.

"Do you want to waste this time?" he asked again.

She shook her head and he watched the tears glistening in her eyes. He put out his hand and she took it and rose.

"Take your shawl," her father reminded her from the makeshift pulpit. "It's cool out there."

Seth wrapped the creamy woolen shawl around her and led her down the aisle toward the back of the hall, wishing he could change their direction, change fate.

"We'll stop at my office and get Bartlett moving," he said, knowing that they didn't have the luxury of time for a reunion. Or for recriminations. "It'll help if he comes with us to Boston."

She stepped outside of the grange hall with him and stood on the top step. "Seth, there won't be any Boston," she said, and allowed him to help her down the steps—the girl who had bristled when he'd held a door for her, who had dashed from pillar to post. "I can't go."

"Of course you can. You and me, and Bartlett and Anna Lisa and Armand, too. As soon as I get Bartlett started on the details, we'll come back here and have your father marry us and—"

Slowly, cautiously, she came down the steps beside him. When she reached the bottom and could let go of the railing, she gently touched his face, a feather against his cheek, a wish against his soul. "Don't do this," she said softly. "Get on your train and go before I lose my . . . resolve."

"And let you die some noble death? Is that your plan? Well, there's nothing noble in dying, Abby, nothing at all. But in fighting tooth and nail? Well, that I could admire for—"

She sighed as if he didn't understand what it was costing her to be so brave. How could she not know how gladly he would pay the price for her, give his own life, if only he could.

"Can you give in to me just this once?" he asked.

She smiled at him, the radiance still there, and laughed. "And you'll never ask me for anything again?" she asked, arching one eyebrow at him.

"That's my girl," he said, taking off toward his office as if he had a bottle of miracles waiting there. She lagged behind, not dawdling, he realized, and he slowed his pace so that she could keep up with him, she who had always danced ahead.

The light was on in the bedroom upstairs, his bedroom, and Seth opened the office door for Abby, followed her in, helped her to a seat, and then called up the stairs at the top of his lungs. "Ephraim? Get down here before I come up and get you and break all your old bones!"

He glanced at Abby, saw her smile, and continued his tirade purely for her amusement. Hell, he'd stand on his head to make her smile. And he'd give his life to see her well.

Bartlett came down the stairs, buttoning his vest as he came, assessing the situation with just a glance. "Didn't I tell you he'd be madder at me?" he asked Abby, confirming what Seth had supposed when he'd put all the puzzle pieces together on the train from St. Louis.

"You bet your old ass I am," Seth said. "Now get your sorry self over to Walker's Mercantile and have him get Mrs. Waitte so she can put you through to

Mass General on the telephone. Tell them we're bringing Abby on the next train and—"

Bartlett sat down in the chair behind Seth's desk, reached into the bottom drawer, and pulled out a bottle of scotch that hadn't been there when the desk had belonged to Seth. "They won't operate," he said, taking two shot glasses out and splashing the liquor into them. "How's the pain, honey?" he asked Abby, affection clear in his voice and his eyes.

"The new medicine lets me sleep," she said, shrugging off her shawl as if they had all the time in the world to sit around and discuss the weather or something equally unimportant.

"They *will* operate," Seth said. "You've got connections there. Pull some strings—"

"Sit down," Bartlett said. It was an order, not an invitation. "And drink this. Do you think no one thought of taking her to Mass. General until you showed up? Do you think Ansel didn't storm in here demanding just what you are? Do you think that Reverend Merganser—"

"My father came to see you?" Abby asked, her hand shaking in her lap.

"Honey, there is no one in all of Eden's Grove who hasn't come to demand I do something for you. I feel as if I should follow up Seth's column in *The Weekly Herald* with one of my own." He shrugged and looked at Seth as if the whole thing was his fault, as if the article on brain tumors had caused Abby's.

"So why didn't you take her to Boston?" Seth demanded. "Why did you let a minute pass?"

"Because too many minutes had passed already."

Seth lifted the glass of scotch and downed it in one gulp. He had failed her, pure and simple. He hadn't seen the signs and now . . .

"My fault," Seth said, rubbing Abby's hand and feeling the tremors in it.

"Yours? Listen, son, there would have been only the smallest chance even months ago. Even if she'd been diagnosed early, even if she'd been in Boston. We only operated on sure bets. And even then our success rate was minimal. Mostly we got our patients from insane asylums, where they wouldn't be any worse off if I—"

"*I? We?*" Seth stared at Ephraim Bartlett. "*You* are a brain surgeon?"

"I *was* a surgeon," Bartlett admitted reluctantly. "And yes, my specialty was the head."

"Fine. Then you'll operate," Seth said, as if that settled it. "Abby and I are going to get married tonight and then tomorrow—"

Abby was looking at Bartlett, and Seth followed her line of vision straight to Ephraim's hands, which he held out. Tremors shook his hands so that the man would have been hard-pressed to hold a pen, never mind a scalpel.

"I'm going to take Abby home to get ready to marry me. Her family ought to be there by now. You and I can work out what we do next when I come back."

Abby pulled her shawl up around her shoulders. "No," she said more firmly than he'd have liked.

"No what?" he asked.

"No, I don't want to marry you. I won't marry you. Are you in a rush to become a widower?"

Could he say aloud the words that crashed in his

head? That he wanted her headstone to say that she was his beloved wife, and belonged to him in that way forever?

"It wasn't a very moving proposal," Ephraim agreed. "None of that flowery stuff or words of love."

"Of course I love her," Seth said. "Why else would I want to marry her, attach myself to that crazy family of hers, and spend my days here in Eden's Grove with her?"

"You don't need to marry me, Seth. Not now."

"Do you think I'm marrying you because I think you're going to die? That I'm doing it for you?" he asked. She should know better, surely she should.

"Well, you didn't want to marry me before I was dying, did you? I mean, you left, didn't you?"

"Of course I did. You tricked me into leaving. You know I wanted to marry you. Even after that ridiculous story about Armand Whitiny—which I will tan your bottom over just as soon as we are alone, by the way—I still wanted you."

Her look said that she didn't believe him.

"What about the ring?" he asked. Didn't that prove it?

Ephraim Bartlett leaned forward with great interest, as if he had any right to be privy to their conversation. "There was that," he reminded Abby. "And remember that you were the one who sent him away, girl."

"You can have it back," she said, pulling it from her finger where it belonged.

"I'll take it for now," he said, holding out his hand and letting her place the ring in it, curling his fingers around her hand as she did. "But I'll be putting it back on that finger later, with God—and God help me— your father, watching."

"Does it matter what I want for you?" she asked, unshed tears glistening in her eyes.

"This is for me, Abby, believe me," he said. "It's always been about what I want, and I'm ashamed and embarrassed to say that it still is. Do this one last thing for me, Abby. Be mine."

And then he opened his arms and she nestled against him, fitting her soft body against his, letting her sobs be muffled by his rumpled suit. "I've always been yours," she said, her words muffled by tweed and closeness and his own sigh.

"That's my girl," he said, pulling a hankie from his back pocket and holding it to her nose. "Now blow."

She did as she was told, and then lifted the biggest, loveliest hazel eyes to him. "I can't give you much," she said, "and I would have spared you the end, but I want every moment I can have with you."

"I'll work on it," he said, and nodding at Ephraim, he took her arm so that he could see her home.

Seth saw her to her door and stood there beneath the porch light, all flesh and blood and real, and despite the pain in her head and the worries in her heart, she reveled in the sight of him.

"I'd like to kiss you," he said, asking permission for what he'd stolen long before.

"I won't break," she assured him, and was swept up into his arms and pressed so tightly against his chest that she began to doubt her own words.

He kissed her, tenderly at first, gently, as if he didn't quite believe that he wouldn't hurt her, and then the kiss deepened, sharpened, turned to something possessive and defiant, as if his very lips, his breath, his love, could keep her alive.

And God help her, she believed him. She kissed him back as if nothing would ever part them, and she pressed herself against him, molding her body to his.

"We'd best get you inside," he murmured against her neck. "I think it may be cold out here."

"Is it?" she asked, feeling only warmth, his warmth, spreading through her, warming places that had been cold since the day she'd told him that she couldn't marry him.

"I can't believe I fell for that Armand business," he said, his hand drifting down her back and cupping her bottom so that she could feel his hardness against her belly despite her layers of skirts.

"I'm a very good actress," she said, leaning her head back to let him kiss her throat, and gasping as his lips went lower still.

"Are you acting now?" His words drifted up to her. Of course she was acting. She was playing the part of a newlywed with her whole life in front of her.

"Seth?" It was Anna Lisa's voice, and suddenly Abby and Seth were bathed in light from the open front door. "Are you certain she can do that?"

"She *can* very well," he said, releasing her and guiding her into the living room where all of the Mergansers stood gawking at him. "But I suppose she shouldn't."

"Sir. Mrs. Merganser," he said with a nod to her

father and mother. "Jed, how goes the flying machine?"

Jed's face lit up, and he said, "It'll fly. I know it will. Of course, some people around here don't believe in miracles, so . . ."

"God's miracles and man's . . . well, man doesn't make miracles," her father said.

"Well, sir, I'd like to see if maybe someone can," Seth said.

It would take a miracle, Abby knew, and she only hoped that Seth could make it happen.

"For Abidance?" her father asked.

"Don't you have something you want to ask my father?" Abby asked, looking at him as innocently as she could manage considering that she could think of little but the way he had kissed her and pressed himself against her, and how, if they really were to marry tonight they could—

Seth cleared his throat. "Seeing how Armand Whitiny has jilted Abidance here," he said with a knowing look that made Armand Whiting cough behind his hand, "I'd like to offer for her hand."

"Don't you want the rest of her?" Jed asked, and Abby loved the low chuckle that came from Seth's chest.

"You want to marry Abidance?" her father asked. "I guess with all that kissing on the porch she didn't have time to tell you—"

"He knows, Papa."

"And you still want to—"

"Tonight. As soon as she's ready," Seth said, taking

her hand in his and kissing her knuckles before guiding her to the sofa.

"I don't need to—" she started.

"Save your strength," he said solicitously, whispering in her ear as he helped her sit, "for later."

"I don't know if this is such a good idea," her mother said. "Abby isn't really up to—"

"Best damn idea I've heard in a month of Sundays," her father said, daring anyone to contradict him or call him on his choice of words. "Jed, you go tell Ansel and Emily to meet us at the church. Mother, you see if there's something sweet you can whip up in a hurry. Patience, you go tell Mrs. Stella we'll need her at the organ, and tell them over at the Grand that they'll need a room. Prudence, you get your sister ready, and I'll just stick close to the groom here and make sure he doesn't leave town . . . again!"

"It was *your* daughter . . ." Seth was saying as they left the house and he sent her a plaintive backward glance while her father railed on.

"Can't," Bartlett said. "Don't you think I wish I could?"

"And if there is no operation?" Reverend Merganser asked as the three men sat around Seth's desk and Ephraim asked them to share what was left of the scotch.

"She'll die," Bartlett said matter-of-factly. "In all likelihood she'd die from the operation anyway."

"So you're saying that there's really no difference,"

the reverend said, eyeing the scotch as if he could taste it across the table.

"Oh, there's a difference, all right," Bartlett said. His speech was slightly slurred, but his facts were textbook perfect. "If she dies on the table she leaves the way we all knew her—brave, full of life, whole. She'll have more time if we let the tumor grow, but she'll lose more of herself every day—the forgetfulness we've all noticed will extend to you," he said, pointing at the reverend. "And you," he added, pointing at Seth.

"She'll forget the most basic of things, lose control over her bowels and bladder and—"

"You have to do it," Seth said. "Now when there's still a chance."

"She doesn't have a chance with me," Ephraim said. "I couldn't even kill her right with these hands."

"Then *you* have to do it," the reverend said, looking right at Seth as if he were the Messiah himself. "You're a doctor. You love her. You can save her."

It was the stupidest, most ridiculous, horrifying thing he'd heard since Anna Lisa had told him that Abby was dying. "I'm not a brain surgeon. I've never taken out more than an appendix, done more than a caesarean section, or lanced a boil. I don't have the training, the skill, the knowledge. . . ."

"He could tell you," the reverend said gesturing toward Ephraim with his head. "You could be his hands."

"You're crazy! I could kill her. Do you understand that?" Seth shouted at him. "My wife, my life, and I could kill her with one tiny mistake."

After what seemed like forever, the reverend spoke

in a small voice, as if he were giving away a confidence. "She got lost on the way to the kitchen this morning. Stood there in the hall with tears in her eyes waiting for someone to help her. You gotta be that help."

"From her pain and from my examination, I'd say unequivocally that the tumor is in an operable location," Ephraim said. "We've got that much going for us."

"That much isn't enough when it comes to Abby," Seth said. No guarantee could be enough. A slight chance was hardly good enough to—

"Everything indicates that it's prefrontal. The best location. She's young—that's in her favor."

"You're asking me to kill her, Merganser—you know that's what you're really asking."

"You ever put a horse down, or a dog?"

"What?"

"Hurts you, but it don't hurt the horse or the dog. They go on to a better place without pain and suffering and sadness."

"I can't have this discussion," Seth said, barely able to breathe. Comparing Abby to some helpless creature turned his stomach, made the bile rise in his throat. "This is my wife we're talking about."

"Not yet," the reverend said, crossing his arms over his chest and licking his lips as if just one glass of scotch was all he needed.

"What's that supposed to mean? That you'll oppose the marriage unless I agree to operate on my own wife and risk her life?"

"Her life's already at risk," Bartlett said. "It would be more like you were risking her death."

"I *would* be risking her death," Seth said. "I can't do that. I couldn't live with myself if—"

"Dr. Hendon," the reverend said, "I never did care for you all that much, but my Abidance thinks the sun rises at your say-so, so I'll remind you that this isn't about you, it's about her. She'd feel safe in your hands. You know that."

Abby would trust him. She would lie beneath the knife in his hand and tell him to do what he had to do.

"Do you remember when I told you about how there was no place to operate safely in Eden's Grove?" Seth demanded. "Did I not warn you that we could all be sorry if I had to do a surgery here?" He swept his arm to encompass the room with its debris, its years of germs.

"The church," the reverend said. "It's spotless for the Easter service."

"It's got lots of windows," Bartlett said positively, as if all that were left to discuss were the details.

"You're both crazy. I don't know how to remove a brain tumor, and if I did, I'd be the last appropriate doctor for Abidance. I'd be too—"

"Involved?" Bartlett asked.

"Choked up?" the reverend said.

"*Could* I do it?" Seth asked Bartlett. "I mean really, man-to-man. Would she have even a chance of surviving?"

"A small chance," Bartlett said softly.

"And of being herself again? Of having her mind intact?"

"Smaller still."

"I can't do it," he said, the little he'd managed to eat

on the train rising up in his throat. "I couldn't—" he started, before losing his dinner in the wastebasket beside his desk.

"And the chances of her getting better if he don't do it?" the reverend asked the doctor when Seth had finished retching.

"None."

"And of her knowing us, saying good-bye to us and all at the end—if he don't pull himself together and operate?"

Bartlett shook his head. "None," he said again.

"But if I operate on her, there's a good chance that she could die," Seth said. And then, just as if she were there, he heard her say that he'd gotten it wrong again. That it should be *She could die, but if I operate on her, at least she's got a chance.*

Chapter Twenty-two

T HE GRANGE HALL WAS FILLED WITH CANDLES. Abby didn't know how they'd gotten there, nor how the chairs had come to be filled or how the flowers for her to carry had come to be waiting on the bench beside the door. It seemed like a dream, a miracle.

And at the front of the hall, waiting for her was the greatest miracle of all—Seth. Dressed in a dark suit that he had apparently borrowed from someone just a little shorter than he, he came with a smile on his lips, to take her arm and lead her down the aisle.

"Thank you," he said softly as he placed her hand in the crook of his arm.

"For what?" she whispered as the wedding march rang out from the old organ that had been pulled from the fire, a little the worse for wear, some of the notes missing, though Abby didn't care.

"For marrying me," he said simply, as if she should have known. "For loving me," he added, squeezing the hand that rested on his arm with his other hand.

She'd taken a good deal of the medicine that Dr.

Bartlett had given her to dull the pain that never left her head, and it had left her a little woozy and unsteady on her feet. Maybe it was the drugs that made the music sound so perfect. Maybe it was the candles that made Seth's face so incredibly handsome. Maybe it was just something a mother said to all her daughters that made her feel like the most beautiful bride.

And maybe it was love.

"Dearly beloved," her father said when she and Seth were finally standing in front of him. "It is late and nearly the saddest day of the year, since it's just about Good Friday, and the truth is that Maundy Thursday's no cause for hallelujah either, but wedging this ceremony in sort of between the two, well, I guess the Lord couldn't have been too happy back then, but I know he's happy now.

"That said, I won't say anything else," her father said.

"We are gathered here to witness the coming together of the flower of the flock, my sweetest, smartest—"

There was a slight gasp from the first row and Abby tried to keep the smirk off her face.

"Now, come on, Patience, everyone knows that Abidance could mop up the floor with you in any argument you two have had since you was old enough to talk. And since she never did, that just proves my point about her being the sweetest, don't it?

"So as I was saying, we are gathered here to witness the coming together of my *sweetest, smartest* daughter, Abidance Faith Merganser and the doctor who delivered a good lot of you and treated the rest of us. And actually cured a whole bunch of us, from time to time." Her father winked at Seth, and he nodded back, but the smile left his face.

Her father rambled on some more, in the way that only her father could, and that his congregation had come to love, or at least tolerate.

Finally he got to the I-do's, which it seemed to Abby, who was more than ready, took forever.

"Do you, Seth Henry Hendon, take this woman, Abidance Faith Merganser, to be your lawfully wedded wife, to cherish her, honor her, obey her, and hold yourself only unto her through sickness and health, for richer for poorer, until death do you part?"

Seth said nothing at first, just looked down at her through eyes so heavy with tears that it took all she had not to look away. Her hands in his, he softly said, "Even death won't part us."

"Well, I guess I can take that as an *I do*," her father said.

"And I promise never to leave you," she said, not caring how the real words went, not believing they could have more meaning for her and Seth than the vows of their hearts.

"Don't go putting the horse before the cart," her father said. "You have the ring?"

Ansel took a step up and handed the ring to Seth, who took the fine gold band with intricate markings on it and slipped it back on Abby's finger. "My mother loved flowers," he said, as if they were the only two people in the hall, as if whether she liked it mattered.

"It's perfect," she said, putting out her hand and smiling through tears as the candlelight gleamed off it.

"With this ring," he said without prompting, "I thee wed, and endow thee with all I possess, including any skill I might have."

It was an odd thing to add, but she knew he would explain it to her later, and she would know it had been just the right thing with which to bind her to him.

And he took her into his arms and kissed her, and people were cheering and crying and her father was shouting that he could kiss the bride. And could he ever!

"*You* were supposed to come to *my* wedding," Anna Lisa said, coming up to hug her along with her sisters and her mother. "And you went and did it first!"

As she was passed around for hugs and kisses, she could see Seth talking with Dr. Bartlett and her father. Several other men and some of the women seemed to join the group, and heads nodded and hands were shaken. After a short time she felt breathless and Emily came to her rescue, saying that she herself needed to sit, and suggesting that Abby keep her company.

"What are they planning?" Abby asked her.

"I heard them talking about the church," Emily said. "Maybe your father is getting Seth to agree to marry you again in the new church on Easter!"

"I'll worry about Sunday on Sunday," Abby said as Seth came to claim her.

"You be careful of my little girl," Abby's mother warned Seth, shaking a fist at him. "You take your time and you be gentle, or she won't be the only one complaining of a headache."

"Mother!" Abby said, knowing her cheeks were flaming.

"Maybe you shouldn't—"

"Mother!"

"I'll take good care of her, Clarice," Seth said.

"Well, she's not all that well and I think—"

"He's a doctor!" Abby said with a humph, a chorus behind her echoing the same words.

"He knows what's best."

"He'll take care of your little girl."

"Mother, you are embarrassing her to death!"

That last comment caused a momentary silence, which was lightened when Patience asked Abby to take good care of the dress because she wanted to wear it next.

It took forever to get Abby out of the grange hall, and, once they got to the hotel, even longer to unfasten the row of buttons that went down the back of her dress. Seth supposed that it was a good thing he had to take his time so that he could get hold of himself and remember Abby was frail and not up to what he wished he could do.

"How are you feeling?" he asked her after he'd managed the last button and before he slipped the sleeves down her arms.

"Like a bride," she said, with a little nervous titter that hardly suited his Abby. He supposed, considering, he was lucky she was herself at all.

"Well, let's get you out of this," he said with a sigh, trying to tamp down lusty feelings that he didn't dare act upon.

She let him undress her, her eyes never straying

from his, hopeful, warm, expectant. On the bench at the foot of the bed lay a nightgown that he suspected had been her mother's, or Pru's from some other wedding night. When he had her down to her chemise and stockings, he reached for the gown.

"Time to get you into bed," he said, sounding more like her father than the husband he wished he could be.

"Aren't you coming?" she asked, sensing that he was pulling away from her, that his plans did not include a consummation of their vows.

"Abby, I—" he started, but his voice caught in his throat when she untied the bow to her camisole and it fell open. She shrugged it off her shoulders and it fell to the floor and she was nearly naked and looking at him with a plea in her eyes that would be hard to ignore.

"I'm dying. You know it and I know it, and I'm sorry about it. But I won't have another wedding night, and I won't ever be better than I am now, and I—"

"Are you asking me to make love to you? Because I really think that you need rest more than you need—"

"I need to be with you, to feel you around me and inside me and I need to forget, just for tonight, or however long I have, that all of this is going to be taken away from me. Don't take it away before I even—"

"Abby, you can't know how much I want you, want to hold you and touch you and—jeez, Abby! Put the gown on, will you?" He held it out to her.

"After," she said, coming closer and unfastening the buttons on his shirt, pushing the suspenders off his shoulders, pulling his shirttails out of his pants.

"Ab—" Her fingers touched his lips, silencing his words.

"Love me, Seth. Make me feel like a bride. Make me your wife."

She'd been irresistible from the start. Now, naked, pleading with him to love her, he had no choice. He'd go slowly. He'd be careful. He'd pet her and kiss her and let her fall asleep in his arms. He didn't have to exhaust her, exhaust himself. He could always stop if he thought he should.

And so he dropped his pants where he stood, pushed down his drawers and stood as naked as she, he with his socks, she with her stockings, and let her gaze at him the way he was gazing at her.

"You're very handsome," she said, running a hand down his chest, letting it fall away after it reached his waist.

"And you are even prettier than you were in your wedding gown, and I didn't think that was possible."

"I'm ready," she said, filling her chest with a deep breath and then turning to pull the covers from the bed, giving him a view of her backside that fired his need nearly to bursting.

"Abby? You're sure?" he asked, fearful now that once he touched her, once he tasted her skin and smelled her hair, he would be lost.

"You asked me for just one thing, remember?" she asked. "Now I'm asking you to return the favor. Pretend with me, Seth. Make me whole and real and perfect for just this one night."

It was enough to break his heart, to take away his

desire, but he fought the sadness, swam up from the despair and smiled. "My pleasure," he said, easing her down onto the bed and crawling between the sheets beside her.

"I love you so much," she said, obviously feeling the same way he did, that "love" was an inadequate word, that it was overused and tossed around and couldn't mean to anyone else what it meant to them.

"You are my life," he said, and since words weren't enough, he captured her lips and silenced them with his own. He kissed her until she began to arch beneath him, needing more, wanting more, and he let his hand drift down over her silky skin until it found her breast. He teased the nipple until it hardened, and then he lowered his head until he could suckle there, drawing strength from her. He toyed with her other breast while he licked and kissed her nipple and caught it gently between his teeth.

Her hands were clutching his back, driving him faster. One hand moved between them and he drew his breath in sharply as she found his chest and ran a fingertip across his own nipple before pushing against him so that he was flat on his back at her silent command.

He thought that perhaps she had had enough, and began to resettle himself to an uncomfortable night when she turned on her side and ran her hand down his chest, across his waist, and finally, slowly, until she touched his arousal. He lay as still as he could while she explored, learned his size and shape and what made him gasp and groan and sigh.

And then she climbed up on him, lying fully upon him, his manhood trapped against the hollow of her belly. "Hold me tightly," she told him and he put his arms around her and pressed her against the length of him.

He murmured something, not that he loved her, or wanted her, just sounds that spoke of now and forever, and she slid off him and pulled him toward her, spreading herself beneath him, guiding him home.

"This is madness," he said, pulling himself away from her only to have her grab at him and reel him back.

"Then let it be madness," she agreed. "Let me have this one night, Seth, this one night as your true wife, and I promise I'll face the rest of it with a smile on my lips."

How could he deny her what they both wanted so much? Reality dissolved in the warmth of her arms, and Seth basked in it, reveled in it, and acquiesced.

He tried to go slowly, gently, but she clutched at him, urging him on, matching him thrust for thrust, calling out his name and God's, until finally they lay sated in each other's arms.

"Thank you," she said softly against his chest where he had cuddled her against him.

He wanted to ask her if she was all right, if she needed anything, if it had been worth it. But he had promised her that for tonight he would forget, and so he stroked her hair, and said, "Oh, no, ma'am—thank *you*."

"I'm a ma'am, not a miss, anymore, aren't I?" she asked sleepily.

"You're a missus," he said, tucking the covers up around her. "Mrs. Seth Hendon. Mine."

"I wish there was a way that I could own you, too," she said, snuggling down and breathing softly those first few breaths of sleep.

"You do own me," he whispered at the air, feeling the sting of tears in his eyes, the cold trek of a tear down the side of his face. "Heart and soul. Forever and ever."

He awoke to the sound of Abby moaning. The sound cut through his sleep like a rusty knife, and he jerked awake and reached out to comfort her, but she wasn't in the bed.

Holy mother of God! Her hand was on the doorknob and she had just begun to open the door.

He leaped from the bed and shut it, pulling her away as he did. "Where are you going?" he asked, his hands on her thin shoulders.

"Just down the hall," she said. "I have to—"

"Abby, honey, you're not wearing anything," he said, his eyes drifting down her naked body. "You have to put some clothing on."

She looked down at herself and her lip trembled. She looked around the room as though she had never seen it before, hadn't commented when they first came in how lovely the curtains were, how pretty the pale yellow walls looked in the gaslight.

"You're at the Grand Hotel. Remember?" he prompted her.

"Of course I remember," she snapped at him. "I'm not crazy, you know."

He kept one hand on her and reached for her robe with the other. "Put this on. I'll walk you down the hall as soon as I get some clothes on."

"Why is it so dark in here?" she asked, looking toward the window. "Isn't it morning yet?"

Brilliant light streamed in through the lace-covered panes, and Seth felt the air rush out of the balloon of hope that had held him aloft all through the night.

Her satchel was on the luggage stand beside the dresser and she began to rifle through it, making little perturbed noises and groans as she did.

"What are you looking for?" he asked, taking the bag from her. "Let me help you find it."

"My medicine," she said, sitting down in the big armchair and lowering her head until it was between her knees. Wrapping her arms around her legs, she pressed her knees together, her head held viselike between them.

He grabbed up the medicine that they had left on the night table and knelt beside her, trying to unwrap her hands and give her the bottle. She'd warned him that mornings were the worst, when the medicine she'd taken before bed had worn off, but he wasn't prepared for this. He could never be prepared for this.

"It hurts," she said, eyes so sad that he would have done anything to take away the pain, knew he would do anything to make her pain stop. "It hurts so much."

"Take the medicine, Abby. It won't hurt much longer. I promise."

• • • •

Poor Seth! Abby tried not to stare at his face, the creases that ravaged his handsome forehead, the tightness that twisted his beautiful lips. It didn't help to look at her father or mother, or at Dr. Bartlett. How had she ever imagined that dying was only a personal thing?

"We could wait a while longer," Seth was saying. "It doesn't have to be tomorrow, or next week, or—"

"Today," she said, unwilling to make everyone live the nightmare longer still.

"Every day we wait, we run the risk of the optical neuritis leaving her blind. The sooner we operate, the better the chances she'll make a full recovery," Dr. Bartlett said. Abby didn't miss the look that Seth shot him. She just couldn't quite decide whether it was betrayal or pure hate. She tried to concentrate, but the medicine had made her dopey. The medicine or the tumor. Who could tell anymore what was causing what?

"Abby, you know that I—" Seth began, but her father interrupted him.

"Today is a good day for it," he agreed. He didn't bother saying that it was Good Friday and if the Lord was ever watching, this would be the day he just might grant a miracle.

"All your life I've let you make your own decisions, find your own way," her mother said. Tears streamed freely down her face and she swiped at them but went on. "Are you so sure?"

"Yes," she said, and felt a relief that had eluded her

since she'd first found out. "Yes," she said again with a rush of air and a smile for Seth.

"You can't mean today," Seth said, a plea in his voice that she disagree. "Surely not so soon. Next week, Abby. Please. Or the week after."

"Today," she said, pressing her palms against her temples. The medicine was wearing off already. "As soon as possible."

"Have you eaten?" Dr. Bartlett asked. When she shook her head, he said, "Good. Today it is."

"This is crazy," Seth said. "I can't—"

"You promised me you'd stop the pain, Seth," she said. She wanted him to know that whatever happened he was fulfilling the promise he'd made her, that she'd demanded of him.

"*Dr. Hendon*," he corrected her with a wink. "I'm your doctor now, so you have to do what I tell you."

"I thought I had to do that when you became my husband," she said, teasing him back. It felt wonderful to joke with him, to talk to him, to see him.

"As if I ever had a hope of you listening to me," he said, ruffling her hair. "In any capacity."

"They're going to have to cut off some of that hair," Dr. Bartlett said and Seth looked stricken.

"It's only hair," she said, burying the pain. "Bring on the barbers."

"I'll do it," her mother said.

Her father looked at his watch.

"You better get over to the grange hall, Papa," she said softly.

"But honey . . ." he started.

"Can you think of anyplace you could do me more good?"

He nodded, kissed her forehead, and then put his hand on the top of her head. "I'll say a prayer," he said, lifting her chin to look deeply into her eyes. "And He'll hear."

"Will I see you before? . . ." she started, then stopped herself. "I'll see you later. Or tomorrow," she added softly.

"You can use the patient room," Dr. Bartlett told her mother. "I'll show you where you'll need to shave, and then, if we can see any protrusions, I'll mark them with some nitrate of silver.

"We'll make a sort of checkerboard on your head, Abby, honey, so that we can see the various fissures and—"

"Kind of like marking a dress pattern," Abby said, trying to be game so that Seth wouldn't decide not to do the operation.

"Just like that," Dr. Bartlett agreed. "But first, just like when you were a little girl, your mama will scrub your head and wrap it up in a bandage to keep it nice and clean."

Seth followed them into the small room, looming over them, fussing, listening as Dr. Bartlett told her mother where the hair had to be removed, and that it had to be shaved right to the scalp. He handed her a bottle of alcohol and said that it might sting the freshly shaved skin, and Abby decided that she would stop listening and put herself in the doctors' hands. And God's.

"You'll need to get some things set up over at the

church," Bartlett said to Seth, who looked as if he'd watched a train wreck and knew he had to help but didn't know where to start.

He left Abby with her mother and put an arm around Seth, leading him out of the office, telling him there was nothing he could do there.

Nothing except lend her his strength, his surety. Except he didn't seem to have those to give.

The cemetery was only a few yards beyond the new church, which stood clean and bright and ready for Easter. Women were removing the flowers that had already been placed there and carrying them to the grange hall when Seth went by.

He found Sarrie's grave easily and was surprised to see a ring of pansies planted just in front of the headstone like a wreath for his sister's hair. He had no doubt who had planted them despite her pain.

He stood reading the words on Sarrie's marker that said she was a beloved daughter and sister, and his heart went out to Ansel, who had been forced to let her go, exert no claim, retain no hold.

"So I suppose you've been watching us all make fools of ourselves down here," he said aloud, brushing a fallen leaf from the pansy ring. "Me running to St. Louis to call out my rival before settling down to lick my wounds, Abby making a wedding gown she never expected to wear."

He supposed that what she had expected was that she would be buried in it, and the thought made it hard for him to swallow.

"There's a good chance," he choked out, "that by tonight she'll be in your care, Sarrie. I'd make her wait, but it would be for my sake, not hers, and I'd be making her wait in pain, and I can't do that. Bartlett thinks there really is a chance. There's a technique they didn't want him to try at the hospital that he thinks might work. It's complicated, but it's something.

"And I've got to do something," he said, turning to go into the church and see to what needed doing. He needed to get the dental drill from Dr. Thayer and sterilize it. He needed to bring in sterile sheets and dressings. He needed to be sure they had everything on hand because they would not want to bring in anything contaminated from outside.

Just before he took off he turned and looked over his shoulder again at the pansy ring. "If it comes to it, Sarrie, you'll look after her till I get there, right?"

Chapter Twenty-three

F OUR HOURS OF SURGERY. TWO HOURS OF
checking vitals and ensuring circulation. Ten
hours of changing drains and doing little more
than watching for a movement behind Abby's eyelids,
or a twitch of her fingers or a sign that his wife would
ever return to him.

Nothing. Had she died on the table and did her body
not know it? Her heart continued to beat as strongly as
ever. Her color was good. And yet she was as unre-
sponsive to his pokes and prods as she was to his words
of love and encouragement.

"Any change?" Bartlett asked, standing now at the
door of the church where he made certain that no one
came close enough to Abby to give her weakened system any more to fight.

"Nothing," he said.

"Doesn't mean anything," Bartlett told him. "Not
yet."

"When do we know the results of what I've done?"
Seth asked.

"I tell you," Bartlett said, "all brain surgeries should

be done by the husband of the patient. If any one of my patients trusted me the way that woman trusts you—"

Her last words—before the ether had put her under—were *Don't look so worried. I'm not.* And then she'd asked him to come closer, and she'd kissed him. *Till later,* she'd said.

Till after, he'd agreed.

Well, it was damn long "after" and he was losing his mind. A million times he told himself that their wedding night had made her worse. That they'd have had more time if he'd never left Eden's Grove. That he should have married her years ago. Everything but that he never should have operated.

She had been in pain. What choice had there been?

Yet another of the Mergansers came to the door. Pru, her children in tow, from what Seth could see from his vantage point at Abby's side.

He couldn't make out Ephraim's words, but he knew well enough what the man was saying—*Too soon to know anything. Vitals good. Reason to hope, blah, blah, blah.*

All day they came, and all day Ephraim gave out the same information. Seth sent him home at dinnertime, and after leaving a note on the door for well-wishers Ephraim finally left him alone with his wife.

"You deserved better than this," he told her, taking her limp hand within his own. "You deserved the sun and the moon and all those other trite things that men promise women if only they'll marry them.

"I wish I knew what to promise you to make you

wake up," he said, checking the bandages on her head and changing them yet again for the sterilized ones that Bartlett had brought with him from Boston, more a souvenir of another life than something he had ever really expected to make use of again.

"Abby?" He could have sworn she flinched slightly when he touched the mixture of carbolic acid, vaselini, and wax to her incision to stop the oozing. "Abby! Blink, wiggle a finger, swallow! Do something so I know you hear me, so I know you're still here!"

In the empty church his voice echoed, mocking him, as Abby lay still as a corpse.

He lit the lamps that they had hung from the rafters so that it shone in the church as if it were the middle of the day, and as he turned each one up he talked to her, nonsense at this point, but his need to hold on to her was greater than his fear of being ridiculous.

"So, when you're all better, I thought we might take a little trip. I know you like St. Louis, so maybe there. Or maybe to the Pacific Ocean?" he asked, gave a moment for her response, and then continued. "I do think you would like the ocean. Or maybe you'd prefer to go back East. I could take you shopping in New York City and you could model the highest fashions for me. What would you think of that?"

He talked until he was hoarse, paced until his legs could carry him no more, and then he sat in the chair beside the operating table on which Abby still lay, and fought his heavy eyelids.

"Maybe I'll just rest for a moment," he conceded. "As long as you're sleeping, anyway."

He must have nodded off for a moment or two, because when he heard the knock at the church doors, it made him start and he nearly fell out of the chair.

"Abby?" he asked, checking her again, making sure that she was still alive, wishing she would open her eyes and know him just one more time.

Who was he kidding? He wanted the rest of his life with her. He wanted them to have children and grandchildren and great-grandchildren. He wanted to rock on a porch with her and watch the sunset and die holding her against his body in a bed that had all but given out beneath a million nights of loving.

The knock came again and he came to the door and spoke through it. "What?" he called through the door.

"It's Jed," Abby's brother called. "Jedidiah Merganser. Abidance's brother."

"She's still sleeping, Jed," he said. He looked at his watch. It was nearly five-thirty in the morning. "Go back to bed."

"I haven't been to bed. I've been working. For the sunrise service. You know."

"Yes, Jed, I know," he said, having completely forgotten that this would be Sunday, Easter Sunday.

"Can I talk to Abby?"

"She's still sleeping, Jed," he repeated. Poor Jed. So many parts of his mind had never matured, but his heart was fully formed.

"Can you give her a message for me?"

"What is it?" Seth asked, anxious now to change Abby's bandages again and look for any reason to hope.

"Tell her to look out the window."

"Out the window? For what, Jed?" he asked.

"For the miracle," Jed answered. "I gotta go."

"It'll be a miracle if she can look out the window," Seth muttered to himself and he made his way slowly back down the church's aisle toward Abby. The longer it took him, the longer he could believe that when he got there she would open those dazzling hazel eyes and smile that gut-flipping smile of hers.

"So it's time to check your bandages again," he said as he approached her. "Don't want any infections impeding your progress after the wonderful job I did."

He tilted her head slowly away from him to get at the edge of the bandage, wondering how with no hair, with her life on the line, she could still be so incredibly beautiful.

"Oh . . ." It was a tiny voice, sad, soft.

And clear as a bell! He ran around the table, afraid to move her head, afraid to speak, afraid to hope.

Her eyes were open and she appeared to be looking out the window.

"Abby! Oh, God, Abby!"

"Am I dead?" she asked softly, looking past him to continue staring out the huge church windows. Was she seeing anything?

"Well, if you are, so am I," he said, not caring that he was crying freely. "Can you see me? Can you see anything, darling?"

"*Darling?* Now I know I'm dead. Jed's flying and you're calling me darling."

He turned to look over his shoulder and sure enough, there was Jed, in his ridiculous machine, floating just outside the church windows, throwing white crosses that sounded like rain as they hit the window-panes.

He turned back to her just as her eyes were closing, a wrinkle furrowing her brow.

"Does something hurt you?" he asked, putting the back of his hand against her forehead to make sure there was still no sign of fever. "Are you in pain?"

"There's no pain in heaven, silly," she said. "But I am hungry. I didn't think there'd be hunger in heaven, did you? Why are you here, anyway? You didn't kill yourself when I died, did you?"

"Abby, honey, you're not dead. You are very much alive." He ran over to the window and opened it in time to hear the most beautiful church bells he had ever heard. Somehow they had managed to uncrate the bells and set them up temporarily in the street, just far enough off the ground to ring them.

"She's hungry!" he shouted out the window to anyone who could hear. "She says she's hungry!"

He heard the crash and Jed's shout of pain, and figured that Ephraim Bartlett could set Jed's bones.

"Tell me how you feel," he said, coming back to her. "Does anything hurt? Are you able to move your fingers and toes and—"

"Mostly I'm tired, Seth," she said dreamily. "Would it be okay if I just rested a little?"

He touched the underside of her foot and watched as her leg reacted, jumping just as it should. There would be time enough for planning and dreaming, all the years to come. "You go ahead and rest, Mrs. Hendon. We have the rest of our lives to catch up."

Epilogue

⚜

S ETH HELPED HIS WIFE OFF THE TRAIN, NOT BE-
cause she needed any help but because it was
the proper thing to do. Not that their marriage
so far had been close to proper. Oh, no, not with Abidance Merganser Hendon and that strong head of
hers—insisting on signing the register at the hotel in
Boston herself instead of letting him see to such matters.

And demanding that he perform his husbandly du-
ties nearly every night for three months!

Well, he thought—and the thought brought a smile
to his lips—that was the price one paid for marrying a
woman so much younger than himself.

"And just what does that Chesire-cat grin mean, Dr.
Hendon?" his wife demanded, her body sliding down
his as he lifted her off the last step and set her down on
the ground.

Before he could answer her, his new family surrounded them, cooing over how well Abby looked, Patience obviously trying to see if there was any hair

under Abby's hat, Clarice touching her daughter's forehead with the back of her hand as if checking for temperature, Ezra beaming, and several children wrapping themselves around her legs.

"Let's not knock your aunt Abby over," Seth warned them, and Abby shooed *him*, not them, away.

"Don't coddle me, Dr. Hendon," she warned him, as if she had ever let him do that, as if she ever would. *Cuddle, yes*, she had told him as they lay in bed at the hotel in Boston, *coddle, never*.

Well, he'd see about that once he had her ensconced in Joseph Panner's old—no, make that *their* new home. And if she intended to help him as a nurse of sorts, she darn well better learn to listen to his instructions.

"At least sit down," he begged, rather than ordered, her.

She pinned him with those big eyes of hers and he shrugged and left her to her family after receiving his own handshakes from Jed and Ezra, and pecks on the cheeks from Patience and Clarice.

On the outskirts of the circle stood Ephraim Bartlett and Ansel, both of them watching the exchange between Seth and Abby with obvious amusement.

"I see you have her well in hand," Ansel teased. "She seems to be very much our old Abidance."

"That she is," Seth said, and allowed himself a satisfied sigh.

"And Carter at Mass. General?" Bartlett asked, taking Seth's hand and shaking it with both of his. "He said she was in the clear?"

"He did," Seth said. "And he sent his regards and his respect for a job well done."

"I did nothing," Bartlett said. "You—"

"I was simply your hands," Seth said. "She'd be dead now," he started to add, but the rest of the sentence got stuck in his throat with a thousand unshed tears he'd had to hold back. He'd have lost her if not for Ephraim, and he'd be forever grateful.

"Been holding on to this for you," Ephraim said, handing him the Dickens book that Abby had given to Seth years before. "Thought you'd want it in the new place."

"Thanks," Seth said, and thought about someday reading it aloud to his children, his and Abby's children. Talk about miracles! The doctors in Boston had said that they saw no reason why Abby wouldn't be able to have all the children she wanted, though they did say something about why in the world she'd married Seth and why she would ever want to bear his kids. And then they'd all had a good laugh—all but Seth, who had to wonder why indeed his Abby loved him.

He wasn't good enough, kind enough, even smart enough for her. But he would love her enough, or try to, for the rest of their lives.

Abby managed to extricate herself from her nieces and nephew and make her way to Seth's side, where she belonged. She took a hug from Ansel that was gentle and careful, as if he couldn't quite believe she was truly all right, and a bear hug from Ephraim, who apparently was sure she was.

"Where's Emily?" she asked. "And Pru?"

"Emily's tending to your very newest niece," Ansel said proudly. "Ephyra Abidance Merganser, named for the man who helped save you and, well . . ."

"Don't you give Seth any credit?" she asked, delighted to see the blush in Dr. Bartlett's cheeks at having a child named for him.

"He got you," Dr. Bartlett said. "What more could he need?"

"He'll need a child named after him," she said simply. "And I'm—"

Seth blanched, grabbing her arm and holding her as if she were suddenly made of glass. She didn't know why he was so surprised. After all, he was a doctor. Surely he knew where babies came from.

". . . Working on it," she finished. "Don't go to pieces yet, Seth."

"Then you're not? . . ." he asked, a bit of color returning to his cheeks, but the smile gone from his lips.

She shrugged. "Maybe," she answered, not being coy but honest.

"Maybe you should—" Seth began, but Ansel and Dr. Bartlett were laughing so loudly at him he didn't have the nerve to finish.

"Can you imagine when she knows for sure?" Ansel asked Dr. Bartlett, poking him in the ribs. Apparently the two had become fast friends while she and Seth were back East. That was nice, since they were to be neighbors now that Ephraim would stay in Seth's old place and she and Seth would move into Joseph Panner's mansion, converting it into the hospital Seth wanted so much.

And from her father's letters, it was clear the town wanted both the hospital and Seth to run it.

The whole group began to drift down the street, past

the church, where they paused to hear the music drifting out the open door. Someone was singing, and Abby climbed the steps of the beautiful new church to see Prudence pounding at a magnificent new organ and singing an alleluia at the top of her lungs.

"Boone sent it," her mother said, speaking right up against her ear so that Abby could hear her over the music. "He struck a mother lode! And he's coming home."

Abby didn't think she could be happier. And then Seth came up behind her, his arms encircling her, and when the music finally stopped, he whispered softly into her ear.

"We're home, Mrs. Hendon. Welcome home."

And she was happier still.

Author's Note

WHEN WRITING HISTORICAL NOVELS, ACCURACY IS AS IM-
portant as characterization and plot. It *is* in many ways,
characters and plot. After all, we are the products of
our time, limited by the progress of the day, shaped by
the world in which we live.

In addition, an author has the trust of her reader,
which is never, at least by this author, taken lightly. I
know that it may have been hard to read *A Heart Full
of Miracles* without thinking that I must have stretched
the truth, played with the dates, made the facts suit my
story. I know that, because as I read and researched,
I'd gasp, shake my head, read passages from dusty old
texts over and over aloud asking if this could really be
so. It was. With the help of John Mangiardi, M.D.,
FACS, neurosurgeon, who pointed me in the right direction to find the documentation I needed; Jennifer
Po, R.N., who brought all the sources to me, answered
E-mails and cheered me on; and Bruce Wilde, O.D.,
who suggested a brain tumor in the first place and told
me to look up Fedor Krause, I now know more about

brain surgery in the late 1800s than I ever thought I would.

Brain surgery like the kind I described was carried out at Massachusetts General Hospital in the last decade of the nineteenth century. The success rate was poor, but just as I said in the novel, there were those who did survive and go on to live normal lives. In 1891, Philip Coombs Knapp, A.M., M.D. (Harvard), a clinical instructor in diseases of the nervous system at Harvard Medical School, as well as physician for diseases of the nervous system to outpatients, Boston City Hospital, member of the American Neurological Association and fellow of the Massachusetts Medical Society, etc., authored a Fiske Fund Prize dissertation entitled *The Pathology, Diagnosis and Treatment of Intra-Cranial Growths*. In his dissertation he not only described the operations in minute (and often stomach-turning) detail but he also recited case studies of patients upon whom he operated—those who died and those who survived. Yes, survived! A twenty-eight-year-old male suffering from headaches, vomiting and vertigo. A thirty-six-year-old female suffering from headache, psychological disturbances, anesthesia of the left arm and face, dullness, beginning coma. A twenty-year-old male with headaches, spasms of the left arm and face, optic atrophy. Certainly there were deaths, lots of them, but there were successes. Why not allow Abby to be one of them?

The hospital situation presented a problem, since many deaths at the turn of the century and before were due to septicemia. That's why I went to great lengths to have them sterilize the church and use the autoclave. I had Seth carefully follow the instructions I found in two medical texts, one written in 1894 by Fedor Krause, and a second from ten years later by Drs. Bergmann and Bruns. Vital also was *The International Medical Annual* for the year 1891 (E. B. Treat, Medical Publisher, 5 Cooper Union, NY, 1891), which contained not only the following quote but some lovely wildflowers that had been pressed between the pages!

Brain surgery is now in a somewhat similar condition to that of abdominal surgery some years ago. Surgeons are afraid of the brain, or too much in the habit of letting the favourable moment for operation go by, on account of their fear of the consequences of interfering with the skull and its contents.

(page 118)

In addition to the references cited above, I also became familiar with the practices at Massachusetts General Hospital from two other sources: an article titled "The Massachusetts General Hospital—Early History and Neurosurgery to 1939" by Fred G. Barker II, M.D., and "The History of the Massachusetts General Hospital from June 1872 to December 1900," by Grace Whiting Myers, librarian emeritus, Massachusetts General Hospital, Boston, Massachusetts.

For more information on the history of brain surgery, you might like to check out the following Web site: *http://www.brain-surgery.com/history.html*, which traces the origins of brain surgery back to the neolithic

Stone Age. (My guess is that while they may have performed the surgery then, they didn't have much of a survival rate!)

Those of you in the medical profession may note some practices that Seth used that seemed improper. Please remember that medicine has come a long way in the past hundred years. We know things now that Seth Hendon was unaware of. All of the medical books of the time insisted that to fight frostbite the skin was to be rubbed gently to return circulation. Today's physicians would be horrified at the thought. But Seth lived then, so I had him rub Joseph Panner's feet. (This is one of those do-not-try-this-at-home things!) No doubt I included other treatments that might raise an eyebrow by today's standards. Most of Seth's treatments (aside from Abby's brain surgery) are found in *Dr. Chase's Last and Complete Receipt Book and Household Physician* (1884, 1887, 1904), *The People's Common Sense Medical Advisor* by R. V. Pierce, M.D. (1909), or the *Century Book of Health* by J. H. McCormick, M.D. (1906).

While medical details give me the willies, I loved every minute of writing Seth and Abby's story. Of course, they went on to have a couple of kids, Abby learned to assist him in his medical practice, and their daughter became a surgeon. And everyone, everywhere, lived happily ever after!

About the Author

With *A Heart Full of Miracles* Stephanie Mittman returns to her favorite place—the midwest of the late 1800s. There's something about the sense of community in that time and place, of people pulling together to fight the fates, that appeals to her strongly. So strongly, in fact, that it's always hard for her to say good-bye to her characters and leave behind the town they live in. So, in an effort to recreate her reality, she and her husband have moved to a small town on Long Island and she is happy to report that the people in the post office, the library, and the drug store all know her by name. Now, if she could just tear herself away from her computer for a while, maybe she could even meet the neighbors!

She loves to stop writing to answer letters and E-mails, so if you'd like to contact her, she can be reached online at www.stephaniemittman.com or by snail mail c/o MLG, 190 Willis Avenue, Mineola, NY 11501.

Stephanie Mittman

"Stephanie Mittman might very well be
the standard against which all future
Americana romance is judged. Five Stars!"

—Affaire de Coeur

"The best of American romance."

—Romantic Times